W9-CCD-869

The Desert Sky Before Us

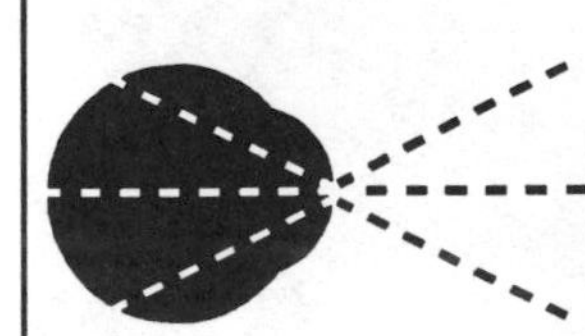

This Large Print Book carries the
Seal of Approval of N.A.V.H.

THE DESERT SKY BEFORE US

ANNE VALENTE

THORNDIKE PRESS
A part of Gale, a Cengage Company

Farmington Hills, Mich • San Francisco • New York • Waterville, Maine
Meriden, Conn • Mason, Ohio • Chicago

This is a work of fiction. Names, characters, places, and incidents are the products of the author's imagination or are used fictitiously and are not to be construed as real. Any resemblance to actual events, locales, organizations, or persons, living or dead, is entirely coincidental.

Thorndike Press® Large Print Reviewers' Choice.
The text of this Large Print edition is unabridged.
Other aspects of the book may vary from the original edition.
Set in 16 pt. Plantin.

**LIBRARY OF CONGRESS CIP DATA ON FILE.
CATALOGUING IN PUBLICATION FOR THIS BOOK
IS AVAILABLE FROM THE LIBRARY OF CONGRESS**

ISBN-13: 978-1-4328-6565-8 (hardcover alk. paper)

Published in 2019 by arrangement with William Morrow, an imprint of HarperCollins Publishers

Printed in the United States of America
1 2 3 4 5 6 7 23 22 21 20 19

For Michelle

“Most deserts have a memory of
the sea. . . .
If the world ends, let me be here.”

— Terry Tempest Williams,
The Hour of Land

39.8517° N, 88.9442° W: Decatur, Illinois

Rhiannon expects her in uniform. White polyester polo. Navy pants. Black orthopedic shoes. The same state-issued clothes Billie's worn each time Rhiannon's visited the Decatur Correctional Center across the six years of her sister's sentence, the same starched shirt and rough fabric given to each inmate upon entry. Rhiannon waits in the car sheltered from low clouds and the constant spit of June rain. The engine running, a commuter Mustang still far less familiar to her than a stock car. She lets the air-conditioning blow out of habit, what would have once been expected at the start of summer instead of this year's steady stream of dulled rain across Illinois.

She glances down at the car's mileage count, a speedometer instead of the close attention she once paid to a tachometer. Revolutions per minute. Maintenance no more than routine now, the five years since she raced nearly as long as the six-year span of her sister's prison sentence. Rhiannon waits at the Correctional Center's curb anticipating Billie with no personal items but the standard-issued bus ticket each inmate receives when released. A cluster of women gathers beyond the Mustang's windshield, their figures clearing into relief each time the wipers slide drizzle from the glass. Women in street clothes. Women without umbrellas, standing beside small packed bags. Nowhere among them her sister. Rhiannon lowers the dial on the car radio to avoid the latest news, the seventh commercial plane crash in the past four months.

A Frontier flight carrying 126 passengers from Los Angeles to Houston: the reason airports are beginning to shut down across the nation and the world.

Rhiannon turns the radio off, a silence that evaded her the night before as she stayed up watching scrolls of headlines on CNN. A trail of wreckage in eastern Arizona, just past the edge of the Apache-Sitgreaves National Forest. No black box recovered. Only speculation, only the garbled voices of air traffic controllers in Los Angeles and Houston reporting what they knew. Rhiannon sat in the dark and imagined shards of metal scattered across the

Sonoran Desert. She sat in the dark and wondered what she would say to her sister the following day and across the coming days of sharing a car for the two weeks of driving ahead of them, their first conversations in six years beyond the monitored tables of the Correctional Center's visiting room.

When she looks up from the radio's dial, Billie is standing with both of her thin-boned hands wrapped around the handle of a suitcase. No umbrella. Her hair rain-damp, her head half shaved to a deep side part, dyed-red strands spilling down her chin. Her hair naturally brown like Rhiannon's but hidden since high school beneath boxed coloring kits and bleaches. Rhiannon recognizes the suitcase: their mother's red-leather Amelia Earhart bag, what she and Billie fought over when they were kids. Their mother's former flight bag to dig sites, what she let them use to store their doll clothes. Rhiannon remembers Billie dumping their Barbies' lace skirts and velvet dresses and filling the suitcase instead with a half-eaten peanut butter sandwich and a paper fan and two undershirts and six dimes, everything a four-year-old thought she needed to travel the country like their mother.

Beyond the bag, Rhiannon recognizes the

hollowness in her sister's face.

She thinks of the route ahead of them, two weeks on the road, trail mix and protein bars already packed in a cooler for the next morning's departure. From Illinois straight across Missouri to Kansas then all the way through Colorado to the border of Utah. The Cleveland-Lloyd Dinosaur Quarry: where their mother spent the bulk of her career unearthing stegosaurus bones, the densest concentration of Jurassic fossils in the entire world. Dr. Margaret Hurst. Their mother a Jurassic paleontologist specializing in the function of stegosaur plates. And this route, what she'd devised four months ago when she learned Billie's release date and realized she wouldn't live long enough to see her daughter come home.

A second funeral.

A favor she called in through the Bureau of Land Management.

A scattering of ashes across the desert though she was already lowered down three months ago in the wet fog of a Midwestern spring, this second ceremony nothing more than a symbolic gesture for a daughter whose prison refused early release for a parent's burial. Rhiannon visualized the route west as she drove from their childhood home in Champaign-Urbana to the

Decatur Correctional Center that morning, a fifty-minute drive down Interstate 72 that had grown routine. The abandoned Sinclair station just past the turnoff for Lodge Park. A cluster of wind turbines spinning slowly in the stark fields, white blades and gray clouds. A drive so much shorter than the route their mother planned for them across four states to Utah, a route she'd whispered to Rhiannon from a reclined hospital bed in her final weeks. *Go west.* Her mouth close to Rhiannon's ear. *It will be good for both of you.* A route Rhiannon hasn't driven in over five years, one she tried to imagine from the rain-sprinkled cornfields along the highway between Champaign and Decatur as the radio's news circulated again and again on the latest downed plane.

Rhiannon pulls the Mustang up to where Billie stands in the weak rain at the Correctional Center's curb. Through the thin light of a gunmetal sky, Rhiannon sees a line of small silver hoops glinting along her sister's ear, what she didn't notice the last time she visited over two months ago. She wonders who pierced her sister's ears, who dyed her sister's hair, a community inside the prison's walls that Billie's hardly ever mentioned. Billie wears threadbare jeans and a black T-shirt, what she must have been wearing at intake six years ago. Billie still a girl then at twenty-six and Rhiannon wonders if her clothes still carry the thick scent of smoke and ash.

Rhiannon shifts the car into park, leaves the engine on, pops the trunk and circles out front. Drizzle pelts her face as she pulls her sister into a stiff embrace.

Nice car, Billie says against Rhiannon's ear.

Are you hungry? is the only thing Rhiannon can think to say.

Billie nods and slides into the passenger seat and Rhiannon circles around to the driver's side of the cherry-red Ford Mustang GT, a car she bought two years into her new job as a textbook sales representative and two years into Billie's sentence, a two-door model the dealership's salesman made sure to remind her would be impractical for a family and kids. *Might be a tight squeeze back there for a car seat.* Every American dealership a microcosm of the racetrack. Assumed roles. The art of negotiation the realm of masculinity, the same as hospitality tents and checkered flags and sponsorship banners and 235,000 fans in the stands of every major speedway, all of them there for the promise of a man behind a wheel. Rhiannon drops into the Mustang and buckles her belt, the silence thick in the absence of the radio's hum.

Where do you want to eat your first real meal? she asks.

I don't care. Billie stares straight ahead. Anything but stale bread and meat.

Rhiannon imagines some diner along the highway where their mother will inevitably come up between them, where they'll finally discuss the details of the coming two weeks. She hasn't seen Billie in nearly three months, a trip they've only discussed through clipped collect phone calls since their mother's funeral. She tries not to notice the heavy chicken skin of her sister's left arm, burn scars snaking up her elbow and disappearing beneath her shirtsleeve. Scars she's never seen before, Billie's prison-issue shirts always long-sleeved and starched. She tries not to notice the other women, bus tickets in their hands, waiting in the rain of the Mustang's rearview mirror.

The Steak 'n Shake off I-72 is sparsely populated, midafternoon on a Saturday in central Illinois. Rhiannon orders only coffee, Billie a tuna melt with fries and coleslaw and an Oreo milkshake. Whipped cream and a cherry, she tells the server, who slides a pencil behind his ear and recedes to the kitchen.

Do you have a parole officer? Rhiannon asks, though she knows the answer is no. As Billie's repatriating family contact, she knows Billie is only required to attend mandated therapy in the state of Illinois upon release.

The server brings Billie's milkshake, an iridescent cherry on top. Rhiannon tries not to notice Billie's first gulping sip through the straw.

Is that really what you want to talk about? Billie asks.

What do you want to talk about?

Billie watches her across the table. Tell me about your life. Travels. Races. I haven't seen you in almost three months. Rhiannon looks down at her mug. Ignores *travels* and *races* and everything she's kept hidden since Billie went to prison for two words far more piercing: *three months.* The span of time since their mother passed away, a blink, quick as the cancer that seized her brilliant brain. The last time Rhiannon saw Billie, their mother was alive.

Work's fine, Rhiannon says. Fine enough to give me two weeks off.

That's a miracle during the busiest season, Billie says as the server slides her tuna melt onto the table. I can't believe you get two weeks away from summer races.

Rhiannon looks out the window at the slate June sky, once thick with heat and Illinois humidity and blue-drenched sun and the heavy crack of thunder. Now nothing but increased gray rain since March, a constant mist, temperatures hovering always in the low sixties. She visited Billie once a month for six years. Once a month and never told her she stopped racing cars right after Billie was imprisoned. That she stopped racing and began selling textbooks, as profitable a job as any in a college town, a job with ample time to take two weeks off in the middle of a university's summer break while NASCAR motored on through June and July. She made her mother promise not to say a word to Billie when she visited Decatur, a promise her mother kept across six full years.

I already planned our route, Rhiannon says. Ready to head out tomorrow?

Billie dips two matchstick fries into the ketchup pooled on her plate. I'm ready.

We can wait a day or two if you need some time to adjust and take it easy.

I don't need to take it easy. Billie's voice is firm. I missed her funeral. Enough bullshit. Enough small talk. Why don't you tell me about her funeral?

Rhiannon watches Billie across the table and wonders what there is to tell. That she'd been the only person for days in their childhood home going through their mother's boxes of clothing and old dishes before their father came down from Chicago wanting her wedding ring, an aquamarine stone she'd taken off just after they divorced, a ring Rhiannon couldn't find anywhere in the sparse jewelry sachets and the one safe-deposit box. That their father still wore its twin. That Rhiannon hadn't seen him in almost two months since he'd been out on training circuits for upcoming summer races. That it rained the entire service. That their father tried his best to talk with his ex-wife's colleagues from the University of Illinois's geology department at the reception following the funeral and that Rhiannon saw they still made him uncomfortable, conversations he'd always avoided for fear of not knowing the right terminology. How they both stood among their mother's friends and relatives who came in from every corner of the country, Rhiannon's cousins and second cousins and her mother's sister from Dallas who stood behind her throughout the entire service, a hand firm but tremoring on her shoulder, and Beth standing beside her without holding her hand.

It was nice, is all Rhiannon says. It was what she would have wanted.

What she would have wanted, Billie repeats.

The server refills Rhiannon's coffee and the heat in Billie's voice dims.

We have to be at the Cleveland-Lloyd Quarry in a week? she says.

More or less. It's not a solid date. The Bureau of Land Management knows we're coming. They'll let us do the service whenever we get there.

You just have to be back within two weeks.

I have a job, Rhiannon says. And you're required to report within two weeks.

I have time, Billie says. No mandatory supervision. No reports to any office.

Rhiannon knows this. Knows everything from the prison's debriefing before Billie's release. How Billie's arson sentence was heavy but not dire enough to require a parole officer, supervision, regular check-ins. How her only postincarceration probation requirement is to see a mental health counselor once a week for the next twelve months. How the appointments have been mandated to start within two weeks of release, another reason for their trip's quick out-and-back. How a program officer visited the house three weeks ago to verify the address and number of bedrooms and number of residents and how Rhiannon had replied *only one resident,* the words three thick rocks in her mouth. How Rhiannon doesn't know what Billie's plans will be once they've driven out to the border separating Colorado and Utah and driven back and Billie takes up residence with her in their childhood home in Champaign-Urbana, the house on Grove Street that Rhiannon returned to when their mother got sick and where she's been sorting through boxes since March, since moving out of the apartment she shared with Beth.

My fines are almost paid, Billie says. My restitution too. We have nothing but time. Time to drive way the fuck out to Utah and all the way back.

Rhiannon knows Billie's fines, the restitution to Illinois College's Schewe Library that she has helped her family pay across the years Billie's been in prison. Rhiannon's sales job so much of what ended up paying for Billie's mistakes, and even still: she's hidden every single textbook before her sister sets foot inside the house. She downs the last of her coffee, grinds she can taste at the bottom of the cup. She signals the server for the check.

■ ■ ■ ■

At home, Rhiannon watches the six o'clock news in the living room while Billie takes a long shower upstairs, the whine of water groaning through the walls of the house. On the news: more footage of the Frontier flight's wreckage in eastern Arizona. A scattering of ripped metal. A tail wing. A trio of seats, a suitcase still packed with rolled socks and folded shirts. Twenty-seven minutes into flight, not even long enough for the plane to reach cruising altitude, the seventh plane in less than four months. A bizarre string of crashes that newspapers and media pundits are still debating whether they're linked or catastrophically coincidental, a continued stream of news that Rhiannon has barely been able to focus on given the crashes' proximity to her mother's death.

The first plane: a disappearance in February, somewhere in the Indian Ocean between the Maldives and Perth where the wreckage was never found, only two months after her mother's initial diagnosis and rapid decline. The second a crash outside of Tokyo in early March amid unseasonable monsoons pummeling the coast of Japan, the news blinking blue on the television screen above her mother's hospital bed only nights before she passed away. Then three weeks later, a plane lost to the desert of the Congo just days after Rhiannon buried her mother in the rain-drenched fields of Greenlawn Cemetery. Then Russia: where ice floes still pocked the Volga River in late April and frigid waters made wreckage recovery next to impossible, Rhiannon poring through her mother's closets and the garage's storage. Then a crash in Suriname only a week later, a 747 carrying 502 people from Buenos Aires to New York, Rhiannon staring blankly at a computer screen in the small cubicle of her office reeling from moving the last of her things out of Beth's apartment. Then a plane crossing the North Sea from Sweden to Greenland in late May, no sign of storms, Rhiannon making preparations for a cross-country trip, Rhiannon blocking everything out but this. And now the US mainland, the seventh plane in less than four months. Rhiannon watches the news and hears the shower shut off upstairs. Airports across the world in a state of ratcheting panic, what her mother seemed to understand as she faded in and out of consciousness during her final weeks. Two planes already lost in quick succession, the reason she insisted her daughters drive to Utah instead of fly.

Her mother kept the television on in her Carle Clinic room on the many nights Rhiannon stayed long past visiting hours in a thinly upholstered bedside chair, the screen's glow candle-flickering blue across the walls. Always old reruns of *I Love Lucy* when the news wasn't on, current events her mother still insisted on knowing. And when her mother was sleeping, Rhiannon watched her dream, eyes trembling in the stages of REM, hands oscillating subtly back and forth. Rhiannon memorized her face. The way her thumbs and pointer fingers clasped together and formed a complete loop. Picking, Rhiannon realized. Her mother was picking in her sleep. A movement as second nature to her as eating. Rhiannon knew the motion well from the countless times she'd visited her mother's office on campus, the pick a tool she remembered best because it matched the tool their family dentist used when she was small. The same utensil Rhiannon's hygienist uses in Champaign-Urbana every six months, a tool Rhiannon knows will gut her on every single checkup for the rest of her life. A dental pick. Her mother running the beveled edge along fossilized bone to remove caked soil, chiseling out slabs of rock and shipping them to Illinois and notching them into sharp relief when she wasn't out in the field at the quarry.

The newscaster on-screen reports the closing of certain airports. The possibility of climate change as a factor, what pundits have been speculating for the past four months. A possibility Rhiannon recognized thumbing through one of the aviation textbooks she sold, what she couldn't stop herself from reading due to her own fear of flying: an atmospheric study indicating increased clear-air turbulence. Jet stream modifications due to warming poles. A rise in air traffic causing wind wakes. Her father had dismissed it all as modern mythology when she mentioned it on the phone between his racing trips from Chicago. But her mother knew the earth. Its sediment and layers. She shook her head and said flights to the quarry had become more turbulent when she was still healthy and traveling regularly to Utah, the weather around every site she'd visited in the last ten years growing more severe, more windswept, more dangerous.

Do we still have cable? Billie asks. Rhiannon looks up and her sister is standing in the living room in a T-shirt and sweatpants, the unshaved side of her hair still wet.

Mom never got rid of it. Watch as much MTV as you like.

Billie sits down on the couch. We had movie night once a month in Decatur. But only family films. *Grease. Toy Story.*

How's the old bedroom?

My posters and hemp necklaces are gone. Other than that, everything's the same.

Rhiannon knows Billie's old bedroom looks nothing like it did in high school. Her mother painted both of their rooms once they moved out, made Billie's a work studio filled with dig tools and Rhiannon's a guest bedroom.

Did you find your stuff in the closet? Rhiannon says. The rest of it is out in the garage.

Thanks. I'll get to it eventually.

Rhiannon says nothing more, her sister's stuff everything she left behind in Jacksonville that had to be moved once she went to prison. A house she'd shared with her ex-boyfriend Tim. Rhiannon and her parents hauling Billie's clothing and books out of the small two-bedroom house a half mile from Illinois College in the rushed panic of Billie in the hospital followed by Billie behind bars. Tim hadn't helped at all, holed away in his campus office so he wouldn't have to see them. Rhiannon's asked Billie only twice across the past six years if she heard from him since and both times her sister shook her head, her mouth a line drawn tight.

Billie glances at the television's footage of the wreck. We weren't so closed off inside to not hear about all this. Is this why Mom wanted us to drive?

Rhiannon nods. She doesn't know what else to say.

What time are we leaving tomorrow?

I don't know. Nine. Ten? You can sleep in if you want.

I'm used to getting up at six. Prison orders. I'll probably be up before the sun.

Rhiannon looks out the living room's bay window. Nearly the first day of summer, tonight a long June evening that should have held an equally long sunset. The window fogged with gray, the same charcoal haze pressed against the windowpanes since March.

I'll set an alarm just in case, Rhiannon says. It should be sunnier out west.

She assumes but isn't sure. She's seen the weather reports, the climate abnormalities in every part of the country. In the Midwest: rain and clouded skies, temperatures at least twenty degrees below normal since spring. In the Northeast: hot and dry, the same as the West and the Southwest where states of emergency have been declared due to drought. And in the Great Plains: so much wind. Gusts reaching 50 miles per hour. Rhiannon feels a hand on her leg, the first time Billie has touched her beyond their first strained hug.

If I didn't say it before, Billie says, thanks for taking me in. Thanks for letting me stay.

Rhiannon turns off the television. She's done nothing but pick Billie up. This isn't her house anymore, both of them interlopers, bedrooms no longer theirs. She's done nothing but map the logistics of a route their mother planned across four states.

Dad may call you tomorrow before we leave, Rhiannon says. I haven't talked to him much, but he knows you're home. He knows we're leaving in the morning.

Rhiannon hears Billie's breath halt and waits for her to speak. What they've never discussed, Billie shutting down the conversation every time Rhiannon brought it up: across six years, their father hasn't visited the Decatur Correctional Center once.

I'm heading to bed, Billie says though it's not even seven o'clock.

Extra blankets in the hall closet, Rhiannon says. In case you get cold.

She stays on the couch and knows they're

too old now but imagines light flooding beneath Billie's closed bedroom door if she followed her upstairs. What she saw so many nights of their childhood shared in this house. Billie reading books in bed when she should have been asleep. Billie obscuring the glow by bunching sheets around her flashlight, by lining a towel along the bottom edge of her door. Never *Gulliver's Travels* or *Peter Pan.* Always books on science, still lining the bookshelves of Billie's bedroom turned office. Books on fossils, just like their mother. Books on herpetariums. Books on the lakes and streams of Illinois. Then in high school, ornithology guides that Rhiannon can only guess quickly became manuals on falconry in college. Birding handbooks. Guides to constellations. The same kind of books their mother was writing, contributions to paleontological textbooks and scientific journals, a language Rhiannon never understood. The same kinds of books found scattered and burned all around Billie in Illinois College's library when she was taken to the hospital and then arrested. Audubon's *Birds of America.* An atlas of world maps, splayed open to Mozambique. The pages of an illustrated history of oceanography flamed down to a fine husk. Rhiannon hears Billie walking around in the bedroom upstairs and then her footsteps fall silent.

Rhiannon leans into the couch's cushions and listens to the hollowed echo of the house, the quiet patter of rain on the roof. So many empty rooms. Closets filled with jewelry, vacation seashells, musty coats and rain boots, old vinyl albums. What she's been sorting through since March, what she and Billie will continue thinning out when they return from Utah. Rhiannon imagines the walls of Beth's apartment less than two miles away, the lithographs and silkscreens surely still on the walls. Beth's artwork. Beth's delicate things everywhere. A French press and tea tins and coffee table books on Jim Dine and Jean-Michel Basquiat. An entire book on the Spiral Jetty, an earthwork sculpture curling out from the shore of the Great Salt Lake, the kind of land art Beth wanted to create. Rhiannon had barely moved anything into their apartment. She pulls her phone from her back pocket. Hesitates. Dials Beth's number anyway, still the top contact in her phone.

Beth picks up on the second ring. How's she doing?

We're both fine. Still scheduled to leave tomorrow morning.

You talk to your dad?

Not yet. I'm guessing he'll call before we leave.

A garbled noise on the line. Beth eating. A Friday night. Rhiannon knows she's called at dinner, knows Beth could easily be with someone else.

Are you ready for the trip? Beth asks.

Not really. But I can't back out. Not now.

Want to come over?

Rhiannon closes her eyes. The light-filled apartment she moved into four years ago and left at the end of March. No fight. No grand severing. Only a slow drift that still feels sometimes like love.

I shouldn't, Rhiannon says. We should stop doing this.

You're the one who left, Beth says though there is no accusation in her voice. A statement of fact. Beth beside her at the cemetery, a hand Rhiannon wouldn't hold to keep everything still and measured and restrained before she dragged her picture frames and her clothes back to her childhood bedroom within a week. A toothbrush. T-shirts. Everything so easy to move. Nothing meant to stay, she knows in hindsight, her racing helmet still hanging in the garage of her mother's house. The one item she never moved to Beth's apartment. A past life she and Beth barely acknowledged.

I miss you, Rhiannon says.

She says it and watches the thick gray rain out the window and listens to the silence of her sister's room through the ceiling above her.

I miss you too, Beth says. Get some sleep. And drive safe out there on the road.

When the line falls silent, Rhiannon tries to picture the route beyond the drone of the living room's television and the boxes of Christmas decorations her mother left behind. Illinois. Missouri. Kansas. Colorado. The road sprawled ahead of them west on Interstate 70 straight out toward Utah, a road she traveled countless times with her father on racing trips, a road unfurling toward their mother, a road unfurling toward goodbye.

What she couldn't tell Billie when she asked, what their mother's funeral had really been: that among bouquets of lilies and the rain and the soft pressure of her aunt's hand on her shoulder, Beth quiet beside her, Rhiannon felt at last what she'd tried so hard to imagine for six years.

What it was that Billie felt in the library.

What it felt like to ignite.

What it felt like to burn.

HURST, MARGARET. PHD. "VASCULARIZATION AND FUNCTIONALITY OF STEGOSAURUS PLATES." PALEONTOLOGY AND THE JURASSIC AGE: A TEXTUAL COMPENDIUM. ED. JONATHAN MCGREG. NETHERLANDS: ELSEVIER, 1999. 22–30. PRINT.

CALL NUMBER: QE860.4 .R16 2009

ABSTRACT

The functionality of stegosaurus plates, two rows of bone along the ridge of the reptile's spine, has long been debated in the fields of paleontology and geology. This paper proposes that among varying theories for the plates' functionality, including self-defense and size augmentation against predators, an alternative might be considered for mate attraction and signal communication. Given the presence of blood vessels in each plate, and the subsequent presence of blushing and changed color, this paper submits that stegosaurus plates were intended to attract potential mates and signal other herd members regarding potential food sources, environmental conditions, and the possibility of approaching danger.

Because the stegosaurus's plates were vascularized, carrying blood vessels rather than containing solely bone and cartilage, blushing among stegosaurus herds is a strong indication that the plates' color was used to attract mates, as well as to communicate signals to other herd members regarding food availability, potential danger, and change in atmosphere or climate. To date, vascularization has been assumed to suggest only temperature control for a cold-blooded reptile. However, the orientation of the plates as well as their flexibility and range of motion suggests that vascularization served multiple functions, including mate attraction and sensitivity to environmental harbingers.

40.1097° N, 88.2042° W: Champaign-Urbana, Illinois

Sometimes from the thin mattress of her prison-dorm bed, Billie lay in the dark and imagined Rhiannon racing the track of the Chicagoland Speedway. Her car a flash across blacktop. Two hundred miles per hour. Gripped tires crackling across the asphalt's heat and Rhiannon lowered inside a single-seat cockpit. A fighter pilot's reflexes: what it took to command a stock car at the highest speeds a land vehicle could reach. Rhiannon had been in the garage with their father for as long as Billie's brain was old enough to make memories, her sister as much a part of the NASCAR world as diesel-soaked rags and cans of gasoline.

Billie shifts on the mattress of the pullout couch in her old bedroom, the metal bar digging into her back still more comfortable than the rungs of a state-issued prison bed. A room that seemed so small to her in childhood filled now with the enormity of being alone, no bunkmates, no constant coughs and yells, the first time she's been by herself in years beyond finding the farthest corner of the prison yard and standing as still as possible, her eyes scanning the trees for hawks. Falconry. The hobby she chose, so different from her mother and sister and father. All around her in her mother's office: rock picks. Chipping hammers. Chisels and tweezers. The tools of a trade lined across the room's shelves and her mother's corner desk. Also on the desk: a single textbook, what Billie knows hides one of the most well-known articles her mother wrote when Billie was still in high school. "Vascularization and Functionality of Stegosaurus Plates." QE860: a call number Billie never came across in Illinois College's Schewe Library or the prison library despite memorizing the Dewey decimal system. Beside the textbook sits a lone stegosaurus metacarpal, one of the dinosaur's smallest bones. What her mother could transport and keep at home, what she showed her daughters when they were small. And the main focus of her life's work: what the stegosaurus's trademark plates were for.

A paleontological controversy, Billie knew. A decades-long debate over whether the plates were used for defense or thermal regulation, for camouflage or self-protection. Growing up, Billie remembers her mother's voice at the dinner table discussing armored plates while her father pretended to listen, a driver himself before retiring to join Rhiannon's maintenance crew. It was only after reading earth science texts as a University of Illinois biology major and then as a circulation clerk at Illinois College that Billie gained a better sense of her mother's work. Her mother believed the plates were vascularized with blood vessels to sense shifts in weather, and also meant to attract mates. No different than a male cardinal's crimson feathers. A mating call. A method of animal magnetism. The same as a red-tailed hawk's aerial dance of courtship.

Birds descendants of dinosaurs, though Billie knew falconry was nothing compared to her mother's work. Birding something Billie pursued instead of chasing Jurassic fossils or the adrenaline rush of race cars, nothing more than a hobby to her mother's career and her sister's fame and her father's lifelong passion for the road. What Billie kept as a pursuit of leisure, her library job a means of meager funding, the only person in her family without a clear career. Birding notoriously a white man's hobby, no different from the world of paleontology or the world of racing. Her teacher, Bud, the only Latino falconer in the state of Illinois. She'd called him on a whim after finding his listing in the phone book one lazy afternoon after house-party hopping the night before, an impulse she knew was sheer curiosity born from her biology classes and not the influence of her mother's work. Billie still wonders what made Bud accept her as an apprentice, so few women in the field, so few of anyone but middle-aged men.

Light rain pelts the lone window of her once-bedroom, a wash of gray water. She sinks into the pullout couch's sheets, flannel bedding Rhiannon must have chosen instead of thin cotton, what should have been more appropriate for June. She watches the walls of her childhood bedroom and tries to remember how young she must have been when she first knew herself as different from a mother and father and sister who were always in motion, every single one of them always doing, always pushing harder no matter the route they chose to push. Her mother in academia and research, already in a doctoral program by the time she met their father, a man who never completed college. How he clung to a trade instead, to oil changes and tire pressure and speed. How Rhiannon absorbed this. Billie wouldn't admit to anyone what she knew from the prison's threadbare sheets, even dreaming her sister on the raceway: that sometimes the Correctional Center felt like a long exhalation. Six years of breathing out despite how hard each day could be, even in a minimum-security prison. Rationed food. Rough guards. Group therapy. The monotony of so many long days. Despite all of it there was still no need to control anything, everything controlled. Eating. Showering. Her only responsibility tending the small prison library's circulation desk ten hours each week. An inmate assistant to the prison's single librarian, Barbara, a woman who kept to herself and browsed online most days, her computer the only monitor with authorized internet access. Work Billie was given for her background in libraries despite academic circulation sharing nothing with a one-room collection of donated books. Children's books. Young adult novels. Books left behind by visiting families. Books dropped off in boxes by well-meaning citizens. Popular magazines. Old issues of *National Geographic* and *Elle* and *The Economist.* Nearly every leisure read in their small collection gifted or discarded, Barbara curating everything else through meager state funds and federal guidelines for inmate enrichment. GED preparation. Parenting skills. Drug addiction prevention and sexual abuse recovery. Billie's single task was to keep tabs on which inmate checked out which book, her only tool a small scanner and sometimes a cart for reshelving books. No picks. No chisels. No hard grip on a steering wheel that controlled an entire engine. Just her palms circling a scanner. How it was enough on days when her shame grew overwhelming. How embarrassed she knew her parents must have been to have one daughter in national races and the other in jail. How the blaze of what landed her in the Correctional Center could distill itself down to something so simple: her hand to the worn spines of donated books.

Not the flashed pavement of the raceway her sister and father shared.

Not the heat-scorched rock of her mother's digging.

Billie rolls over in the flannel sheets and tries to imagine the Cleveland-Lloyd Dinosaur Quarry, a trip impossible to picture after an interminable block of unchanging days. The quarry where their mother spent most of her professional life and where Billie's been just once, in ninth grade when her mother took her on a dig while Rhiannon spent her senior year spring break in Atlantic City with her friends. Billie remembers the hazed peaks of mountains, the dry-crackled air. The wide-open desert of Utah, a Martian landscape of snow-packed summits and a single salt lake. When they arrived, Billie knew her mother wanted her to feel a spark of passion, some sense of what she wanted from her life. Rhiannon already racing. So many books squirreled away in Billie's bedroom. She remembers her father saying sometimes when she picked up books on dinosaurs *maybe you'll be just like your mother* and Billie watched her sister pull on her driving suit and felt a cloud of pressure descend, the same pressure she felt standing at the quarry, the thick desert heat bearing down as her mother showed her how to dust red rock and reveal fossilized bone. Fifteen. Billie not even done with her first year of high school. She remembers nothing from the trip except that the quarry was an alleged predator trap, the reason it held the highest concentration of Jurassic bones in the entire world. Where so many Jurassic carnivores were found alongside the herbivores they were drawn to feed upon, a mud pit that caught and smothered hundreds of dinosaurs at once.

Billie sits up, feels the wetness of her still-damp hair. Glances at the rain-fogged windows, a streetlamp on Grove Street pressing light against the panes. She sits at her mother's desk and runs a palm across the stegosaurus metacarpal, bone velveted in layers of sediment. She notices the back of her own hand, still unblemished, skin that smooths up toward her elbow before starting to pucker. Third-degree burns rivuleting her forearm, breaking into rippled waves up her shoulder and across the left half of her back. The left side of her abdomen equally raked, her left leg a long scar of thick skin. A doctor told her postgraft that she'd been found lying on her right side, passed out on the Schewe Library's floor from smoke inhalation. Books scattered around her. Blistered pages. Burned bindings and ashen lettering. An overnight custodian had pulled up to the library lot and seen smoke billowing from the windows and called the fire department and Billie wonders even still what police made of the black eye, how doctors justified the dragged cut down the side of her face unaffected by fire. The side pressed into the library floor's carpet, unburned. The side that forced her from Tim's apartment to the library's doors.

Billie picks up the metacarpal, holds its

surprising weight. Her mother's tools filling a room she no longer fills, a room Billie once filled, a room holding nothing more of either of their dreaming. She hears Rhiannon walking around downstairs, the soft creak of the hardwood floors. A home that across six years still smells the same, cedar and cinnamon bread, her mother's baking trapped in the floorboards and the walls.

And in the closet: raptor-size anklets. A single hood. Jesses and a bow perch and a lure line. Her falconry equipment. What her family didn't let Tim keep when they collected her things. And Alabama: Billie's red-tailed hawk. She'd cut the bird's line. Watched the hawk hesitate only a moment before taking noiselessly to the dark, before Billie herself took to the street toward the library. Across so many nights watching the small window above her prison bed for the faint blink of stars, Billie felt the phantom grip of Alabama's talons still grasping her arm through the raptor glove.

She leaves the closet closed. Listens for the sound of another voice downstairs. Wonders if Rhiannon will have Beth over before they leave for two weeks. A woman Billie's never met, an entire relationship begun while Billie was in Decatur, so much of her sister lost to a chasm of time. Billie hears nothing, just the sound of her sister's weight moving across the floor, and reaches down into the Amelia Earhart bag her mother brought to Decatur on her last prison visit four months ago. What she slid across the table in the Correctional Center's visiting room just after she was diagnosed. What once held Billie's doll clothes. What the warden let Billie keep, her sentence nearing its close.

What contained a GPS device.

What contained a journal filled with coordinates, one on each page.

Go to these places, her mother said. *Don't look ahead in the pages. Don't ask questions. Please, just do as I say.* A road trip, her mother said, immediately upon Billie's release. The coordinates locations she wanted her daughters to visit along their route.

Billie took the journal, a small notebook no bigger than a Moleskine.

One page at a time as you find each location, her mother said. *For now, just the first page.*

Billie opened the book. On the first page: no notes, no map, no indication of city or state. Just a coordinate, latitude and longitude, and a single drawing beside it. A drawing of a dinosaur. A thin sketch. The only page she promised her mother she'd look at until they were well on the road.

Her mother didn't have to say it. Billie knew Rhiannon didn't know about the GPS or the journal. She guessed her mother had her reasons, ones Billie wanted to protect. And Billie hated to admit that it felt good having a secret to keep, to not be the one family member on the outside looking in.

Their mother had squeezed the journal into her hands. Billie didn't have to ask why her mother wanted them to drive. She'd seen the news on the airplanes in the Correctional Center's television room. But she didn't know anything of what these coordinates were, what her mother intended for them to see along the way. Billie took the digital GPS. She took the journal. She took them pretending she would see her mother again. She'd let her mother walk away through the metal detector and the double-paned glass, to a quick decline in a hospital bed that only took four weeks.

What began as a secret was now a promise.

Whatever it was their mother wanted for them, Billie would see that they did it.

She sits at her mother's desk and opens the journal and runs her hand over the ink-stained coordinates of the first page. Her mother's handwriting a precision across years of holding picks and brushes, a penmanship grown blurred with radiation and a tumor's pressure, her brain a bomb all these years just waiting to explode. And in the final two weeks, a tumor so large it pushed against her frontal lobe and shut down her motor control and slurred her speech. Billie spoke to her by a wall-hung phone only twice after her final visit, both times her voice barely audible. *Billie.* The syllables smeared. *Billie. You are so loved.* What Billie couldn't bring herself to say back if it meant the last time, the word an unaccustomed stone in her throat. Billie hanging up the hallway's phone, pressing her forehead to the receiver. She glances out the window at the evening rain and imagines the funeral at Greenlawn, the blooming March irises, Rhiannon and their father standing in bone-wet cold. Her fingers find her mother's tools upon the desk, rock picks and trimming chisels and tiny hammers. How she wants to dig them into her skin. Break the earth of her body. Excavate the scars. Exhume everything she's done that kept her from being there in the cemetery.

Billie looks at the journal's first page. The first coordinate. A northern degree followed by a western degree, latitude and longitude, neither of which mean anything to Billie without a map. A small sketch of a Tyrannosaurus rex beneath it. A stick drawing. Her mother's only hint of what they might find when they reach this first stop, one Billie will map in the morning once they're on the road. Billie knows Rhiannon will balk. This part of the plan she wasn't let in on, this change in their route. Rhiannon's rigidity surely their mother's reason for giving Billie the journal instead.

Billie runs a palm up her left arm, the skin a rough ridgeline beneath her fingers. Its similarity to a stegosaurus's back the only bridge Billie could forge between her mother's life and hers in the end. She imagines her father in Chicago, over two hours from Champaign-Urbana, gone from their childhood home for over sixteen years. Divorced when Billie was a sophomore in high school, just a year after she visited the Cleveland-Lloyd Quarry with her mother. Her father's voice: one she hasn't heard since she left for Decatur. A voice Rhiannon expects her to speak to in the morning if he calls.

Billie curls into the sheets and hears the hum of the television downstairs through the floorboards. The past six years: a break from the pressure to do anything at all, but also a long tenure of contemplation. That if she'd done something meaningful and good with her life, she wouldn't have gone to prison. Wouldn't have been living in Jacksonville. Wouldn't have met Tim. What she would have been instead: following her own path just like her mother, her sister, her father.

A thick scent of coffee drags Billie from sleep, a knot of pain pulsing in her back against the couch's pullout bar. Intermittent sun speckles through the window behind a wall of heavy clouds but there's no sound of rain. Rhiannon is already dressed when Billie heads down to the kitchen in her pajama shirt and underwear, sleep hazed enough to forget the pocked skin along her left leg until Rhiannon's eyes catch upon her bare thigh.

Billie stops. Sorry. I'll grab some pants.

No, it's fine. Don't worry about it.

Billie climbs down the last step, the first time she's felt self-conscious about her body in years, her prison mates used to her scars. Billie remembers swapping clothes with Rhiannon in high school, pulling off ripped jeans and exchanging tees, an effortless undressing that here in the kitchen feels all at once guarded. Rhiannon hands her a mug of coffee. Then a bowl of yogurt, a plate of eggs. Strawberries. Blueberries with cream.

I figured you couldn't get any of this in Decatur, Rhiannon says. She sits down at the kitchen table with her own plate. Billie sees she's waited to eat though she's been up awhile, her hair nearly dry but the tips still wet. Jeans and a tank top. Ready for a long drive. Billie takes a bite of eggs scrambled with cilantro and avocado and Sriracha and sour cream. Nothing stale. Not four-day-old bread, not near-sour milk.

Thanks for making breakfast, she says.

Rhiannon picks up her fork. The car's packed. Water, protein bars. I put a bunch of trail mix and fruit in the backseat. I just have a backpack in the trunk. There's plenty of space in there for whatever you want to bring.

Do you have music?

Rhiannon gestures toward the garage. My phone's already hooked up. I made a huge playlist. You can add tracks if you want.

Billie shakes her head. She and Rhiannon haven't traded music since high school. The benefits of an older sister. How it made you cultured. Let you know Joy Division, NWA, PJ Harvey, Tori Amos. Their parents also record collectors. Their names the product of their parents' old albums. Rhiannon: their mother's obsession with Fleetwood Mac.

And Billie: her father's love for Michael Jackson, shortened from Billie Jean.

Sleep okay? Rhiannon asks.

Like a rock. Billie sips her coffee. Are you seeing Beth before we go?

We broke up.

Billie looks up. When did that happen?

Just after the funeral. I moved out.

Billie doesn't know what to say, her bare legs beginning to prickle with cold. The strangeness of a once-familiar house and an empty bedroom. A girlfriend she's never met but felt she knew through anecdotes and stories every time Rhiannon visited.

Are you okay?

I'm fine. We're still friends. Or whatever else in between.

Billie wants her sister to say more but she doesn't. Rhiannon stands and the telephone rings, the landline their mother insisted on keeping. She knows who it is by the tone of Rhiannon's voice as she picks up the phone. When Billie finally looks up, Rhiannon is watching her, her hand holding out the receiver.

Billie doesn't want to take it.

Out on bail? her father says when she takes the phone.

Just getting ready to leave, she says.

About a two-week trip?

Two weeks. No more, no less.

Just wanted to tell you I'm glad you're out, he says and Billie hears the central Illinois twang, the nasal vowels and the truncated syllables, the *yer* instead of *you're* despite sixteen years in the city. The Chicagoland Speedway his home track since it opened just after Billie graduated from high school. Where he moved full-time once it was clear there would be no reconciliation postdivorce, where he still works servicing cars and venturing out on a road team for traveling races.

You girls be careful out there, he says. What with the weather and all.

We're not girls anymore, Billie says. A small grenade she can't stop herself from throwing. Rhiannon looks up from washing dishes at the sink.

Be that as it may, her father says, just be careful out there.

Billie hands the phone back to Rhiannon and heads up the staircase to get dressed and hears her sister letting their father know where they'll be and when. His voice nothing like Tim's and yet the Illinois drawl flames a heat inside her that rises with each stairstep she takes. Tim all Illinois, born and bred. Their relationship a tilted seesaw. An imbalance that crowded the walls of the prison, that became a motor for never again. The dull ache of a black eye. The sharp blow of a fist splitting skin. The can of gasoline that would burn everything down.

When Billie pulls her suitcase out to the garage, Rhiannon is standing in the entryway of the raised garage door, the sky oystered in clouds behind her. Billie hoists her suitcase into the trunk and keeps a daypack slung over her shoulder.

There are water bottles in the backseat, Rhiannon says. And I put two thermoses of coffee in the front cupholders. We can refill them at motels and campsites. I have enough money for motels all the way, but I packed a small tent just in case. Just let me check the house one last time. You have everything?

Billie nods and Rhiannon heads back into the kitchen while Billie throws her hiking daypack in the passenger seat. At the bottom, her mother's journal and the GPS device. Her sister's phone already hooked up and mapped west. Sunglasses in the visors. Water bottles in the backseat of the two-door coupe beside a soft-pack cooler filled with apples and trail mix. Billie forgets how often Rhiannon has seen the road. She glances around the garage: so many tools, bags of soil, clay pots. Two road bikes suspended upside-down from hooks screwed into the garage's ceiling. And on the far side of the garage, two racing helmets hung against the wall.

Billie recognizes the one on the left: a helmet their father gave Rhiannon when she first started racing in Soap Box Derby events, painted in lightning bolts and coated with dust. The one on the right, Billie's never seen: a larger helmet lacquered in constellations and covered in cobwebs when she lifts it from the wall.

Is this your helmet? Billie asks when Rhiannon returns to the garage.

Rhiannon looks up, her face unreadable. It was, she says. I haven't used that one in years.

Where do you keep all your stuff now? Your suit and your gear?

It's still at Beth's apartment. Rhiannon locks the kitchen door behind her. I'll get it back when you and I return. I keep some stuff at the raceway too.

Are you still at the Vermilion Speedway?

I practice there. Chicago's better, but I haven't gone up the last few months.

You sure two weeks away is okay for the racing schedule?

Rhiannon drops her hands. It's fine, Billie.

To be honest, I've taken a step back from circuits this summer with everything that's happened. I need this break too.

Billie places the helmet back on the wall's hook. Rhiannon climbs into the driver's seat and turns on her phone's map and says nothing more of the raceway and Billie lowers herself into the passenger seat before Rhiannon backs the car out of the driveway. Billie drags her fingers against the passenger window's glass as they pull away from Grove Street, their childhood home receding in the rearview mirror.

Heavy fog dusts the flatlands as they drive west on Interstate 72, stratus clouds resting low on the cornfields. Billie knows this land stretched in every direction from the Decatur Correctional Center's prison yard where she sometimes went for short walks, the stark view impeded only by the fence's whorls of barbed wire. She knows the way the seasons shifted beyond the prison's fence from summer to winter and back to summer, the muscle memory of a girlhood spent entirely in central Illinois. She can tell by the corn's height how much of summer is left. In June: empty fields, pointillistic rows of planted seeds. Short stalks in July. Waving greens by August, taller than every high school boyfriend Billie ever had. She remembers the sharp cut of corn silk, tassels caught in her clothing running through the fields as a teenager with some boy, shirts caked with dirt from the silt of stalks and from lying down in the high grass. Mosquito bites and sweat. The scent of citronella and aloe. The droned whine of cicadas across the fields of August, the Illinois sky a broken-open eggshell above them, a landscape Billie memorized even amid the alcohol haze and cigarette smoke of high school. Her brain a map of hills and patches of oak trees and undulations of rolling corn, an atlas of childhood that became the learned requirements of a falconer releasing a red-tailed hawk: to know the height of trees, the respite of clearings, what bramble might snag a bird if it didn't return when called. Rhiannon's car passes a field of wind turbines, bone-white blades cutting circles in the clouds, and Billie recognizes the same turbines she sometimes saw from her prison window if the sky cleared just right. They are nearing Decatur. Billie realizes the coordinates of their mother's journal will determine their route west and determine it quickly. She reaches down for the journal in her bag before Rhiannon turns to see what she's doing.

What's that? Rhiannon asks.

I wanted to wait until we were on the road, Billie says.

For what? What did you bring?

Billie opens the journal and glances at the first coordinates. She doesn't know enough of latitudes and longitudes to know where these coordinates point. And the T. rex drawing: Billie has no clue what it means. She rummages in the daypack and pulls out the GPS.

Billie, I have the map. I know where we're going.

Billie presses the coordinates into the handheld device and it beeps, their destination located. The center of St. Louis. Billie looks up and sees an iridescent-green road sign marking only eleven miles to Springfield, where they'll have to turn if they want to change their route and head south.

Pull over, Billie says.

What?

Just do it.

Rhiannon shifts into the right lane and pulls onto the shoulder, the highway's rumble strips vibrating beneath the Mustang. She brings the car to a stop but keeps the engine running, her foot on the brake pedal.

Jesus, Billie. What?

I need to tell you something.

Rhiannon looks straight ahead and Billie sees her jaw working inside her mouth, her teeth tightening against one another.

Mom brought me something, Billie says. For the trip.

Brought what? When did she bring you something?

Mom brought me a journal.

Rhiannon looks at her. What the fuck are you talking about?

A journal of map coordinates.

For what?

She brought me this journal and GPS specifically for this trip.

When? When did this happen?

Four months ago. She came to see me.

What, and you're just telling me this now?

I know you want the quickest route. But, Rhee, this is mapping us to St. Louis.

That's south. Rhiannon shifts the car into park, the engine idling. We're heading west, she says. Straight across the top of Missouri.

There's a whole journal, Billie says. A journal of coordinates. Places she wants us to visit along the way. At least that's what she told me.

Rhiannon pulls the journal from Billie's hands. Opens it to the first page and runs her fingers over their mother's handwriting.

The same penmanship that once scrawled their names across brown lunch bags, that marked birthday cards mailed to Billie's college dorm room and to Jacksonville and to the screened postal facility in Decatur every single year. Billie studies Rhiannon's face, the tremble of her lip, a brief flinch before she begins turning the pages.

Don't look ahead, Billie shouts.

What do you mean, don't look ahead? Where the fuck are we going?

She made me promise not to look ahead. That we'd take each page one at a time.

One at a time? How many are there?

I don't know. She didn't tell me.

Jesus, Billie. That could take weeks.

She knew we'd have to get back within two weeks.

Rhiannon glances down at the journal's first open page. But there's no location, she says. Only coordinates and a drawing.

I know. Billie looks at her hands. I think she wanted us to have some fun. As much as we can on a trip like this.

Rhiannon closes the journal and throws it against Billie's lap.

Why didn't you say anything? Is this some kind of fucking joke?

Rhiannon presses her fists against her closed eyes, like she's trying hard not to break herself open.

We don't have to do it, Billie hears herself say.

Rhiannon pushes herself back against the driver's seat and blinks up at the car's ceiling.

Of course we have to do it, she whispers.

Billie touches the back of her sister's hand and Rhiannon pulls away.

You should have fucking told me.

I know. I just didn't want you to say no.

I mean earlier. Four months ago. You should have told me then.

When, Rhee? It's not like you came by. You haven't visited in nearly three months.

You should have told me, Rhiannon repeats.

Cars whip by on the highway. They sit in silence. NPR blares on low, the last radio signal Billie knows Rhiannon has hoped to catch before they travel beyond range. Storms developing late. Continued flight investigation across the weekend in Arizona until a black box is found. Airports continuing to shut down. O'Hare. Lambert. General Wayne Downing in Peoria. The sound of a radio a revelation, something Billie took for granted and then forgot. Their news at the Correctional Center always television, always screened to prevent surprise and the possibility of inmate conflict. Billie breathes inside the car and hears the rise and fall of her sister's lungs in the driver's seat beside her.

We take 55 south from Springfield, Rhiannon finally says.

So you'll do it?

We take 55 south to get to St. Louis, is all Rhiannon says.

Billie closes her eyes. Rests her hands on the journal. Feels nothing but relief. Keeps her eyes closed long after she feels Rhiannon shift the car into drive and the rumble strips shake as the Mustang pulls back onto the road.

The river is a ribbon of dulled light beneath a matte-gray sky. Billie remembers coming into St. Louis as a kid and rounding the hilled bend of Interstate 55 and seeing the Mississippi River sudden and wide, as big as an ocean from the landlocked plains of Illinois. The Arch a halo on the riverfront, what her mother surely saw being built from her hometown of Godfrey across the river along the bluffs. Where Rhiannon and Billie visited their grandparents as children, picking white peaches in summer and spotting bald eagles in winter.

Rhiannon turns off the radio. What does

the coordinate say?

Thirty-eight degrees north, ninety degrees west, Billie says. Approximately.

Where in St. Louis? Tell me where to go.

Billie lets the GPS map them straight into the heart of St. Louis, the highway winding past Busch Stadium where they saw St. Louis Cardinals games as kids.

Get off here, Billie says when the GPS beeps. Rhiannon pulls the Mustang off the highway and straight into Forest Park.

Are you serious? Rhiannon says. We've been here a million times.

The park a staple of their childhood, larger than Central Park in New York. Weekend day trips down to St. Louis for the park's free institutions. The Art Museum. The History Museum. The St. Louis Zoo. They pass the zoo's entrance and Billie remembers feeding the giraffes with Rhiannon and their grandparents, rough purple tongues pulling in stalks of leaves. Washington University sits at the park's western edge, where their mother earned her doctoral degree and where she met their father, working then at the Gateway International Raceway just across the river in Madison. The raceway Billie imagines was their mother's version of cutting loose through graduate school, where she went sometimes with friends to forget the halls of academia. Where Billie guesses her mother's friends warned her away, even then, from starting a life with a man wedded to transience. Billie guides Rhiannon through the park until the Mustang is idling in a lot near the outdoor ice skating rink. She glances out the window at a group of people playing sand volleyball, what the rink has become in summer months despite the Midwest's rain.

Why are we here? Rhiannon says. What the fuck are we supposed to find?

Come on, Billie says. Let's get out and walk.

They follow a paved path that circles a pond populated with clusters of mallards. Two men stand at the pond's edge casting fishing lines. Three teenagers sit on a blanket beside the water taking advantage of a day without drizzle. To stroll along a path: unthinkable from the boxed-in walls of Billie's bunk in Decatur. Everywhere people outside, a small miracle. Billie scans the tree line for hawks, an instinct. Rhiannon walks ahead, her gait impatient. She slows when the path begins to ascend a steep hill.

Are you sure this is right? Rhiannon says.

Positive. This is where Mom went to school. Where she met Dad. We spent half of our childhood in this park. Surely there's something here she wanted us to see.

Rhiannon brushes her hair from her face. A road bike buzzes past them in the opposite direction. Rhiannon keeps walking and Billie follows until her sister stops short and Billie nearly runs into her.

Rhiannon steps onto the damp grass, her face tilted up. Billie follows her gaze. What they've seen before as kids. The St. Louis Science Center. Home to the city's planetarium, to penny funnels, to a chick hatchery and gas-filled beakers and rising balloons that demonstrate the magic of helium. Home also to dinosaurs. Reconstructed skeletons. Indoor replicas of pterodactyls in motion. And an outdoor park filled with resin dinosaurs that she and Rhiannon climbed on as children.

Except one: only one dinosaur too tall for them to scale. A tail that as kids they crawled across until it sloped upward, too steep to climb. Rhiannon stands at its base, squinting up. Their mother's drawing. The Tyrannosaurus rex.

JOHNSON, BRIAN. PHD. "WENDELL SCOTT: NASCAR'S FIRST BLACK RACER." AN UNEQUAL PLAYING FIELD: AFRICAN AMERICAN ATHLETES IN THE 20TH CENTURY. ED. DEBRA HILL. UPPER SADDLE RIVER, NJ: PRENTICE HALL, 2010. 121–129. PRINT.

WENDELL SCOTT: INITIAL BIOGRAPHICAL INFORMATION

Born on August 29, 1921, in Danville, Virginia, Wendell Scott became the first African American NASCAR driver and the first African American winner of the Grand National Series. He learned the mechanics of cars through his father, who was a driver for two white families in Virginia, and eventually began running his own auto body shop after WWII. He began attending stock car races, though he was at first barred from participating due to assumptions that only white racers were allowed on the track.

Because black drivers were sometimes recruited in Danville's Dixie Circuit to race white drivers, Scott eventually began racing in his hometown. After he brought his car to Winston-Salem to compete in a NASCAR race, however, the organization would not let him enter. He raced in non-NASCAR competitions and speedways until 1954, when his reputation for speed and skill brought him onto the national stage of NASCAR competitions.

In 1961, Scott moved up to Grand National, NASCAR's highest series, and became the first African American to win this series in 1963. He was not announced as the winner at the time despite finishing two laps in front of the second-place leader. The trophy went to the second driver, Buck Baker, and though Scott was named the official winner two hours after the race, his family received the trophy in 2010 — forty-seven years after Scott's win, and twenty years after he died.

38.6311° N, 90.2703° W: St. Louis, MO

Rhiannon wants to be thinking of her mother. Wants to stand beside a resin dinosaur she and her sister climbed across as kids, a sister she hasn't stood beside in six years. Wants to not be hurt by her mother's secret, that she gave the journal to Billie, that she kept all this hidden. Rhiannon wants to look at the T. rex and know what a pair of coordinates and a drawing mean but she stands with Billie inside the dinosaur's shadow and thinks only of the Gateway International Raceway just across the Mississippi River.

One of her first major races. Barely out of high school. A race in the NASCAR Nationwide Series, a minor-league circuit to prove her worth for the top-ranked Sprint Cup Series. Banked asphalt. Pooled mirages. The simmering heat of June. Billie still in high school and back in Champaign with their mother while their father stood nearby on the sidelines, the crew chief of her seven-man pit team. Two tire changers rolling out new wheels. A lone gas man adding race fuel, a catch-can man detaining the overflow. A jack man ratcheting the car and wiping the grille clean. Two tire carriers taking the changed tires away. Only seven team members allowed inside the pit-stop crew, her father calling orders from behind a regulation wall. A team that at the Gateway still had no faith in her driving, the only woman in all of NASCAR at the time. What Rhiannon hated most about racing and what she couldn't have known as a girl in her father's garage when she first fell in love with the speed of cars: NASCAR a minefield of every form of discrimination, the crowd unaccustomed to anyone behind the wheel who didn't look like them. No drivers of color. No gay drivers, one of the first secrets Rhiannon ever learned to keep. And so few women. Janet Guthrie in the 1970s. Shawna Robinson in the 1980s, a driver no one talked about when Rhiannon was small. Sara Christian a competitor in NASCAR's inaugural 1949 race, a man finishing the race for her. So few women, all of them white, and everyone else in every book she found: nothing but faces upon faces of white men except the one man who became her role model.

A driver named Wendell Scott.

The first black man to race in NASCAR. The first African American to win a major race. His family accepting the trophy posthumously, an award he didn't even get to claim while living. What enraged Rhiannon to read in high school and what she read again so many years later while selling an order of textbooks on sports barriers in the twentieth century. For Rhiannon in the twenty-first: slurs of gender. The condescension of *sweetheart.* The hurl of *cunt.* The expectation that she was someone's girlfriend and not a driver, surely so different from what Wendell Scott endured on the racetrack as the nation pushed toward the civil rights movement, but even if their fights were similar yet so very separate, she held him as her hero. The Wendell Scott Trailblazer Award now a NASCAR recognition, an award established for marginalized drivers making gains in the field and bestowed by nomination from other drivers, what her male peers never deigned to do for her. Her whiteness a privilege. Her sexuality concealed, at least on the track. And her gender only tolerated, even after her first major win at the Gateway International Raceway.

Twenty cars huddled together around an oval track, a proximity that made Rhiannon forget how fast they were moving. One hundred seventy miles per hour. The interior of the car an oven, Rhiannon pressed behind the steering wheel into the bindings of a roll cage. Rhiannon drafted the leading two cars before maneuvering ahead on the race's final lap and inching past the checkered line in first place. The sound of the crowds: a stunned silence before hesitant cheering. A woman climbing from the winner's car, the briefest of pauses before grudging applause, what she guessed Wendell Scott also heard and worse when he won the Grand National in 1963.

And the sound of her tires pulling off the circuit and into the crew pit: the same rumble of pulling over in Illinois and letting Billie tell her what the fuck was going on. In the feeble glint of the afternoon sun, the statue of the Tyrannosaurus rex looming above them, Rhiannon glances at her sister. At the ripples of scars cascading down her bare left arm.

This is it, Billie says. The exact spot of Mom's first coordinate.

Rhiannon nods. Finds it hard to speak. She pictures a library's flames, what she imagined from her car's cockpit on her first race after Billie's sentencing. The Indianapolis Motor Speedway: the race that took her out of racing. The dead heat of August, Billie locked inside the Decatur Correctional Center less than two months. How Rhiannon had already set qualifying records at Daytona, how she'd placed in the season's NASCAR Sprint Cup Series at Talladega and Pocono and on to Kentucky and the Texas Motor Speedway through May and June, how the checkered flag was in sight.

Billie squints at Rhiannon. What do you think this means?

Her sister standing beside her, here and now. Her sister: the reason for the end of a career. How she'd only meant to clip the stock car beside her and her tire blew and catapulted her car against the racetrack's walls. The car flipping, the tire exploding, her wheels spinning out. Her father on the sidelines. The asphalt's heat so close to the fuel tank and the car spiraling across the raceway and she remembers wondering what flames would feel like catching the protective layer of her uniform if the car caught fire. If it would be a benediction. The same as Billie. A split second of spark, the car buckshot against the speedway's wall. Then her father's hands beneath her arms, pulling her out.

She'd lost the race.

After Billie left, she'd lost every single one.

Rhiannon looks at Billie standing scarred in the shadow of the T. rex replica and for a moment feels the deep pit of resentment rise in her chest before she catches it in her throat and swallows it, her sister beside her a miracle despite everything.

Rhiannon sighs. I don't know, Billie. I don't know what any of this means.

Billie touches the T. rex's leg, reptilian skin sloping down to four thick talons. She crouches and sits on the tail and glances up at the dinosaur's frame.

Can you believe how fucking small those claws are? she says.

Rhiannon shields her eyes. Looks up. What she recalls her mother telling her of the T. rex, a Cretaceous dinosaur, the age following the Jurassic period of her mother's work: the arms used for grasping a mate in copulation. What her mother knew by studying the mating habits of ancient reptiles. Her life's work, a term that rattles in Rhiannon's brain. Life's work. St. Louis a city Rhiannon hasn't visited since she stopped crossing the country on the racing circuit. St. Louis a city where her mother's career began in graduate school and where Rhiannon's flamed before fizzling out.

■ ■ ■ ■

The bar is dark when they walk in. Neon signs. Damp hardwood floors. Two televisions behind the bar, one broadcasting an afternoon Cardinals game and the other on mute running CNN, headlines blaring the crashed plane and the continued closures of airports. Paris's Charles de Gaulle. Tokyo's Narita. New York's JFK. Billie takes a seat at the bar and orders a Bud Light and Rhiannon pulls up a stool beside her.

Come on, Rhiannon says. You can do better than a Bud Light.

We're in St. Louis. Home of the King of Beers.

You've been away for six years. Order something better. Billie signals to the bartender and changes her order to a

Schlafly pale ale. Rhiannon asks for an IPA and two orders of cheese fries, a late lunch. The bartender hands each of them a beer and Billie slides her pint against Rhiannon's glass.

Cheers, Billie says. To the road trip.

To the road trip. And to your first beer in years.

Billie looks at her. You think I haven't had alcohol in six years?

I've read Decatur's policies. It's not allowed.

That doesn't mean we didn't have our ways.

Despite herself, Rhiannon smiles. Your ways? Like what?

Hidden contraband. Bootleg bullshit. One of the girls in my dorm worked in the kitchen and made her own moonshine out of cornmeal and sugar.

Lucky you, Rhiannon says. The fries arrive and she grabs a bottle of ketchup.

Moonshine aside, I haven't had any beer in a long time. And I don't think I've had a Schlafly since college.

Rhiannon remembers Billie's dorm room at the University of Illinois. A concrete tower of double rooms, nothing like the luxury high-rises skyrocketing around Champaign-Urbana now. Nothing like her own college experience, no dorm, only living with her father in Chicago between races and going part-time to the city's University of Illinois campus. A degree in communications that she barely finished. Billie's experience back home far more traditional, living in the dorms at their mother's insistence. The full experience. Four years of college. Where Billie met Tim, a doctoral student in European history, before following him to his first job at Illinois College in Jacksonville. Rhiannon glances around the bar, an establishment at the edge of Forest Park and St. Louis's Central West End. A neighborhood she knows her mother lived in for a period of time while studying at Washington University, the bar just old enough.

Do you think Mom ever came here? Rhiannon says.

I doubt it. Not her style. She wouldn't slum it here.

It's not like she came from money. And she met Dad during those years.

Yeah, that was a phase. One she shouldn't have bet on by marrying him.

Rhiannon notices the bar's pool table, empty of billiard balls. She tries to imagine her parents here, a bar they likely never set foot in. The dynamics between them always tenuous, how she and Billie grew up well aware of their father's discomfort around their mother's academia. How Rhiannon sensed his pride in their mother's research as much as she saw his misgivings, his lack of education a cross he bore against their mother's doctoral degree even though she, too, was from small-town Illinois, the only member of her family to graduate from college. Rhiannon remembers her mother saying that her parents came to her PhD graduation, a world they didn't understand. Her doctoral robe, bunches of fabric they called her wizard cape. The fact of their showing up good enough. Rhiannon wondered sometimes if her mother simply grew accustomed to tough love. Rhiannon saw how her father showed it: *your mother can't be at your school play because of course she's working late again.* Rhiannon wonders if she ever did the same to Beth, a learned response. Wonders if Beth's brought anyone over since Rhiannon left. She looks at Billie. Knows Tim is surely still somewhere in Jacksonville.

Was Tim a phase? Rhiannon asks.

Billie keeps her eyes forward. I'm not going to talk about him.

You never do. You never have.

Billie glances at Rhiannon. What does it matter?

Because I'm supposed to look out for you. I don't want you to repeat any mistakes. And I don't know if you consider him a mistake.

You really think you're looking out for me? By bringing this up? Why now?

Rhiannon picks at her plate of fries. She doesn't know why she's bringing it up now. She watches drops of condensation slide down her pint glass and knows it isn't Billie she's interested in needling. The fire a fluke, an act of desperation. A mistake Billie won't repeat. Rhiannon doesn't know what happened between Tim and Billie, if he simply disowned her after she went to prison. Rhiannon knows only that she's irritated.

Why didn't you tell me about the journal?

Where she wants anger in her voice, there is only hurt.

Billie sets down her beer. I just wanted to get out here with you. I wanted that first. And before you think worse of her, don't think she was hiding anything.

How can I not think that? She knew about this for nearly four months and said nothing to me.

You think this is all about me, a funeral for my benefit. I guarantee you, it's not. She didn't say much when she came to Decatur, but she did say this — that you were wrecked. That you needed to get the fuck out of Illinois.

I am out of Illinois. I'll be out of Illinois for two weeks.

And isn't this better? Here we are.

We could've had beers in northern Missouri, Rhiannon says and thinks of the route she planned straight across Missouri and up through Nebraska. She thinks of the Gateway Raceway, the blade of driving past it.

But here in this bar, there's a calm in returning to St. Louis that she doesn't expect. Where they visited their grandparents. The hum of baseball on the bar's television the same as every Cardinal series they watched as kids. The burned melt of cheese fries, the hops and carbonation of beer. Beth always drank whiskey. Rhiannon hasn't had a beer in years, hasn't left the state of Illinois in months. And Billie. Her sister here beside her. Her sister here.

What do you think this means? Rhiannon says. The park. The T. rex statue.

I have no fucking idea.

I've only got two weeks off, Billie. And we need to get back within fourteen days for your first therapy appointment. There's no leeway on that.

Billie nods. We'll be back in time. Even with a different route.

Rhiannon sips her beer and watches a foul ball sail into the stands on-screen.

When they leave the bar, the sky has darkened in whorls of green and gray, a thunderstorm rolling in from the west. Though it means more rain, the low sound of approaching thunder comforts Rhiannon. What's been missing in Illinois. The summer thunderstorms she remembers, the lightning and heavy clouds of a Midwestern childhood. The interruption of television broadcasts for weather updates. The front porch where she sat with her father watching cumulonimbus clouds push in. Her mother inside but watching from the window, Billie beside her, how no one ever retreated to the basement no matter how many storm sirens screamed. How thunderstorms were better than television. How thick drops of rain gusted in sideways, blowing open blinds, wetting window screens and splashing the pavement beyond the driveway. How long it's been since Rhiannon's seen anything but gray rain and anemic clouds.

Think we should wait it out? Billie says as they approach the Mustang, still parked near the Science Center. I know you're nervous about the weather given the news.

We're not flying, Rhiannon says, the first lack of worry she's felt since hearing the news. I haven't had the chance to drive through a storm all summer.

The wind picks up and Billie glances toward the T. rex. Do you think there's anything we're missing? We don't even know why she led us here.

Rhiannon climbs into the car. We looked. I don't think there's anything here but a reminder. A place to start.

Billie situates herself in the passenger seat. What kind of reminder?

I don't know. This is where she spent her childhood. This is where her career began. And this is where we began too. Our entire family. Where she met Dad.

She didn't study the T. rex.

But it's on our route. And these are the only outdoor dinosaurs in the whole city. Besides, she studied them a little by looking at every dinosaur's mating habits.

Billie watches out the window as Rhiannon follows the road out of Forest Park, trees whipping leaves to the pavement. A few stragglers remain on the paved trail. Two runners. A lone biker pedaling into the wind. Rhiannon watches a garbage can blow over and roll into the street and pulls onto the highway headed straight west into Missouri. I-70: the same interstate she took so many times with her father. Lightning flashes beyond the windshield and splinters down the horizon, a bolt of electricity breaking apart a sky that has gone almost black.

What's the next stop? Rhiannon says. Whatever it is, we still need to be in Utah within the next few days.

Billie opens the journal, grabs the GPS. The sky splits open with rain and the windshield wipers kick into high gear and Rhiannon feels a wave of sadness, the St. Louis skyline receding in the rearview mirror. Where their mother studied. Where their father first built his racing career. Where she began hers only years after she first taped a picture of Wendell Scott to her bedroom wall, a page she copied from a library book. The Gateway Raceway where she first hurtled her car across 110-degree asphalt toward a finish line no one thought she could cross.

Smoky Hill River, Billie says. Russell Springs in Kansas, right along I-70.

What the hell is in Russell Springs?

Like I would know.

How far?

Over six hundred miles. Almost nine hours.

Rhiannon glances at the dashboard clock. 3:04 p.m. We might be able to make it, she says. We'll see how far we can get. Is there a drawing by the coordinate?

Some kind of fish. Something big. With fins and teeth.

Fins? We're in the middle of the fucking plains.

A fossil is my best guess.

Rhiannon sighs. Wonders why their mother couldn't make legible notes, couldn't have just told them where they're headed and why.

Whatever, she says. Put on any music you want. We'll be in the car awhile.

Billie chooses Bob Dylan. *Highway 61 Revisited,* far mellower than what Rhiannon expects. Billie's childhood bedroom once filled with Black Flag posters and Minor Threat LPs. The jangle of Dylan's harmonica fills the closed car. Gusts of wind push against the side of the car and the St. Louis suburbs thin out to waves of green hills. Billie sinks into the passenger seat and traces her finger along the water droplets streaking the window and Rhiannon watches the road ahead through the downpour, thunder rattling the earth around them, the red taillights of the car ahead their only guide west.

The storms abate along Interstate 70 just as Rhiannon passes signs for the University of Missouri. Signs she passed along this same highway during what would have been her college years, spent instead taking piecemeal online courses and driving every major roadway chasing NASCAR series wins. Rhiannon knows the I-70 Speedway just past Columbia, Missouri's only asphalt oval where she sometimes raced in regional competitions. Billie still in high school then. Billie now asleep in the passenger seat beside her, lulled by the rain. The Dylan album long over, replaced by the in-and-out static of public radio. The weather report: clear skies in Kansas City but reports of a tornado touching down in Owensville, sixty miles behind them. *The sky is volatile,* the reporter says before segueing from weather to more coverage of the downed plane and Rhiannon lets the words ring through her brain in the car's silence. Her mother's unthinkable decline. The hurried end of her relationship with Beth. Billie's release. The journal. Rhiannon's hands grip the wheel, the only semblance she feels of any control at all. The radio drones: major airports closed. Air travel suspended. A black box recovered in northern Arizona, the latest development. Officials investigating its recordings for any link to the crashes of six other planes worldwide across the past four months.

The landscape rolls in half-lit waves beyond the window as Rhiannon listens to the broadcast's summary of the other six planes. Black boxes have been pulled from four of the crashes, every one of them holding the voices of pilots shouting sudden clear-air disturbances. Unprecedented turbulence. Air currents gusting beyond the most modern advances in aerodynamic technology. Voices of surprise then a quick cutting off, what was reported across all of the recovered boxes.

Billie shifts in the passenger seat beside her, still asleep, and Rhiannon recalls the last commercial flight she took. Always white-knuckled, always a nervous flyer. She specified a window seat every time to watch the clouds and know why the plane jolted each time it passed through a mass of white. A race car so contained, one lone driver. The commercial plane a conglomerate of so many factors beyond anyone's control. The ground crew: so many different people who oversaw wings and lights and fuel and wheels, so many different places where one thing could go wrong. The same as a pit crew, though she knew every single person on her team. The flight attendants anonymous, the throngs of people shuttling in, a pilot in the cockpit she'd never meet. Air traffic control. The strange dings and bells in flight. Rhiannon hated everything about flying and had taken to sitting in the window seat unable to read or do anything at all, watching only for coming clouds and for any small movement a plane could make.

Her mother knew this. Her mother teased

her. So accustomed to flying multiple times each month to dig sites and conferences. Rhiannon always drove between raceways but had been flying since Billie's incarceration, an occupational hazard of selling textbooks. And then her mother's chiding tapered off once her own travel grew bumpier in the past few years, flights west filled with turbulence.

Rhiannon's last flight: five months ago. A trip between Chicago and New York to meet with sales executives at the textbook corporation's headquarters. A two-hour flight, a windless day. Completely smooth through clear skies until the plane shook everyone on board halfway in, the man beside her roused from sleep, the teenager in front of her pulling headphones from his ears. The plane dropping swift as a diving bird, overhead bins rattling open, the drink cart crashing down the aisle, the flight attendant shouting, the bellwether Rhiannon watched to know what was routine and what was not. Her stomach hollowing out as the plane blew sideways and the man beside her braced the seat in front of him, no more than ten seconds of extreme turbulence, but in those ten seconds before the pilot gained control and the plane leveled off and the flight deck issued an apology, Rhiannon was absolutely certain the plane was going down and that she would die in the air so far from a planet that held everyone she loved.

When the plane landed, wheels gripping the runway like talons, Rhiannon promised herself she would never fly again.

One month later, the first of seven planes crashed to the earth.

Signs for Kansas City shimmer along the road. As they near the state line, the thunderstorm's thinning clouds break the last of the day's glow into shards. Billie sleeps beside her and Rhiannon watches the western sky above the highway and lets herself think of her mother. Feels for a moment what her mother built into this trip for her: not just a second funeral for Billie, but a car. Transportation without fear in a vehicle that feels like home. Her hands to the wheel as if her mother were guiding her across the Midwest.

When Rhiannon hears Billie wake, the sun has set but the sky remains streaked with fading ribbons of light beyond the windshield. Billie rubs her face, reaches into the backseat, and pulls out an aluminum bottle of water.

How long was I sleeping? Billie says.

Almost all the way across Missouri.

Billie squints out the window. Where the fuck are we?

The middle of Kansas. We passed Topeka a while ago.

Rhiannon surveys the land spilling all around the car. Land for miles. The Great Plains. A browned panorama of small badlands and pocked fields of dimly lit sunflowers. Rhiannon glances at her sister and wonders what this looks like to her, these roadways a diagram burned into Rhiannon's brain. She realizes that even before Billie went to Decatur, she'd never lived beyond the state of Illinois, not even in college and the following years in Jacksonville. Only trips here and there. The quarry at fifteen. Family vacations. Billie watches out the window and Rhiannon feels a brief stab of jealousy for a single horrible moment that her sister can see this land for the first time.

How far are we from Smoky Hill River? Billie asks.

About two hours, according to the GPS. It's nearing nine o'clock. How hungry are you?

Very. We could stop at the next town for the night.

The next biggest town is Salina. Fifteen miles down the highway. Might be our best bet. We can head over to the river in the morning.

Salina, Billie repeats. I've never even heard of it.

When they pull off the highway at one of Salina's three exits, a strip mall greets them past the first stoplight. One storefront is illuminated in a line of darkened windows, its neon sign advertising a restaurant: La Cantina. Rhiannon glances farther down the street and sees only darkness.

How about Mexican food? Rhiannon asks.

Billie nods. Mexican it is.

Inside the restaurant, they slide into a vinyl booth and a server drops a plastic wicker basket of tortilla chips on the table. Rhiannon orders only water, Billie a margarita rimmed with salt. Soft music pipes through the speakers above them and above the restaurant's only two other patrons, a couple populating a booth in the back.

How does it feel to be out here? Rhiannon says.

What, you mean on the road?

On the road. And outside of Illinois.

I always knew I wouldn't be in there forever. Billie breaks a chip in half and dips it in salsa. You'd be surprised how fast six years goes, even with nothing to do but wait. Even still, this feels crazy.

The pang of jealousy sharpens in Rhiannon's chest. How so?

All of it. Those coordinates. The land. How fucking wide open it is. How I never noticed. Billie runs a hand through her short hair. And Mom, she says softly. How somehow the land looks different. How I know she's not here.

Rhiannon thinks of the St. Louis skyline fading in the rearview mirror.

How did you do it? Billie says.

Rhiannon doesn't know what Billie means as their food arrives. Two plates of chile rellenos. The server walks away and Billie's voice softens.

How did you stand watching her go?

The question is a blow, one Rhiannon could have anticipated sometime across the drive, but still it beats the breath from her lungs. The same seizing she felt beside the hospital bed while her mother slept and the television droned on the wall above them. In the flickering light Rhiannon felt the world already absent. A dropping out of every scaffolding the earth held. A quiet panic from the bedside chair as her mother's fingers worked dig sites through the dreaming of her sleep, a bricked silence that pressed against the room's windows and the ceiling and the floor.

I didn't, Rhiannon says. I didn't stand it all.

At least you got to say goodbye.

There is no such thing.

Billie says nothing, the restaurant's music the only sound between them.

Rhiannon glances at Billie. What happened when she visited you last?

Nothing happened. She gave me the journal, the GPS, told me what to do with them. Then she left when visiting hours were over. There was no fanfare. We both pretended like it wasn't the last time.

Billie sips her margarita and Rhiannon feels the tip of a knife needle her chest. Billie watching their mother walk away. Billie pressing her hand to the visiting room's glass window once hours were over, what she'd done so many times after Rhiannon came to see her and time was up. Any jealousy she felt dissipates. Rhiannon pushes her fork across her plate and wonders which of them had it worse. Whether it was harder to pretend not to say goodbye, Billie knowing for sure she'd never see their mother again. Or whether it was harder to watch her waste away, the chemo treatments, the appetite loss and the brittleness of bone and the falling away of hair in chunks.

How it ravaged her completely.

How it turned her animal.

How Rhiannon kept it locked inside her as she sorted through her mother's closets.

I wish it could have been different for you, Rhiannon says.

Billie looks up. I can't imagine you had it any better.

She would've visited you again, Billie. I don't think any of us had any idea it would happen so fast.

Has Dad helped?

He's come down a few times. He'll help us go through her things, but there's nothing he wants. They've been divorced for sixteen years.

Rhiannon doesn't know why she doesn't mention their mother's wedding ring, that their father wanted it, that she looked for it in every jewelry box in her mother's bedroom and couldn't find it. Billie says nothing and slices her stuffed relleno with the side of her fork.

I know you're angry with him, Rhiannon says. You have every right to be. But I think he just wants to help you, make sure you're transitioning okay.

Nice of him to think of me now.

Rhiannon doesn't know what to say. Doesn't know why her father never visited Decatur across six years, even when he drove down to Champaign from Chicago to visit.

What about Beth? Billie says.

What about her?

Is this just a break? For a little while?

I don't know what it is, Rhiannon says. She grabs a tortilla chip from the basket and thinks of countless nights on Beth's couch watching cooking shows and nature documentaries and home improvement reruns. Whether it was losing her mother that drained away any shred of love she had to give or whether it was the final linchpin of a slower collapse. Beth pressing closer and Rhiannon a wall, knowing herself a fortress. Beth asking about her racing. Rhiannon shutting down the conversation every time. How she made her mother promise to never mention it in Beth's company. Rhiannon doesn't know what would have happened if her mother had never gotten sick. Reruns and popcorn. If her mother was only an excuse to leave.

I'm just not good for anyone right now, she says.

You're good for me.

Rhiannon looks up and her sister is watching her.

I'm exhausted, Billie says. I don't want to go where we're going. I want to say goodbye the right way and I don't want say goodbye at all. But I'm out here. I'm on the road. I'm on the fucking road, Rhee.

Rhiannon wants to feel something. Wants to take in this moment beyond the stiffness of embracing her sister outside the prison when she picked her up. But she feels only curiosity, nothing else. What it is that makes her sister feel this much.

What it was that made her once burst into flames.

Come on. Billie sets down her napkin. Let's get out of here and get some sleep.

Rhiannon signals for the check. When they step out to the car, streetlamps hold the only points of light along the dark street. Slumped mailboxes. Tall grass. Wind winnowing through town from the open plains. Rhiannon drives with the windows down, the weather noticeably warmer from the cool damp of central Illinois, until the Mustang comes upon a motel with a neon vacancy sign still blinking. The Salina Inn. Free breakfast. Free Wi-Fi. A pool. Rhiannon pays fifty-five dollars for a double bed, the pool an indoor atrium they pass on their way to the room. When they open their room's door, there is brown shag carpeting and dim lighting and the stale scent of cigarettes.

Billie sits on the bed's edge. I want to go swimming.

The pool's probably closed. You brought your swimsuit?

I found an old one in my closet last night. Of course I brought a swimsuit. And pools are never closed at places like this.

I didn't even think to bring a swimsuit.

Come on, Billie says. Just wear your underwear.

Rhiannon hesitates. This day already nothing of what she planned. But she pulls off her T-shirt and jeans before she can make herself stop and then they are sneaking back down the hallway toward the atrium, Billie in her bikini, the entire length of her left leg a long scar. Rhiannon's bra and underwear mismatched. The atrium a wall of humidity when Billie opens the door. A small Jacuzzi in the corner. An enormous water slide tubing into the deep end of the pool. Bright orbs of pool lights. Rhiannon watches as Billie stands at the pool's edge and regards the diamond glow of the water. Eyes rimmed like she might cry and Rhiannon wonders when Billie last swam. Rhiannon doesn't wait. She is here. Illinois is behind her right now so she might as well be here. She runs past Billie and jumps into the deep end and feels the rush of water push against her bra and when she surfaces Billie is tunneling down the slide and shooting headfirst into the water and Rhiannon hears the reflex of uncontrolled laughter ricochet off the atrium's walls right before the water takes her sister in.

HERNANDEZ, LINDA. "IS CLEAR-AIR TURBULENCE CAUSING BUMPIER FLIGHTS?" TECHNIQUES IN COMMERCIAL AVIATION. ED. FREDERICK GAINES. COLUMBUS, OH: MCGRAW-HILL, 2013. 24. PRINT.

CALL NUMBER: TL691.8 .G21 2013

IS CLEAR-AIR TURBULENCE CAUSING BUMPIER FLIGHTS?

According to a recent study by a team of meteorologists at the University of Florida, incidents of dangerous turbulence on commercial planes causing injury to passengers and crew have been on the rise in the past two years. The study suggests that clear-air turbulence (CAT) is the cause, the meeting of bodies of air traveling at widely different speeds in otherwise cloudless skies. This can cause severe turbulence in commercial planes and is suspected to be the cause of 80 percent of turbulent flights resulting in injury to passengers and flight attendants between 2011 and 2013.

One reason CAT may be increasing is more flying routes, causing air wakes between planes that cumulatively disturb the atmosphere. Some meteorologists also speculate that climate change may be causing CAT, a warming atmosphere creating greater pockets of varying air temperatures and speeds that could clash. It is still too early to determine whether either of these possibilities are true, or whether this is merely coincidence. Air travel remains completely safe in the continental United States and worldwide.

38.9111° N, 101.1758° W: RUSSELL SPRINGS, KS

Billie sits on a picnic table outside the Salina Inn, sun sifting through the morning clouds. Wind pushes across the plains and ripples through the cornfields lining the motel's parking lot. Rhiannon still sleeping. With a cigarette and a paper cup of weak coffee, Billie watches light creep up the Kansas horizon. She can count on one hand the number of Camels she's smoked across the past six years. Just three — all of which Billie smoked in bathroom stalls — from her first bunkmate, Skylar, a wiry girl with a reputation for smuggling. Decatur's contraband queen: four years for small-business embezzlement until she was transferred to East Moline a quarter of the way through Billie's sentence and a sullen arsonist named Tina took Skylar's place and kept to herself.

Like with like. Her prison mates called their bunk Arson's Corner. Prison mates

Billie never got to know beyond cursory meals and handing each other soap in the hard-water showers, women Billie sometimes let herself believe she was better than in her worst moments. She'd grown up in a good family. She deserved more after making a single mistake. It was easier to believe the other women had made more than one mistake and that there was such a thing as a good or bad family but when she was honest with herself on dark nights when she couldn't sleep and a square of sky poked through the small window above her dorm bed, she knew that despite the injustice of Tim getting off without consequence and still standing in front of college classrooms and masquerading as a role model for students that she too had gotten off easy, her sentence lighter than those of the women around her. Arson more violent than drug possession, what so many of the women in Decatur were in for. Minimum security. The prison filled with women swept up in the remnants of the war on drugs, pulled apart from their families just for carrying marijuana. She couldn't have set a building on fire if anyone else had been inside but in the rage of dragging a can of gasoline across the deserted streets, her brow bone broken and her face bleeding down her sweatshirt, she knew on those worst nights in her dorm bed that she couldn't have been sure. She could have harmed someone. There was so much less harm in selling a drug, a pang that kept her withdrawn from other women and holed away in her own bunk.

After Tim, she felt no need to know anyone else.

A couple pushes through the Salina Inn's lobby doors, a burled man walking five feet ahead of a small woman rolling a suitcase, and Billie can't help but see it even six years later. The man's sharp directives. The woman throwing her suitcase in the trunk of a beat-up Geo, the man taking the driver's seat. Subtle disparities Billie once told herself to disregard. Tim's razor tongue. Labeling her women friends idiots. Calling her useless when she forgot to take the trash out. What she let herself ignore until the first time he shoved her, a quick blow of violence. His phone ringing one night while he was in the shower, a phone she'd checked but hadn't picked up. His hair still wet when she told him she didn't recognize the number, thought nothing of it at all until she was already pressed to the wall with his elbow to her throat. His skin still damp against her neck, eyes hollowed and emotionless with rage. A violation of privacy, he'd screamed, his face unrecognizable so close to hers. Billie watches the couple climb into their car and rolls her tongue on the blunt taste of cigarette ash, the same taste of smoke that crowded her throat before she passed out in the library.

She'd worked for two years in a circulation position Tim negotiated when he joined Illinois College's history faculty, an extension from her hourly wages at the University of Illinois's undergraduate library where she'd bided time for two years after graduation while he finished his dissertation. Then two years of isolation in Jacksonville. No one around but the Schewe Library's patrons, Illinois College students sliding their textbooks across the circulation desk without looking at her. No acquaintances but Tim's new colleagues, faculty members who talked over her at parties because she only had a bachelor's degree. Every friend from high school and college still in Champaign. Her mother, too. Her father and Rhiannon always out on the road. No one there to restrain Tim's growing *stupid*s and *bitch*es and *slut*s, no one to tell her they were just words but dangerous ones. How she wanted to tell someone but couldn't, her sister making sports headlines, her mother publishing groundbreaking articles. The shame of making nothing of herself funneled into the acceptance that she was nothing if Tim kept telling her she was. Jacksonville a hiding place for discolorations. Mounting bruises. The wide wash of empty Illinois cornfields: the relief of anonymity. Until a shove became a cracked tooth became a dislocated shoulder became a knuckle splitting her brow. Until she took to the lamplit streets wild-eyed and bloody, her chest filled with nothing at all. Until she stormed to the library, the only shelter she knew, after stopping at the Marathon gas station and buying one freestanding canister of gasoline.

A matchbook in her pocket, the only thing she remembered to take from home.

The library's key dangling on the chain wallet belted to her jeans.

How she stood in the center of the stacks hyperventilating, her right eye a bloodshot mess. Five years wasted. Five years bearing the weight of words. Five years of gaining nothing but a knowledge of falcons, some stupid agility with birds. Gasoline in her hands. All around her: books on ornithology. Deep-sea exploration. So many pages of information and every one of them routing her nowhere, only to a fist, only here, her face hidden beneath her hoodie, what she'd pulled over her eyes at the gas station to conceal what was fractured. Blood creeping down her cheek, a velvet stain already permeating the shoulder of her shirt. She pulled the books from the shelves and tore them open and ripped up every page she could find and scattered them around her and shook the gasoline until she felt a hot dampness seeping through her clothes and against her skin.

Pulled the matchbox from her pocket. Struck it lit.

How she threw the match and how quickly a flame spread across the floor and swept across the library's carpet and the scattered books and climbed her shoes and jeans and stretched up her body as she watched the silent streets beyond the library's bay window and then the world burned clean and dissolved.

Sometimes from her bunk, quarantined from every other woman to let herself feel the shame and learn from it somehow, Billie watched peregrine falcons wheeling in the sky and wondered if it wasn't the library's custodian who first called the police, what the deposition said, but the clerk at the Marathon station: a middle-aged woman Billie saw squint hard beneath her hoodie before handing over change for the gasoline.

A look Billie came to recognize only later, the look of a woman who knew. The look Billie can't stop herself from giving the Geo as it pulls out of the Salina Inn's parking lot.

The lobby doors open and Rhiannon appears with a cup of coffee, her hair still wet from the motel room's dimly lit shower.

Not much in a way of breakfast, she says.

I'm fine with protein bars in the car, Billie says. And this shit coffee.

Rhiannon sits on the picnic table beside Billie. I still can't believe there's no rain out here.

Billie follows Rhiannon's line of sight toward the plains, russet-colored hills that undulate with the gold of sunflower fields. A span unimaginable from the bunk of a prison, a landscape Billie only intuited in the late dark of last night's arrival. In the morning's thin sun, the Kansas prairie rolls for miles.

Ready to hit the road? Billie says.

Already showered and packed. I wore hiking boots, just in case.

What do you think we'll find?

It's a drawing of a marine reptile. You can expect a dig site.

I don't remember Mom ever coming to Kansas.

I don't either. She never studied reptiles. But that doesn't mean she wasn't here. She had a whole life before we were born.

Or maybe she was never here. Maybe it's just some bullshit roadside attraction.

Rhiannon stands. We'll find out if we get on the road.

Billie crushes the last of her cigarette into her empty coffee cup, the air warm enough that she sheds her hoodie for the tank top beneath. She forgets the damaged cells of her shoulders pulling in the prairie's sun, forgets that her skin gives anyone in the inn's lobby a reason to look.

Russell Springs is farther than Billie guessed, nearly three hours west of Salina. The Mustang passes the sign for Smoky Hill River just before noon, a brief drive south of I-70 and a stone's throw from the Colorado border. No trees in sight, only wide-open fields of rippling wheat and specklings of soybeans. The GPS leads them to a parking lot for someplace called Smoky Valley Ranch, the sign marking what appears to be a hiking trail leading out into the plains.

Jesus, Rhiannon says. I'm glad we filled up in Salina.

The coordinate is a little farther, Billie says. Somewhere out there in the fields.

Rhiannon looks dubious. To Billie, the plains beyond the windshield are like staring into the sun. So magnificent they hurt. So much space.

Where do we start? she says.

Rhiannon nods toward a one-room building beyond the passenger-side window.

Visitor center, she says. Looks like the trailhead is over there.

When they approach the building, Billie sees a trail marker and a hiking register. Not a single name penciled in. Inside the visitor center, a lone man sits at a desk reading a mystery paperback, a box fan whirring behind him.

He looks up when they walk in. What can I do for you ladies?

Rhiannon speaks first. We think we're looking for a trail. Fossilized reptiles, we're guessing. Where can we find those?

The man closes his book. You've come to the right place.

He pulls out a trail map and hands it to Rhiannon. He says there's a one-mile loop and a five-mile loop, that both will take them past Cretaceous sea deposits.

Smoky Hill River was once the sea, he says. The Age of Reptiles. The map tells you more, but you'll see everything along the way. Not to mention spectacular views of the river valley on both loops.

Billie hangs back and looks at the center's displays of the valley's fossil record and rock sediments. The Chalk Badlands. The entire Smoky Hill River Valley a pocked landscape of bluffs formed by an ancient sea.

Be sure to take water, the man says. And watch out for rattlesnakes.

Billie follows Rhiannon from the visitor center toward the trail.

Rattlesnakes, Billie says. Are you sure we want to do this?

We're fine. He probably just has to say that as a precaution. Rhiannon squints down at the map. We should take the shorter loop. It's probably enough to see what she wants us to see so we can get back on the road. Where are we headed next?

I didn't map it yet. Surely Colorado, since we're so close to the state line.

Maybe Denver. We can map it when we get back to the car.

Billie looks across the open plains, the river valley's badlands poking up through fields of prairie grass. Denver's only a few hours from here, she says. If that's where we're headed, we can still be there by dinner. We have plenty of time.

Rhiannon sighs. Two weeks, Billie. That's all I have.

Yeah, and an extra hour in Kansas isn't going to make you late for work.

Rhiannon glances at her. Fine. Five-mile loop?

Billie holds the GPS in her hands, the coordinates still leading them somewhere out into the fields. They set out on the longer trail, Rhiannon in front against the valley's high winds while Billie follows with the map.

This says we could see prairie chickens or swift foxes, she says.

What about the fossils? Rhiannon shouts. What kind of fossils are we looking for?

This says large turtles and sharks. And giant clams.

We're not looking for clams. What dinosaurs?

Billie runs her finger down the map's list. Mosasaurs and plesiosaurs.

Like I know what those are.

Cretaceous dinosaurs, Billie says, what she remembers from the science wing of the Schewe Library, books she opened on slow afternoons. Section QK. A decimal system she memorized from working at three different libraries.

These fossils are more recent than Jurassic fossils, she calls to Rhiannon. Even if this wasn't Mom's era, maybe she studied these first.

She keeps walking, the wind whipping prairie grass against her exposed legs. Rhiannon passes back water and trail mix. A small toad hops across the dusted path. Billie feels sweat beading at her temples, the first she's broken in years beyond the squats and sit-ups of her prison bunk. The trail begins to climb, a steady creep to the edge of the river's dust-brown bluffs. Rhiannon reaches the precipice first, an expanse overlooking the valley of western Kansas. Cutting through the bluffs below: the Smoky Hill River. Larger and wider than Billie anticipated, a rushing oasis through the dry prairie. Rhiannon steps up to a small wooden placard staked into the dirt.

Cretaceous formations, she reads aloud. This must be what we're looking for.

The GPS beeps in Billie's hands, the coordinates reached almost squarely. This is where we're supposed to be, she says. Do you see anything?

Rhiannon kneels at the edge of the ravine and runs her hand over the rock. The sun breaks clear of the thinning clouds overhead, a full sun Billie hasn't seen in months from the dreary gray of Illinois. Light bounces off the reddish-brown rock of the river valley and Billie looks down to see Rhiannon crawling on her knees along the bluff's edge.

This looks like some kind of reptilian fossil, she says. She skirts her hands across a wide swath of puckered rock. Billie crouches beside her and traces the ridges. The faint outline of four fins, a round body. A neck stretching out long and far, the marine version of a brontosaurus. Billie glances at the trail map.

Plesiosaur, she says. Exactly where the map says it is.

Rhiannon sits beside the fossil's outline. And Mom's drawing?

The journal is back in the car burrowed in Billie's daypack, but she remembers the contours of her mother's sketch.

This is it, Billie says.

Do you see anything? Can you remember anything she ever said about marine fossils or Kansas?

Billie sits beside her sister and lets her legs dangle off the bluff's edge. I don't remember anything, she says. She went on a million digs. She could've been here anytime. She could've even come out here when she was in graduate school.

Rhiannon squints down at the water. Goddamn, it's hot out here.

Did you ever think you'd say that after all the rain in Illinois?

Rhiannon leans back, tilts her face to the

sun. It feels nice.

Billie takes in the sweep of their view. Red bluffs. Marbled blue sky. The sun diamonding off the rush of the river. She closes her eyes and listens. No noise. No cars, no highways. No guards yelling. No chatter of dorm mates. Only the water's liquid rush and the wind's pulse and the rise and fall of Rhiannon's breath beside her.

What do you think this means? Rhiannon says.

Billie doesn't know. Doesn't care. Wants only to sit with the sun warming her face way out here. Rhiannon stands and returns to the staked placard and Billie hears her hiking boots scuff through the dirt path, pebbles and gravel. Hears her footsteps stop at the sign, her metal water bottle clanging open, her breath catching and sharpening.

Billie, come here.

Billie turns and Rhiannon is crouching in the dirt and pushing her hands through short tufts of crabgrass and pulling out what looks like a small ammunition box. When Billie reaches her, Rhiannon is holding the box in her palms.

What is that? Billie says.

I don't know. There's some weight to it. I think there's something inside.

Do you think it's for us?

Billie, I don't know.

Is it locked? Can you open it?

Rhiannon presses against the box's plastic, a small latch that quickly pops open. She lifts the plastic lid and looks inside and Billie sees a folded piece of paper on top.

What is it? Billie asks.

Rhiannon unfolds the paper and Billie sees what's scrawled on the sheet before Rhiannon can speak. A drawing of a reptile alongside a set of coordinates. The exact latitude and longitude plugged into the GPS in Billie's hands.

Jesus Christ.

Rhiannon looks at her. Did you know about this?

I would have told you if I did. She only gave me the journal.

Rhiannon glances down at the box. There's something else in here.

She sets down the piece of paper, holds up the plastic box.

Unearths a locket on a short golden chain.

What the hell is that? Billie says.

Rhiannon pulls the chain from the box. I've seen this before. I know what this is.

What? Billie says. What the fuck is it? Her voice sharper than she wants. Rhiannon peels open the locket, a gold disc no bigger than a quarter. A locket Billie remembers seeing her mother drop into her nightstand jewelry box at some point across their childhood. Rhiannon sits in the grass, her jeans chalked with dirt. She hands the locket to Billie. Inside, on one half: a picture of their mother as a teenager. Her hair dark and full, her cheeks rose bulbs. The other side their aunt. Two years younger than their mother, a cherubic-faced adolescent.

That's Aunt Sue, Billie says dumbly. Her mother's only sibling, an aunt Billie hasn't seen since Thanksgiving the year she moved to Jacksonville. Living now in Dallas. She glances at Rhiannon and sees she's near tears.

How is this here? Rhiannon whispers. How the hell did she get this out here?

Maybe a colleague. If she planned this months ago, maybe someone on regular dig sites to these places.

There's no way she could've come here herself. Rhiannon sits up. Fuck. This has to mean we missed something in St. Louis.

What, you mean another box?

Of course that's what I mean. And we've already fucked it up.

Tim's brother lives in St. Louis. At least he did when we were in Jacksonville. If it really matters, I could call him. I could have him go check for us.

Rhiannon wipes dust from her face. Don't do that.

He was always nice. I'm sure he would do it. Especially given the circumstances.

Mom had this in her jewelry box when we were kids, Rhiannon says. I remember asking her once where she got it. She said Aunt Sue had one too.

Did you see her? At the funeral?

Rhiannon nods. She stood right beside me.

Billie looks across the river bluffs, the jeweled water cutting down through the valley. What do you think it means? she says. Why this? Why here?

I have no idea.

Maybe we could ask Aunt Sue. She's the one who was around Mom most in their younger years. Maybe this locket means we should call her.

Rhiannon shakes her head. I didn't know Mom knew how to geocache.

Billie looks at her. Geo what?

Rhiannon's face finally cracks into a faint smile. Geocaching. It wasn't really a thing yet six years ago. And there probably aren't many boxes hidden in prisons.

What boxes? What the fuck is geocaching?

Hiding boxes at specific coordinates. Sometimes the boxes contain messages, little treasures. It's a hobby. People find coordinates on websites and hunt around designated locations until they find boxes like these. They log their names in the boxes and put them back for other people to find.

This isn't for other people, Billie says. This one has our coordinates, our drawing.

She probably just borrowed the idea. She made a kind of game for us.

What for?

Rhiannon sighs. Maybe so we'd forget we're driving to her funeral.

Billie sits up in the grass. So every coordinate has a box like this? All the way to Utah? And we have to figure out what the fuck it means at every stop?

I don't know. We can call Aunt Sue when we get to wherever we're staying tonight. Rhiannon stands. But at least we found it. We found the box. And we should probably get back to the car and get on the road.

Billie looks to the sky where the sun is just beginning to tilt toward the west. A ferruginous hawk soars above them, a bird of prey Billie knows from manuals and her training with Bud. A master falconer originally from Santo Domingo but trained in Nebraska where he grew accustomed to working with this species in their native range, his manuals filled with them despite

Billie's work with the red-tailed hawks of the lower Midwest. The bird circles above them and Billie stops herself from holding out her arm. No landing place. No glove. Rhiannon starts back on the loop that will return them to the visitor center, the small box in her hands, and Billie follows. When they reach the trailhead, Rhiannon grabs the hiking register and flips back through six months of names and nowhere among them is their mother. Billie watches Rhiannon's gaze sweep the river valley before she takes the pen and signs their names on the day's blank ledger.

The date. The time. Proof that they were here.

When they reach a BP station just past Brewster, a small town near the border of Colorado, Rhiannon refills the dwindling tank and Billie steps into the food mart's cool air. The sun high, pushing toward late afternoon. I-70 the route they've continued following toward Colorado, Billie promising to map the next coordinates once they reach the state line. She leans her forehead against the cool glass of the mart's refrigerators and regards the lighted rows of beer and soda and water. So much choice. The America she's forgotten, a sprawl of endless highways, any variety of Pepsi she wants. She pulls out Rhiannon's cell phone, a touch screen Rhiannon let her play with on the drive to Smoky Hill River until she learned how to use it. The last one she owned nothing but a flip phone, long disconnected but packed somewhere in her discharge bag with a contact list that still holds his name. She finds the internet browser on Rhiannon's phone and then the white pages and then St. Louis, a name unique enough that she finds him swiftly: Oscar Doherty. McCausland Avenue. Age 35–40. Tim's brother.

Billie presses the number and dials before she loses her nerve.

Oscar, it's Billie, she says when he answers. Billie Hurst. Tim's Billie.

He breathes sharply across the line and she hates herself for identifying who she is like this. Tim's Billie. As if he'd owned her.

No collect call, Oscar says. I'm guessing you're out?

Look, I hate to call, she says. But you're the only person I know who can help.

Billie imagines him standing in his kitchen, the same kitchen of the same house where he made scrambled eggs and pancakes for her and Tim when they visited. So many weekends. Jacksonville so close to St.

Louis. A familiarity that made her feel like he was her own brother and how quickly a familiarity vanished. Oscar single then and Billie wonders now if he has a partner, if he has a family.

His voice is guarded, his once-easy tone stilted. What can I do for you?

Billie tells him about her mother, about Utah. She tells him about the coordinates and where they are and what they found in Russell Springs and how they left something behind in St. Louis.

I know it's a big favor, she says. But you're so close to Forest Park. I was wondering if you could just check.

There is stillness on the other end of the line and Billie doesn't want to imagine what Tim's side of the story was. Whether Oscar ever knew the scope of his brother's violence or if Tim only told them he didn't know how crazy she would turn out to be.

The Science Center, he finally says.

The dinosaur park out back.

I know it. Just give me the coordinates.

Billie feels the tight coil of her stomach flood with relief. She glances around the food mart, the clerk behind the counter eyeing her as she paces the aisle of packaged chips. She dictates the exact coordinates to Oscar. Gives him Rhiannon's number.

I can't tell you how much I appreciate it, she says. Just let me know what you find. We'll be on the road for at least the next week.

If I find something, you want me to hang on to it?

I guess. Whatever it is, we can grab it on the way back to Champaign.

Oscar pauses a moment. How are you doing?

Billie doesn't know if he means their mother or something else. I'm fine.

I'm glad you're out. Glad you're doing okay.

Billie can see Rhiannon through the food mart window recapping the gas tank and she feels the urge to hang up before the conversation leads to Tim.

Thanks again, she says. Just give me a ring if you find anything.

You gonna buy something? the clerk shouts and she pulls a package of Ruffles from the shelf and a Coke from the cooler. She takes the snacks to the cash register and glances out the window, Rhiannon already back behind the wheel.

I called Tim's brother, Billie says when she climbs inside the car.

Rhiannon nods at the bag of Ruffles. We already have a million snacks.

He said he'll check for us. I gave him the coordinates.

Rhiannon turns out of the gas station. How was it to talk to him?

He didn't say anything about Tim.

Rhiannon doesn't ask anything else. She pulls back onto the highway and finds the local public radio affiliate, what would be a rush-hour news update if they were anywhere near a city with traffic. Instead there is news of continued widespread rain across the Midwest, a tornado touching down last night in central Missouri. Then national news: indication from the Arizona flight's recovered black box that the plane hit clear-air turbulence minutes before spiraling a sharp descent, the same exact finding of four of the past months' crashes.

I'm glad we're driving, Rhiannon says.

Have you ever even heard of clear-air turbulence?

It's a term they've been using the past few months. Something new. Some new kind of unexpected turbulence due to wind wakes and climate shifts.

It's windy as shit out here, Billie says. Though probably nothing to speeding around a track at two hundred miles per hour.

Rhiannon says nothing and Billie imagines

the lone television room in the Correctional Center where she and the other inmates gathered on hard couches to watch regulated programming. Family movies. Talk shows. Never sports events, what would have let her see her sister's races. But sometimes local news that in the past months let Billie know something was changing in the atmosphere. Speculation from broadcasters of pilot error, the possibility of mechanical failure. If the planes were manufactured in the same facility. A problem of parts or labor. Something tangible to pinpoint, the question of climate change still a debate that left so many news anchors skeptical, a question Billie could have answered as she saw the sky shift across six years above the prison yard from bright-summer blue to mottled gray.

I haven't flown in months, Rhiannon says. Mom knew it, too, that I wouldn't have wanted to fly.

Billie looks at her. Where have you flown recently? I figured you'd always drive.

Vacation, Rhiannon says quickly. Beth and I went to Punta Cana last year.

You think you'll call her?

I don't know. Probably just to check in. Let her know where we are.

You think you'll get back together?

Billie, I don't know. Things are so complicated right now. I'm just going to give it time. She glances over. Did you date anyone in prison?

What, like other women?

Anyone. Six years is a long time to be alone.

After Tim, I wanted to be by myself for as long as I could.

What do you mean?

Billie drinks her Coke and looks out the passenger-side window. Fields of sunflowers line the highway, lemon blankets catching the slanting sun. She remembers the first time Rhiannon told her in high school that she didn't feel anything for her boyfriend, nothing like the lust they were supposed to feel as teenagers sneaking into cornfields because there was nowhere else to go. Robert. The goalie of the men's varsity soccer team. He and Rhiannon dated all through high school and broke up right before graduation. Billie remembers Rhiannon telling her from a phone in Chicago that she was attracted to women, that she thought she might be in love with another girl in one of her few in-person communications classes. Billie still in high school, still running around with nameless boys across Champaign's deserted back roads but old enough to know what this was, a hard confession, the words spit from her sister's mouth like knocked-out kernels of broken teeth. How Rhiannon told her first, then their mother and at last their father. Billie thought of that phone call again and again from the closed-in walls of Decatur and from her chair in a circle of chairs at group therapy where the weight of the women's stories around her made her feel too ashamed to speak. Women separated from their children. Women who'd gotten out only to get back in because no one would employ them. How she wanted to hear her own voice spill a secret about a split-open eye and a can of gasoline and how she only went to three group sessions before quitting and how she imagines telling her sister here in the Mustang shuttling across Kansas everything caught beneath her tongue. But *Tim just wasn't right for me* is all she says and Rhiannon doesn't press and for once Billie wishes she would. They pass a green highway sign of city distances. Forty-one miles to Burlington, Colorado.

We're nearing the state line, Rhiannon says. We should map the next coordinate.

Billie pulls out the journal and the GPS. Opens the booklet to the next page beyond Russell Springs, a new coordinate etched beside a new sketch.

What's the drawing? Rhiannon asks.

Billie looks at the arched back, the telltale plates. What she recognizes immediately from a childhood of living among her mother's diagrams and photographs.

A stegosaurus, she says.

Where is it? Where are we headed?

Billie plugs in the coordinates. Cañon City, she says. Colorado, south of Denver.

Should I stay on 70? How far is it?

Billie pushes the map icon on Rhiannon's phone and types in the town's name. We stay on 70 into Colorado then veer south on Highway 24, she says. Looks like we won't go through Denver, but at least we'll go through Colorado Springs. Two hundred thirty-five miles. This is showing a four-hour drive.

Rhiannon glances at the dashboard clock. Four thirty, she says. If we don't stop anywhere, we can be in Cañon City by sunset.

Or we could stay in Colorado Springs for the night.

Or we could just camp in Cañon City.

Billie wrinkles her nose.

Oh, come on, Billie. You're not paying for any of this.

Because I can't.

Your counselor can help you find a job when you get back.

Yeah, that will be easy. At least in the state of Illinois I can still vote.

I'd rather save money, Rhiannon says. It should be beautiful camping out here.

I'm sure it's beautiful in Colorado Springs, too.

Why don't you live a little? When was the last time you camped out under the stars? When was the last time you even had the chance to do that?

Billie watches the fields of sunflowers whip past the window. She lets Rhiannon listen to the radio. She holds the locket in her hands and wonders where her mother even learned about geocached boxes, one more secret she didn't tell her daughters. She lets Rhiannon hurtle them across the state line into Colorado where the sunflowers recede and the sun sinks fast ahead of them over waves of mountains that begin to rise.

KIM, MARTHA. "RED-TAILED HAWK." NORTH AMERICAN ORNITHOLOGY: A GUIDE TO THE BIRDS OF AMERICA. ED. JAMES BURCH. NEW HAVEN: YALE UNIVERSITY PRESS, 1994. 223–229. PRINT.

CALL NUMBER: QL670 .G520 1994

THE RED-TAILED HAWK (*BUTEO JAMAICENSIS*)

The most common bird of prey in North America, the red-tailed hawk has a wide habitat range and can be found in every continental state year-round. Red-tailed hawks are broadwing birds, with wingspans approximating four feet in length. They boast wide, short tails and brownish-red feathers with gray or white chests. Often spotted soaring high above fields or perched along fence posts, redtailed hawks seek open country for the purposes of hunting.

Red-tailed hawks typically reuse their nests, which they build at the tops of trees or on the ledges of tall cliffs. Made of branches, foliage, and dry leaves, their nests are typically up to six feet high and three feet wide. Mothering hawks incubate clutches of one to five eggs for up to forty-five days, and mated pairs often stay together for life.

Because red-tailed hawks are so common in the United States, they are the most widespread choice in America for work with beginning falconers.

38.8673° N, 104.7607° W: Colorado Springs, CO

The Rockies: crests protruding off a rolling landscape.

The Rockies: plates of armor sloping across a stegosaur's back.

Rhiannon sees the resemblance as they drive west and the Kansas hills sharpen into Colorado ridges. The sun drops toward the rising mountains and breaks across the horizon line and Rhiannon watches the peaks take the shape of the Jurassic spine her mother knew so well.

A spike-studded herbivore, meant to hold its own in an age of predators. Rhiannon remembers every bit of information their mother shared, every bone and spike she brought home chiseled into relief from dust and rock. She knows the controversy over the stegosaur's plates, what her mother was still trying to research from her hospital bed. Whether the ridges were meant as armor or temperature regulation in trapping air that would have cooled the dinosaur's blood, or if they were meant to enlarge the size of a small herbivore among so many carnivores. Or if they flushed with color to warn off predators, the very reason her mother argued across her career that the plates were intended to attract mates: that if they were vascularized to regulate temperature and signal environmental dangers, then they could have blushed red to announce an invitation, the same as cardinals and bowerbirds, the dinosaur's direct descendants.

Do you remember your trip to the Cleveland-Lloyd Quarry with Mom? Rhiannon asks.

Billie shifts beside her in the passenger seat. What, in high school?

Is that when you went?

Yeah, while you were on that spring break road trip to Atlantic City.

How do you even remember that?

Because it's the only reason you didn't come too.

Atlantic City: Rhiannon's senior year of high school. A trip she hasn't thought of in years. Four girls in a car traveling from Illinois to Ohio to Pennsylvania to New Jersey, Rhiannon already racing, the future spread out before all of them. Rhiannon still dating Robert, the goalie of the varsity soccer team, a relationship across all four years of high school readying to break across the finish line of graduation. What brought them together in the first place, Rhiannon knows: a shared love of sports and nothing more.

Atlantic City: the first time Rhiannon ever kissed another girl.

No nameless faces, no underage bars, just her friend Mandy along for the trip. Cheap motel, threadbare sheets. Mandy beside her getting dressed, their other friends Geneva and Lauren already down the street at the bar. Mandy sitting on the double bed half clothed in a nude bra and ripped jeans and Rhiannon leaning across the bed and brushing her mouth against hers, the taste of watermelon Puckers, what they'd been drinking all afternoon. Mandy pulling back. Mandy staying quiet the rest of the trip. The two of them drifting apart as they slid toward graduation and into the humidity of an Urbana summer and Robert leaving for Indiana University in August without saying goodbye. Regardless of Mandy, regardless of reciprocation: that moment in the motel room felt wide open.

That was the last road trip I took, Rhiannon says.

Yeah, but you've been on the road so

much for races.

That doesn't really count.

You never went to the quarry? Billie asks.

When would I have gone? I was racing so much already in high school. Just small circuits, but I don't even remember when Mom started making regular trips out there.

Ninth grade was the first time I went out there. The only time.

Do you remember anything?

Not much. A lot of dust and red rock. And wind. Billie hesitates. I remember her wanting me to feel something.

Rhiannon glances over. What do you mean?

I don't know. Like a trip out there would give me the same passion she had. For anything. How the desert lit her up. I think she wanted me to feel that too.

Rhiannon pulls down the driver's-side visor against the low western sun. I'm sure she just wanted you to see her work and take you on a vacation. To someplace completely different from Illinois.

Maybe. But you were already racing. It was clear you had a path ahead of you. I think she worried about me. Dad clearly did too.

Rhiannon says nothing. This brief silence the same tension between them when they were growing up. Billie's bird books and ocean atlases so much closer to their mother's interests, a language Rhiannon thought they shared and she couldn't breach. Their father taking her under his wing instead, a disciple of diesel and speed. And his six years of not visiting Billie: what Rhiannon assumed was disappointment in her prison sentence and not passive aggression for her to find a passion like he had.

Thirty-five miles to Colorado Springs, Billie says as they pass an iridescent green highway sign. Rhiannon imagines Interstate 70 north of them, veering off toward Denver, Highway 24 the exit they took somewhere back near Limon. Highway 24 more desolate, fewer gas stations. A two-lane highway that widens to four as they approach Colorado Springs, the largest city for miles.

Want to stop? Billie says.

I told you. I'd rather camp.

But we're still nearly two hours from Cañon City and I'm starving.

Rhiannon glances in the rearview mirror, the flatlands of eastern Colorado a wash of navy dark disappearing behind them. She knows Billie doesn't want to camp, even the cheapest of motels more comfortable than the hard rungs of a prison cot. The overcast skies of Illinois, a kind of claustrophobia. Rhiannon imagines how uncluttered the Colorado wilds will feel, the stars a splattered canvas above them.

I'll make you a deal, she says. We camp. But you can choose whatever you want in Colorado Springs for dinner.

It's not like I know what the hell is there.

I've been there a handful of times on race routes. There's a nice downtown.

Billie rotates the gold locket in her hands, what she's been holding since they crossed the state line. A locket Rhiannon's mulled over from the Kansas plains into Colorado. Billie leans down and picks up the journal from the passenger floor.

We could always look ahead, Rhiannon says. It's not a crime to know where we're headed.

I know. But she made it clear that she wanted us to be surprised by each stop.

Why? What difference does it make?

What, you think I have answers? We found a locket today and we don't know what it means. We didn't even know there was anything in St. Louis. Geocaches. Whatever the fuck you called them. I don't know what they mean, but I know Mom. I know she wanted us to follow these points, one by one.

Fine, Rhiannon says. We're making good time anyway. It's only Monday. We can be in Utah by tomorrow if we want.

If we want. We'll see where we're headed next.

Rhiannon glances to the side of the highway as they pass signs for Falcon. Population: 10,500. Highway 24 a route she's never driven despite knowing America's roads, even blue highways beyond every major interstate, Falcon a town she's never seen.

Did you ever come across books on falconry in the prison library? she says. Were you able to keep up your practice at all, even if just by reading?

No one donated any. We had one book on a bird refuge. And one on North American birds, with a single entry on red-tailed hawks. Barb wouldn't buy a falconry book for us. It's not exactly a marketable trade for repatriating.

Do you ever think of flying hawks again?

I don't know if I'd even know how to land one now.

Rhiannon watches wide swirls of clouds catch the last of the sky's salmon light and pictures her sister with the leather glove on her arm, how her red-tailed hawk somehow knew to return. Alabama. Billie never hunted, what Rhiannon knew was the intended purpose of falconry. Billie never explained what it was that drew her to birds of prey though Rhiannon suspected she only wanted to watch them take flight, to feel the heavy weight of talons leave her arms.

The map says to just keep taking Highway 24 straight into town, Billie says.

Rhiannon glances down at the locket in Billie's hands. I'll call Aunt Sue while we're there and have guaranteed cell service.

Billie nods and Rhiannon presses the Mustang onward toward Colorado Springs and straight into the first line of mountains they've seen.

Rhiannon parks near Colorado College, the streets empty of liberal-arts students gone for the summer. Liberal arts a world still so foreign to her despite working in textbook sales, an in-state public school always the implied option for her and Billie due to their mother's tuition remission working for the University of Illinois. She and Billie walk south toward downtown through growing clusters of June tourists. People with fanny packs, with hiking shoes, with wide-brimmed sun hats and Garden of the Gods T-shirts. They walk the downtown streets until Billie stops in front of a local brewery, live music billowing from a rooftop patio above them.

How about this place? she says. We could sit outside.

Rhiannon nods. Your choice. Lead the way.

The host seats them at a small corner table on the rooftop and asks where they've traveled from. High tourist season. An educated guess that they're not locals. Billie tells them Illinois and the host says they've chosen the right night to come through. Monday evenings: happy hour until close. Rooftop music until 9 p.m. Billie takes the draft list and Rhiannon scans the menu as the host walks away.

They have sweet potato tots, Rhiannon says. And a mushroom po'boy.

And a mile-long beer list, Billie says. One of my bunkmates warned me about this. She was in and out of prison three times. She said you want to eat everything when you get out. She said she gained fifteen pounds the first time and twenty the second.

Billie has hardly ever mentioned any of her prison mates and Rhiannon wants to ask more but doesn't. The view from the rooftop scans a panorama of the Rockies. Their server comes and Billie orders an IPA and the po'boy, Rhiannon a burger and a summer-seasonal apricot ale. A bluegrass trio serenades the crowd from the opposite corner of the patio, the soft plucking of mandolin and guitar floating across the tables. Rhiannon sips her beer and watches the last of the sun's light lean on the mountain peaks to the west.

Nice view, she says.

I haven't seen the Rockies since high school, Billie says.

When you came with Mom to the quarry?

No, we flew. I came to Boulder sophomore year on that awful annual ski trip.

Rhiannon smiles. I passed on that one.

Yeah, who needs a charter bus full of teens with raging hormones when you can race across the country on your own?

Rhiannon remembers the spring break trip sponsored each year by Urbana Public High, an overnight chartered bus from Champaign to Colorado. Her friends went junior year while she stayed behind to train with her father, an embarrassment at the time that she chose to spend vacation on a racetrack, and that so many of her friends had ski equipment while she and Billie would have to rent. The start-up expenses of racing taking any extra income her parents had, Rhiannon borrowing her father's gear but still needing her own suit, a helmet in her size. She doesn't know if Billie felt similarly embarrassed on her class trip to Colorado. Once Rhiannon left for Chicago, Billie still in high school, she lost track of her sister's relationships, her friends. That she'd ever gone to Boulder.

I blew Mike Steffen on that trip, Billie says. The back of the bus. Once everyone else went to sleep.

The kid with the platinum hair? The one in that Rancid rip-off band?

He had a horrible goatee. No band.

He sounds like a charmer.

Billie smiles. No one said we make good decisions when we're fifteen.

Or when we're thirty-five.

Rhiannon's words slip before she can catch them.

Billie looks up. You think of Beth as a bad decision?

Rhiannon sighs. I don't even know if she's what I mean.

Then what? God, Rhee, you did it. You race cars. You did want you wanted to do. What bad decisions could you have possibly made?

Rhiannon watches the sun slide against the Rockies beyond the rooftop, thick light that as it disappears takes with it the day's warmth. What Rhiannon's forgotten about the west: that the nights bring a chill. The bluegrass swells across the patio and all at once she feels tired. A six-year charade. Billie still believing she drives. And what for, a lie she made her mother keep every time she visited the Decatur Correctional Center, an omission in her own conversations with Billie that here in Colorado, the mountains before them, seem completely meaningless.

I'm not racing anymore, Rhiannon says.

Billie sets down her pint glass. You mean this summer.

No, I mean I'm not racing anymore, Billie. Not since you left for prison.

Rhiannon watches her face change as the server approaches with their food.

What do you mean, not since I left for prison? Billie says when the server walks away.

I mean I haven't raced, Billie. Not at all. I haven't raced since you left.

Are you kidding? she says, the pitch of her voice rising.

Keep your voice down.

You've been lying to me?

You lied about this trip, Rhiannon says, an argument she knows will go nowhere. You lied about the coordinates. The journal.

Jesus Christ. I lied for one day.

Four months. You've known about all this

for nearly four months.

And you've been lying to me for six fucking years.

Rhiannon sits back. Look, you had other things going on. So many other things.

Yeah, you lied for my sake. You're the saint at this table. Jesus, Rhee, you make it sound like you stopped racing because of me. Not since I left?

The bluegrass band wails and the sun sinks behind the mountains and Rhiannon feels her chest ignite with heat. I didn't want to upset you by telling you while you were there, she says. You had your hands full.

My hands full? You're a fucking coward. Do you even know what prison is like? Some days I just sat for an entire afternoon watching the light change on the walls and you visited every month for six full years and you never once said a word. Billie stops speaking, her palms pressed to the table. Oh, Christ, and Mom. You made her lie, didn't you? Every fucking time she came to visit?

Lower your voice. And calm the fuck down.

Stop telling me to calm down. Stop trying to control this conversation. This is one thing you can't control. Did you make her lie?

I didn't make her lie.

Fine, let's split hairs about this. You made her omit.

What do you care? Rhiannon says, loud enough that two women at the next table look over. Yeah, I lied. But what difference does it make what I did or didn't do while you were in prison?

If it doesn't make a difference, then why didn't you tell me?

Because it was my decision. Mine. My career has nothing to do with you.

Well, you sure as shit made it sound like this had something to do with me.

It was a hard time for all of us, is all Rhiannon can think to say.

For all of us. Billie pushes her chair back from the table. Right. I was the one in Decatur. I was the one sleeping in a dorm room with cockroaches and eating shit food and staying confined to a quarter-mile radius for the six longest years of my life. I'm sure it was a real fucking hard time for you.

Billie, sit down.

Fuck you.

Billie pushes herself away from the table and disappears into the restaurant's interior. Her sandwich sits untouched across the table, her pint glass half drained. The bluegrass swells above the rooftop, across clusters of tables pretending not to notice. Rhiannon closes her eyes and breathes in and tries not to think of Billie's temper taking her far from the rooftop and from the restaurant, untraceable. No cell phone. No way of finding her at all in her rage, what Rhiannon thought she wouldn't have to expect. A can of gasoline. A library. Rhiannon watches the sun drag light behind the jagged peaks of the mountains and drinks her beer, her burger going cold.

Billie is nowhere inside the restaurant when Rhiannon pays their bill. Nowhere near the upstairs bar, where she half expects to find her sister drinking a pint alone. Nowhere downstairs among the tables of tourists and nowhere upon the park benches dotting downtown Colorado Springs just outside the restaurant. Rhiannon checks the digital map of her phone: Cañon City, an hour away. Dusk's last light still phantoming the sky, still enough time to make it to the campsite and set up their tent if she can find Billie and soon. She glances up the street then back toward the car, no sign of her sister in either direction. She sits on a bench outside the brewery and waits for

Billie to retrace her own steps and come back.

Rhiannon watches families pass along the downtown sidewalks and tries to imagine Billie lying in her prison bed, a bunk she never saw. The showers, the cafeteria, the stale food. The visiting quarters the only corner of Billie's world Rhiannon ever witnessed. She wonders what Billie imagined beyond the prison walls, what gave her hope. If Rhiannon kept up the lie out of shame or to keep her sister dreaming.

A couple walks by holding hands and Rhiannon thinks of Billie's hesitation to call Tim's brother. Rhiannon tries to remember the last time she saw Tim, his absence strange when she and her parents cleared Billie's things from his house. Billie kept herself tight-lipped about their relationship well before her sentence but changed the subject every time Rhiannon asked about him during monthly visits.

Her phone buzzes in her hands and for a moment she believes it's Billie.

You girls doing okay? her father says when she answers.

We're fine. Just stopped in Colorado Springs for dinner.

That's a bit south, isn't it? Why didn't you just go straight through Denver?

Billie wanted to see Pikes Peak, Rhiannon hears herself say. She hasn't been out on the road in so long. We're taking a short detour.

How's your sister doing? Everything going okay?

She's fine, Rhiannon lies. We're making good time.

How's the weather out there?

Dry. We drove through one thunderstorm in Missouri, but it's been all sun since.

Enjoy it while you can. There's nothing but rain here in Illinois.

How's Chicago?

Nothing new to report. We're going out on a new racing circuit next week.

How's Bryson doing this year?

Like you don't already know.

Rhiannon leans back on the bench. Her father knows she wouldn't ignore the season's races and point tallies. Bryson Townes: the new NASCAR phenom her father's been working with for the past two years from rookie to midrange racer to top-seeded pole placer. Only twenty-three. An African American racer, still as rare in NASCAR as women. A history of racing in his family, the same as Rhiannon. She knows how good Bryson is. Solid finishes the past two years. And this summer, top-three placements in

Daytona and Martinsville and Talladega. She watches the first stars begin to pepper the sky above the downtown streetlights and wonders for a moment if Bryson's spring and summer racing routes took her father anywhere near Smoky Hill River.

Dad, did Mom ever make you take things for her on your trips?

What kinds of things?

Rhiannon sighs. Mom gave Billie this journal. A journal full of coordinates. Places we're supposed to see on our way out here.

What do you mean, coordinates? What kind of journal?

I don't know. But it's why we're in Colorado Springs. We're taking a different route out to Utah, one Mom clearly designed for us a few months ago. I thought you might know something about it.

How different of a route could there be?

She's outlined coordinates for us. All across the west. She's mapping us on her own route out to Utah.

I don't know anything about it. But I wouldn't be your mom's first choice for keeping some kind of secret.

That makes two of us, Rhiannon says.

Your mom told Billie but not you?

She gave Billie the journal sometime this spring.

What Rhiannon doesn't say: *on her last visit to Decatur.*

Her father is quiet for a moment. What are you finding at these coordinates?

We found a locket in Kansas.

A locket? There are things left at all these places?

We've only found one thing so far. Look, do you know anything about this? Just tell me. We can't figure out how she got these things out here. If you did it, just tell me.

I told you, I don't know anything about this.

We went to St. Louis first. Yesterday afternoon. We didn't know then that we were supposed to find some kind of hidden object at each place.

Where in St. Louis?

The T. rex statue outside the Science Center, Rhiannon says and hears her father fall silent on the other end.

The one by the pond?

I guess there was a pond. What, Dad? What do you know?

Her father sighs. That lake. That's where I proposed.

Rhiannon sits in the dark of downtown, the streets silent beyond the bench, surprised by the hard lump thickening in her throat.

You never told us that. How did we not know that?

You never asked, her father says. It was well into her doctoral degree, almost near her graduation. We spent a lot of time at that park.

And the T. rex?

Must be a coincidence. Honestly, I didn't know it was there. I only realized later when we took you girls down to the Science Center when you were kids.

Rhiannon wants to scream. A coincidence, the last thing this is. The dinosaur what her mother drew in the journal and not a wedding ring, not a pond.

You didn't find anything in St. Louis? her father says.

We didn't even think to look. It was our first stop. She left just coordinates and drawings. There's no indication at all in this journal that anything was left or hidden.

I didn't help her. Your mother always had her own ideas and plans.

It's getting late, Rhiannon says. I should go. I'll keep you posted on everything.

Let me know where you are. I'll be on the road this week, but I'll have my phone. Don't hesitate to call if you need anything.

Rhiannon hangs up and watches the Big Dipper slowly appear in the night sky above

Colorado Springs's deserted streets. The only constellation she knows without Billie here to identify them. No sign of Billie anywhere, no sense of where to even begin looking for her. Rhiannon looks down at her phone, the inability to reach her sister maddening, the locket surely coiled inside one of Billie's pockets. She flips through her contacts, past Beth, the first in her list of favorites. Continues scrolling until she finds Aunt Sue.

The phone rings seven times, so long that Rhiannon readies herself to hang up when she hears her aunt's voice.

Rhiannon?

Hi, Sue. It's me.

It's so good to hear from you.

Am I calling at a bad time? Rhiannon says. She rethinks the time: already past dark in Colorado. One hour ahead in Dallas, nearing ten o'clock.

No, not at all. Your uncle and I were just watching TV.

Uncle John. The only reason Sue moved to Texas. Sue born and bred in Illinois, an accountant, her husband a pharmaceutical representative whose work took him to Dallas. Rhiannon always liked him but her mother labeled him a workaholic. He didn't make it to the funeral, an Oakland business trip he couldn't reschedule. Aunt Sue always made several trips back to Champaign when they were growing up because of an impermeable relationship with their mother, older by two years, a sisterhood Rhiannon watched as a child wondering if she and Billie would have the same.

This is going to sound crazy, Rhiannon says. I have to ask you something about Mom.

The noise of the television falls silent in the background. What about her?

Did she say anything to you about a trip? Us going out to Utah?

I knew she was planning a second funeral for Billie and for you, Sue says. The sound of the word *funeral* catching on her tongue. Nearly imperceptible.

She told you that?

She'd been planning it for a few months.

Did she tell you anything else about the trip?

Like what? Where are you calling from?

We're in Colorado Springs, Rhiannon says. Look, we found a locket. In Kansas. Billie says it belonged to Mom. It has your picture in it and hers.

Where did you find it?

That's what I'm calling to ask. Does the Smoky Hill River mean anything to you?

I've never heard of it. That's where you found the locket?

She planned an entire route out here, Rhiannon says. She gave us a journal of coordinates with objects hidden at each location. We just realized it today. We found the locket at Smoky Hill River, not far from the Colorado border.

Your mother and I got those lockets when she was in graduate school, Sue says softly. It was the first time we ever lived in different states from each other.

Rhiannon closes her eyes, the pain in her aunt's voice still raw and burning. She knows both of them went to Illinois State before her mother moved to St. Louis right after graduation on a full scholarship to begin her doctoral work. Rhiannon imagines Sue left behind, the start of her junior year in college: the first year without her sister.

Is there anything special about the locket? Rhiannon asks.

Rhiannon hears Sue smile by the tone of her voice. What isn't special about it?

Do you know why she would've left it in Kansas?

What's the Smoky Hill River? Why did she send you there?

Marine fossils. It's a river and trail, but she drew some kind of amphibian in the journal. It's apparently a hotbed of ancient reptiles.

But she studied stegosaurs.

I know. That's exactly what we said.

Aunt Sue is silent. Rhiannon can hear the sound of cabinets opening and closing in the background.

Wait a minute, Sue says. Marine reptiles.

The moon begins to climb over the buildings of downtown and Rhiannon feels her blood spike. Hope. That Sue might remember something.

What's the name of the town? Where Smoky Hill River is?

Russell Springs.

That's it, Sue says. I wouldn't have even thought it until you said it. I remember the name. It's where I mailed the package to your mother to send her the locket. Some P.O. box in the middle of nowhere. I remember imagining a truck having to drive all the way from Illinois to find it.

You mailed it from Bloomington?

It was her first year of graduate school. Before she specialized. I was still in Bloomington. A junior. It was our first year apart. I got her the locket and had to mail it to some dig site so she'd get it on her birthday. It had to have been Kansas.

Rhiannon imagines her mother walking

into a desolate post office in the middle of the plains. Hair messy, skin caked with dirt. Barely hiding the glow of her youth. Spring winds rattling outside, her birthday in the center of April, what a March funeral made her miss by three weeks. Tan pants. Hiking boots. Hands pulling open the envelope and finding the locket.

So it was a gift, Rhiannon whispers.

I bought one for myself, too. I still have it.

Billie's hanging on to Mom's half for now.

How is Billie? I'd love to talk to her.

She went to bed early, Rhiannon lies. Otherwise I'd put her on the phone.

She's adjusting okay?

She's doing great.

Your mother would've wanted you both to have that locket. Sue laughs. You'll just have to decide which one of you gets to keep it. The weather okay up there? We've had only clouds and dust in Texas.

No rain. Just a storm in Missouri. And a lot of dry heat up here, too.

You girls be careful, Sue says. You take care of each other out there.

Rhiannon hangs up the phone and watches the rising moon to blink away her aunt's voice. Taking care. What Rhiannon hasn't done, barely a day into their trip and Billie already nowhere she can find her. The locket tucked somewhere in her sister's pocket, a totem of love. What she realizes she lacked by not telling Billie she quit and by hearing nothing of Billie's life in prison, if her sister made friends or had anyone at all to rely on. Barb. The only name Billie mentioned among surely other work relationships in the prison's library. The moon throws light down upon the Colorado streets where Rhiannon hears all at once a commotion and looks down the block and Billie is there, Billie is a mirage beneath speckled stars, Billie is outside a bar shoving a bouncer in the chest and unleashing a scream that verges on breaking into tears.

SHAH, SAMARA. A BACKYARD GUIDE TO CONSTELLATIONS. HAUPPAUGE, NY: BARRON'S, 2010. PRINT.

CALL NUMBER: QB806 .B12 2010

SUMMER CONSTELLATIONS IN THE NORTHERN HEMISPHERE

Lyra
A four-star constellation directly overhead, shaped almost like a parallelogram.

Cygnus
Known as the Northern Cross; Deneb, its brightest star, forms the "Summer Triangle" with nearby stars Vega and Altair.

Boötes
A ten-star constellation shaped like a herdsman; pursues the two bears, Ursa Major and Ursa Minor, two other constellations in the summer night sky.

The Milky Way
Not technically a constellation but a light-filled band shimmering with star clusters and nebulae; visible on the southern horizon away from city lights.

38.8673° N, 104.7607° W: Colorado Springs, CO

Billie notices his mouth first. Something she never used to notice on men. She remembers only Tim's broad shoulders, marine-blue eyes, a jawline hidden in the half shadow of stubble. She remembers nothing of his mouth and how it once moved across her body but she notices the slight curl of this man's lips, the way they pull back across his teeth. A grin of cockiness, accustomed to getting what it wants. Billie wouldn't have fallen for it in college but it's been nearly a decade since a man looked at her like this. Tim first noticing her on the University of Illinois's campus quad. Autumn sun winking down. Her back to an oak tree's trunk. Her invertebrate biology textbook sprawled on her lap between classes and a Frisbee thrown against the nylon of her backpack and the pages of her book darkening with a form standing over her. But here in Colorado Springs, just some bar called Cowboys. The first place Billie sees when she leaves the brewery.

A shitkicker dive. Country music. Billiards and darts and line dancing.

Billie sits at the bar alone drinking a Bulleit on the rocks, the whiskey's sweetness doing nothing to temper her rage. A sisterhood slimmed down to monthly visits that pushed distance between her and Rhiannon, but not like this. Billie feels her hands tighten around her glass recalling the number of times Rhiannon sat across from her at the visiting room's tables and said nothing. Billie explicitly asking about her racing circuit each summer. Rhiannon overtly lying. Billie lets the whiskey swill beneath her tongue and tries to focus on the taste and texture, an imagined luxury from her prison dorm, until the man with the grin sidles up to the barstool beside her.

You lost, little girl? he says. Billie looks up and rolls her eyes. A tired line. One she'd have ignored under any other circumstance but there is his mouth. Scuffed boots. Black-suede cowboy hat. He asks if he can buy her another whiskey and she lets him, for nothing else than the sound of ice cubes swirling against glass.

You come here often? he says.

Did you really just ask me that?

You don't look like you're from here.

Just drove in from Kansas.

A Midwestern girl. Legs as long as those fields of corn.

Billie stifles the impulse to laugh, these dumb lines. But she can't stop herself from glancing down at her legs, from making sure she's wearing jeans that conceal her scars. Her tank top baring her arms though she's sure the bar's lights are dim enough to hide their puckered skin.

What's your name?

Betsy, she lies. You?

You can call me Jesse, he says.

As in Jesse James.

If you want it that way. He grins again. A grin that despite its heavy smugness still draws Billie in, the whiskey doing its work.

How long are you in town? Jesse asks.

Just for the night. A quick in and out.

I like it that way. He smiles and Billie stops, thinks for the first time to get up and leave. But keeping Rhiannon waiting somewhere out on a rooftop patio makes Billie play along. The music swells around them and couples pair off beneath the disco ball hanging above the dance floor and Jesse holds out his hand.

You dance?

Billie glances at the dance floor. I could

be persuaded.

She drains the last of her whiskey and Jesse takes a single shot of tequila, licking lime and salt from his knuckles. His tongue skirts the back of his hand and Billie is at once repulsed and drawn to him. She imagines a bathroom stall in the back, his weight pressed against her, something quick, something anonymous. Enough to forget her sister and remember what it was to be wanted and to forget the scars and a prison dorm and the small window of light above a bunk's bed. She lets him lead her to the center of the dance floor, winking bulbs raining light down upon them. The heat of other couples pressed around them. Billie's hair slicks against her forehead. Jesse takes her hands and drapes them around his neck and lets his palms lock on the waist of her jeans.

You know how to line dance? he says against her ear.

Not a chance.

She feels him grin against her cheek and lets herself move with the guitar's twang. Six years. She never let anyone touch her at Decatur. Tim enough for a lifetime, the black eye gone within a week but the cut down her face a ghosted scar for months. The skin of her left arm and left leg and abdomen grafted for a year beyond sentencing, hospital care the prison let her take. Transplanted skin. Peeling healthy layers from other parts of her body, transporting them to so many burns. Risk of nerve damage. Infection. The first months of prison a complete blur. She closes her eyes and the music pulses and for a moment the hands upon her are Tim's hands. When they were tender. Nights in bed and the windows open and the sound of cicadas and a breeze blowing in and his arm thrown across her body, fingers skirting her stomach in his sleep. Jesse's hands tighten around her waist and Billie thinks of Tim's fingers clenching her arm, his right hand knuckling into a fist, what happened so fast that Billie only remembers being on the floor, her vision fuzzed to nothing but a dim view of the hardwood.

He'd first shoved her against the wall in Jacksonville, elbow to her throat. Grabbed her arm too hard a few times when they still lived in Champaign, what she shouldn't have ignored. She assumed every couple experienced rough patches, until they moved to Jacksonville. He'd worked late on campus so many nights, what he blamed on the responsibilities of a new faculty member, until he came home at three a.m. after drinking with colleagues and she asked why he didn't call and he pushed her to the ground and kicked her stomach and made her first understand this wasn't normal. He'd said he was drunk. Would never do it again. Then only weeks later: the library.

He'd come in the front door well past dinner and she asked why he hadn't called, the spaghetti she'd made already cold, and he threw down his bag and knocked her to the ground and walked back out as quickly as he'd come. Hardwood. Tim's sneakers receding across the floor. Billie sitting up and holding her head and pulling herself up and out the door, the spaghetti still sticking to a pot on the burner. The first place she went: out to the backyard with a kitchen knife. Alabama in her weathering pen outside. Billie touching the side of her face knowing by its uneven shape that the brow bone was broken. She watched Alabama through the weathering pen's chicken wire. Opened its door. Unhooked Alabama's jesses. Took the knife and cut the line clean. She watched Alabama blink back at her for only a moment before stepping to the edge of the weathering pen and taking soundlessly to the night sky. Billie dropped the knife in the grass. Billie dropped the knife and headed toward the gas station and the library.

Billie pulls her head from Jesse's shoulder on the dance floor.

What's the matter? he shouts over the music.

Nothing, she shouts back. I just need some air.

He pulls her toward the back of the bar where a doorway leads from the bathrooms to a patio. Billie follows him outside and swallows the cool night air, the sun lost to the mountains beyond downtown. Stars salt the darkness above them. Arcturus twinkling just past the ladle of the Big Dipper. Summer stars she knows from the books of so many libraries. The moon climbs the tree line beyond the deserted patio and shimmers above the streetlights.

Jesse pulls her toward him. You want another drink?

No thanks. I just need to sit for a minute.

How many drinks you had? Little Midwestern girl still adjusting to the altitude?

Billie ignores his tone, the slow drawl. She sits at a table near the patio's edge where the lights are low enough for her arm's scars to stay hidden and Jesse pulls a chair up beside her, a hand on her leg.

You want to get out of here? he says.

The stars shimmer above them and Billie imagines Rhiannon alone on the brewery's rooftop. She wonders if she's still there. If she walked up and down Colorado Springs's downtown streets growing more and more panicked. If she called the police, the last thing Billie realizes she wants.

I should go, Billie says. I mean, get out of here on my own.

Hey there, Betsy, he says. We were just getting to know each other.

We're heading out early tomorrow.

We?

My sister, Billie says, the first truth she's told all night.

So there are two of you. Jesse grins. Double the fun.

All at once his smile loses its magnetism. Billie stands. It was nice to meet you.

Jesse grabs the belt loop of her jeans and pulls her down and Billie scans the patio and realizes they are alone.

We were just getting started, he says. He begins to twist his fingers from the belt loops to the underside of her waistband.

Billie pulls away but his hands are quick, too quick for her mouth to form words. He draws her back and his fingers find the button of her jeans, her zipper, the thin band of her underwear. His arms bind her shoulders and she kicks back swiftly before she grasps that this is happening, that a man is shoving his hand into her jeans. She kicks her legs back and her shoes find the bend of his knee and his hands lose their grip as she pulls away but not before he reaches out and grabs her hard by the left arm.

Don't fucking touch me, she screams.

He grips her arm tight and then recoils.

Jesus, what the fuck is wrong with you? he yells.

Billie thinks he means her pulling away, as if all women want to be groped like this. But he just stands there staring at her arm beneath the patio's dim light as she refastens her unbuckled jeans and she realizes he means the dimpled scars of her skin.

Get the fuck away from me, she says, pushing her way toward the door.

She hears him behind her. No one wants a gnarled-up cunt like you anyway.

She is upon him before she can think to get herself to her sister and to the safety of another town. She feels her nails digging into his skin and her fist meeting his mouth and the rush of everything Tim kept her from doing for so many years, her mind a mess of believing a man's words. She keeps punching until Jesse screams and she feels the sharp heave of someone pulling her from him, her left knuckle wet with the crawl of his blood, her arms pinned, her body dragged toward the exit.

Her voice hoarse. Her vision dark. She feels herself shouting, so much louder than the weak trill of Jesse's screams. She feels herself shouting *it was him it was fucking him he's the one who shoved his fucking hands down my pants* and hears only the low boom of *you best get the fuck out of here before he presses charges.* And then there are hands on her shoulders, not a man's hands or the thick weight of a bouncer's arms. Something gentle. Her sister's voice. *It's okay, Billie.* Rhiannon's voice taking charge, taking her away toward the empty streets.

The car is a capsule, the windows closed. The moon pooling light beyond the windshield. Billie sits in the passenger seat, Rhiannon beside her in the driver's seat, the engine off. Billie feels her body keeping itself locked tight, feels the pressure of her lungs trapping her breath.

He tried to hurt me, she hears herself whisper.

I know. Just tell me what happened.

What do you think happened?

Billie, what did he do?

Nothing, Rhee. He didn't do anything at all.

But he tried to.

And I stopped him. Billie turns to her sister. Jesus Christ, Rhee, I stopped him. Any way I could. What would you have done?

The same thing. I would've done the same thing. I would've knifed him in the fucking throat. But, Billie, you just got out. You can't start fights in bars. You'll be right back in Decatur before you can blink.

I didn't start a fight. I didn't start anything. It's not a crime to have a drink.

I know it's not. Don't misunderstand me. You didn't do anything wrong. I just want to keep you here. Out here. Not in there, not locked up.

Billie watches the moonlight glint down on the silhouettes of mountains. Pikes Peak: a tall slope she knows is just beyond Colorado Springs. A summit she's never seen. So many things she's never seen beyond the lined beds of a prison dorm.

He mocked my scars, she says.

He's an asshole.

He called me a cunt. He put his hands down my fucking pants.

Rhiannon stays silent and when Billie looks at her she's staring straight ahead.

One hand clenched around the gearshift, tight enough to reveal the thin bones of her fingers in the moonlight.

Did that ever happen to you? Billie says.

Not like that. But racing wasn't exactly friendly to women. I just wish you could press charges.

I can't prove anything. No one saw anything. And you heard the bouncer. That guy could press charges instead.

Fuck that guy.

We can go, Billie says. You wanted to get to the campsite by nightfall.

Rhiannon watches Billie, her face a question, and Billie looks away.

I'm sorry, Billie. I'm sorry I lied to you.

The lie seems meaningless now to Billie, but she says nothing.

I didn't want you to think less of me, Rhiannon says. For quitting. And I wanted you to believe everything would be the same when you got out.

Billie doesn't look at her. Doesn't see how anything is the same at all now that she's out. She nods, the only forgiveness she can give. The place on her arm where Jesse grabbed her still smarting as Rhiannon turns the key in the ignition, the highway waiting for them to leave downtown.

Skylite Campground: tents only. No hookups for RVs. No water, no electricity. Just an outhouse and a shower on an unlit path through the woods. Billie leaves Rhiannon at the campsite to use the restroom and ignores the bruise on her arm beneath the outhouse's lone lightbulb, the skin already purpling, and in the single stall considers her period for the first time since Rhiannon picked her up. She counts backward. Nine days. She can expect her period in nine days. What required such exact planning in Decatur, each inmate allotted a limited number of tampons. One of the male guards, a burly asshole named Dan, punishing certain women by withholding their monthly allotment. Billie one of those women. Taunting her daily push-ups, telling her they wouldn't get her anywhere. *You think little biceps like those will save you in here?* He withheld every tampon she needed so she confiscated toilet paper rolls instead. Every woman did who didn't have enough pads each month, the cardboard a substitution. Billie knows there are no tampons in her daypack. Nine days. They might be back in Illinois by then but she grabs a toilet paper roll from the outhouse just in case. When she returns to the campsite, Rhiannon is staking the two-person tent swiftly in the dark, a small flashlight clenched between her teeth. Billie pulls their bags from the Mustang's trunk and helps Rhiannon toe the stakes into dew-softened ground. Rhiannon unzips the door flap and climbs inside and Billie follows her, the roof's gauze meshed in moon glow.

Think we'll need a rain cover? Billie says.

The forecast is clear. And look at those stars.

Billie looks up and finds Ursa Minor. The tent's dome an open mouth of darkness, nothing like the rectangle of sky from her prison bunk.

What do you see? Rhiannon says.

Little Dipper. Polaris. Common June constellations.

Think we'll see the Milky Way out here?

Maybe. Though it might be easier in Utah. Fewer people. Fewer lights.

Billie watches her sister pull a pair of sweatpants from her bag, the night cool beyond the day's heat. Rhiannon unrolls her sleeping bag and the spare for Billie. She grabs her toiletry bag. A small electric lamp. A can of beer she throws to Billie.

Here, she says. I bet you could use this about now.

Billie pops the tab, a craft beer from DeKalb that Rhiannon has stored in her bag all the way from Illinois. The beer warm but welcome, the whiskey's buzz long gone. Billie takes a drink. Hears Rhiannon snap open a can beside her.

Rhiannon climbs out of the tent and sits in the grass, knees pulled to her chest. The sky is dark but Billie can tell from the incline of the ground that they're on some kind of ridge, its height unclear until she crouches beside her sister and sees the lighted valley of Cañon City below them, the faint silhouette of the Rockies in the distance.

Nice pick for a campsite, she says.

I told you camping wasn't all bad.

It's hard to believe how dry it is out here after so much rain at home.

Rhiannon nods. I barely want to listen to the news tomorrow.

I watched the news in Decatur. It was hard to tell from there just how scary this is. All those airports shutting down.

It's a good thing we're driving. Aside from the boxes we're supposed to find, I think Mom planned it this way. To keep us on the ground.

Billie keeps her eyes on the mountains. I'm sorry I left you at the restaurant. I'm sorry I got so angry. You lied. But I shouldn't have stormed out.

Yeah, you shouldn't have. Especially not

right now.

Billie looks at her through the dark. Why did you really quit?

Rhiannon sighs. It's not your fault that I quit. My concentration was just shot after you left. Racing suddenly seemed so stupid. So selfish. I started losing. I wasn't making money. I met Beth soon after that.

Was she a reason you quit?

No. But life with her was so much easier than being on the road.

So you made safe moves.

That makes it sound like a cop-out.

But that's what you mean.

Rhiannon takes a sip of beer. I don't know if that's what I mean.

Billie imagines her sister in Champaign all those years while Billie took communal showers, ate stale bread, rationed toilet paper, circulated books in a prison library so far from the college institution where she once worked. The visiting center. Every month Rhiannon came to visit. Her face a shield revealing nothing.

What have you been doing all this time? If not racing?

I sell textbooks.

Billie laughs. Are you serious?

Billie hears Rhiannon laugh too in the dark. Can you imagine a life more boring?

I'm sorry, Rhee. It's not boring. It's just so different from racing, but I wouldn't say it's boring.

Come on, Billie.

What? Some people are very passionate about books.

Rhiannon laughs again. Like you?

What, you mean working with books, or burning down a fucking library?

I guess Mom made book lovers out of both of us. Even if you explicitly chose them and I just worked my way back to them.

Billie says nothing. Their mother, nothing she wants to discuss tonight.

It's a job, Rhiannon says. It's fine. But I miss the road.

Well, you're out here now.

Crickets trill in the far-off grass. A barn owl screeches softly from the trees, a sound Billie can distinguish even still from great-horned and barred owls. Alabama. A cord she cut in desperation. Tim coming home and finding her gone and harming her hawk a risk too great to take. Or else him sending Alabama to some kind of facility that wouldn't take proper care of her. No. Billie set her free. Rhiannon breathes beside her and the pain in Billie's arm dulls to a quiet ache.

I lied too, Billie says before she can stop

herself. The night wide open, the valley puddled before them. She throws it from her mouth before she can keep it inside of herself forever.

Rhiannon glances over. What did you lie about?

Billie feels her hand tremble holding the can's aluminum. About Tim.

What about Tim?

About what he did. About why I did it.

Billie, what? What did he do?

Billie turns toward Rhiannon and skates a finger down the right side of her face in the moonlight. He broke my brow bone, she says. Right before I went to the library. He broke open my eye and knocked me to the floor.

Rhiannon watches her. Rhiannon says nothing. Rhiannon reaches out and runs her hand over the scar's ridge, just below the bone.

Jesus Christ, Billie.

I couldn't take it anymore.

Why didn't you tell me?

I didn't tell anyone. The police never caught it. They assumed it was an injury from the library.

I don't care about the police. Why didn't you tell me?

Because it's not about you.

Of course it's not. Goddammit, Billie. That's not what I'm saying.

Then what are you saying?

I could've helped you.

Helped me do what? You were on the road. And Mom and Dad? I couldn't tell them. No fucking way. I was already a fuckup to them before I moved to Jacksonville.

You weren't a fuckup.

No? It was obvious. They always wanted so much more for me.

Someone hitting you isn't fucking up. Someone hitting you isn't your fault.

But I chose him. I let him do it.

Don't fucking say that. Please.

Well, it's true, isn't it?

Rhiannon looks at her. Was that the first time he hit you?

Billie says nothing.

Was that the first time? Rhiannon shouts through the dark.

No, Billie says softly. That asshole tonight calling me a cunt was nothing compared to the things Tim said and did.

What did he do? Billie, what the fuck else did he do?

I don't want to talk about this. Not tonight.

Well, you brought it up. You should have

said something. You could have shortened your prison sentence. You might not have gone to prison at all.

Are you kidding? None of those men in that courtroom would have believed me. And it's not like I fought back in self-defense. I tried to burn down a goddamn library. And are you saying this is my fault?

Rhiannon rubs her hands across her face. No, Billie. Jesus. None of this is your fault. But I wish you would have said something. There was a reason for what you did. The courts should have known the reason.

Well, it's real fucking helpful to hear what I should've done.

I'm just talking out loud. I can't believe he did that to you.

You can't change it. You couldn't have protected me.

I could have if I'd have known.

You can't control everything. You think you can, but you can't.

Rhiannon is silent and Billie wishes she could take the words back.

Look, it was so lonely there, Billie says. It was so fucking lonely in Jacksonville. She sets her beer in the grass and keeps her eyes on the mountains' silhouettes. I couldn't bring myself to tell anyone. I just sat with it. Until he did what he did and I decided that

I'd kill myself first before I let him do it for me.

She expects Rhiannon to speak, to scream something back, to tell her what she should have done with her loneliness. But her sister says nothing, sets down her beer and holds Billie's hand in hers.

I'm so sorry, Billie.

Billie watches the dark of the mountains until they blur.

I wanted to die, Rhee. What he did made me want to die.

Maybe not. Maybe you knew burning down the library wouldn't kill you.

What, you think it was a cry for help?

I didn't say that. But maybe you knew you'd live. Maybe you knew someone would see you and drag you from the building. Maybe you knew it was a way out. That either way, what you did would put an end to your relationship.

Billie can't speak. Can't believe that what she's held on to for over six years has fled her mouth. What she dreamed from a prison cell, how her tongue would ever form the words to say it.

I'm sorry I wasn't there, Rhiannon says. I'm sorry you went to the library instead.

The library. Billie closes her eyes and sees nothing but a trail of flames ziplining across the carpet. Scattered books.

I wanted better, she says. I wanted so much better than that for myself.

It wasn't your fault. Tell yourself that. Tell yourself again and again. None of what he did was your fault.

The barn owl has gone silent, the city lights below them a patchwork of grounded stars.

Tim's brother, Rhiannon says. God, Billie. I shouldn't have made you call him.

You didn't. I offered.

If he calls back, I can handle it. It's my phone. You don't have to pick it up.

I'm fine, Rhee. It's been six years.

We can figure out another way to find out what Mom left us in St. Louis.

I said it's fine. Oscar was always nice. He probably never even knew his brother was such a piece of shit.

I know someone else who can help us if Tim's brother can't. I talked to Dad. Tonight. He said he'd drive through St. Louis for us.

You called him?

He called while you were at the bar.

I bet he was proud that his felon of a daughter was on the loose in Colorado.

I didn't tell him. He only asked how you were doing.

I bet he did. What else did he say?

That he didn't know anything about the journal. That he proposed to Mom near that lake by the Science Center when she was in grad school.

How did we never know that? Is that why she led us there?

Maybe.

Then what about the T. rex?

A coincidence. That's what he said. I don't know if I believe that. Anyway, he said he'd be on the road this coming week. Maybe through St. Louis. If so, he can find what we missed instead of Tim's brother finding it.

I said it's fine.

Rhiannon picks up her beer. I called Aunt Sue, too.

Jesus, Rhee. You made the fucking rounds.

She wanted to talk to you. I said you were sleeping.

Billie pulls out the locket, still wedged in the front pocket of her jeans. Did she say anything about this? Did she tell you why it was along a riverbed in Kansas?

Actually, she did. She says Mom was studying marine fossils her first year of grad school. Aunt Sue sent her the locket on her first travel dig.

Despite everything, her arm still aching,

Billie feels her body lighten.

So there's a reason the locket was there, she says. A reason that makes sense.

I don't really know what it means. I don't know why Mom wanted us to have the locket. But yeah, I guess it means there's some reasoning to these coordinates.

And it means there's something in St. Louis, too, that we didn't find.

Maybe. Like I said, I can have Dad take a look.

I said I can handle it. I'm sure Oscar will call me back.

Rhiannon pours the remains of her beer in the grass. It's getting late. We should get some sleep. Do you know how far the next coordinates are from here?

Not far. I'll map the exact route in the morning.

Billie stands and Rhiannon stays seated, her gaze on Cañon City's valley.

I'm glad you told me, Billie. I'm sorry I couldn't be there for you sooner.

Billie nods. The sound of crickets filters through the darkness of the woods. She doesn't know what to say so she reaches down and Rhiannon takes her hand and Billie pulls her up.

Sunlight billows down and warms the tent's

mesh and Billie awakens with the thick taste of cotton in her mouth. Too many drinks. On her left arm, a swath of blue green that looks like a small lake spilled across her tricep. Jesse's fingers. A bruise that will surely stay for days. Rhiannon is nowhere in the tent, her sleeping bag already gone. Billie unzips the tent's nylon flap and Rhiannon is sitting in the grass overlooking the ridge with her hands curled around a thermos.

Coffee? They had it for free at the check-in station.

How long have you been up?

Long enough to take a shower and get packed. Are you hungry?

Not really. We could just eat protein bars this morning.

Rhiannon fills the thermos cap with coffee and passes it back and Billie sits beside her sister, the grass dewed and wet against her bare feet. The mountains are clear in the distance behind a thin wall of summer haze, the valley below already crammed with cars circuiting the streets. A Tuesday morning. A workday filling the road with traffic. Billie has long forgotten the schedule of nine-to-fives.

I'm ready when you are. Rhiannon glances over at her. You okay?

Billie rubs her face. Just let me hop in the

shower too.

By the time they pack the Mustang, the sun is already high in the western sky. Billie takes out the GPS and plugs in the set of coordinates from their mother's journal.

The coordinates are just past town, she says. Sort of back the way we came.

And the drawing is a stegosaurus?

Yep. Hopefully this one will be more self-explanatory.

The GPS takes them north of Cañon City along a road dotted with signs for the Gold Belt National Scenic Byway, a paved throughway that turns to dirt-covered switchbacks the Mustang steadily climbs. The Rockies on all sides. Billie navigates while Rhiannon steers around the road's turns, the car jumping on divots and rocks. Not once out on these roads has she revealed any slippage in her skill. Billie grips the door's handle, the valley teetering beyond the edge of the guardrails, and navigates them six miles outside of Cañon City until they reach the coordinates' destination: a single sign. The Garden Park Fossil Area.

Have you ever heard of this place? Rhiannon asks. She pulls the car into a sparse parking lot populated only by wooden signs pointing to different fossil sites.

Never, Billie says. Maybe Mom mentioned it, but I wouldn't remember.

Looks like there are several quarries here. Any sense of the one we need to find?

The one with the stegosaurus, Billie says blankly. How many can there be?

Rhiannon parks the car in the shade of a juniper tree and squints across the parking lot. Visitor center over there, she says. We can ask inside.

Billie follows her toward the building, larger than the visitor center at Smoky Hill River but still unimpressive, a site clearly passed over by Colorado tourists. A woman in a brown uniform and ranger hat sits behind a lone desk inside the center.

You ladies need help?

I think we're looking for a quarry, Rhiannon says as they approach the desk.

Well, this is the place. You know which one?

How many are there?

Six. Each one's got a different story. Do you know which story you're looking for?

The one with the stegosaurus, Billie says. Unless that's all of them.

Just one. The Small Quarry is the one you want.

Which way is that? Rhiannon asks. And is there anything we need to know about the

Small Quarry before we go?

You'll need sunscreen, the woman says. Not a lot of shade out there.

I mean history, Rhiannon says. I'm assuming we'll find stegosaurus bones. But is there anything special about this particular quarry?

The woman pulls a pamphlet from a drawer and slides it across the desk.

Most of the information is back in town at the Dinosaur Depot, she says. Not the most official name, I know. But it's the museum where tourists go.

Then who comes out here? Billie asks as she takes the pamphlet.

People who want to see the original sites. The actual quarries. Also hikers. Lots of good trails out here. Anyway, the Small Quarry is where one of only two complete stegosaurus skeletons has been found. The skull intact. Plates all in a line.

Plates? Billie asks.

Their mother's specific area of study: surely what they've been brought here to find.

One of the only places in the world where the plates have been found in a full row, the woman says. Other quarries, they've been found scattered around the skeleton. If you want to see the site, take the first trail out the door to the right.

Thanks, Billie says and opens the pamphlet to the map of a trail that will take them a mile into the quarry's hills. She heads toward the door and readies to fold the pamphlet into her pocket when Rhiannon takes it from her hands and runs her finger down its text, halting on the paragraph explaining the trail's history.

June of 1992, Rhiannon says.

And? Billie says. Does that mean something to you?

No, but it's recent. I thought these sites were all dug before Mom's time. Nineteen ninety-two was well into her career. Do you think she was here?

I don't know. We were around then. Don't you think we'd remember?

We were kids. We didn't know where the hell she went.

Excuse me, the woman calls behind them. Did you say your mother? What career?

Rhiannon turns around. Our mother studied stegosaurus bones.

What was her name?

Margaret Hurst. She worked for the University of Illinois geology department.

The woman's face changes. Are you ladies her daughters?

Rhiannon says nothing and Billie steps in. We are.

Welcome to Colorado. And I'm so sorry for your loss.

Billie feels herself motionless. Did you know her?

Your mother's a household name around here.

Billie watches the woman. Rhiannon has gone silent beside her.

The woman smiles. The Small Quarry is where the first stegosaur skeleton was found fully intact, she says. And your mother's the one who discovered it.

GORDON, RICHARD. "URBANA HIGH SCHOOL GRAD TAKES SECOND PLACE IN NASCAR NATIONWIDE SERIES." THE CHAMPAIGN-URBANA NEWS-GAZETTE. 21 AUGUST 2007: G1. PRINT.

Urbana High School Grad Takes Second Place in NASCAR Nationwide Series

In a close finish at the Talladega Superspeedway, local driver Rhiannon Hurst took second place in the NASCAR Nationwide Series' championship race after racer Chase Derrington pulled ahead by a .01 margin. Derrington took the first-place trophy, while Hurst took home a second-place win.

"I was close," Hurst said in a postrace interview. "But not quite close enough."

Hurst, a graduate of Urbana High School, has made a name for herself in NASCAR as she ascends the ranks of the Nationwide Series. Having once driven in local and regional races, she has had a breakout year on the Nationwide circuit by placing tenth, fifth, fourth, and now second in the series' races.

Hurst is the only currently active female driver in NASCAR.

Her father, Jim Hurst, a retired NASCAR driver and former resident of Champaign-

Urbana, now serves as his daughter's pit crew manager. "It's an extremely respectable finish," he said. "Rhiannon's primed for debuting in the Sprint Cup Series. Just wait until next year."

38.4419° N, 105.2209° W: Cañon City, CO

Rhiannon wants to feel relief that this woman knew their mother, that she and Billie have an answer before they hike a trail to find the meaning of a scrawled coordinate. Their mother one of the first to find a full stegosaurus skeleton, a star in the field of paleontology. She wants to feel relief but there is nothing, the woman's words bouncing hollow through her brain.

Household name.

A term her father once used for her on the racing circuit.

Climbing the ranks of every NASCAR race from tenth place to fourth to grandstand finishes. Standing on the platform in third place and then second, pushing her way toward her inaugural first-place win that became wins that became sweeps. So much easier than what Wendell Scott endured, his photo still taped to her childhood bedroom wall. Easier than what Billie has revealed, what Tim did to her, what she silently withstood in Jacksonville. Still, how many times interviewers asked who she was dating, whether she wanted kids, if a stock car was harder to control for a woman's small hands. Shirtless fans yelling *cunt* from the stands during pit stops. All of it unwanted fuel to prove she could do it. *You're gonna be a household name, Rhee,* her father said as they drove across Indiana and Oklahoma and Texas, a term her mother echoed in anticipation of everything their daughter would become.

And now this park ranger's voice makes it clear: their mother's reputation. What Rhiannon could've guessed but her mother never directly said. That she'd been famous in her field. That she surely wanted this for her daughters. Billie's visit to the Cleveland-Lloyd Quarry some hope that the desert would infuse one daughter with some sense of drive, the other already making a name for herself before spiraling out across the Indianapolis Motor Speedway and leaving behind her helmet and her racing career before it truly started.

The heavy weight of expectation, of being a girl who does.

It blankets Rhiannon as the ranger stares at her and Billie.

Why is it called the Small Quarry? Billy is saying.

Bryan Small, the woman says. One of your mother's assistants. He's the one who stumbled on the stegosaurus skeleton first. Being who she is, your mother let him take the name recognition for the discovery.

Being who she is, Rhiannon thinks, not knowing at all what this woman means. If her mother was someone different out here than who she was in Illinois.

Were you here when she was here? Billie asks.

The woman laughs. I guess my face shows my age. I was here. Just starting out then, in conservation and forestry. I've met a lot of scientists out here. Your mother was always one of the nicest.

Rhiannon tries to smile. Any information should be welcome, any story to celebrate the memory of her mother, but this woman's words are a swift needle. *Was.*

I was sorry to hear about her passing, the woman says. You ladies out here retracing her steps?

Rhiannon wishes the ranger would stop calling them ladies. A household name, she wants to say. I could've been a household name. We're making our way out to Utah, she says instead and pulls Billie toward the visitor center's door. This is on the way.

Definitely stop in on your way back, the woman calls after them. I'd be happy to answer any questions you have about the quarry or your mother's work.

Rhiannon smiles thinly and Billie follows her out the door toward the trail and Rhiannon paces ahead and Billie walks quickly to keep up, the sun beating down across the treeless hills.

What was that all about? Billie says, catching her breath at an overlook along the trail. And Jesus Christ. Slow the fuck down.

Rhiannon stops and looks across the valley. Nothing tall on the horizon, only sagebrush that reaches her waist. The Rockies a jagged line in the distance, a paleness matched by the growing smog of the sky.

You notice how hazy it is today? Rhiannon says.

Hey, Billie says. Answer me. What the fuck was that all about?

It was about nothing, Billie. Nothing at all.

Oh, come on. That woman just wanted to help us.

Did she? By telling us how well she knew Mom?

It's not a competition of who knew her best. It's okay if that woman knows things we don't know.

Did you know?

Know what?

About this skeleton she found, Rhiannon says. That Mom was so famous.

Billie pulls a water bottle from her daypack. No, I didn't know.

You think that's why she sent us here? So we would know she was a household name?

That phrase. Rhiannon can't help the mocking tone that fills her voice and Billie stares at her, a realization sliding across her face.

So that's it, Billie says.

Rhiannon watches the valley, its small cars and sunlit metal.

It pisses you off. That Mom was so well known and you're not anymore.

Rhiannon wants to feel angry that Billie's said it out loud, that she was never famous like their mother. The desert's dust fills her lungs, so much grime and silt. She closes her eyes and a mass of black dots clusters at the edge of her vision and she is at once on her knees trying to swallow so much thin air. A twilight of fainting. A precursor she's experienced only one other time in her life, out on the track after spinning out.

Jesus, Rhee. What?

Rhiannon wants to speak but can't. She

sets her hands on her thighs and keeps her eyes on the ground. Why this. Right now. Why not standing at the edge of her mother's casket. Why only upon hearing something that elated her when her father said it and now only scalpels her chest, the words blading the breath from her lungs.

Drink this, Billie says, shoving her water bottle in Rhiannon's face. It's probably altitude. We've only been in Colorado a day. You haven't had time to acclimate.

Rhiannon takes the bottle and the huddle of dots remains.

Put your head between your legs, she hears Billie say.

Rhiannon sits back in the dirt and lowers her head to her knees. She can't remember the last time she was at this high an altitude, every business trip from Champaign heading east by plane. Where there were no mountains. No raceways. Only the smooth gleam of a textbook's hardcover, only the glad-handing of shook deals and the listless transfer of business cards between palms.

She feels her lungs slacken, the tension in her chest beginning to ease.

It's the altitude, Billie says again.

I don't know if it is, Rhiannon hears herself wheeze.

Then what? God, Rhee, get ahold of yourself.

Billie, I'm aimless.

Curled into her body, her voice muffled. Loud enough for her sister to hear.

I'm so fucking aimless, she says again. I'm not racing. I'm not in a relationship anymore. I'm not anything at all.

Billie's hand is on her back and for the quickest of moments it feels like her mother's hand and Rhiannon wants to disappear. The sharpest hurt she's felt since the funeral, watching her mother be taken in by the earth. The weight of expectation. Of failure. Of hanging up her helmet and selling textbooks and Billie recovering inside a prison cell, her busted eye healing and her heart hardening. How Rhiannon could have pushed herself back onto the road instead of giving up while Billie had nothing, so much privilege Rhiannon let swirl down a drain. She feels Billie's fingers moving soft against her back. This land filled with her mother's once-footsteps, her once-hands. How they chiseled bone. How they made things happen. Hands buried now below the earth.

You're grieving, Billie is saying. It's okay. It's okay to feel lost.

I've been lost for six years. This has nothing to do with Mom.

But even as she says it and wipes the trail's swirling dust from her face Rhiannon knows it has everything to do with their mother. If their mother were still here, Rhiannon could have gone on like this for years, for decades, for the rest of her life. She would have still been becoming. She would have still been a child. Her mother just down the street from her and Beth's apartment until she wasn't anymore and Rhiannon was back on Grove Street going through her closets and donating her coats and unearthing box after box of things that smelled only of something lost, a childhood of plastic model cars and painted soapboxes and one lone biography on Wendell Scott, the picture of him on her bedroom wall ripped down.

You're not lost, Billie says. You have a job. You have a partner if you want her. You have a home. If anyone's lost, it's me. Look at me, Rhee.

Rhiannon imagines Billie in the library. Flames licking the walls all around her.

At least you acted, Rhiannon says. At least you knew to do something. At least you knew to do it fast. It's been years since I've wanted anything.

You can do anything you want. Nothing's stopping you.

Nothing's stopping me but knowing in the first place what I want. Nothing stopped me the whole time you were in Decatur. Nothing's stopping me now.

Our lives aren't the same. Yours is yours. And you aren't responsible for what happened before or after I went to prison.

But I wish I would've known. What Tim did.

Yeah, Billie whispers. I wish you would've let me know some things too.

Rhiannon watches the thin sky beyond the trail's cliffs and tries not to think of what else hides in the boxes of her mother's things in their childhood home: newspaper clippings. Every race Rhiannon won. What her mother saved. What Rhiannon found in one box tucked into the back of her old bedroom's closet and promptly closed.

You have no idea, she says. You have no idea what it's been like in that house, going through all her things. Every elementary school essay, every school project, every declaration of what I wanted to be. Do you know how many times they asked us in school what we wanted to be when we grew up?

I get to go through all that when I get back. A nice reminder right out of prison.

Rhiannon opens her eyes and looks at her

sister. Despite everything, she laughs.

We'll figure it out later. Billie laughs too and extends her hand. Come on.

Rhiannon lets herself be pulled up and despite her laughter tries not to notice the sadness in Billie's face. Six years Rhiannon had that Billie didn't. Each day a cubicle but rising nonetheless to an open road if she'd wanted it. An open road she chose not to take.

The sky continues to haze as the trail leads them up through tufts of juniper and piñon to a roped-off section of limestone cliffs marked by a sign. Billie stops ahead of Rhiannon and wipes the back of her neck beneath her shaved hair.

This has to be it, Billie calls.

Rhiannon catches up and squints at the cliffs. There's nothing here.

Billie runs a pointer finger across the sign and Rhiannon scans the roped area. No sign of fossils or a full skeleton. Not even evidence of chisels or pickaxes. Only the pocked surface of rock, the same as everywhere else along the path.

This says the skeleton is at the Denver Museum of Nature and Science, Billie says.

Then why didn't Mom send us there? We were headed that way.

This is where she found it. The museum's probably full of people, the skeleton off-limits. Mom was actually here.

Rhiannon stoops and touches the rock just beyond the rope. The pamphlet said 1992, she says. God, Billie, we were just kids. What does the sign say?

That the skeleton was found completely intact. The skull, the tail, the plates. That its completeness settled long-debated issues about the tail spikes and plates.

Rhiannon feels her face flush with heat: long-debated issues. Controversy over the plates' function, their mother's life work.

That's why she wanted us here, Billie says. There's your answer right there.

The limestone is cool beneath Rhiannon's palm. What her mother chipped away with a rock pick hammer, what she dusted off with brushes to find the plates intact.

Maybe this was a start, Billie says. The beginning of a life-long mission to determine what the plates were for. And to prove everyone else wrong.

Rhiannon pushes her hand against the rock. The start of her mother's entire career, a heat Rhiannon wants to feel pulsing through the limestone.

Billie pulls the GPS from her bag. These are the coordinates. Exactly. Do you think there's a box here?

Rhiannon stands. The one in Kansas wasn't far from the information placard. She looks at Billie. I can't believe we're already talking like this. Are we really looking for plastic boxes buried in the middle of nowhere?

Billie ignores her. If there's something here, it shouldn't be hard to find. We're the only people out here.

She leans down and checks the base of the sign and Rhiannon kicks through the thin grass and roots of clustered sagebrush. The heat bears down on her shoulders, splitting through the sky's wisped clouds. She bends down to pull the water bottle from Billie's bag and sees it tucked beneath the underbrush of a juniper: a gray box, small and plastic, barely visible in the weeds.

Billie, she says.

Billie crouches beside her and pulls the tiny box from the undergrowth. Do these have locks? she says.

No. They're hidden well so they won't need them. It should pop right open.

Billie pushes a small latch and the box unfolds. Inside is another slip of paper with the matching coordinates and a rough sketch of a stegosaurus, exactly what their mother drew in the journal. Beneath the paper, what Billie pulls out: a tiny fragment of rock that to Rhiannon looks like the tail of a miniature whale.

Billie holds the rock up to the weak sun. What is it?

Some kind of fossil, Rhiannon says. Honestly, I have no idea.

The heat is all at once monstrous. Heavy as the leaden x-ray blankets of the Champaign dental office Rhiannon and Billie visited as children, where their mother once acquired picks in bulk for digs.

Rhiannon wipes her brow and sighs. You know who'd know what that is?

The visitor center looks even smaller through the growing haze when they make their way back, the woman still inside at her desk.

You ladies find what you were looking for?

Rhiannon places the fossil on the desk. Any idea what this is?

The woman picks up the rock and eyes Rhiannon. Did you take this from the site?

Billie approaches the desk. We didn't take anything. Our mother left it for us.

What do you mean your mother left it for you?

Geocaching, Billie says as if she's familiar with the term. She's left us items all across the country. We found this one right by the dig site.

You drive or fly? I wouldn't want to be flying right now.

Rhiannon avoids the question. We're going where she wanted us to go.

It makes sense your mother wanted you here. This was her place. Her discovery. One of the main reasons the entire Garden Park Fossil Area exists.

Rhiannon points to the fossil their mother left for them that this woman now holds. Can you just tell us what this is?

My name's Lucy, by the way. Yours?

Rhiannon sighs and tells her each of their names.

Nice to meet you both, Lucy says. At any rate, this is a tail spike. One of the smallest found on the stegosaurus.

Our mother studied plates, Billie says. Any idea why she left us a tail bone?

Your mother found one of the only full skeletons intact, which includes the tail spikes. The orientation of the spikes proved the tail's limited range of motion.

What does that matter? Rhiannon says. What does it have to do with the plates?

Another paleontologist by the name of Bakker argued that the stegosaurus could stand on its hind legs to grab food, using the tail as support. Your mother's skeleton proved that couldn't be the case. The tail was too rigid. And the reason the tail was too rigid? Directly due to the positioning of the plates.

How were they positioned? Billie asks.

Upright, right along the spine. In alternating nodes. They anchored the tail. A tail that provided a clear, irrefutable picture of how the plates were oriented.

Billie looks at Rhiannon. So this could've been the start of everything she studied.

Rhiannon envisions their mother here, these same paths. Her hands stumbling upon pocked rock, finding a full skeleton she must have known would change her life.

She looks at Lucy. Did the skeleton prove anything else? Besides offering information about the plates and the tail?

That's about it, Lucy says. Though the Small Quarry did reveal evidence of the late Jurassic climate. What might have caused the stegosaurus's extinction. Evidence of a mass drought. The bones showed that the stegosaurus could have died by lightning.

Rhiannon zeroes in on Lucy's words. Climate. What her mother knew about the planet by examining its past. How in the last months of her life she'd warned Rhiannon against flying for work, advice she assumed came from her mother's dig-site flights and not from decades of studying ancient climate patterns.

Have you heard anything more about those flights? Rhiannon asks.

Which one? the woman says. The one that went down in Arizona?

We've been in and out of radio range, Rhiannon says softly. I wondered if you'd heard anything about all those planes.

The last I heard, some airports are staying closed, but others might be opening back up to keep making money. Why?

Rhiannon doesn't answer. Thanks again for your time. We appreciate it.

You hitting the road? Anything else I can do to help you ladies?

Rhiannon holds her tongue. You've been a tremendous help.

Billie takes the fossil and places it in her pocket where Rhiannon knows the locket still hides. Any place I can fill up my water bottle here before we hit the road?

Restroom around the corner. Lucy smiles. I guess I can let you keep that fossil.

Rhiannon grins back to hide the quick anger that flashes through her brain.

You know where to find me, Lucy says. If you have any more questions about your mother and her work.

Lucy shakes their hands. Rhiannon waits outside while Billie fills her water bottle and tries to imagine her mother here before they leave. The woman who pushed them from her body. Showed them peonies, the flight of honeybees, the thin wings of bats in their backyard. The woman whose passion for the way things worked led one daughter to a racetrack and the other to birds, and so many years later led both of them here.

Rhiannon keeps heading west on Highway 50 outside of Cañon City until they find a roadside bar and grill. Tammy's Café, just beyond the outskirts of a town called Texas Creek. POPULATION: 47, according to the flashing highway sign for slowed speed, beside signs for ATV tours and rafting outposts along the Arkansas River.

We're really doing it, Billie says across a vinyl booth after ordering a burger with onion rings and a strawberry milkshake. We're really out here. Two Hurst ladies.

Jesus, I thought she'd never stop saying that.

What's wrong with being a lady? Don't you consider yourself a lady? I like being a lady way out here. Just two ladies.

Rhiannon glances out the restaurant's bay windows, the growing fog a thick weight upon the mountains. The Rockies surround the highway and block direct sun. Cars whiz past the café windows, the weak afternoon light glinting off their metal roofs. The server slides Billie's milkshake onto the table along with a frosted-aluminum cup that holds extra ice cream and hands Rhiannon a glass of water.

At least she gave us good information, Billie says. She wasn't all bad.

I just don't want to hear it right now, Rhiannon says. How well someone else knew Mom. I already feel like I don't know her at all.

Why? Billie says. She did all this for us.

Maybe. But why didn't she just tell us about all this when she was still here?

Billie shrugs, her mouth to the straw, the milkshake diminishing inside the glass.

Rhiannon watches her across the table. Why do you think she gave you the journal? Why you and not me?

What, you think you're more responsible? That it should've gone to you?

That's not what I'm saying. But why do you think she chose you? Why choose anyone? Why not just tell both of us about these plans?

Billie glances out the window and avoids Rhiannon's eyes.

What? Just tell me. What did she tell you?

She didn't tell me anything. Nothing at all. But come on. You can guess.

What can I guess? Rhiannon asks as their food arrives.

Mom was proud of you. Billie knifes ketchup onto the open face of her burger bun. It's clear she was prouder of you than me. But I think she knew I'd be more willing to deviate from a path.

What, getting out here? Come on, Billie. I've deviated just as much as you from any path she thought I might take.

But you've always been focused. In your career, and in everything else. Maybe Mom knew you'd say no. Maybe she knew you'd just want to get out here and get back.

Rhiannon looks at the BLT in her hands so Billie won't see the unexpected burn of tears in her eyes. That their mother could think less of her, in any way at all. That their mother knew her well enough to know the same determination that once kept her on a racetrack would keep her on a highway straight out to Utah, narrowed to the road and nothing else.

She was just as determined as I was, Rhiannon says.

Yeah, she was. She had a plan. She pursued a single track her entire life. But determination isn't the same as being able to stop and look around. I think she did that. She was curious. I can't imagine she kept that curiosity focused on dinosaurs alone.

Rhiannon thinks of their mother's backyard garden. A bat box fastened to their oak tree. A cluster of cork to draw bees. A jungle of peonies, the bulbs of alliums. Flower heads cottoned like small planets, full of voices her mother once told her lived on the surface of plants. *An entire world in there,* her mother whispered and Rhiannon believed her, that flowers contained neighborhoods. An imagination so crucial, Rhiannon realizes now, to reenvision a prehistoric era. Her mother's desk filled with bone fragments and crinoids and anatomical sketches of a dinosaur she'd never seen. And her world beyond work, Rhiannon recalls: movie nights. Twilight walks. Weekly flamenco lessons at the YMCA. The same as Billie's red-tailed hawks and biology books.

You're just as curious, Billie is saying. You just don't let yourself explore it.

Rhiannon looks at her sister across the table. Right now I feel aimless. I don't feel curious about anything at all. I don't think that's what Mom wanted either of us to feel.

I'm more aimless than anyone, Billie says.

I think Mom knew it. She knew I'd just be getting out, that I'd have a vested interest in wandering and enjoying. Billie holds her sandwich up. Like this burger. This fucking burger. It's still hard to believe. There was nothing like this in Decatur. Nothing like those fucking mountains out there either.

Billie motions her burger toward the window. Mountains and more mountains beyond them, peaks rising behind the gentler slopes that dot the highway. Mountains Rhiannon once passed along the interstates of America like they were nothing.

She glances at Billie. Are you doing okay?

Why wouldn't I be?

That bruise. He grabbed you harder than you said.

Billie rubs a hand across her left arm, covering the blue-green mark and the pocks of her scars. I'm fine, Rhee.

Would you tell me if you weren't?

Probably not. Billie smiles. But I've seen worse than that asshole at the bar.

That's what worries me. That you wouldn't say if anything was bothering you.

Billie ignores her. She picks up an onion ring and dips it into a small pool of ketchup on her plate. Why'd you ask about the planes?

When?

In the visitor center. Why'd you ask Lucy about the news?

I like to be informed.

Bullshit. There's a reason.

Rhiannon sets down her BLT. Mom knew I was scared to fly. I thought that's why she organized the trip like this, all road and no planes. But Lucy mentioned the Jurassic climate. Drought and lightning. What might have caused an extinction.

So?

So Mom studied climate change her entire life.

Billie looks at her. And you think that has something to do with the planes.

Not directly. But I'm sure she connected her research to what's been happening. She didn't want us to fly out to Utah. That's clear. But maybe she wanted us to understand not just her career but something else.

Billie takes a sip of her milkshake. Like what? Some connection between the Jurassic climate and this bonkers weather now?

I don't know. But the weather's changing so drastically. Those planes aren't a coincidence. We've never had a summer like this. Constant rain since March. And this drought out here. And fuck, Billie, all those planes. Airports have actually closed.

Some are opening back up. That's what

Lucy said.

So, what, you're not scared? Are you worried at all about the news?

Billie rolls her eyes. I was in prison. It's not like we ever thought about vacationing from there. So, no. I haven't given plane travel much thought.

This isn't about vacations, Billie. Seven plane crashes in four months. Rain in Illinois. That storm in Missouri. This haze and fog. Rhiannon gestures out the window. Have you ever seen a sky like that?

Billie glances toward the mountains where thick smog jackets the peaks. I haven't seen any sky beyond Illinois in years. I don't know what's normal.

Well, that's not normal, Rhiannon says as a hard gust of wind throws itself against the window and rattles the panes. We should get back on the road. Where's the next coordinate?

I left the GPS in the car.

What's the drawing?

Billie pulls the journal from her bag and a roll of toilet paper falls out before she stuffs it back into her daypack.

What was that? Rhiannon asks.

Billie looks up. What was what?

Are you carrying toilet paper with you?

Billie looks down at her bag, her face

unreadable. My period might come on this trip. I wanted to be prepared.

Did you take that from the motel?

From the campsite.

Billie, I have tampons. And we can just stop at a convenience store.

For the first time since Rhiannon picked her up, Billie looks embarrassed.

They took our tampons sometimes, she says. I forgot we could just buy them out here.

Rhiannon feels ridiculous. The things her sister never talked about for six whole years and the things she's processing that Rhiannon can't fathom. Not the openness of mountains. Not a highway's freedom. A tampon. Something so fucking simple.

We can get whatever you need, Rhiannon says. Just tell me and we'll stop.

Billie nods and opens the journal to the next page. From across the table, Rhiannon sees what looks like some kind of scrawled horseshoe, a small sliver drawn above it in the shape of a crescent.

What do you think that is? Rhiannon says.

I have no idea. It's definitely not an animal.

That crescent looks like a moon. But the rest of it?

Maybe a break from fossils and hiking. I

wouldn't mind that.

Another pulse of wind shakes the panes and Rhiannon signals the server for the check.

Rhiannon continues west along Highway 50 and lets the stereo hum. She's heard enough news for now and the playlist lights upon Fleetwood Mac, her namesake. Billie fiddles with the GPS in the passenger seat until the device beeps.

Where are we headed?

Billie sits up. Turn around.

Rhiannon looks at her.

What?

I said turn around. This coordinate's routing us south.

Rhiannon flips on the hazard lights, the shoulder's rumble strip shaking the Mustang as she pulls over. A white SUV behind them honks.

How far south?

Billie taps the route into the digital map on Rhiannon's phone.

Carlsbad, she says. At the southeastern corner of New Mexico, almost to Texas. This is showing an eight-hour drive.

Rhiannon wants to scream. Are you fucking kidding me?

It's not a far backtrack. It looks like we

take Highway 69 south from here, a few miles back near Texas Creek.

A few miles back. Then hundreds of miles south.

Eight hours south, Billie says. We have time. We'll still make it to Utah.

Yeah, by the middle of next week. Jesus, Billie. I thought she'd at least create a route that makes sense.

Billie studies the digital map and makes adjustments. It's thirteen hours between the Cleveland-Lloyd Quarry and Carlsbad. We could do that in a day's drive.

Assuming we're going straight there. There's probably some other stop along the way.

Even if there is, it's only Tuesday. We can still be there by Friday and drive straight through on Sunday, all the way home. Just over a week on the road.

Rhiannon eyes the jagged peaks beyond the steering wheel, the Mustang ready to drive straight through the Rockies. What she did so many times with her father, mountain passes through Colorado between speedways. How he always let her rest in the passenger seat between races, her brain catching on whatever passed beyond the window. The shapes of clouds. Sunflowers in Kansas. Wildflowers along the highways in Colorado. The same curiosity her mother had. What hasn't lit Rhiannon up in years. Everything in her life: A to B. Utility. Nothing more than getting things done.

Tonight in Carlsbad, she hears herself say. Maybe one night somewhere on the way back up tomorrow, Cleveland-Lloyd by Thursday. But, Billie, this is far more driving than I ever imagined. I'm going to need to change the oil soon.

I can drive if you want, Billie says.

No, you can't. You don't even have a license.

Billie smiles and Rhiannon bursts out laughing.

You think that's funny? Billie says and Rhiannon watches her begin to laugh too.

I'm sorry, Billie. I know it's not funny. But all of this is just so fucking unreal.

Billie is still laughing. What the fuck is in Carlsbad?

Probably some other dig site. I don't know. I've never been there.

Rhiannon shuts off the hazards and makes a U-turn and there is a shift that takes her by surprise. She feels no frustration. This detour not the disappointment she expected. What floods her body instead is pooled relief to drive away from Colorado and feel her hands on the steering wheel for an eight-hour stretch, the Small Quarry behind them. What a household name meant for her mother. What it almost meant for her.

JAMESON, CARRIE. "CARLSBAD CAVERNS NATIONAL PARK." AMERICA, THE BEAUTIFUL: A GUIDE TO NATIONAL PARKS. CHICAGO: RAND MCNALLY, 2008. 14–19. PRINT.

CALL NUMBER: GB561 .G70 2008

CARLSBAD CAVERNS NATIONAL PARK

Located within the Guadalupe Mountains in southeastern New Mexico, Carlsbad Caverns National Park is the fifth-largest cave in North America. The main cavern, made of limestone, is nearly 4,000 feet long and 255 feet high. The cave contains gypsum, a formation marked by limestone's reaction with sulfuric acid, as well as speleothem formations including popcorn, draperies, and soda straws.

Approximately 250 million years ago, what is now Carlsbad Caverns was the coastline of an inland sea, its marine life forming the Capitan Reef. The Caverns are currently occupied by very few organisms except seven species of bats, including the most common species, Mexican free-tailed bats. Once populating the cave by the millions, the bats' numbers have diminished in recent years due to suspected damage from DDT pesticides.

32.1753° N, 104.4439° W: Carlsbad, NM

New Mexico is a lunar landscape, the setting sun pressed against Billie's west-facing window as the Mustang guns south across the desert on Highway 285. Rhiannon's playlist fills the car. Bob Dylan. The Guess Who. Jefferson Airplane. Every song an anthem of their childhood, their mother's records merged in marriage with their father's LPs. The Moody Blues. Electric Light Orchestra. Michael Jackson, Billie's own namesake. She watches out the window as the landscape flattens from mountains to low ridges to dusted plains. Raptors wheel in the sky above them. A Cooper's hawk. An American kestrel. Billie recognizes their wingspans, smaller than a red-tailed hawk.

Billie wondered from her prison bunk and still wonders way out here where Alabama flew when she cut her loose. If she found a mate and built a nest. If Billie was right in letting her go, what Bud once told her some falconers did to let their birds live free in the wild. If Alabama was still out there somewhere in Illinois or if she migrated south or died years ago, struck by a car or hit by lightning or caught in the spiked whorls of a barbed-wire fence. Billie's arm smarting as they travel south. A plum-size bruise. The feel of Jesse's hands sliding down her pants. The toilet paper in her bag. How stupid. Billie forgetting what she could just buy. And still lodged in her brain the muscle memory of Alabama taking flight from the encased glove of her left arm, the weight of a red-tailed hawk all feather if not for the grip of talons. Hawks already less a part of her life by the time she moved to Jacksonville, Tim so frustrated with falconry's strict routines and live-rat purchases that he forced Billie to keep Alabama outside in a poorly constructed weathering yard, barely regulated, and not in the mew he insisted Billie keep in the laundry room where the humidity was far too high for a hawk.

Billie remembers holding Alabama for the first time. Only six months old, raised at a breeding facility in central Illinois where Bud acquired her for Billie's keep. Alabama so much lighter than Billie anticipated, all feathers and soft peeping. She earned her permit and completed Bud's yearlong apprenticeship and passed her exam and built an indoor mew. The Illinois Department of Natural Resources visiting her two-bedroom in Urbana, checking enclosures for humane treatment. Billie wiring the outdoor weathering pen herself, airtight mesh and pipes, unlike the careless pen she made in Jacksonville. The only one Tim let her build, his salary funding their rented home, a weathering yard full of chicken-wire holes big enough for cats to claw through. What Tim made her keep quiet because he didn't want to spend more. Alabama's first indoor mew in Urbana had been pristine: inspected, state approved. An opening for sunlight. A suitable perch. Jesses and anklets. Enough space for her full wingspan. A small pan for water and bathing. A freezer for food. Everything Billie set up in the second bedroom of her rented house as if preparing for the birth of a child.

And Alabama herself: the hawk Billie named not after a band but for a state she'd never seen. She'd driven across Arkansas and Mississippi and Georgia once on a family road trip on their way to Disney World but had missed Alabama where she imagined the stars falling in curtains of light, the same magic as a hawk she could send to the sky. Not to hunt. What she knew the intended purpose of falconry was. Just a hawk she could feel leaving her arm, its weight taking to the Illinois blue.

You want to stop for dinner somewhere? Rhiannon says.

Billie shakes her head. I think I'm good.

I think Roswell's the next big town. If you're tired we can stop there for the night.

I'm good if you are, Billie says. And anyway, it's June. Longest days of the year. The sun won't fully set for another few hours. We can make it to Carlsbad before then.

Rhiannon nods. I'll just need to stop for gas.

Billie wants to laugh that they're stopping in Roswell, a place she's never seen but has read about more times than she can count. Books on planets: the 523s of the Dewey decimal system. Alien life. *Are we alone?* They reach the outskirts of Roswell where buildings begin to populate the horizon. The Mustang passes the city limit sign and a huge wooden UFO where a minivan is parked, a family of three posing for a picture.

Looks like we're in for a treat, Rhiannon says.

Highway 285 takes them straight through

the center of town, a highway turned business district that Billie expects to roll out again into vast plains of nothing once they pass the city's limits on the other side. Rhiannon slows the car, every gas station and grocery store decorated in outer space. Wooden cutouts of green aliens flanking each driveway. Arms waving customers inside. Flying saucers soaped into the windows of McDonald's play palaces. Meteors painted on a Wendy's atrium.

This place is no joke. Rhiannon points at a sign along the road. Want to stop at the UFO Museum?

I'll pass.

Billie, I'm joking.

I'm fine with just a gas stop. Gas and a bathroom. Maybe a soda.

Rhiannon finds a Chevron station, the cheapest gas listed. Her phone beeps in the center console as she pulls in, back in range. Billie looks down: a voice-mail message.

I'll fill up the tank, Rhiannon says. You can take a bathroom break first.

Rhiannon hands her a five-dollar bill and Billie opens the passenger door and feels her legs stretch against the pavement. Nearly five hours in the car since Colorado. She makes her way toward the gas station's food mart when Rhiannon calls her back.

Billie turns around and Rhiannon is holding her phone to her ear.

It's for you, Rhiannon says. If you want to take the call.

Billie, it's Oscar, the message crackles when she places the receiver against her ear. His voice piercing. It could be Tim's voice if Billie closes her eyes. She reminds herself that she told Oscar to call, that she asked for this kind of message. He reports what he found in Forest Park: a small plastic box wedged beneath the T. rex statue's tail.

Rhiannon stands at the fuel pump beside her as Billie calls back before she can lose her nerve. The phone buzzes in her ear, the same drone of the Correctional Center's only public phone. A line down the hallway from her bunk, one allotted call per week. Billie waiting always for someone to pick up on the other end of a line, Rhiannon or her mother or sometimes Bud. Never her father. Never Tim. Never his voice. Never again. Bud the only man she communicated with for six years beyond the prison's guards, a voice that reminded her of Alabama: that she'd been someone before Tim.

Thanks for calling back, Oscar says when he picks up on the fourth ring. You were right. There was a plastic box right under the statue.

Billie steels herself. Did you open it?

I didn't see what was inside. I didn't know if you'd want me to look.

Rhiannon shifts beside her and Billie knows she wants to hear what Oscar found.

Do you have the box with you?

Right here.

Open it, Billie says.

She hears the muffled sound of Oscar fidgeting with the plastic box. She envisions his home, imagines a partner though she knows nothing of his life. There's a drawing, he says. It's a T. rex, and some kind of coordinate.

The drawing matches the first page in the journal. What Billie's expected, though she's still surprised to hear it.

Dig further, she says. What's beneath it?

The fuel pump snaps and Rhiannon pulls the wand from the tank. Cars rush past the station along the business district, a whir of heat and dust.

It looks like some kind of ring, Oscar says.

What kind of ring? Billie asks and Rhiannon stops moving beside her.

It's a blue stone. I'm not sure what kind.

But Billie already knows what kind as soon as he says it's a ring. Aquamarine. The birthstone for March, the month their mother married their father in a late Illinois snowstorm. The month she died. Their parents' wedding a ceremony and reception at Pere Marquette Lodge across the Mississippi River from St. Louis. Just outside Godfrey, Illinois, where nearly everyone in their mother's family still lived, their father's family traveling downstate from Pekin. Their parents anticipating crocuses for the ceremony. A foot of snow arriving instead. The Lodge nearly shutting down but both sides of the family traveling regardless for a Pabst keg and a fried chicken buffet and a ring that's been missing from her mother's hand since their parents divorced when Billie was a sophomore in high school. Billie hasn't seen her father in years but the last time she did, he still wore his ring, a small point of ice blue set in a thick band of gold.

You want me to mail it to you somewhere? Oscar says.

No, Billie says. We won't be anywhere out here for more than one night.

Then what should I do with it?

Keep it. Just for now. We'll be making our way back through the Midwest early next week. Is it okay if we swing by?

Oscar is silent for a moment. Only if you think that's okay with you.

Billie holds her breath before she speaks and wonders what Oscar's been told. That she's fragile. Unstable and crazy. Still an ex-felon, Tim scot-free in Jacksonville.

Just give me your address, she says. I'll call you early next week to let you know when we'll be heading through St. Louis.

I'll keep it safe until then. If I'm at work, I can take a quick break to meet you.

Billie wants to ask where he works but stops herself. This glimpse of her former life. She shouldn't know, shouldn't want to know. She only says thanks instead. When she hangs up the phone, Rhiannon is still standing at the fuel pump watching her.

A ring, Rhiannon says. Mom's fucking wedding ring.

Right underneath the T. rex tail.

Billie.

It's fine. We didn't know what it was we were looking for. Don't worry. He'll hang on to it until we get there.

Do you know how long I spent looking for that ring?

Billie looks up and Rhiannon is trembling, her hands drawn and knuckled.

Before her funeral, Rhiannon says. Dad wanted it and I couldn't find it anywhere.

Why? They were divorced. And who gives a fuck what Dad wanted?

I do, Rhiannon says. I fucking care. God, Billie. Get over yourself. It's been six years.

I don't know why Dad didn't call and didn't visit you but he's still our father. He's the only parent you have left.

And that makes him a hero? Billie shouts, anger climbing her throat.

Keep your voice down, Rhiannon hisses. People are looking.

Who gives a fuck if people are looking?

Look, you have a right to your feelings. But Dad does too.

He has a right to judge me? He has a right to not even show up once?

No, Billie. He doesn't. I don't have any fucking idea why he never came. But he's not a bad man. He doesn't hate you. And he has the right to see that ring one last time.

Why didn't you tell me you were looking for it? Or that Dad wanted it?

I didn't think it mattered. I couldn't find it anyway.

Billie glances toward the food mart, the five-dollar bill still wedged in her hand. Mom hid it in Forest Park well before her funeral, she says. Or had someone else do it for her. It obviously didn't matter to her if Dad wanted it or not.

She probably didn't even know he wanted it.

That lake by the Science Center is where

Dad proposed. You said so after you talked to him. That's clearly why she left it there.

I know, Rhiannon says. But she drew a T. rex. Not the ring.

Yeah, just to help us find the box.

Maybe not. Maybe her career was always more important to her. At least in hindsight. More important than a marriage ever was. Maybe she wanted us to know that.

Billie sees in Rhiannon's face a trace of regret, her hands curled as if still gripping the steering wheel. Hey, Billie says. We have no idea what she wanted us to know.

Rhiannon squints toward the rush of cars whistling past on the highway. I feel like this whole trip is Mom's way of shoving all this in my face, she says. Everything she discovered throughout her career. All these places she saw, all these roads I once traveled and haven't been on in years. Even marriage. Leaving us this ring. That she could leave it behind just like I left Beth.

I don't think so. I don't think that's it at all.

What else could it be?

Maybe this isn't about you. Maybe this isn't about either of us.

How not? She built this entire scavenger hunt for the two of us.

Billie looks south down the highway where

they're heading. She has no idea what their mother is trying to tell them. She thinks of visiting hours, her mother's weak palms pressing the journal into her hands. Her eyes already tiring and growing weak but her face still bright. Not a face of punishment, retribution. Never the face of hoping her daughters would discover only regret on the road.

Rhiannon drives south across New Mexico with no music, her gaze fixed on the road. She doesn't open the bag of M&Ms Billie grabbed for her inside the Chevron station. She only drums her thumbs against the top of the steering wheel as Billie watches the sun sink deeper into the desert, light banded over fields of creosote and mesquite. Billie leans her head against the window, Oscar's voice still banging around in her brain.

Did you ever want to get married? she asks.

I know you were gone awhile, but Beth and I wouldn't even have been able to get married in Illinois until this year.

Then traveling to another state for a marriage license. Did you ever consider it?

Not once. We never talked about it at all.

Did you want to talk about it?

I think she might have wanted to. But I'm

not really the marrying kind.

Billie laughs. The marrying kind?

I'm serious, Billie. Do I look like someone ready for marriage?

You could be.

Rhiannon sighs. I think you need some permanence to make that kind of decision. I've never really felt permanent.

Across nearly five years of dating her? You never felt permanent?

Maybe for a while. But who can really feel permanent selling textbooks?

I'm sure a lot of people can. Maybe you conflated Beth with a job you never wanted. Maybe you'd have felt differently about her if you were still racing.

Rhiannon keeps her eyes straight ahead. Your circumstances were completely different, but did you ever feel permanent living in Jacksonville? Like it would last?

Tim talked about marriage sometimes. In hindsight, I think I always knew it wasn't right. I don't know if it was him calling me a cunt or him shoving me against a wall that made it clear he wasn't the one for me.

Billie means it as a joke but Rhiannon looks at her, the first time she's looked away from the road since they left Roswell.

How? Rhiannon says. How did you first know it wasn't right?

Billie thinks of Alabama's makeshift weathering pen in the backyard. Tim's long hours on campus. The expectation of a clean house, cooked meals. What she can't believe she abided across those years, among everything else.

There was always something hollow in my stomach, Billie says. An intuition. I tried sometimes to push it away. That was the only permanent thing I felt in Jacksonville.

I think I felt that, Rhiannon says. A hollow. As soon as I left the racetrack.

You could've kept racing. No one stopped you.

I know. Knowing that is the worst thing.

Billie watches the road and lets herself ask what she's been wanting to ask since they left Cañon City. What did stop you?

I really don't know. It wasn't Beth. And marriage or not is beside the point. We never talked about my past. She never asked. At first I thought she wasn't interested but I never brought it up. I didn't want to talk about it.

You think?

What's that supposed to mean?

Billie sits up. You're good at a lot of things, Rhee. Talking about how you're feeling isn't one of them.

I'm talking now.

Yeah, to me. Not to Beth.

Rhiannon sighs. Sometimes I think she never really even knew who I was.

What stopped you from talking to her about this for so long? You were together for over four years.

Rhiannon hesitates. I think I was ashamed. That I chose something safe. That I didn't just get back in the car and try again. That I was a fucking coward. That I felt the entire time we were together that she was far more passionate about everything than me. All these exhibitions. All these coffee table books everywhere in our apartment about art. I used to be so much more interesting.

What made her interesting to you?

She's a printmaker. She was excited about it. It was sometimes so hard to walk into her studio knowing my helmet was gathering dust in Mom's garage.

The sun slips low against the western horizon, the fields around them ablaze.

You could forgive yourself, Billie says softly. That's a good place to start again.

You could too, Rhiannon says and Billie runs her hand up her left arm and the rippled scars and the lake bed of her bruise. What she hears Rhiannon saying: more doing. That Beth did things. That Rhiannon wished she had too. Billie closes her eyes and tries to root down into the same intuition that told her years ago Tim wasn't right. Wonders if it can tell her out here in the nowhere of New Mexico what she should do now with her life. The one saving grace of prison. Just being. She opens her eyes and feels them sting and tells herself it is only the piercing light of the desert sky.

Dusk settles around them as the Mustang pulls into the entrance for Carlsbad Caverns National Park, where the coordinates have led them. Not a dig site. Billie should have known. Carlsbad known for its caverns, New Mexico's only national park. Despite their late arrival beyond regular hours, they join a line of cars filtering in. The road curves through plateaus dotted with sagebrush and limestone that Billie knows hide miles of caves beneath the surface. What she read about in one of the prison library's donated books on national parks. The caverns a once-inland sea, so much like Smoky Hill River. Another ancient bed of marine fossils, the reason Billie imagines her mother has sent them here.

Does this road ever end? Rhiannon says as the road's mile markers lengthen through the darkening hills.

Billie checks the mapped coordinate.

We're getting close.

It's well past visiting hours. Surely we're too late for a hike.

I don't think so. Billie watches the trail of red taillights ahead of them. All these cars are here for a reason.

Whatever it is, we can still camp for the night and come back early in the morning if we need to hike out somewhere. Can we camp here?

Billie isn't sure, no posted signs, no cell service since they left Roswell. But the landscape is desolate beyond the park, a vast flatland of desert rolling out beneath a sky that will soon heavy itself with stars. A sky that won't care if they pitch a tent. The caravan of cars slows as a large building appears on the plateau, what Billie assumes is the park's visitor center and cavern entrance. Even in the dark Billie can see the vastness of the valley below, a wide horizon of red rock and desert sage and intermittent pinpoints of lighted homes. She glances down at the GPS in her hands, their route still inching toward its exact coordinate. Rhiannon follows the line of cars and parks in the building's lot, the Mustang's windshield overlooking the dim valley. Billie pushes open the passenger door, the air windless, surprisingly cool. Illinois another country from here. Constant rain, impossible from the dryness of the New Mexico desert.

Where are we supposed to go? Rhiannon says.

Billie slides the GPS into her pocket, its position a near match though it still hasn't beeped their mother's exact coordinates. She nods toward families leaving their cars and funneling onto the sidewalks past the closed visitor center.

We're not quite there, she says. I'll keep the GPS on me to let us know when we've reached the exact mark, but I'm guessing we should just follow those people.

They fall into step behind a family with two small girls. Billie watches them toddle and tries to remember if their own parents ever took them to national parks. She recalls only Illinois state parks. River bluffs. Thick oak trees. Maples turning crimson. Their father carrying her on his shoulders through the woods, nearly impossible to remember, her father so close, her small fists gripping his sweatshirt. She and Rhiannon pass a ranger who waves them along, the sidewalk transitioning into a black-topped path that leads off into the plateaus.

This path must lead to the cave's entrance, Rhiannon says.

What could we possibly see there at night?

We're obviously not hiking. Look at all these kids.

The path stretches off into the hilled landscape until the flow of people backs up at a staircase leading off a precipice and down toward something Billie can't see.

This must be it, Rhiannon says.

Must be what? What the fuck are we here for?

When Billie reaches the top of the staircase, she sees the cave's entrance at the bottom of the stairs. A yawning dark where swiftlets circle up from the cave's mouth in dusk's fading light. People all around them, families and teenagers and couples on vacation. People descending the stairs and filtering into rows of limestone seats, a natural amphitheater in the shape of a horseshoe that surrounds the mouth of the cave.

A horseshoe: their mother's drawing.

The crescent curved into the notebook's corner the same as the half-moon rising beyond the cave's entrance.

No hike, no fossil. Only an outdoor amphitheater and the coming night.

Arriving right on time, the moon already high, just as their mother intended.

Billie should have known. The Carlsbad bat

flight. It appeared in so many of her earth science books, one of America's natural wonders. The GB560s in the call number system, the library's section on caves. Carlsbad one of the only places in the country where Mexican free-tailed bats flew out by the thousands each night and gathered food until the sun rose and they returned, roosting here through summer before returning to Mexico in winter. Only other two locations where they lived: Bracken Cave in San Antonio. The Congress Avenue Bridge in Austin. Both of which Billie has only seen in the glossed pages of a library's books.

Rhiannon sits beside her at the edge of one of the amphitheater's stone rows, far enough to the periphery that neither of them can see the mouth of the cave. Billie has let the GPS guide them exactly, the device at last beeping when they reached the row's edge. *Do you see anything?* Rhiannon asked when they sat down, but Billie saw nothing. Scanned the stone beneath her shoes, the edges of the rows around them. No trace of a hidden plastic box. Tufts of sagebrush and juniper bushes obscure their view of the cave's mouth though a ranger standing at the front of the amphitheater promises ten thousand bats will be visible from every seat. The ranger is a young woman providing facts to the crowd about the free-tailed bats' diet and hunting habits. Facts Billie stops herself from calling out over the din of children, everything she recalls from so many hours reading books to pass the time at the library. Echolocation. Mother bats finding their young among thousands by call alone after hunting beetles and wasps, as many as two hundred pups per square foot stuck to the cavern's ceiling. Rhiannon shifts beside her on the stone bench, the roughness of her jeans rubbing against Billie's bare leg.

I'm getting hungry, Rhiannon says.

Billie watches the deep indigo of the sky above the cavern. The sun's long gone, she says. The bats should be circling out any minute.

Circling?

That's what they do. The cave's entrance is small and steep. They need to circle out together to get enough lift to leave.

Tell me more, nerd. Why don't you go shove that ranger out of the way?

The ranger tells the crowd to stay quiet. Says the bats will circle from the cave behind her. She tells the audience to let her know by rotating their hands in a circular motion and that the bats will fly over the amphitheater and out over the valley to eat two hundred tons of moths and bees in one night.

I wish I could do that, Rhiannon mumbles.

Come on, Rhee. We'll be out of here soon.

I don't know why we're here in the first place. A thousand-mile detour, and for what? There aren't even any dinosaur bones here.

She clearly timed these stops just right for us to arrive here at dusk. She wanted us here for a reason.

Any idea what that reason is? And are we even sure there's a plastic box hidden somewhere here? Look at all these people, Billie. How the fuck are we going to find it?

Billie doesn't want to think of the effort it will take among so many people. Despite the GPS beeping this row exactly, Billie scans the ground again and sees nothing as the audience near the cave's entrance begins to rotate their hands and circle their arms in the air. The crowd falls silent and the ranger moves away from the entrance where bats begin to emerge.

The crowd is so quiet that Billie hears the desert air shift with the movement of wings. The bats corkscrew and rotate out of the cave, an airless tornado, wings slicked in the half-moon's light. Billie watches children clutched in their parents' arms, brought to this isolated place just to see. Despite the weather, the planes. A toddler eyes the bats from her father's lap, the grip of her small hands clenching the bunched fabric of his knees. Billie's own father so fucking far away. An Illinois forest. Billie settled on his shoulders as he identified oak leaves. Sugar maples. Eastern bluebirds. Turkey vultures. Monarch butterfly chrysalides. He made sure she knew every secret the woods kept. Those same Illinois woods doused in rain and Billie wonders what autumn will even look like this year, a permanent flood. The bats pulse from the cave in cyclones and Billie wonders if they'll even be here in fifty years, in twenty, the weather changing and their habitat shifting and the wind across the desert rising. The half-moon glares down, hooking light on the intermittent gleam of webbed wings and Billie feels her throat catch. Rhiannon touches her leg. Billie can't bring herself to look at her sister.

The ranger said this could last for two hours, Rhiannon whispers. I'm ready to go whenever you are.

Billie nods. Families begin to filter from the amphitheater. Billie wants to stay but gives her sister this. A sister who's picked her up from prison and taken off work and driven her halfway across the country. Billie follows Rhiannon toward the central staircase. She traps the sound of the bats' wings in her brain, the soft silence of membranes and webbing. Her father's shoulders, autumn leaves rainbowing his feet as they walked through the damp woods. Alabama taking flight from her forearm. As she walks she hears the scrape of plastic, her shoes kicking weight at the edge of their row. A recognizable shape. They might have seen it if there'd been fewer people when they first sat down in their row. Billie looks down. A mottled-gray box. Nestled beneath the lip of a stone seat, only feet from where they sat.

The same kind of box as the Smoky Hill River, the Small Quarry.

Beyond bats, what their mother intended them to find.

Billie sits in the passenger seat, the engine off as cars stream from the parking lot behind them. Headlights fill the Mustang's interior. Rhiannon holds the small box in her hands. She unfastens the latch, the sound of popped plastic. Billie hears the rustle of paper, what she knows is the coordinate and drawing. The stone amphitheater, a crescent moon. A match for the sketch inside the journal. She hears Rhiannon digging inside the box then the sound of something soft, almost inaudible.

I think this one might be for you, Rhiannon says.

Billie looks over and the box is lying discarded in Rhiannon's lap. The paper nudged aside. In Rhiannon's hands: the feather of a red-tailed hawk.

A wing feather. Burnt color, marked by telltale tiger-striped barbs. White wisps funneled to the tip of a beta-keratin quill. The same down of Alabama's coat, a weight Billie can feel still beating against her palms.

Hawks winter here, Billie says dumbly. In New Mexico. They winter here.

Come on, Billie. Mom didn't send us here to see where birds winter.

Then why did she? Billie looks out at the dark ocean of the valley, the lighted pinpoints of distant homes. And God, why bats? Bats aren't even birds.

Maybe she knew you'd know something about any kind of animal with wings.

There were feathered dinosaurs in the Jurassic. Maybe she did research here.

Jesus, Billie. We both know what this means. This feather's clear as fucking day. It's for you. It's about you. This stop isn't about Mom at all.

What, to remind me that I used to do something? Billie looks at her sister. Just like you? She didn't have to send us way the fuck down here to remind me that I'm not like you or her or Dad. Why the fuck are we out here?

Rhiannon is silent and Billie takes the feather from her hands. The bats surely still beating toward the moon and outward to the valley. Billie closes her eyes and there is only the soft pulse of their webbed wings, the hardest sound she's heard since she cut Alabama's line and listened to her take flight in the backyard's stillness. It cracks her open. The feather in her palms. The bats cycloning through the dark above them. It cracks her open like her mother knew it would.

ORENSTEIN, BRIAN. "ECHOLOCATION IN MICROCHIROPTERAN BATS." NORTH AMERICAN ORNITHOLOGY: A GUIDE TO THE BIRDS OF AMERICA. ED. JAMES BURCH. NEW HAVEN: YALE UNIVERSITY PRESS, 1994. 22–26. PRINT.

CALL NUMBER: QL670 .G520 1994

ECHOLOCATION IN MICROCHIROPTERAN BATS

Microchiropterans are an order of bats distinguished from megabats by their smaller size, their use of sonar, and the presence of a tragus, a small point on the external ear that funnels sound. Microbats use echolocation to find food, usually in complete darkness once night falls. They generate sonar through their larynx and nasal passages, bouncing off potential prey to determine distance. Because a single crèche habitat can contain up to two hundred bats per square foot, mother bats also use echolocation to find their pups.

32.1757° N, 104.3766° W: WHITES CITY, NM

Rhiannon lets Billie help her pitch the tent in the dark. This second night of camping, not what Rhiannon promised: she vows to find Billie a clean hotel once they finally cross into Utah. They've parked the Mustang in Whites City, an RV park named after the man who allegedly discovered Carlsbad Caverns. So many towns out here bearing the names of explorers. The same as racing, the same as paleontology and falconry. The mythology of American men, the West never intended for anyone else, never meant for her or for Billie. They've stopped here for a lack of options and dined at the RV park's restaurant. Rhiannon ordering a burger and cold fries, Billie across the booth eating only soda crackers. And now she thrusts herself into pitching the tent and Rhiannon wonders if she even knows how to anchor a stake into the ground.

I can take care of this, Rhiannon says.

Billie twists two aluminum poles together. I'm fine.

Rhiannon says nothing more and wonders what it was about the feather that shook her sister so hard. A message from their mother, as clear as anything else: that Rhiannon wasn't the only one who needed a soft push. But Billie's silence is a surprise. Rhiannon can't remember the last time she saw her cry. Not in high school over boys. Not over fights with friends. Not even in Colorado Springs, her reaction only rage. When they at last raise the poles and the tent's mesh stretches into a dome, Billie grabs their sleeping bags from the trunk and unrolls them on the tarp and they lie in the tent's dark, the rain flap open and filled with stars. The half-moon glows through the ceiling's mesh, each constellation a string of small pins.

Which ones are those? Rhiannon asks.

The bright one is Arcturus.

Where's the Big Dipper?

Billie points higher along the tent's ceiling. It's farther up in the sky, she says. We can't see it. The Big Dipper's handle slopes down to Arcturus.

Rhiannon huddles deeper into her sleeping bag, the desert growing cold. How did you learn all that?

You know how I learned it, Billie says. I read a lot of books.

But it's been years since you've been able to stargaze.

I had a window. Billie nods at the rain flap. A small opening like this one.

Rhiannon hesitates. Billie, what's wrong?

Nothing's wrong. I'm fine.

You didn't seem fine in the car. You don't seem fine now.

Billie rolls onto her side, her back to her sister. Rhiannon hears her sigh. I can't believe Mom led us down here just to throw the past in my face, Billie whispers.

I don't think she meant to make you feel bad.

It's not just Mom. It's everything.

What's everything?

Billie is quiet for so long that Rhiannon thinks she's fallen asleep. Rhiannon watches more stars begin to salt the sky, the moon's light pulsing through the rain flap.

What has your relationship with Dad been like? Billie finally says.

You mean lately?

I guess so. The last six years.

It's been fine. We don't talk about a lot of things. We don't talk about Beth or Mom. But we understand each other. He understood what racing meant to me.

I don't think Dad understands anything about me.

That's not true.

It is. It's completely true.

Is that what's bothering you?

I don't know. It was hard to hear his voice the other day. Everything is hard. It's so fucking hard to be out here. It's a lot. All at once.

I know, Rhiannon whispers.

Those bats should have made me think of Mom. She's the one who led us down here. She's the one who left that feather for me to find. But all I could think of was Dad. Walking through the woods with him when we were little. How I always thought it was Mom who made us want things, but now I'm not so sure.

They were so different. It's clear Dad was threatened sometimes by Mom's accomplishments. But they both wanted things. They both had drive.

I know. And knowing that out here, right now? I just feel lost. I feel so much pressure to feel something. To do something. From two people who aren't even here.

Rhiannon nods in the dark. Every time I talk to Dad, he mentions Bryson Townes. The new driver he's helping to train. He keeps saying I could have been like him. I could have still been on the circuit winning every race.

At least Dad gets what you do. I don't feel like he ever got me at all.

Rhiannon turns to her. When did you ever feel closest to him?

Billie rolls onto her back and looks up into the darkness. I remember what it was like to hike with him. That's what I kept thinking about at the cave. How there was a time when he showed me how to love everything outdoors.

That was all you. That was your thing. Yours and his and Mom's.

But you and Dad had racing. I still remember the first time he set you down in a Soap Box Derby car.

You remember that? You couldn't have been older than three.

I knew that was your time. Your space. Dad and I had the woods. But ever since I became a teenager, I don't think he's known how to talk to me.

It's not like he and I talk about relationships or anything else in life.

But you talk about racing.

You think telling me I could've been great is talking about racing?

At least it connects you. He understands you. He never visited me once.

I know.

Billie turns away from the sky and looks at Rhiannon. Do you?

I don't know why, Billie. I never asked him. We never talked about it.

Do you know how much that hurt?

Rhiannon shakes her head.

I always thought it was because he hated me.

He doesn't hate you.

It's been so much easier to hate him back.

Billie, he wanted so badly to talk to you the other morning.

But not for the past six years?

I know. I don't know why he never came.

Because he was ashamed of me.

You had your reasons for doing what you did. Remember that.

And you had your reasons for leaving the racetrack. But you didn't burn down a fucking library. He's always been prouder of you.

Rhiannon sighs. Is that what this is about?

Jesus, Rhee, no. But come on. You did something, the same way they both did something with their lives. I've never been able to do anything.

Did. I did something. Something I'm not doing at all anymore. And what you're saying isn't even true. They were both so proud of you. And anyway, don't discount completely different circumstances.

What circumstances?

No one ever hit me.

I could have left Tim sooner. And it's not like I had a big wellspring of drive before I met him.

No one ever thinks to leave sooner. Jesus, Billie. It wasn't your fault.

Look, I know. But what I'm talking about precedes even Tim. It wasn't the library or prison that distanced me and Dad. I felt lost to him as soon as I entered high school.

You were a teenager. Teenagers aren't supposed to do anything.

You did. You were already racing in high school.

Rhiannon is quiet a moment. You could call him.

I don't want to call him. I want him to call me.

Rhiannon imagines their father in Illinois, not knowing at all that the wedding ring he sought has been hidden for months beneath a statue in Forest Park.

Didn't those bats make you want to die? Billie whispers and Rhiannon doesn't know what she means but the stars above them are so luminous they make Rhiannon feel humbled and small. Everything out here so much larger than them, her brain catching on what it was to forget herself in something. The wonder their parents wanted for each of them: Tires skidding against the pavement. A wheel's torque curving around a racetrack. Or else the weight of a falcon on Billie's arm. Miraculous. The same as a swirl of bats cycloning toward dusk.

Rhiannon awakens to morning heat filtering through the tent's mesh, her mouth dry and her head heavy with dreaming. A dream of Beth. Beth folding clothes for donation piles. Beth helping her sort through discarded recipes and forgotten photographs and old holiday cards. A reverie, Rhiannon disentangling every one of her mother's boxes on her own. She imagines Beth in the small studio of their former apartment making woodcuts from the materials of the Midwest. Maple and oak. Wheat and prairie grass. *Art working in tandem with the land,* the language Beth used on so many of her artist statements. Why she was drawn to a land sculpture like the Spiral Jetty, an art book always on their coffee table that Rhiannon barely noticed, her mind focused instead on mechanics and facts. The precision of racing. The sale of textbooks, all numbers and invoices. Rhiannon sits up and shakes away the dream and Billie is nowhere, her sleeping bag already rolled. When Rhiannon unzips the tent, Billie is sitting in the grass, knees triangled against the ground, holding the feather in her palms.

Morning, Rhiannon says.

Billie glances back. Sleep well?

I guess I did. You?

Better than I thought I would. But I wouldn't mind sleeping in a bed tonight.

That's fine. I budgeted enough for motels at least half the nights. You okay?

Billie smiles. Mom's really offering us a swift kick out here, isn't she? All these hidden objects. These wide-open spaces. So much fucking time in the car, Rhee. She knew we couldn't avoid it.

Avoid what?

Billie looks at her. Ourselves. Mom knew we couldn't avoid ourselves.

Rhiannon thinks of her dream, Beth beside her. I know, she says.

Billie twists the feather in her hands. Is it possible to feel elated and horrible all at once? I'm out here. I'm fucking out here but Mom's gone. It was so much easier to pretend like she was still here when I was in Decatur.

How?

Nothing ever changes there. But out here? Billie motions to the sky. We've been in a different state every single day. Everything's changing. And Mom's not here.

Rhiannon closes her eyes. Everything changing. Her relationship. Their family. Billie here now. A locket. A stegosaurus's tail bone. The weather.

Where are we headed next?

North, Billie says. Surely north. That's all I know.

Did you look at the journal?

Not yet. The GPS signal has been intermittent out here, but we know we have to head back the way we came. Highway 285 is the only route north.

There's cell service in Roswell. That's not far, and it's on the way back. We can reroute when we get there. You hungry?

Billie shakes her head. I can wait. We can stop later to break up the trip.

Then let's pack up. We can eat in Roswell. It might be the biggest town until we cross into Colorado and Utah. And anyway, I need to change the oil. We're nearing the three-thousand-mile mark. Engine problems are the last thing we need out here.

Billie nods and Rhiannon turns to break down the tent and leaves her sister in the grass, the feather still twirling in her hands.

■ ■ ■ ■

In Roswell, Rhiannon drives until she spots a Valvoline Instant Oil Change, a chain she knows will be expensive but quick. It's only Wednesday, plenty of time to get to the Cleveland-Lloyd Quarry and back to Illinois but Carlsbad is a detour she didn't expect, gas she hadn't anticipated burning. The sun hazes over again as they travel north, the sky a marble of blue and dust.

She pulls into the Valvoline's garage, a tunnel of gauges and hydraulic jacks not unlike the service centers of pit stops. Rhiannon could change the oil herself, a skill she learned from her father in high school. But it would take dirtied clothes, so few shirts she's brought on the road, and time she and Billie don't have. She lets the mechanics tell her where to pull up the car and stop. Billie sits beside her holding the GPS, waiting for its service to catch up with Rhiannon's cell phone back in range.

A man in a gray jumpsuit approaches the driver's-side window. Morning, he says.

Rhiannon nods. Just an oil change, please.

You in the system?

We're passing through. Just need a quick change.

The man pulls out a clipboard and Rhiannon notices how young he is, maybe nineteen, his beard only thin stubble. You want the full-service synthetic?

Just your standard.

He leans into the window. I'd really suggest the synthetic blend, ma'am, especially for the Mustang you have here. Desert's hard on a car.

I know. Rhiannon smiles. Like I said, just the standard.

Really, I'd recommend the synthetic. Plus a full-service maintenance check for you girls out on the road for the transmission fluid, the brakes, the tire pressure —

Standard oil, Rhiannon says. I have a tire gauge in my glove box. And your maintenance check comes with every oil change, standard or premium.

The man pulls away. Fine. Standard oil it is.

Rhiannon rolls up the window.

Bet you've heard that pitch before, Billie says, not looking up.

These fucking mechanics.

You can't expect them to know who you are.

Does it matter?

Not to them. Billie grins. You're just a little lady in a little car.

Rhiannon feels the thorn of her anger diffuse quickly. *You girls.* The road all machismo. Route 66. Harley-Davidson. Born to Be Wild. The myth of American freedom. And NASCAR, a sport she first loved as a child before knowing she shouldn't. Each speedway a microcosm for everything she hated about this country: thrown beads. Playboy bunnies. An entire thoroughfare of McDonald's and Burger King, not a single tree in sight. Coors Light. Beef jerky. Men taking up every inch of space like they ruled the raceway, men naming every monument and town out here after themselves. A legacy of owning. Rhiannon recalls the Confederate flags bannered above RVs. The slurs tossed casually between men sharing beers. The palpable racism. The tangible homophobia. The sport's long history of white male racers, what fans would call an upheld tradition and what she knew to be the fragility of gatekeeping. Rhiannon feels her hands tighten around the Mustang's wheel, ashamed of everything about racing that she nonetheless once loved. The speed of the engine. What made a car work. Being part of that culture made her culpable regardless. She glances at a sliver of sky barely visible from the Valvoline station. Beyond hatred and discrimination, NASCAR criticized consistently for emissions and pollution, for lead additives in gas. The mechanic moves around the car, checking the tires before popping the hood and inspecting the fuel levels, and Rhiannon feels liable even here out on the road, the Mustang's emissions adding to an already-turbulent atmosphere. Billie keeps her head bent over the GPS and Rhiannon looks away from the mechanic and checks her cell phone, nearly one full day out of service range and barely any emails. She recalls her dream. No messages from Beth. No checking in at all. What she expected but the silence still smarts.

There it is, Billie says, holding up the GPS. We're back in range.

Billie pulls the journal from the bag near her feet and flips it open to the next page and Rhiannon can't help but strain to see the number of pages beyond the one Billie opens, how many more coordinates their mother has planned. She leans back against the headrest as the Mustang hums with hydraulics, the mechanic working below the car. Maybe Billie was right. Maybe their mother gave Billie the journal for a reason. Rhiannon would have flipped to the last page. The coordinates useless, a collection of locations they'd never stop to see. Billie leans over the journal and Rhiannon realizes what she hates to admit: that despite the miles and a bar fight and the unexpected need to change the oil, this version of the trip wouldn't have happened without Billie.

Billie extends the journal's next page across the center console. This is where we're headed next.

Rhiannon glances at the open page's new coordinate, latitudes and longitudes that make no sense to her. And the drawing: a crude scrawl of small footprints, one after the other.

Looks like tracks, she says. Just like Smoky Hill River. Some kind of dinosaur.

Billie grabs Rhiannon's phone and plugs the coordinate into the digital map.

Where are we headed? Rhiannon asks. Straight to the quarry?

Almost. Looks like we're stopping in Moab first.

Southern Utah? At least it's on the way.

Have you been there before?

The car drones with the surrounding sound of the service station's motorized equipment and Rhiannon recalls only the wideness of the Sonoran Desert in Arizona. Not Utah. On all her roadway travels Rhiannon has never seen Arches or Canyonlands or any of Utah's national parks, all of them too far off the interstates. She remembers only standing at the edge of the Grand Canyon, a brief stop she and her father made on their way back from a competition in Las Vegas. Her first two years of college. Intermittent online courses to make up for time spent away from Chicago. She'd broken up for the first time with a woman, a girl named Shawna in her freshman-year Anthropology 101 class, one of her only in-person courses and a lecture hall of nearly four hundred people and Rhiannon happened to sit right next to the first girl she dated openly for just over a year until Shawna called her crying from Chicago saying that she'd cheated, that she'd met someone else. A boy, Rhiannon remembers now, as clearly as she recalls taking the phone call late in Vegas after she'd won second place in an early race of the Nationwide Series season and standing the next day at the edge of the Grand Canyon with her father and feeling her eyes burn, the swift dagger of heartbreak.

I've never been to Moab, Rhiannon says. How far away are we?

Billie sighs. Nine hours.

Any cities between here and there? Or should we just eat here?

I'm still not that hungry. Albuquerque is the next biggest city. Another three hours, if you can wait. It's still early. I know it's a long drive ahead, but we can be in Moab by dusk if you want to set up camp.

We don't have to camp. I know you'd prefer a hotel.

Last night wasn't that bad. I can handle another night outside.

The mechanic resurfaces from beneath the car and Rhiannon glances past him to the sky through the tunnel of the garage. A milked film of dust, far less clear than the night before, so many crystalline constellations above the tent. Her stomach roils and she fishes in the backseat for trail mix, still three hours until lunch. As she turns she catches sight of a small television in the corner of the garage, antenna-fuzzed but still clear enough that Rhiannon sees the news: continued coverage of the last downed plane, continued reopening of airports around the country, what she let herself forget for one night out of range beneath a swirl of bats and stars.

Albuquerque is latticed with cars, the sun slicked across a gridlock of metal. Rhiannon turns the air-conditioning on full blast, the Mustang trapped between a semi and a truck as they circle the city's beltway and curve around downtown. She looks for a quick lunch turnoff. She's kept the radio off and let Billie control the music selection, her choice an entire playlist of Heart. *Little Queen* once one of their father's favorites. Rhiannon remembers the album blasting through their garage in Urbana when she first learned how to manage a stick shift. She doesn't know if Billie associates the songs with their father but doesn't ask.

I'd say pull off anywhere, Billie says. Before we leave the city limits. Any stop will push us beyond the lunch rush by the time we're back on the road.

Rhiannon is surprised by the number of cars on a Wednesday at noon, Albuquerque larger than she anticipated. Roswell's flattened desert has given rise to peaks off to the east, jagged mountains that in the high sun are hazed with dust. In the creep of traffic, Rhiannon spots a blue sign listing the next exit's restaurant choices. food: Waffle House. Taco Bell. Blake's Lotaburger. Nothing Rhiannon wants but an indication that other restaurants can't be far.

Any requests?

Maybe not diner food this time, Billie says. Something with vegetables.

Rhiannon pulls off the beltway and drives a grid of streets, traffic backed up at every stoplight, until she spots a Vietnamese restaurant at the corner of a strip mall. She pulls in and Billie gets out of the car as soon as Rhiannon cuts the engine.

Jesus, Billie says, stretching her arms above her head. The blunt edges of her bruise still visible but lighter than they were the day before. She leans her back against the car and touches her toes. I wish you'd parked farther away. I could use a walk.

I'm sure we're hiking, Rhiannon says. As soon as we get to Moab.

Fine with me. Billie heads toward the strip mall. I'm getting soft out here.

Rhiannon eyes her sister's muscles as she walks ahead, the sinewed lines of her legs. There is nothing soft at all about her sister, only the brief flood of emotion Billie let her see beneath Carlsbad's stars. When they enter the restaurant, Rhiannon chooses a booth in the corner and Billie orders a tofu-vegetable stir fry and iced Vietnamese coffee, Rhiannon a bowl of pho even though it's nearly a hundred degrees outside.

How far is Moab from here? Rhiannon asks once the server walks away. And what does the route look like?

Six hours. Looks like mostly two-lane highways.

Rhiannon nods. Lower speed limit. But hopefully fewer cars.

The server brings Billie's coffee and Rhiannon's water and Billie takes a sip and extends the glass across the table. You want to try this?

I'm good with water.

Billie takes in half the pint glass through a pink straw, cold coffee mixed with condensed milk. This is amazing, she says. We barely had sugar at all in Decatur.

What about care packages? Mom sent those chewy SweeTARTS you always liked.

Yeah, I liked them in grade school. But they rationed our packages. We weren't exactly living high on the hog out there.

Rhiannon unfurls the silverware from her rolled paper napkin and all at once Beth crowds her brain again. The last time Rhiannon went out for Vietnamese, with Beth just before moving out. The place on the corner near Beth's apartment. A Friday night standard where they went for spring rolls and pho.

I wish you could've met Beth, Rhiannon says before she can think better.

Billie looks up.

I could've brought her to Decatur. I never did.

Ashamed of the family felon?

I'm serious, Billie.

You could've brought her anytime. Why

didn't you?

The server arrives with their food and Rhiannon all at once wants to stop this conversation. Billie unsheathes a pair of wooden chopsticks and picks a piece of tofu from her plate and waits for her sister to respond.

I said I never thought of Beth as permanent, Rhiannon says. If she wasn't, there was never any reason for you to meet her.

Across more than four years of living with her?

It never seemed that long.

Maybe not to you. Billie prods a mushroom with the chopsticks. I can tell you that four years is a long fucking time.

Well, I didn't want to introduce you to someone who wouldn't stay.

You moved out three months ago and you're still talking about her. She seems like someone who's stayed.

Breakups are hard, Rhiannon says. Her words ring dumb in her ears.

Maybe it's not really a breakup.

I moved out, Billie. I've been living with Mom's things for two months.

You moved out. But you still talk. I heard you on the phone in Illinois.

The metal spoon scalds Rhiannon's tongue. She rips up basil and mint from the plate beside her bowl and throws them in with a squirt of lime to diminish the soup's heat. Two months. Two months beyond moving only clothing and linens from Beth's apartment, everything she owned except the racing gear that stayed hidden in her mother's garage for four years. Almost everything in the apartment belonging to Beth, two wide couches and a dining table and a flat-screen television and all of Beth's art supplies. Rhiannon could fit what she owned in the Mustang, everything she'd accumulated across four years that amounted to nothing more than always having been prepared to leave.

It's a breakup, Rhiannon says. I don't see much sense in going back.

Then why is she still listed as the number one contact in your phone?

Rhiannon looks up. How do you know that?

I didn't think it was a secret. You've let me use your phone to map every single place we've traveled.

Rhiannon stirs her soup. I had a dream about her last night.

What kind of dream?

Whatever it was, it felt real. She feels more real to me now out here than she ever has these last few months in Urbana.

Do you think things could be different now? Would things change between you if you were doing something different?

Like not selling textbooks? I don't know.

That's not what I mean.

Rhiannon sets down her spoon. Then what?

I mean doing something different with how you communicate. Rhee, you shut people out. You've always been impossible.

Like you have room to talk.

You said you never even talked to her about your racing. I'm guessing that's just the tip of the iceberg. How well did you ever really let her know you?

Rhiannon keeps her eyes down so she won't have to look at her sister, won't throw back in her face the first impulse she has: that they're both impermeable. That Billie shut herself away for six fucking years, a can of gasoline she must have known would keep her separated from everyone she loved. And Rhiannon, six years of doing nothing but keeping secrets from her sister and from Beth. Two people she should have kept closer than anyone else. Beyond the failure of leaving the racetrack: the failure of failing them both.

Rhiannon stops at a BP station near the

restaurant, the gas gauge already low. So many miles. As much distance as she can put between herself and Champaign. *You shut people out, Rhee.* Six years of nothing but strained monthly visits, six years of secrets and omissions and walls and still Billie knew. That Rhiannon could keep things hidden. Because what did it matter. Even if Beth knew how good she'd been out on the road, even if she knew the oval tracks and the crowds that grew to know her name, the outcome would have been the same. College textbooks, college town. Urbana her life's plan as soon as Billie burned down the library, Rhiannon's concentration broken of everything. Beth's apartment. Beth's lithographs and silkscreens. Beth beside her on the couch. Beth's mouth on her skin. Rhiannon lifts the fuel pump's lever, Billie still inside the car, and feels the weight of the past five years fall heavy all around her. Beyond not letting Beth know the heat of the asphalt or how the interior of a stock car blistered at two hundred miles per hour, she recognizes all at once the two-way street of distance: that she never took the time to know Beth's world either. The specific mission statements of each gallery show. The particular media she used for each one. The books on their coffee table.

What the fuck the Spiral Jetty really even was.

Rhiannon leans against the Mustang's window where Billie sits in the passenger seat. I'm going inside for a minute. Want anything?

I'm good, Billie says. Already peed in the restaurant.

Keep an eye on the fuel gauge. I'll be back in a second.

Billie nods and Rhiannon crosses the parking lot to the BP's food mart, the sun blaring down, the sky a dome of clouds trapping heat. She lingers by the salted snacks, peanuts or Chex mix or potato chips for the long drive ahead. She steals inside the single stall of the women's restroom and pulls out her phone before she can stop herself.

The tone rings. Three times, four. Midday on a Wednesday. Enough time to think better and hang up but Beth answers.

Just breaking for lunch, Beth says. Where are you?

At a gas station in Albuquerque.

New Mexico? What are you doing way down there?

Long story. We're on our way up to the quarry now.

Still scheduled to be back next week?

Still on track. I just wanted to call. We might be out of range the next few days.

Beth is silent and Rhiannon wonders why it matters to tell her they'll be out of range. Neither of them beholden to the other. What she forgets again and again every time she loses her will and rips the Band-Aid open and calls.

How's Billie doing?

She's fine. We're both doing fine.

Rhee, why Albuquerque?

I'll tell you more when we get back, Rhiannon says and regrets it immediately. Making plans as if plans are hers to make. She leans against the bathroom counter, the scent of oversweet air freshener choking the windowless room.

Is it sunny out there? Beth asks.

Sunny and dry. Nothing like Illinois.

Rain here. Every day. As if you couldn't guess.

A thin shell of hurt lines Beth's voice and Rhiannon tries not to read into her words. What kind of rain she means, literal or figurative. She knows Beth dated far more women before her, Rhiannon's dating history a paltry list of relationships she can count on one hand. She knows Beth could move on fast if she wanted. Rhiannon rests against the sink and closes her eyes against the harsh fluorescence of the overhead lights.

I miss you, she whispers.

I'd fly there if I could, Beth says. The first words she's said in months that reveal anything at all of how she's felt since Rhiannon moved out.

Airport still closed?

Our little Champaign airport is. Peoria too. Chicago might be opening back up. Saw it on the news this morning. You doing okay?

Rhiannon wonders what kind of okay Beth means. The news. Her mother. The trip itself. Shuttling toward Utah just to attend another funeral without Beth beside her, not anymore. The wide sweep of an unfamiliar desert. Nothing like the cornfields of Illinois. Nothing like the warm pressure of Beth's hand on her hand.

I'm fine, Rhiannon says.

I wish you'd tell me if you weren't.

I'm fine. Really. How about you? How's everything there?

Not bad. Preparing a few prints.

What kind of prints?

A meditation on rain. So much of it. If I'm focusing on Illinois land, it has to account for this. The prints are for a show in Detroit this September.

You never told me that.

You never asked. And I didn't know if it mattered anymore.

Between the lines of Beth's words: if Rhiannon matters anymore, if their relationship is something to be saved. In the thick bright of the gas-station bathroom, a curtain of loneliness falls dark around her.

I'm proud of you, Rhiannon whispers.

I'm proud of you, too.

For what, Rhiannon wants to say. For crossing four states, for pulling her sister from prison and driving all the way out to Utah just to escape packed boxes and the echo of an empty house.

I'm so sorry I left, Rhiannon says. Her voice breaking across the words.

Beth is silent. The line an ocean.

I'll see you when you get back, she says before she hangs up.

The bricked traffic of Albuquerque thins out, three lanes of highway winnowed down to two as the Mustang veers northwest toward the Four Corners, the cross of the American West. They pass signs for the Santa Ana Pueblo, the Zia Pueblo. The rightful residents of this landscape, Rhiannon can't help but think, and not the names of explorers on every western monument.

She purges the ghost of Beth's voice from the attic of her head. The flatness of her tone. A blank book, unreadable. Billie naps in the passenger seat, mouth open, the map on Rhiannon's phone charting their progress offline as they travel out of cell range. The sky thickens overhead the farther north they travel and Rhiannon turns on the radio, scans the dial until she finds the local news.

She finds Beth was right. Between news of a monsoon squall in Papua New Guinea and a worsening drought across the Sahara are reports of airports opening back up. Los Angeles. London. Tokyo. Chicago, just like Beth said. The cost of shutting down too great a risk for declining airline sales worldwide. The news station reels sound bites from press conferences with the FAA, with the United States president. America's take on ensuring that travel remains safe, that airlines maintain business without fear. Then smaller snippets of interviews with climatologists and radio commentators, whether it's known for certain if the clear-air turbulence that brought down four of the planes where black boxes were recovered can be attributed to climate change and disordered weather patterns. Rhiannon glances at the wide sky beyond the windshield. She can't recall any planes streaking the sky since she and Billie left Illinois. The sheared sun splits thin through a heavy haze as they travel north toward Colorado's border.

Rhiannon shuts off the radio and lets silence fill the car. *I'd fly there if I could.* She wonders if Beth will fly to Detroit for her show. If she'll be forced to drive. What the sky will be like by then, if Beth's voice will still feel as familiar in September as it does now. If there will be any words at all between them when she and Billie return. Rhiannon feels the Mustang's machinery humming beneath her, a familiarity she once knew. Shuttling with her father from one raceway to the next, both of them accustomed to the silence of a race car. No music or idle talk, only the flatlands of the Midwest, only cornfields rippling out into plains and then mesas and then canyons. Billie continues sleeping. The mountains disappear to the east. New Mexico ripples out into badlands, a tent-rocked terrain so much like the Dakotas. Uninhabited wilderness, nothing but junipers and piñon trees and unseen coyotes bedding down in the dust. Rhiannon sees signs for Mesa Verde National Park, 116 miles, just past the New Mexico border into southern Colorado. The clouds keep thickening as they travel north and a heavy wind picks up.

Rhiannon drives through the afternoon's quiet haze. The Mustang approaches and crosses the Colorado border along Highway 491. The wind throws itself against the side of the car, battering the highway from both sides, and Billie remains asleep beside her until the Rockies appear in the northern distance, a far-off range coming into view through a thick line of smog.

Are we already in Colorado? Billie says, sitting up.

Passed the border an hour ago.

Why is it so cloudy?

Probably the same haze we saw from Cañon City. All of Colorado has been hit with drought and dust this summer.

The gas lever leans low and Rhiannon watches for signs of approaching towns.

We should fill up again soon, she says. Colorado mountain towns are small but at least they have tourists. The road ahead into Utah may be pretty desolate. You hungry?

Not for a full-on meal. But I could use something small.

Rhiannon drives until she spots an old Sinclair station, just past a sign that lists the next town as Cortez. The last outpost before the highway curves through the jagged wall of the Rockies ahead, as if Highway 491 will run straight into the mountains and end. Rhiannon pulls into the station and Billie hops out, the wind lurching the passenger door open behind her.

Jesus, Billie says. I'll watch the car if you want to take a break first.

I'll be quick. And I'll grab food. What do you want?

Maybe something with caffeine. I don't want to sleep the whole way.

Rhiannon lets the pump run while she steals into the food mart. She pulls two Cokes from the wall of refrigerators and two Airhead sticks from the candy bins, Billie's childhood favorite. She sets her items on the checkout counter, the only person in line, the station deserted.

Are you Rhiannon Hurst?

Rhiannon looks up at the boy behind the counter. He's young, maybe early twenties, round plugs stretched into his ears. For a moment she wonders if she's given him her driver's license before realizing her wallet is still tucked in her back pocket.

What?

Rhiannon Hurst. The driver.

Rhiannon stares at him, the surprise of standing here in rural Colorado, this boy knowing her name.

I watched you race on ESPN when I was a kid, he says. Words that shock her, the first man she can recall ever mentioning her career. Her fans so often only girls at raceways, and so few of them, the small daughters of NASCAR diehards. Words that sober her for how young the boy must have been then, how long ago it was.

Thanks, she whispers.

I can't believe it's you.

Rhiannon pushes the Cokes and candy across the counter. Just these, please.

Are you heading north?

On our way to Moab.

You might want to rethink that. Highway's closed ahead.

Rhiannon glances out the mart's windows. Where?

Just past Cortez. About five miles down. Wildfire in the San Juan Forest just to the east. The smoke is so bad that visibility isn't much through the mountains. They're closing the road for the night until the winds die down.

The brief vanity of being recognized vanishes. The haze. The clouded sky. Not drought alone but wildfire, what Rhiannon feels stupid to not have considered. The news filled with monsoons, tornadoes.

Is there another route? she asks.

You probably won't get much farther west than here tonight, not anywhere in Colorado. The wind's blown the smoke west and south, even all the way to New Mexico. Should diminish by tomorrow. You been listening to the news?

Just earlier in the afternoon. There wasn't any mention of a forest fire.

Probably because the news is mostly covering those planes. The fire's picked up these last few hours. You'd have seen the roadblock ahead anyway, a few miles down.

Rhiannon looks out the window at the Mustang where Billie sits inside the car, the fuel gauge stopped. Are there any places to camp around here?

Air quality's not great tonight for that. Plenty of motels in Cortez up ahead.

The boy hands her the receipt and slides her sodas and candy across the counter. Any chance I could get your autograph?

Rhiannon hasn't been asked in over six years. When she finally nods, the boy pulls a pad and pen from behind the counter and Rhiannon quickly scrawls her name.

He glances out the window. You stay safe.

Rhiannon nods and leaves the store, the door's bell echoing behind her.

In the car, Billie is reclined in the passenger seat biting her nails. Rhiannon throws her an Airhead. Keeps the boy's recognition to herself.

Road's closed ahead, she says. We'll need to stop in the next town for the night.

Billie sits up. Why?

Wildfire nearby. The guy inside said it would be clear tomorrow.

Billie turns on the radio and scans the dial until she finds the local news broadcast and Rhiannon hears a staid male voice reporting from a Durango public radio affiliate. The sweep of the fire, the entirety of the San Juan National Forest and parts of the Rockies. A fire that must have picked up once she finally turned off the radio past New Mexico's border. A fire she'd have heard about if she kept the radio on, a new route she might have been able to find two hours ago. The voice on the radio keeps reporting. Droves of firefighters and helicopters. The result of statewide drought and high winds, a summer without water finally erupting across Colorado. Wildfires common every summer. This one beyond control, enough to shut down an entire highway. The reporter stops short of climate speculation, the news immediate and breaking, the broadcast delivering only mandates for motorists to pull off the road.

So that's the reason for this haze, Billie says.

The good news is that we're not camping. The air's too thick. At least you'll get your hotel for the night.

Billie picks up Rhiannon's phone and scans the digital map. This pushes us back a day, she says. If we still stop in Moab.

How far is Moab from the quarry? That has to be our next stop beyond southern Utah. Surely Mom wouldn't send us outside the state again.

Three hours, Billie says. Stopping tonight will put us in Moab by tomorrow afternoon. Then the quarry on Friday, assuming we also spend the night in Moab.

That's fine. We're still on schedule. A week out, a week back.

Rhiannon drives until they pass a green highway sign for Cortez. Then a flashing-orange road block, the two-lane highway bereft of vehicles traveling from the opposite direction. A cluster of cars backs up once they reach Cortez, the first line of traffic Rhiannon has seen since they left the outskirts of Albuquerque. She pulls off and follows the trail of brake lights, leaving behind the barricade of the closed highway.

Keep your eyes peeled for a vacancy, she says.

Billie nods and watches out the passenger-side window, her Airhead unwrapped in her hands. Rhiannon drives in the line of cars past several gas stations and a row of tourist trading posts. *There,* she hears Billie say. A red-blinking vacancy sign to the right of the windshield. The Mountain Ridge Inn. The Rockies rising beyond Cortez's main thoroughfare, still visible through the growing haze.

BEARD, JOHANNA. PHD. "WILDFIRE." WEATHER AND CLIMATE. ED. DEAN TRUJILLO. CAMBRIDGE: HARVARD UNIVERSITY PRESS, 2010. 22–25. PRINT.

CALL NUMBER: G552 .7 TRU

WILDFIRE

See Also: brush fire, desert fire, peat fire, vegetation fire

Wildfires are classified as uncontrolled fires, often in dry areas with combustible vegetation. They are distinguished from other fires by their scope, their unpredictability, and their ability to quickly change direction and jump highways.

Recent shifts in climate suggest the potential for wildfire growth. In order for a wildfire to occur, what is known as the fire triangle must be present: an ignition source, combustible vegetation, and oxygen. Typically, high moisture and humidity prevent combustion. But prolonged drought can cause more highly combustible environments, leaving habitats vulnerable to fire's quick spread.

37.3498° N, 108.5767° W: Cortez, CO

The scent of stale cigarettes. The thin polyester lining of the bedspread. The room's dim lighting. Billie sits on the edge of the mattress and takes in every sensation of a roadside lodge, this one far more ramshackle than the Salina Inn in Kansas. Cortez off the beaten path, a smaller highway, fewer tourists and passing traffic. The Mountain Ridge Inn unaccustomed to the influx of people waiting at the reception desk, forced into a night's stop. The wall unit kicking sour air across the room in refrigerated intervals. The water heater pulsing through the wall, Rhiannon showering in the rusted bathroom, the door closed and trapping steam. The analog television transmitting a fuzzed signal, the local news and nothing else. Road closures. The heaviest areas of smoke. Local reports giving way to news of airports opening back up. Tokyo's Narita. San Francisco's SFO. Marrakesh's

Menara. Billie sits on the scratched bedspread and takes in the news and everything about the motel room. Everything in it meaning movement. Its empty dresser and threadbare sheets intended for traveling, nothing else. Nothing like the cinderblock walls and flame-resistant bedding of a prison cell.

The water shuts off and Rhiannon steps out of the bathroom, a towel wrapped around her hair. Well, we have a free night we didn't bank on, she says. Anything you want to do?

What, here? In this grand metropolis?

Rhiannon nods toward the television. Any news on the fire?

Just the same as what the front desk said. That firefighters are on it. That it should die down by morning, at least enough to open the highways.

Rhiannon sits on the bed's edge. Jesus, this is fucked.

This isn't necessarily connected to the planes or all the rain, Billie says though she doesn't know if she believes the words leaving her mouth. She glances at the television's footage of helicopters circling a stretch of burning forest. Reminiscent of FAA investigators circling burning wreckage, what she saw on the prison's single television.

There's a bar next door, Rhiannon says.

Billie laughs. Right. The motel bar is always the hot spot in any town.

Fine. What would you rather do?

Billie leans against the room's window, the air unit blowing cold against her arms. The sun drops across a row of chain restaurants and gas stations along Cortez's main drag, the Rockies barely visible in the distance beyond a thick layer of smoke.

We have a free night, Billie says. Just like you said. Let's do something fun.

Like what?

Get dressed. We'll drive that sad strip out there until we find something.

Once Rhiannon pulls on jeans, Billie follows her out of the motel and into the car. Neither of them dressed for a night out, hiking gear and T-shirts the only clothing they've packed. But Rhiannon is finally game for something beyond sticking to a schedule and Billie finds herself grateful. Every night since she left Decatur filled with purpose, from packing to decoding the journal to figuring out each next step. Rhiannon drives the town's small strip until Billie points to a bowling alley set back from the road. Lakeside Lanes. A windowless warehouse, the parking lot half empty.

Inside the alley, Rhiannon pays for two games and bowling shoes while Billie heads to the bar in socks, a twenty-dollar bill in her hand. The building lit in neon beer signs, only two men sitting at the bar. A few lanes populated with families, what looks to Billie like summer vacations on hold for the night. Van Halen warbling from the overhead speakers above the hollow sound of bowling balls knocking pins. Billie sits at the bar beside the two men who watch their bottles and not her.

What are you having? the bartender asks.

A pitcher. PBR is fine.

You sure you don't want the Oskar Blues instead?

Billie looks up. Short dark hair. Darker eyes. About her age. A towel slung over his shoulder, a caricature of what a bartender should be.

I would if it were cheaper.

The bartender leans against the counter. What if it were?

The music blares. Billie eyes him. His face far warmer than Jesse's face in Colorado Springs, her bruise fading but still there, a thin blue lake on her arm.

I'm listening, she says carefully.

One pitcher of Oskar Blues, he says. Eight ninety-nine.

The two men don't meet her eyes as the bartender fills a pitcher with thick-foamed beer and Billie wonders if they're regulars who have seen this before, this bartender in the habit of cutting women deals for a price.

Thanks, Billie says when he slides the pitcher and a pint glass across the bar.

You drinking all that alone?

Billie nods toward the bowling lanes, where she can see Rhiannon at a console setting up their game. My sister's over there. We're just passing through.

He hands her a second glass. The wildfire, right?

We're on our way to Utah, Billie says, wishing as soon as she says it that she could take it back. The road ahead is closed. We're hoping it opens back up tomorrow.

Billie moves toward the lanes with the pitcher and two glasses. Colorado Springs. Six years gone and she's learned nothing of men. The bartender far more mellow than the man in Colorado Springs but she should keep her mouth shut, even if his eyes and the chiseled line of his jaw make her want to let down her guard. Billie places the pitcher on the small table beside Rhiannon, their names already blinking in the console, two marbled balls waiting in the return.

I got a ten and a twelve, Rhiannon says.

You can take your pick or use both.

Billie fills the pint glasses and hands one to Rhiannon. Slips into her alley-issued shoes, the same size as Rhiannon. Same shoe size, same shirt size, same jeans size though across so many years of prison-issued meals and push-ups on the concrete floor beside her bunk Billie wonders if she's lost too much weight for their clothing to still match.

Rhiannon takes a sip. This isn't PBR. Drinks must be cheap in Cortez.

The bartender gave us a deal, Billie says and Rhiannon looks up.

What kind of deal?

Give me a break, Rhee. He was just being nice.

I'm sure he was. Rhiannon says nothing else and Billie knows she's thinking of the thick bruise on Billie's arm.

We're fine. You're here with me. And he was only being friendly.

Just be careful. Rhiannon glances at Billie. You're up first.

Billie slides her fingers into the grip of the twelve ball and walks to the edge of the lane, fluorescent light slicking off the surface all the way down. Mineral oil, she remembers from a donated book on bowling in the prison library, meant to catch the grooves of a urethane ball. Three pounds of feathered muscle leaving her arm: the same release of a bowling bowl poised on the edge of a lane. Judas Priest blares down from the speakers. The sound of knocked pins echoes across the alley. Billie swings back her arm and lets the ball go and it glides down the lane and rolls through the center, a perfect split. Billie waits for the tongue of the ball return to cough up the twelve. The weight of a bowling ball far heavier than Alabama's feathers but her brain reeling, her hands releasing something after six years of holding nothing.

If you rotate the ball toward one side, Rhiannon tells her, they'll knock across the lane and hit the other pins.

I know, Billie says. You're not the only one who understands math.

Billie grabs the twelve again and draws back her hand and lets the ball fly down the lane and hears the sound of pins cracking against one another. Opens her eyes. Pins rolling around on the slick surface. One still standing.

Not bad, Rhiannon says behind her.

Billie smiles. Let's see what you can do.

Rhiannon grabs the twelve from the return and poises herself at the lane's edge. Sizes it up in seconds, lets the ball release. Billie watches as her ball clears every single pin.

Nice strike, Billie shouts. Been bowling with Beth these last few years?

I haven't bowled since high school.

Billie remembers Arrowhead Lanes, the Urbana alley she frequented in junior high where every kid went to smoke cigarettes and drink shared beers that college students bought for them, the staff watching only for teens bringing disposable flip-flops to steal pairs of bowling shoes. Rhiannon never there. Rhiannon already racing in high school. She grabs the pitcher and pours herself more beer and Billie sees the clench of her fingers around the handle. Muscle memory. What it took to maneuver machinery across a raceway instead of wasting away her teenage years sneaking Coors Lights and shitty cigarettes.

Billie bowls three more frames until she has a score of 29, Rhiannon a turkey of three strikes. The pitcher drained. Billie's stomach begins to growl. I'm going to grab another pitcher, she tells Rhiannon. Maybe some food. You want anything?

Fries, Rhiannon says. And for you to keep a safe distance from that bartender.

The bar is empty when Billie enters, the two men gone, the bartender leaning against the counter watching a small television in the corner. Rockies baseball, Billie can see. A game still scheduled in Denver despite a cloud of smoke sweeping the entire state.

Baseball fan? Billie says.

The bartender looks at her. Just need a break from the news.

The wildfire or the planes?

Both. They've been cutting between them all night. More Oskar Blues?

Only if I can pay full price.

Crowds are light tonight. Not many people coming out with the air like this. My manager won't care. It's not a problem.

It's a problem for me.

The bartender looks up and Billie stops herself from meeting his eyes.

I didn't mean to creep you out, he says. It's just not often a girl like you comes in.

A girl like me? Please. I saw those guys who were in here. They seemed pretty used to seeing deals offered to any woman who walks in.

I'm not like that, the bartender says. His face so honest Billie believes him.

Full price, she says. And an order of cheese fries too.

She slides another twenty across the counter and the bartender takes it.

My name's Nick, he says. Yours?

Billie, she says before she can take it back.

The truth this time. He fills another pitcher with Oskar Blues and charges her full price, eleven ninety-nine.

I'm off at ten, Billie. He places the change in her hand. If you're free.

She says nothing and walks back toward Rhiannon with the pitcher but leaves a five-dollar bill on the bar, a 40 percent tip.

After they finish two games and two plates of fries, the music dies down inside the alley along with the sound of bowling balls against pins, the other families gone. Rhiannon crushes both games. The two of them the last customers, Billie's head swimming with four pints of beer but not enough to keep from stopping by the bar and whispering to Nick the name of their motel and that she'll be at its bar.

Inside the car, the air outside tasting faintly of ash in the dark, Rhiannon turns on the engine and pulls away from the parking lot.

You told him where we're staying, she says. You told him, didn't you?

Come on, Rhee. It's been so long. Let me have some fun.

Fun like Colorado Springs? Fun like finding you screaming on the street?

He's not like that.

How do you know?

I don't know. He just seems different.

From who?

Billie watches the stoplights flash along the street as they make their way toward the motel. From Tim, she says. From that asshole in Colorado Springs. From Dad.

Rhiannon glances over. Now you're wrangling Dad in?

He never visited, did he?

You've known Dad for thirty-two years. Dad never hit you. Dad never left a huge bruise on your arm. And that guy, you've known him for what, three hours? Is he coming up to our room?

Jesus Christ. I'll just have a drink with him at the bar. Nothing else.

Well, I'm fucking tired. I'm going to bed as soon as we get back.

There are two keys. You can watch *The Tonight Show* while I have one more drink. Or else the news, to make sure we get the hell out of here in the morning.

Rhiannon looks at her. Just make sure there are people around. I'll be right upstairs if you need me.

Okay, Mom, Billie says and a silence blankets the car. She wishes she could grab the words back from the air. Their mother. Billie realizes they've barely talked about her. How she at last slipped away inside a hospital room. How beyond the library fire Billie's never felt the urge again to destroy herself except on the day of their mother's funeral. Only an hour up the road from Decatur to Champaign. What might as well have been the distance between continents. Billie standing in the prison yard, her hands gripping the chain-link fence so hard that the metal cut her skin. She glances at Rhiannon in the dark of the car. Wants to ask how she's doing. But there is no space, no time, the motel approaching beyond the Mustang's windshield. Rhiannon hands Billie a key and leaves for their room. Billie hesitates a moment before stepping into the motel bar, a sadder affair than the one at the bowling alley. The bartender behind the counter an older man with a beer belly, his head a half-bald sheen. Billie orders a well whiskey and waits at a high-top table, the local news blaring on a small television behind the bar that smoke is still heavy above town.

And then Nick is there in the bar's doorframe. Billie nods toward the counter and he buys himself a whiskey. He approaches and sits beside her at the table, his playfulness gone, replaced by something like vulnerability. He grins and looks down into his glass.

I've never done this before, he says.

What? Met up with someone after work?

Not someone I didn't know.

You know I like beer and cheese fries.

You know what I mean.

The bar's television is the only sound billowing through the bar. Billie touches Nick's arm. She can't stop herself from the luxury of human contact, can't conjure the caution she should've had in Colorado Springs though somehow here with no music and no ambiance at all there's still something safe, a man's warmth moving through the thin barrier of his skin. And something else moving through hers: want. What she hasn't felt in years.

So what's bringing you two out to Utah?

Funeral, Billie says.

Nick doesn't flinch. Sorry to hear that.

Our mother passed away three months ago. It's more of a symbolic ceremony.

Where are you driving from?

Illinois.

Long drive. I'm sorry about your mother.

The television's crackle fills Billie's head and she imagines Rhiannon curled up on the hard mattress of the motel bed, late-night television flickering through the room. Billie doesn't want to talk about her mother.

For one night, she doesn't want to think about coordinates or dig sites or the objects their mother left behind. She wants to drain her whiskey. She wants to focus on the sensation of someone else's skin. She wants to remember what it was to feel wanted.

We can get out of here, she says. Words she's never said in her life but Nick doesn't shy away. She tightens her grip on his arm and leads him from the bar to the dimly lit hallway. Rhiannon upstairs in their room. Rhiannon watching local news and talk-show television and only steps away if Billie is wrong, if Nick isn't what she thinks. She leads him out the back door to the motel's pool where the lights have been killed, opening hours long over. The hum of chlorine filters. The soft lapping of water in the night's wind, the smell of smoke. Billie hoists herself over the pool's locked gate and Nick follows, the fence's wrought iron clanging against his sneakers in the dark.

Billie pulls off her shirt and lets the dappled light of the streetlamps beyond the patio reach her arms. Muscle. The ridges of scars. Nick watches her and Billie wants to pull her shirt back on but doesn't move. He could turn away. Go home. Call her ugly. Call her worse. He reaches down instead and unfastens the zipper of his jeans.

Billie moves toward the rippling water of the darkened pool. If she could, she would extend this moment forever, stay here inside this night, never go to Utah. She slides out of her own jeans, her sneakers. Steps into the water, sun-warmed by so many June days beneath a drought-choked sky. She sinks beneath the surface and lets the water coat the grooves of her arms, the second pool she's entered in three days as if she were a child again, as if she could slip into the water and be reborn.

Through the dim noiselessness of the pool Billie feels hands on the bare skin of her stomach. What she imagines it was like to float in her mother's womb. Pressure wells in her chest, her mother nowhere on this earth. In her place, hands encircling Billie's waist. She breaches the pool's surface and the shocking cool of the night air meets her face and Nick's arms circle closer around her, his chin resting against her shoulder's scars. *Don't,* she wants to whisper. But he pulls her closer, runs his hands across the scars' lunar fields. His mouth finds her left arm, a puckered line, and trails toward her neck. Scars he'd be senseless not to feel. Scars he shelters against his tongue.

Billie closes her eyes and his hands skirt up her stomach to her chest. The weight of his palms feather-light. Unbearable. A weight she's kept at bay to keep herself safe. She lets her hands find his hands and wants to peel them from her skin as much as she wants to grab them and press them harder to her chest.

She turns around and faces him. Streetlight floods her arms and her mouth is against his mouth. His tongue as weightless as his hands. Her legs wrap around his body and her hands press against his face. Beads of water. The hum of the filter. The soft splashing of waves in the dark. She pushes against him, his back to the wall of the pool and then he is inside her and her body is a torrent of want.

Desire: a spark she hasn't let herself feel. Not books. Not the memory of violence. Something else worth burning. Nick pulls his mouth away from her neck and meets her eyes, his face so close to her face. A face she knows she won't see again. A face she brands into her brain.

When Billie at last slips back into the motel room, the lights are out but the television glows blue against the walls. Her hair still wet, her T-shirt and jeans pulled on, underwear balled in her front left pocket. Rhiannon sits up in bed, the local news murmuring on low.

Did he show up?

We had one drink downstairs. We went out to the pool.

Did you have sex with him?

Billie sits on the edge of the bed. Jesus, Rhee.

Whatever happened, I hope it was better than Colorado.

Billie pulls off her sneakers and pushes herself back against the headboard beside her sister. Yes, I had sex with him, she says. Yes, it was better than Colorado.

Billie expects Rhiannon to drill her about safety. About condoms and strange men. But Rhiannon only smiles and Billie can't remember the last time they talked about sex, if it was in college or in high school.

Well, I'm glad for you.

Glad? Billie shoves a pillow at her.

It's been a long time. And probably a while since it was any good for you.

Billie leans into the pillows and tries to remember what it was like with Tim, if there was ever a time when it was good. You can't even imagine, she says.

It's not like Beth and I were having tons of sex at the end.

You haven't slept with anyone since?

No. I haven't had any interest. Or met

anyone interesting.

Do you want to?

The television's blue light pulses against Rhiannon's face.

I don't know, she finally says. I thought I could move on. I thought we were done, that she wasn't right for me. But now I'm not sure about anything.

What does that mean?

Her sister hesitates. I called Beth earlier today. From the gas station in Albuquerque where we stopped. I called her from the bathroom.

And?

She said she misses me. I told her I was sorry I left and she said nothing. She said she had to go and she hung up.

Billie watches a weatherman on-screen sweep his hands across a map of southern Colorado. Maybe you just caught her off guard.

Rhiannon sighs. The bottom line is that no, I don't think about having sex with anyone else. I'm glad at least one of us had a good night.

I guess I did. It was nice. It was distracting.

Rhiannon nods toward the television. They're calling for clearer skies tomorrow.

Billie glances at the grid of the five-day

forecast. Tomorrow is the day they'll finally cross into Utah. A day that all at once feels like a heavy weight.

I had fun bowling, Rhiannon says softly.

You better have. You swept both fucking games.

Rhiannon looks at her. Someone recognized me today. A clerk at the gas station. He knew my name. That I was a driver. He said he watched my races on ESPN.

Does that surprise you? You were good. Of course people know who you were.

It's the first time a boy has ever asked me for an autograph. And no one's remembered who I am for nearly six years.

Billie leans back against the headboard. How did it feel?

I don't know. Weird. I don't know what else to say about it.

How about proud?

Take a shower, Rhiannon says. Your hair's getting the pillows wet.

Billie pulls off her shirt, her jeans. What time are we leaving tomorrow?

As soon as we get up, so long as the highway is open.

Billie grabs her sleep T-shirt and boxers and slips into the bathroom. She turns on the shower and steps in and lets steam fill the small room. She wants to stay weightless. Unanchored. She runs her hand across her left arm, the bruise nearly gone, the dappled scars still holding the ghost of Nick's mouth.

HERNANDEZ, MARK. "DARK-SKY PRESERVE." INITIATIVES IN ENVIRONMENTAL PROTECTION. ED. OLIVIA YU. TALLAHASSEE: FLORIDA STATE UNIVERSITY PRESS, 2016. 99–102. PRINT.

CALL NUMBER: GE196 .P24 2016

DARK-SKY PRESERVE

Given increased light pollution in urban areas, dark-sky preserves are designated areas, often around observatories or natural landmarks, where artificial light is restricted. They allow visitors the opportunity to view skies as our ancestors once viewed them, without inhibition of modern light and city noise.

The first permanent dark-sky preserve was established in 1999 in Ontario at the Torrance Barrens. Natural Bridges National Monument in southern Utah was recognized in 2007 as the world's first International Dark Sky Park. In 2015, nearby Canyonlands National Park was designated as a dark-sky preserve.

37.3498° N, 108.5767° W: Cortez, CO

Rhiannon sits at a small table in the window of the Mountain Ridge Inn's lobby below an overhead television. She cradles a Styrofoam cup of weak tea, her continental breakfast of white toast and one ripe banana already gone. A dreamless sleep. No Beth. Beyond the window, the sun strains through a thick sheen of haze. Wildfires still burn in the San Juan National Forest, firefighters and military Black Hawks still battling the blaze. But winds have shifted east and north, the western edge of the state clear. *Highway opened back up at five a.m.,* the hotel clerk told Rhiannon when she came downstairs, Billie still sleeping. *You should be good to go.*

From the lobby's window, Rhiannon watches a family of four pack up their SUV. North Carolina plates. She wonders if they planned to drive or if the news has made them take the road. Two small children. A girl Rhiannon assumes is nearing kindergarten and a toddler with bright brown curls. Rhiannon wonders if this is what she and Billie looked like on their few family road trips when they were small, their parents packing up the car and checking the route and placing Billie in a car seat and Rhiannon beside her watching out the window. Rhiannon remembers one trip to the Ozarks in southern Missouri and another to Disney World, her father driving them all night while their mother slept in the passenger seat. Their mother. Billie asked if she wanted to talk. Rhiannon wonders if it's Billie who wanted to talk. The national newscast billows across the breakfast bar from the overhead television and Rhiannon looks up at the headline scrolling beneath two anchormen. GLOBAL WARMING TO BLAME FOR PLANE DISASTERS? Men in suits. Their banter betraying their answer to the question: global warming just a theory. Erratic weather traceable back to the nineteenth century. Pilot error. A series of unfortunate coincidences. Rhiannon glances at two women drinking coffee and one man eating a stack of waffles by himself, none of them paying attention at all to the newscast.

Rhiannon pulls her cell phone from her pocket. 8:24 a.m. An hour ahead in the

Midwest.

Rhee? Her father picks up on the second ring. Where you girls at?

Southern Colorado.

You haven't gotten very far since you last called.

We took a detour down to New Mexico.

Your mother sending you on a wild-goose chase?

You could say that. How's everything in Chicago?

Not much changed since Monday. Still rain. You girls where that wildfire is?

Did it make national news?

A brief spot. Nothing big, but I noticed it since I knew where you two were.

We're in a town called Cortez. Stopped last night because the highway was closed. It reopened this morning. We're heading into Utah as soon as Billie wakes up.

How's she doing?

Fine, Rhiannon says. Good, actually. We're stopping in Moab today and plan to head to the quarry tomorrow.

I'll be out that way this week myself. Not quite to Utah. But I'll be in Dacono.

A track Rhiannon knows well. Dacono north of Denver. The Colorado National Speedway. She should have guessed her father would be on the road, June right in the middle of racing season. Her father on the raceway sometimes nine months out of the year, what Rhiannon assumed in part led to their parents' divorce.

Is Dacono your only race route this week?

With a brief stop in Kansas City on the way, he says. Bryson's racing well.

Rhiannon's followed Bryson Townes's races, knows he placed in Talladega's top ten just before Memorial Day weekend. She knows the name of every contender her father could have mentioned.

Bryson looks like he'll be good, she says.

He's great. But no one's as good as you.

The way he lets her know he still misses her on the team never sounds like a guilt trip. But this morning the road stretches open and a boy has recognized her in a gas station and Rhiannon feels a heat in her throat creeping down the line of her chest.

Will you be heading through St. Louis on the way?

Does that matter?

We found something. Rhiannon hesitates. We found Mom's wedding ring in St. Louis. The one you were looking for.

What, she buried it in one of those boxes? In Forest Park? I thought you couldn't find what you were looking for there.

We couldn't. Billie called Tim's brother

and had him find it.

Tim's brother? What in hell are you talking about, Rhee?

Billie called him. He lives there. He went and found it for us.

Shit, you could've just called me. I'll be driving straight through there.

Her father falls silent and Rhiannon wonders if she should've told him about the ring at all.

We're picking it up in St. Louis on the way home next week, she says. I'll be sure to keep it safe for you.

No need. Your mother clearly wanted you girls to have it instead of me.

Maybe. It's hard to tell out here what she wanted.

You two stay safe, is all he says.

We will. You be safe too on the road.

Love you girls.

Before Rhiannon can wish Billie on the line to hear their father say it, he hangs up and the sound of the breakfast room's television fills the space his voice has left.

By the time Billie comes down to the lobby, her hair a tangled mess and her hips hugging the same dirt-scuffed jeans she's worn every day of their trip, the breakfast bar's open hours are nearly over.

Someone slept late, Rhiannon says.

Billie combs a hand through her hair. Is there at least coffee left?

Coffee and probably waffle batter, if you want to make one.

As if we had waffles in Decatur. Of course I'm making one.

Billie gets up and Rhiannon watches her fill a small Dixie cup with cream-colored batter and pour it into the iron griddle. She grabs a plastic packet of syrup and a Styrofoam cup of black coffee and makes her way back to the table, no one else left in the lobby except one man watching fly fishing on the overhead television, the morning news replaced by midweek programming.

How far to Moab from here? Billie asks.

I just checked the route this morning. No more than two hours.

Billie glances out the window. Are the roads clear?

Sky's better this morning. Still not great, but the winds have shifted off east. The front desk told me Highway 491 reopened this morning.

Billie sips her coffee and grimaces. God, Rhee, this shit is terrible.

How's the waffle?

It's a waffle. Full of sugar and carbs. Delicious.

Two hours means we'll have most of the afternoon in Moab.

Which means we should plan for a hike, given Mom's drawing.

A line of dinosaur tracks, Rhiannon says. Some kind of trail, just like Kansas.

Just like Cañon City. Probably just like the quarry, too. I bet Mom will make us hike five miles just to get to the spot she picked out for her funeral.

Rhiannon falls silent as Billie carves through her waffle with a plastic fork.

I talked to Dad this morning, she finally says.

Billie looks up. And what did he have to say?

He'll be out racing this way next week. Outside of Denver. He offered to stop through St. Louis to pick up Mom's ring.

You told him it's there?

I also told him Tim's brother would take care of it.

Billie takes another drink of coffee and stares out the window.

You're going to have to talk to him at some point, Rhiannon says. She expects Billie to say something smart, but Billie just looks at her.

I know, she says.

Look at you. Have sex once and you're

cool as a cucumber.

Billie smiles. Fuck you.

Dad asked about you, Rhiannon says and stops short of telling Billie what else their father said. *Love you girls.*

Billie slices the waffle, her plastic knife carving a line into the Styrofoam plate. Sorry I slept so late. We can get on the road as soon as I finish this heaping plate of sugar.

You'll hike it off, Rhiannon says and looks at the mountains beyond the window. Fly fishing blares on the television above them. No more news. No more wildfires, no more planes, what Rhiannon hopes stays at bay but knows won't hold. What the newscasters said: an unfortunate fluke, nothing more than a series of terrible coincidences. All of it bullshit. Rhiannon drops the last of her tea in the breakfast room's trash.

The two-lane highway winds from Cortez toward Utah with far less fanfare than the major interstates Rhiannon and her father crossed between racing competitions. She remembers state signs stretched like rainbows across six lanes. Welcome centers. Rest stops and bathrooms and free maps. But here on Highway 491 is a beacon no bigger than a speed-limit sign: WELCOME TO

UTAH, LIFE ELEVATED. The panoramic wall of the Rockies receding in the rearview mirror. Billie's chosen the soundtrack, a loop of the Grateful Dead's greatest hits, what Rhiannon knows is one of their father's favorite bands though she says nothing as they drive into southern Utah's crimson lunarscape. Red-rocked mesas, layers of age Rhiannon can see from the car. The planet's history marked in the gradations of sediment, strata their mother could read in the scalloped sweep of desert land. Rhiannon glances up at the bright blue, no more smoke and no spitting gray rain, this sky unblocked by trees and the small-town steeples of Illinois churches. More cars clog the road as they turn north toward Moab on Highway 191, packed full of families traveling to Arches and Canyonlands. No matter the wildfires and the drought.

We may need to camp tonight, Rhiannon says. I've heard Moab is small. If there are only a few motels, they may all be booked.

That's fine. I got my hotel fix last night.

Rhiannon nods. I bet you did.

Billie smacks her arm as they pass signs for Hole in the Rock, what Rhiannon can see beyond the passenger-side window is a tourist trap. An old house built into the base of a plateau littered with cars and outdoor tables full of cheap souvenirs. Dinosaur bones. Ants trapped in amber. Broken-open geodes. Similar to the roadside attractions Billie sought on their trip to the Ozarks when they were kids. The world's largest nylon ball of twine near Branson. The world's largest fork in Springfield. The two-lane highway's traffic backs up as they roll into Moab, three blocks of storefronts and old bars and a line of campgrounds and cheap motels. A Rodeway Inn boasts a chain-linked outdoor pool painted blue and ringed in plastic palm trees. Signs announce Jeep tours and canyoneering and ziplines. Rhiannon sees the kaleidoscopes of blinking neon as they travel down the main strip: NO VACANCY. Every single motel room booked. She pulls into the dirt lot of a campground just past the northern edge of town.

Moab Valley Campground, Billie says. Our home for the next twenty-four hours.

Assuming they have space.

Looks like they have cabins.

Look at the traffic, Billie. This is high season. Camping will be cheaper.

I told you I was fine with camping.

Rhiannon leaves Billie in the car and enters the campground's front office, nightly rates posted on the wall behind check-in. Tent, no hookups: thirty dollars. Deluxe cabins, the only availability beyond pitching their tent: one hundred and thirty. Rhiannon sets a twenty and a ten on the counter and pulls the Mustang through the circuit of mud-caked roads until they find their campsite, an unassuming patch of dirt.

We should set up the tent now, Rhiannon says. Who knows how long this hike will take, and it'll be even busier here later on when we get back.

Fine with me. Just so long as we eat something soon. I'm starving.

Late night of activity? Extra exercise?

Billie rolls her eyes. Give it a fucking rest.

She helps Rhiannon pitch the tent, the stakes sliding easily into the desert's silt, a consistency that to Rhiannon feels almost like the sand of a beach. Utah once an inland sea: Rhiannon knows this not from her mother's research but from racing. The Salt Flats to the north. An evaporated sea west of Salt Lake City, almost to the border of Nevada. A swath of public land Rhiannon has only seen in pictures, gleaming-white fields of salt. One of the country's premier land-speed record sites where racers have gone to set down history, the landscape's utter flatness a track for breaking records. Rhiannon knows the highest land-speed record for a woman: 512 miles per hour. For a woman. Words Rhiannon heard far more than she ever wanted. She imagines her hands guiding a stock car across the rough grain of the Salt Flats as she drives the tent's metal stake into the dust-strewn ground.

What do you want for lunch? she shouts to Billie, obscured by the tent's domed nylon, staking the other side.

Whatever, Billie shouts back, her voice muffled. Something quick on the way out to the coordinates.

Do you know where the site is? I just mapped us to Moab, nothing else.

Do you have service here? If not, we'll need to find a lunch place with internet.

Rhiannon pulls her phone from her back pocket, two cell bars poking up in the screen's left corner. I have service, she says. Want to map us to the coordinate? I can finish staking the tent.

Billie emerges from the other side and Rhiannon hands her the cell phone and Billie pulls the journal from her bag.

North, she says. Just ten miles up.

The signs back there said Arches and Canyonlands are up that way too. You think the site is in one of the parks? I can bring cash for the entrance fee.

Billie shakes her head. This coordinate is

mapping somewhere right between the two parks.

Rhiannon stands and rubs the dirt from her jeans and feels the sun baking the back of her neck. Let's get going. Whatever you want to eat on the way is fine with me.

Billie smiles. Fast food?

Fine. There probably isn't much else. Let's go before it gets too hot to hike.

After a brief stop at Taco Bell, Rhiannon motors the Mustang north up Highway 191 where they pass the Colorado River and the Arches entrance, a line of cars jammed behind the entry booth and snaking up a plateau of switchbacks into the park.

Jesus Christ, Billie says. High season is right.

I'm glad this coordinate isn't in either of the parks. If it was, we might've needed to go early tomorrow morning instead to beat the crowds.

The highway flattens out beyond the Arches entrance into sweeping desert plains on the right of the car, tall buttes on the left that block the sun. The map on Rhiannon's cell phone leads them straight up the highway toward the coordinate, a location she isn't sure they'll be able to clearly spot from the road. The Mustang passes a dinosaur museum on the left, a T. rex standing in the building's yard. So similar to the same statue in Forest Park, holding the secret of their mother's wedding ring. Rhiannon steadies the Mustang along Highway 191 until Billie tells her to slow down, their turn approaching. A near-invisible turnoff if not for a small sign: MILL CANYON DINOSAUR TRAIL.

I fucking knew it was a hike, Billie says.

Like that was hard to guess. We're in the nation's capital of hiking.

I'm not complaining. But you'd think Mom would surprise us.

Surprise? God, Billie. We've been to Carlsbad, to Cañon City. She planned a whole fucking scavenger hunt. This trip has been nothing but a surprise. You want to know what surprises me? Someone who just got out of prison being so unimpressed.

The Mustang approaches a gravel parking lot, no other vehicles anywhere, every other tourist exploring the national parks. The sun high in the sky, midafternoon. Beyond the windshield, two staked signs. MILL CANYON. DINO TRAIL. Both with arrows pointing right.

Is this the coordinate? Rhiannon asks.

Billie nods to where the signs point. A little farther up that way. Between the two,

I'm guessing the Dino Trail is what we want.

Billie grabs her daypack and a water bottle refilled at the campground to fend off the sky's hanging heat. Rhiannon sees no visitor center, the trail far smaller than the neighboring national parks. Utah more desolate, the land cracked open. Rhiannon approaches the trailhead and pulls a pamphlet from a single staked box.

Are there tracks in that brochure that we're supposed to find? Billie shouts, already ahead of her on the trail. That's what the drawing was. Little dinosaur feet.

Rhiannon glances at the pamphlet. Mill Canyon a former floodplain of silt and sandstone. Jurassic fossils embedded in every rock, a riverbed burying the bones of drowned animals. Allosaurus. Camptosaurus, a sketch on the leaflet that to Rhiannon looks like a brontosaurus. And right beside it: a stegosaurus. Telltale spiked plates.

Stegosaurus tracks, Rhiannon shouts back. That has to be it.

She follows Billie along the trail and regrets forgetting to pack a hat. A lone St. Louis Cardinals cap buried somewhere in her childhood bedroom, central Illinois loyalties on the dividing line between Chicago and St. Louis. Billie trudges ahead of her, sweat Rhiannon can see beading at the base of her shaved hairline. The sun sinks west toward the adjacent plateau and Rhiannon wishes they'd set out just an hour or two later, late enough for the rock to cast a shadow across the trail. Billie is silent, the only sound the scuff of their hiking shoes against dirt. Rhiannon wonders how much more silent it was when their mother was here: if she came in high season or if she came in the desolation of January, the only sound high winds sweeping west and her work boots crunching against snow and ice.

Billie stops short ahead of her. Well, that wasn't long.

What?

I thought we'd be out here for hours. Billie points to a small sign. DINOSAUR BONES TRAIL. The trail's length indicated in small lettering: only one hundred fifty feet long.

I thought we'd be hiking more, Billie says. But the coordinate points just ahead.

It's hot as fuck. I'm fine with a quick hike.

This isn't a hike. This is shorter than a walk to the mailbox.

Rhiannon follows Billie along the short trail, the creek bed nothing but silt beneath her feet. Grains of sand bounce into her hiking shoes, small pebbles she can feel beneath her socks. Billie crosses the creek bed and Rhiannon trails behind her until Billie stops at a short wall of bulbous sandstone marked by another sign.

What does it say?

That this is an outdoor museum of paleontology, Billie says. That there are no guardrails or fences. That it's up to us to keep the fossils intact.

Where are they?

Billie plants her hands on her hips and scans the panorama of rock.

There, she says. Clear as fucking day.

Billie points at a trail of small tracks indented in the sediment that at first glance look nothing like footprints. Thin grooves carved out by water. Recesses in the rock. When Rhiannon moves closer she sees the shape of digits and talons.

Which ones belong to the stegosaurus?

Billie points to a set of prints high on the rock. Those.

How do you know?

I've spent enough time looking at them in books.

Billie leans closer to the rock, her hand nearly touching the trail of tracks. This is the coordinate, she says. Do you see anything? Do you see a box?

Rhiannon scans the ground surrounding the short plateau of sandstone, the afternoon's sharp light crowding her vision. She kicks her hiking shoes through the silt and wisped prairie grass. She hears the tin-pulse of liquid and metal, Billie pulling her water bottle from the daypack to drink. Billie hands Rhiannon the aluminum canister and she takes a sip, her head tilted back. When her eyes realign on the landscape she spots a small gray plastic box bedded down against the wall of sandstone in the shade.

There, she says. She points and Billie crouches down and grabs it.

That wasn't hard to find, Billie says. It's the only thing out here that isn't the color of sand.

Rhiannon finds a short ledge and pulls the sweat-damp pamphlet from her back pocket. These tracks the result of so many dinosaurs drowned at once in a former riverbed, similar to what she knows of the Cleveland-Lloyd Quarry: a predator trap of bones fossilized in sandstone, a floodplain that became mud that caught so many dinosaurs at once. And here, according to the pamphlet, the exact same kind of rock. Billie fiddles with the box's plastic latch and Rhiannon wonders if their mother began studying Jurassic traps here, if this was the first of what became her career's focus at Cleveland-Lloyd. If she took trips downstate across the course of her career to compare bones, to see what differed between northern stegosaurus bones and southern digs or if this was simply a stopover at some point in her life. Billie opens the small box and drags out a card-size drawing of the dinosaur tracks, the same as the sketch in the journal. She hands it to Rhiannon and keeps searching and Rhiannon wants to know what's inside as much as she doesn't. The feather in Carlsbad. A blade that pierced Billie, this box containing the possibility of another knife. But when Billie pulls out what's hidden in the box and holds it out in her hand, Rhiannon sees nothing in the object. No meaning at all.

A laser pointer, Billie says. A fucking laser pointer?

Rhiannon takes the black wand from Billie's palm. How do you even know what this is? she says. It looks like a pen to me.

Don't you remember these from college? Professors used these all the time to highlight information on PowerPoint slides.

I wasn't in as many college classes as you were.

Well, I remember these from biology lectures. But I have no clue why she'd leave one of these out here for us.

Rhiannon holds the pointer up to the late-afternoon sunlight. Maybe something about the University of Illinois? Maybe something about her teaching?

What about her teaching? Did you ever sit in on one of her classes?

Just one. Sometime in high school, though I don't remember what it was about.

I sat in on one during college. Billie wipes away a line of sweat gathering on her forehead. It was an introductory paleontology class. She had a slideshow showing the students what tools to use for digs. I don't remember a laser pointer at all.

Rhiannon bounces the pointer in her palms, testing its mass. Lightweight. She has no idea what this object is supposed to mean.

Well, we have a short walk back and all afternoon to figure this out, she says.

What, you don't want to sit here and enjoy this heat wave?

Not a chance. Come on.

Rhiannon moves away from the wall of sandstone, the tracks and layers of rock receding behind her. Her mouth dry. Her skin flushed with the heat of the high desert. Her impatience beginning to flare, with their mother and with this newest detour and with the inscrutability of these hidden items. She starts to walk back to the car, Billie still behind her with the plastic box in her hands.

When the sun begins to set after they've returned to the campground and taken quick showers, Rhiannon drives them down the main strip into the heart of Moab's three-block downtown.

Hungry yet? Rhiannon asks.

Billie sits in the passenger seat with a knee pulled to her chest. Still burning off two Taco Bell burritos, she says. How about a drink first?

The few drinks Rhiannon's had with Billie since they left Illinois have already surpassed anything she and Beth ever drank across the last months of their relationship. Beth's kitchen: no liquor cabinet. No rack of wine bottles. No six-packs stored in the fridge. Beth drank only bourbon on the rocks, and even then, only intermittently at best. Rhiannon realizes across four years of living together and across so many years on the road with her father and their team that sometimes resulted in nights out after races but more often in only early nights at cheap motels to get back on the highway before sunrise, she hasn't been to many bars at all as an adult, a woman nearing the age of thirty-six.

She parallel-parks along the sidewalk in

front of a pizzeria and a closed bookshop. The sun sets directly down the street, sharding light against the row of storefront windows. Billie walks beside her along the sidewalk above a narrow creek, a shock of water that surprises Rhiannon in the middle of the desert. The creek winds past Woody's Tavern, a stand-alone bar with darkened windows, a neon sign blinking OPEN above the entrance. Rhiannon glances at Billie. Her sister nods and pulls the door open.

Four pool tables line the floor just past the entrance door. An empty stage, unlit. A single couple sits in the back near the restrooms. Billie takes a seat at the bar beside two plastic baskets of popcorn, what Rhiannon assumes are free to all paying customers. She sits beside Billie, thick stools sidled up to a wooden bar scratched heavily with names. The graffiti of past patrons. Initials knifed inside hearts. Billie checks the taps behind the bar and orders a Uinta, what the bartender says is local out of Salt Lake City. Rhiannon asks for the same, the bartender a middle-aged man with dark hair and a goatee. He walks away and fills two mugs and Rhiannon glances at the two televisions behind the bar. No news. Only an NBA playoff game, the orange beacon of a basketball shuttling across a court. The bartender returns with their beers and Billie slides hers against Rhiannon's in cheers.

This tastes weird, Billie says. Three-two beer.

Lower alcohol content.

Billie grabs a handful of popcorn. Three-two? What the fuck does that mean?

Three-point-two percent alcohol. We're in Utah. Every beer on tap in the entire state is watered down. You can thank the state's liquor laws.

How do you know about that?

Traveling on circuits. We stopped once or twice in Salt Lake City. It's the same with buying alcohol in supermarkets. Only liquor stores carry regular alcohol.

I guess I wouldn't have noticed when I was here with Mom in high school.

Rhiannon glances at a cluster of John Wayne photographs on the wall behind the bar. A small shrine to the American West of romanticized cinema. The last great American cowboy. Reminders everywhere that this land was colonized and made for men. Rhiannon looks away.

Do you remember anything else about your trip out here with Mom? Anything that would explain what that laser pointer means?

I just remember that we camped. The

quarry's in the middle of nowhere. We didn't do anything but look at fossils. I don't remember anything about the trip that had anything to do with a laser pointer.

Rhiannon glances at Billie. You want to talk at all about last night?

What about last night?

Nick. The guy from the bar. Did you get his number?

Not a chance. I'll never see him again.

But you had fun. Why wouldn't you call him again?

Because where could it go? He lives in Cortez. Cortez fucking Colorado, Rhee. We have nothing in common. It was just one night and nothing else.

How can you do that?

Rhiannon says it before she hears the judgment in her voice.

Billie looks at her. What, you've never had a one-night stand?

And you have, before last night? When would you have had time? You were with Tim and then you went to prison.

Right. Like I was a total celibate before I met him.

When? High school?

High school and college, too. God, it's not a big deal. You act like marriage is a requirement for having sex. Nick was just one night. It was nice to be with someone who wasn't interested in being a total asshole for once. Stop acting like such a prude.

I'm not.

You've never had sex with someone you didn't love?

The corner jukebox blares to life across the tavern. The woman from the couple down the bar has slid quarters into the machine. Johnny Cash. A song Rhiannon doesn't know but recognizes the voice. The woman returns to the bar and the man places a hand on her back and Rhiannon wonders if she could have been so open with Beth out here, the small towns of the West meant for men but also for men and women, a landscape she crossed on the racing circuit knowing it would never embrace her. A woman who would only ever love other women, no kind of western romance at all.

No, she says. I haven't had sex with someone I didn't love.

It doesn't matter either way. And you can now. Why don't you?

Because I don't want to. And because we're out here. We're in Utah. My guess is that people like me aren't too welcome here.

But they are in Champaign? Central Illinois is the liberal capital of the world?

It's better than this. Look, I feel like shit,

Billie. I feel like shit because I can't tell if I've wasted five years of my life with Beth or if I just miss her. If I miss her terribly.

Why don't you just call her?

I did. I told her I was sorry I left and she hung up on me.

It was just one phone call.

One phone call. One phone call and years of treating her like trash.

Is that what you think?

Rhiannon sips her beer. I know I've been a terrible partner.

I know terrible partners. I don't think you've been that.

There are lots of ways to be a terrible partner.

And there are lots of ways to make amends.

The song ends and another begins, a Hall & Oates ballad Rhiannon remembers from their father's record player when they were small. She glances up at the shrine of John Wayne photos. The West never a place for a driver like Bryson Townes, either. She imagines Bryson on the road this week shuttling across Kansas to Colorado, charting a career despite a wall of history against him. Not the same as her own path, but similar. And her mother, making a name for herself among so many male paleontologists, chiseling her small stake into the West.

I miss Mom, Rhiannon says.

She hears herself say it before she can take it back.

I know, Billie says.

I miss her. I don't know if there's anything else to say.

Of course there's more to say.

Rhiannon looks at her sister. Then why don't you say something? I'm out of words. And it seems like you want to talk about this more than me.

Fine. Billie smiles. Why a laser pointer? What the fuck do you think it means?

I have no idea what it means. To be honest, we don't even know what a hawk feather means, or a stegosaurus tail bone.

The sound of the jukebox fills the bar, the television on mute. Rhiannon should be thinking of their mother and the laser pointer and figuring out what it means but she imagines Beth in Illinois instead, Beth stooped above her printmaking press. Beth carving a fine knife into Midwestern oak that would become the grooves of a woodcut. The book Beth kept on their coffee table: the Spiral Jetty somewhere in this state. An earthwork of basalt circling out into the Great Salt Lake, what inspired Beth, how art could work in tandem with the land. How Beth meant creation to be a gentle thing, her hands shaping the sleek divots of a woodcut. Rhiannon wonders if Beth has ever stood on the shore of the Great Salt Lake, the sculpture spiraling out before her, what Rhiannon never even thought to ask. Beth traveling to Detroit for a show in September. Beth making a name for herself too. Beth on the other end of the line from a bathroom in the middle of New Mexico before hearing Rhiannon's words and hanging up.

After they drink three more beers, the alcohol content low enough to keep them inside the tavern for two more hours, and after they've eaten so much popcorn that neither she nor Billie want dinner anywhere else, Rhiannon pays the bartender and they step outside the bar onto Moab's quiet downtown streets.

I thought it would be busier out here, Billie says.

High season. Early risers for hiking. Early to bed.

Billie slides her arm into the crook of Rhiannon's elbow and the feel of Billie's skin against hers is a thin blanket against the desert night. They walk linked down the sidewalk, Billie's forearm moving softly against her side. They pass over the creek, the water slipping through the dark and catching sleek slivers of moonlight. Rhiannon feels the weight of Billie's head lean against her shoulder.

Goddamn, Billie says. Look at that fucking sky.

Rhiannon looks up and the sky is a dark canvas splattered with the glow of stars. Winking beacons. Summer constellations she's sure Billie knows by heart.

What are we looking at?

Billie points overhead. Boötes. Crystal clear right up there. And that's the hunter following the two bears across the sky. Ursa Major and Ursa Minor.

Where are those?

Billie slides her hand across the sky. There. Ursa Minor contains the Little Dipper and Polaris. The North Star. But you already knew that.

You'd be surprised at how little I know about stars.

When they reach the car, Rhiannon sits for a minute drinking the last of Billie's water bottle stashed in the backseat. Buzzed from so many beers, but still sober enough to drive. She pulls the Mustang onto Moab's main strip and guides the car down the street and into the Moab Valley Campground.

Billie strips her clothes inside the tent and pulls on a sweatshirt and leggings while Rhiannon sits in the dirt outside, the wash of sky above them like nothing she's ever seen. Even before Illinois grew into a haze of low clouds, Rhiannon knows this about herself: she never thought to look up. Never thought to take interest in the fine detail of something like a Spiral Jetty. Her world always asphalt. Her eyes always to the ground.

Billie emerges from the tent and sits beside Rhiannon in the dirt. Look at that, she says. She points up at a gauzed streak across the sky, what looks like a faint river of light pulsing through the stars. The Milky Way, Billie whispers.

We can see it from here?

That's what it is.

Rhiannon watches its shimmering band, what looks like a thick cloud braided across the dome of the night sky. She watches the ether of light and something clicks, even through the lingering buzz of alcohol.

Where's the pointer?

Billie pulls it from the front pouch of her sweatshirt.

Rhiannon takes the laser their mother left them and trains it up into the darkness.

Despite how far the constellations are and how distant the long stretch of the Milky Way, the first time Rhiannon's ever seen it, the green glow of the pointer's vector extends from her hands and reaches the sky.

An astronomy laser, Rhiannon says. Not a pointer for classroom lectures at all.

Billie takes the pointer from Rhiannon's hands. You're fucking kidding me.

That's exactly what this is.

Billie guides the pointer's light along Milky Way's speckled band.

Over two hundred billion stars up there, she says. Can you believe it?

Rhiannon can't. Billions of stars, as unimaginable as her mother no longer here. A realization that punches her in the gut as Billie steers the pointer across the sky. Rhiannon falls silent in the dark. She lets Billie talk, lets her identify every star she sees. Nebula. Star nurseries. White dwarfs and red giants. Rhiannon has no idea what Billie means but knows their mother saw a sky just like this one when she was here. That she left them this pointer for a reason. That she too surely watched splashes of constellations over southern Utah. Billie palettes the pointer across the stars and Rhiannon leans back and looks up.

HSU, DAVID. PHD. "THE CLEVELAND-LLOYD QUARRY." MAJOR SITES OF NORTH AMERICAN PALEONTOLOGICAL DISCOVERY. ED. ALICE SHAPIRO. MISSOULA: UNIVERSITY OF MONTANA PRESS, 1996. 25–29. PRINT.

CALL NUMBER: 561 PR425.16

THE CLEVELAND-LLOYD QUARRY

The Cleveland-Lloyd Dinosaur Quarry, located in the central Utah valley, contains the largest and densest concentration of Jurassic-era fossils in the world. Over fifteen thousand bones have been excavated and studied in this area, a mere fraction of what paleontologists suggest are actually buried in the region.

An alleged predator trap, the Cleveland-Lloyd Quarry is speculated to contain so many fossils due to some kind of natural hazard that held herbivorous dinosaurs captive, attracting carnivores who also then succumbed. The cause of this natural hazard is still being debated among paleontologists. Due to the high concentration of allosaurus fossils in the area, a predator trap is speculated due to the pack-hunting behavior of these particular carnivores.

Beyond a preponderance of allosaurus fossils, other bones excavated in the area indicate the presence of marshosaurus, stokesosaurus, camarasaurus, and stegosaurus.

38.5725° N, 109.5497° W: Moab, UT

When Billie wakes inside the tent, dry-mouthed with the lingering cotton of too many beers, Rhiannon is still bundled inside her sleeping bag. Billie unzips the tent's front flap, the sun still hidden behind the tall buttes that line the Moab Valley Campground. She steps outside, the dirt cool beneath her bare feet, and watches the predawn sky mineral with streaks of coral light.

The scent of campfire. Diminished smoke. Small groups of other patrons clustered around morning fire pits heating coffee. Billie shoves her hands inside the pouch of her sweatshirt and her fingers catch on the laser pointer, still stashed in the folds of her clothing. She can't believe it took them all night to figure out what it was for. She remembers standing in the backyard of their childhood home, her mother's telescope a fixture among the lawn chairs and garden beds and clotheslines. What Billie hasn't thought of in years, and what she almost forgot: while Rhiannon spent hours in the garage with her father and engines and a set of tools, Billie followed her mother outside to identify Illinois birds and moths in the yard, and at night, the Midwest's constellations.

Every Dewey decimal number Billie has memorized first paved by the woodpeckers and sphinx moths and the bright point of Jupiter over the backyard's dusk every June, everything her mother pointed out and Billie absorbed. Her mother and her father. Separate lives in the end and yet the one thing they did together was make sure their daughters were curious about the world, what she hates to admit about her father. Amid the coming sunrise, Billie realizes she's the one who's wanted to talk about their mother without knowing at all what to say. The hawk feather, stashed now at the bottom of her daypack. What her mother left her inside the plastic box in Carlsbad and what Billie assumed was a jab. But here, the laser pointer's weight in her hands and the morning light creeping up the sky, it doesn't feel like a dig so much as a reminder. Of what they shared. That Billie learned the woods and its trees and the shapes of its leaves from her father but she learned the sky from her mother, its stars and birds, what became Alabama's weight alighting on her arm.

Hey, Rhiannon says behind her, emerging from the tent.

Wild night at Moab's hottest tavern, Billie says. Hungover?

Hardly. I told you three-two beer was a good thing.

Sleep okay? I'm starving.

That's what happens when you eat popcorn for dinner.

You want to grab breakfast somewhere?

Rhiannon nods. Places along the main strip should be open once we pack up the tent and get going.

Billie helps Rhiannon pull out the stakes and stuff the sleeping bags into the Mustang's trunk. By the time Rhiannon pulls out of the campground, the sun has risen in sharp bands that break from the surrounding buttes.

That place is open, Rhiannon says as they approach a single-room diner. She parks behind the restaurant and tells Billie to bring her daypack, what Billie knows means bringing the journal inside to map their next coordinate. Beyond the restaurant's front door, six of seven tables are already taken.

Rhiannon was right: early hikers. She motions for Billie to take the last table in the corner while she orders at the counter. Scrambled eggs and sausage. Sunny-side up and polenta for Billie. From the table Billie watches her sister take charge, Rhiannon a commanding presence accustomed to overseeing a pit crew, what Billie notices she mostly hides now in the regularity of daily life.

Rhiannon approaches the table with two mugs of coffee. Billie pulls the journal from her daypack, the hawk feather somewhere inside the bag with the laser pointer and the locket and the stegosaurus tail bone and Billie wonders how many more items they'll collect before they return home. She places the journal on the table between their two coffee mugs and flips it open to the page past the coordinates for the Mill Canyon Trail and its accompanying drawing of dinosaur tracks. On the next page: what looks like another dinosaur. Tall. Standing upright.

Another T. rex, Rhiannon says. We already found one in St. Louis.

Billie rotates the journal away from her sister and recognizes the shape, its large jaws and forelimbs.

It's an allosaurus, Billie says. Similar to a T. rex.

How would you know?

Billie points. The forelimbs are larger. The T. rex had notoriously small arms.

You can tell that from a drawing?

Billie flips back to the first drawing and coordinate, her mother's scrawl of the T. rex statue in Forest Park. Can't you tell?

Not really.

It doesn't matter. At least we know this is the Cleveland-Lloyd Quarry's coordinate. That we're headed directly there.

A server arrives with their breakfast and drops the plate of polenta in front of Billie, the eggs and sausage in front of Rhiannon. Hot sauce? he asks. Ketchup?

Rhiannon asks for both and looks at Billie when the server walks away. How do you know for sure this is pointing us to the quarry?

Allosaurs are Jurassic dinosaurs, Billie says as the server returns with two glass bottles. Just like the stegosaurs Mom studied. The T. rex came almost a million years later, in the Cretaceous period.

That's a nice PBS lesson. Rhiannon shakes Tabasco over her eggs. But it doesn't tell me anything about the quarry and how you know it's what Mom means here.

A predator trap, Billie says. Mom told us a million times. I don't remember much from my trip out there in high school, but I remember that most of the bones in the quarry are allosaurus fossils. They were predators. Mom studied stegosaurus fossils there because the allosaurs preyed on them. That's why there were so many of them there.

Fine. Rhiannon spears her sausage. But can we still check the GPS?

Billie pulls out the handheld device and taps in the coordinate.

North, she says. Two and a half hours. Exactly where the quarry should be.

Rhiannon smiles. We're finally almost there.

Billie slices her polenta. She doesn't know if this is the last coordinate. She refuses to flip the page though she suspects this entry is the last one. She imagines her mother sketching a final page in her hospital room while Rhiannon slept in the armchair beside her, Billie miles away. She imagines her mother drawing the bones of a dinosaur she spent years with in the quarry, bones she knew she'd never touch again.

The stretch of road between Moab and the Cleveland-Lloyd Dinosaur Quarry is their shortest distance but also the most desolate. The landscape flattens past Green River from southern Utah's buttes to the central plains of the state, a wide visibility that reveals distant mountains ridged off Highway 191. Billie counts twenty-six mile markers, one to the next to keep her brain occupied, not a single gas station or rest stop along the road between them. Her fingers clutch the Mustang's armrest only when Rhiannon veers into the oncoming traffic lane to pass slow cars. From the map on Rhiannon's phone, Billie can see the indirectness of their route: they nearly pass the quarry on the way up, plateaus to the west impassable and preventing their quick cutover. They'll bend northwest and route back down, directly south again to Cleveland-Lloyd.

Rhiannon keeps the radio on until the airwaves flatline, enough time to hear the news. Nearly every airport in the world reopening, airlines avoiding the risk of losing revenue. Two commentators debate the pull of capitalism against the ethics of safety and Billie notes no mention of the Colorado wildfire, so many other droughts and tornadoes drawing larger headlines. A mile-wide twister in central Mississippi the night before. A prolonged summer drought in

Southern California, testing the watershed. Greater devastation than wildfire. Greater property damage and economic loss.

Did the library fire ever make the news? Billie asks.

Rhiannon glances at her from the driver's seat. What?

The fire at Illinois College. My fire. Did it make the local news?

Maybe in Jacksonville. Not in Champaign. We were two hours away.

Nothing happens in Jacksonville. I'm sure it was all over the local news for one day and that's it.

Rhiannon lowers the radio's volume. Does that matter to you?

I guess not.

Would you have wanted it to be on the news?

No. Billie hears the frustration in her voice. I'm just surprised by all this news coverage of weather and air disasters. The news only cares if something huge happens. If people lose their homes. If people die. I'm not saying that any suffering is worth more or less attention. But isn't it strange that domestic violence never makes the news? Or nature? Nobody cares about a woman with a broken face. Or about a wildfire that's killed millions of trees.

Rhiannon looks at her. The news doesn't cover everything that's important.

I don't need you to say that. This is important. Billie gestures toward the radio. So many planes. The weather of a whole planet. I'd say that's important.

So is never knowing that someone's sister lived in an abusive situation for years.

How could I have told you?

Maybe you couldn't have. But I wish you would have.

Billie watches another mile marker pass by.

Are you feeling better? Rhiannon asks.

I'm fine. My arm is fine.

That's not what I mean. The hawk feather Mom left you. You were so upset.

Billie watches out the window. I can't believe we're almost there. I thought I was ready for this, but I don't know if I am.

Rhiannon nods. I know.

You went to her funeral, Rhee. This isn't even a real one. What could you possibly not be ready for?

This is different. You and I are together this time. And Billie, you've been here before. I've never seen this place. I've never seen this quarry that meant so much to her.

It's not like I remember it that well.

But you've been here. The Small Quarry

was hard enough. To see how much she was revered. I don't know what it will be like to see the place where she actually spent most of her career.

Billie watches a line of mountains in the distance and says nothing and Rhiannon turns on a new playlist. Soul and blues. Sam Cooke and Etta James. Billie remembers flying into Salt Lake City and driving south through Provo and Spanish Fork along the length of a range she later learned was the Wasatch Mountains, the same mountains that approach out the window. She wonders if their father ever made the trip here. If she's the only person in their family who's seen the quarry. She watches the desert sweep past the passenger window and wonders if her mother felt more free out here, a landscape that let a woman roam beyond the closed-in tree lines of Illinois.

Rhiannon suggests stopping in Price, the last outpost with food and gas, before they make the final push to Cleveland-Lloyd. Two new grocery bags of precooked hot dogs and canned baked beans and apples and coffee sit in the backseat as Rhiannon steers the car up the gravel road leading to the quarry's entrance, everything meant for making meals on the intermittent fire pits dotting the Bureau of Land Management.

Do we even have outdoor cookware? Billie asks.

Rhiannon nods, the car bouncing over the rocked road. I packed a small set. I hope camping is okay for one more night. There's nothing else out here.

Is there a specified campground?

Not like in Moab. Out here, it's just BLM land. More rustic, no showers. They'll surely have a place where we can camp for the night.

Rhiannon winds the Mustang up the unpaved road until she reaches the Cleveland-Lloyd Quarry's visitor center, a small building Billie remembers from her trip in high school. How it surprised her that there was any building at all out here, the middle of nowhere. A wide vista of Utah's central valley visible from this elevated height. The GPS beeps, their destination reached. Billie doesn't know who's expecting them and what she and Rhiannon should anticipate in return. Who from the Bureau of Land Management has organized this second funeral. Who knew their mother well enough to extend this favor to her two daughters.

Did Mom tell you anything about how this funeral would go? Billie asks.

Not really. She just said that when we arrived, they'd tell us what to do. Did she tell you anything?

No. She just gave me the journal.

That's more than she gave me.

What about ashes? Mom was buried. What ashes are there to scatter way the fuck out here?

Goddammit, Billie. Rhiannon's voice is sharp. I don't know.

Billie feels all at once stupid that she asked. Rhiannon parks the car beside the visitor center and Billie follows her through the front doors. Inside, a mounted allosaurus stands directly in front of them: what their mother drew on the journal's page. Panels line the walls explaining bone excavation and the makeup of the quarry's terrain. In display cases around the center's perimeter sit the enormous skulls of dinosaurs. Camarasaurus. Diplodocus. All herbivores orbiting the allosaurus, the quarry's primary carnivore. Rhiannon drifts off to find a bathroom and Billie meanders around the railing that guards the allosaurus skeleton and makes her way to a display case that holds a single, large skull.

The stegosaurus. Billie wonders if her mother's hands touched the smooth fossil behind the glass. Twenty-three feet long,

Billie silently reads. One of only four stegosaur remnants found in the Cleveland-Lloyd Quarry compared to forty-six allosaurs, the predator trap she remembers her mother explaining. She leans closer to the placard on the wall behind the stegosaurus's display case: *a paleontological puzzle,* the sign says, no intact skeletons found anywhere on the grounds of the quarry. The mounted allosaurus a reconstructed anatomy, a sham of display that was never found this way. Billie wonders why their mother spent more time here instead of the Small Quarry where she found an entire stegosaurus skeleton, and here, only a scattered four. Billie knows there's a plastic box somewhere and that if it were anywhere, it would be here by the stegosaurus skull. She looks to the ground. So much easier than Carlsbad. Just behind the display case lies a small gray box.

Rhiannon approaches from the bathroom. Is this the stegosaurus?

One of four. Billie crouches and picks up the box.

You found it already?

This is the only stegosaurus display in the entire visitor center. She hands the box to Rhiannon. You want to open it?

Rhiannon takes the box and pops open the plastic latch. Inside: a slip of paper, the same as every other box. A hand-drawn coordinate and the allosaurus drawing. Rhiannon pushes the paper aside and pulls out a single jigsaw puzzle piece. She holds it up to the light of the visitor center's windows and Billie sees the vague outline of an illustrated dinosaur on the piece.

What the hell is this?

I bet I can guess, Billie says.

She takes the jigsaw piece from Rhiannon's hands and holds it to the informational sign behind the stegosaurus's display case. Paleontological puzzle. A literal match in their hands for the figurative mystery of how the bones were found.

Rhiannon looks at Billie. Is this a joke?

No. I think she means this place is literally a puzzle. Probably one she spent her entire career trying to solve.

What's so puzzling about this place?

Billie points to the sign. This says seventy-five percent of the dinosaurs found here were carnivores. And that none of them were found intact.

You mean complete?

Not like the full skeleton Mom found at the Small Quarry.

Then why did she spend so much time here? If there aren't even that many stegosauruses here? And if she found a full skeleton in Colorado?

Why would I know?

She gave the journal to you.

And that means I know something?

You've been here before. Do you remember Mom saying anything about what was so mysterious about this place?

It was so long ago, Rhee. I told you, I don't remember much.

Rhiannon sighs. Come on. Let's just ask someone where we need to go.

Billie slides the puzzle piece into her daypack and follows Rhiannon to the front desk where a park ranger sits behind the counter, a young man in a beige sunhat who looks like he's still in high school.

Excuse me. Rhiannon approaches the desk. We were hoping you could help us.

The young man looks up, the brim of his hat low above his eyes.

This will sound weird, Rhiannon says, but we're here as the daughters of Margaret Hurst. She was a researcher here. We're here for her funeral.

Billie expects the young man to look confused, to pick up his desk phone and seek the advice of a supervisor, but his face changes.

You're Dr. Hurst's daughters? I'm very sorry for your loss. It was truly an honor to work with her.

Billie looks at him and feels a quick sting in her rib cage, what Rhiannon must have felt talking to the woman at the Small Quarry: that everyone in every park across America knew their mother, and that they all know more about her work and what these coordinates are telling them than either she or Rhiannon do.

Did you work with her? Rhiannon asks.

Just for the past few years. I'm still relatively new to the field.

Billie can't stop herself from thinking it: relatively new. Embryonic. This boy seemingly at least fifteen years younger than her, surely still in college on some kind of prolonged summer internship. But he tells Rhiannon he's a doctoral candidate in paleontology at the University of Utah and Billie's stomach plunges as he stands and extends his hand to Rhiannon. A PhD student, the same as Tim was. And so fucking young. Billie lets him shake her hand and feels ancient standing at the desk.

My name's Marcus, he says. Yours?

Rhiannon says her name and Billie mumbles hers.

Follow me, Marcus says and motions for them to follow him away from the counter. Billie wonders if it's okay for him to leave the front desk even though there's no one here, thirty miles from the nearest two-lane highway.

Marcus leads them through a door behind the desk and into a small back office with two computer-laden cubicles. One is empty, Marcus's workstation. Only two employees. At the other desk sits an African American woman holding a turkey sandwich in her hands, the first woman of color they've met on their trip, Billie realizes. So few groups of women at each campsite, especially women of color. The American myth of the West a whitewashed landscape. Marcus coughs and the woman sets down the sandwich, a private moment Billie knows she and Rhiannon have disturbed.

Dr. Wallace, Marcus says. There are two people here excited to meet you.

Billie wonders if she's ever heard this name before, if there's any way she met her while visiting in high school. Billie's brain draws nothing as the woman turns and instead of extending a handshake she drops her sandwich and envelops her and Rhiannon in the soft blanket of a hug.

Inside a trailer down a dirt path behind the visitor center, where Dr. Wallace tells Billie and Rhiannon she lives during summers of research, she makes them tea on a red-coiled hot plate despite the temperature outside nearing ninety degrees. The trailer is tiny, large enough for single living and nothing more. A one-person kitchenette, an airplane-size bathroom. A fold-down table where Billie and Rhiannon sit, a low door in the back that Billie assumes leads to a twin bed. The scent of cinnamon and cardamom drifts up from the mug in Billie's hands. Dr. Wallace sits on a bench across from them, no tea, her elbows resting on her knees.

How much did your mother tell you about our work out here?

Not much, Rhiannon says. Only that she spent most of her career here.

I came here when I was in high school, Billie says. Were you here? I'm sorry, I was so young that I don't remember.

I was here. Though honestly, I was probably out in the field so much that it's no wonder you don't recall.

Dr. Wallace, did our mother call you? Rhiannon asks. In the last few months? Did she set up this entire second funeral through you?

Call me Angela.

Angela, Rhiannon says. It seems like you knew our mother well.

Angela nods. Your mother called me three months before she died. I'm still sorry I couldn't make it to Illinois for the funeral. She mentioned her plan for you girls. She set up this entire thing through me and the BLM.

You girls. Billie wants to be irritated but there is nothing. This woman's voice a balm where the Small Quarry's ranger wasn't. Nothing like being called a lady.

Did you hide all the boxes, too? Billie asks.

Angela looks at her. Boxes?

The geocache boxes, Rhiannon says. Our mom created a kind of scavenger hunt for us, plot points of coordinates all across the West. We've been everywhere this week. She hid boxes for us at each location. Are you the one who helped her drop them off?

Angela sits back. I don't know anything about that. I only helped her with coordinating this funeral here for you two. What kind of plot points are we talking about?

Places that meant something to her throughout her career, Rhiannon says. And throughout her life in general, I guess.

Angela smiles. So you went to Cañon City?

Rhiannon nods. The Small Quarry.

That place made her famous before she

began focusing her studies here.

Billie wants to ask Angela about the jigsaw piece. The quarry's paleontological puzzle. Why her mother spent so much time here when there were no intact skeletons anywhere in these excavations. But Rhiannon steps in before she can speak.

Do you study stegosauruses too?

Angela shakes her head. Your mother was my very best colleague in the field. But we didn't study the same thing. I don't study any particular dinosaur or bone at all. I'm out here piecing together the strangeness of this place.

Billie watches her. What do you mean?

Your mother never told you about it? The predator trap?

She told us, Rhiannon says. But not that there was any mystery to it.

Angela stands and disappears through the small doorframe to the bedroom at the back of the trailer and Billie wonders if Rhiannon has offended her. Billie sips from her mug, the tea still far too hot. Rhiannon stays silent. Angela returns with a posterboard split into a pentagon of five equal drawings, what looks like educational material for patrons to the quarry's visitor center. She sits back down across from Billie and Rhiannon and holds the posterboard upright on her knee.

This place is the largest concentration of Jurassic bones in the entire world, Angela says. And even still, no one knows why so many are here in the same place.

Why are there no fully intact skeletons here? Billie says. We didn't even know until this week that our mother discovered one in Cañon City. She never told us. We only knew that she came to this quarry. Why did she come here if there were no intact skeletons, and only a few stegosauruses?

Angela grins. So you've done your research on this place.

What's the mystery? Billie pulls the jigsaw piece from her daypack. Our mother left this for us here. This was hidden inside the visitor center for us. What's so mysterious about this place that she spent so much of her career here?

Angela doesn't answer but points to the upper-left corner of the posterboard where, above a paragraph in print too fine for Billie to read, a cluster of sauropods stands in a pool of sinking mud.

There are five main theories for why so many Jurassic bones are here, she says, and why nearly all of them are predator bones. This first theory is the muddy bog. This one. The floodplain turned to mud, where herbivores like your mother's stegosauruses got trapped in a mud field that became a feeding frenzy for allosaurs.

Is that what you believe? Rhiannon asks.

Let me go through all these first, Angela says. She trails her finger down to the lower-left corner where a group of dinosaurs, both predators and herbivores, lie dead along the shore of a cartoon-blue river. Theory two, she says. A former riverbed. The possibility that these animals died elsewhere and washed up over time on the same sand bar and fossilized. That they were all eventually pushed downstream from other habitats.

Wouldn't that make sense? Billie says. Wasn't all of Utah once an inland sea? I thought the Great Salt Lake was a remnant of an ancient ocean.

Hold on, Angela says. She slides her finger to the central drawing in the pentagon of boxes: scattered dinosaurs lying lifeless on a sunbaked stretch of desert. The third theory is poisoning, she says. That all the dinosaurs here died together from a single contaminated waterhole, and not from any kind of predation.

She moves her hand to the lower-right drawing, a similar sketch but with living dinosaurs roaming the desert's sand and dust, no carcasses in sight. A very similar theory, she says. Theory four speculates that the animals died not from poisoning but from drought. If the land was mostly desert, they'd have all been here seeking the same water source. It might account for why the bones have been found in so many different orientations and states. Instead of contamination, some might have died of thirst, others by attack from competition.

That sounds plausible, Rhiannon says.

But why no intact skeletons? Billie asks. Wouldn't poisoning or drought still leave full skeletons for paleontologists to find?

Not necessarily, Angela says. Like I said, predation due to competition would have scattered the bones, especially if carcasses were discarded left and right. This wasn't a mass extinction, like an asteroid or meteor. It was isolated to this area. Scavengers from other habitats could have come in and decimated the bones.

Billie nods to the fifth drawing: the only one without dinosaurs, nothing but a sea of illustrated blue water. Flood, I'm guessing?

Exactly right. Angela's hand slides to the upper-right corner. This last theory suggests that a widespread flood drowned these dinosaurs and deposited them all here.

Does the geology support that? Billie asks. What kind of flood might have happened during the Jurassic period?

It's hard to say, Angela says. But it's a good question. I mean, look at all these different theories. We're talking about a total flood or else a total drought. Opposites. But the Jurassic period was such a large span of time. Sixty-five million years. Angela glances up and nods out the small window of her trailer. Look outside, she says. Look how much our weather has changed in just the past few years.

Billie peeks at Rhiannon whose gaze has drifted beyond the trailer to the scorched span of desert all around them. Changing weather. Rhiannon surely thinking about the planes, the wildfire that kept them overnight in Cortez. Billie doesn't know what to think, this landscape as fascinating as anything she's read about in any library book, but she wants to know about their mother. Why she was here. Why she's led her daughters here beyond the guise of a funeral.

What do you believe? Billie asks.

I don't really know. The bones are so dispersed that none of them really indicate anything unifying. Vertical orientation indicates mud bog, that they were trapped upright. Some fossils have been found that way, while others have been found horizontal, which supports a theory of water flow. Still others are oriented completely randomly, which could indicate poisoning or drought. I work in paleontology for the University of Utah. Marcus is one of my research students right now. Neither of us knows what to believe. Have you girls been up to Salt Lake City yet?

Rhiannon shakes her head. We drove up from the south.

Part of my work at the university is contributing to the Cleveland-Lloyd exhibit at the Natural History Museum of Utah there. Kids and their parents can cast their vote on which theory they believe.

What's the winning vote? Rhiannon asks.

Angela smiles. If you'd believe it, all five are split pretty much evenly.

Billie looks up. What did our mother believe?

We're dealing with so much time here, Angela says. Sixty-five million years. Your mother never said it outright, but I think she entertained the possibility that multiple events might have happened across the entire era these dinosaurs would have been alive.

You mean she thought several disasters happened? At different times?

Angela sets down the posterboard. I don't

know. She never said definitively. I think she wanted to stick to her corner. Stegosaurs. She knew I was studying the mystery.

Then what was she studying, if not the mystery? Billie says. Why was she here?

Angela looks at her. I'm sure you know your mother studied vascularization. Blood vessels in the plates. What they were for.

Rhiannon nods. She said they were intended to attract mates.

Blushing for attraction, Angela says. That's true. But here, she was also studying vascularization as temperature control, and as a potential detector of environmental changes. She thought the plates might have served all three functions. And here, beyond the thrill of finding an intact skeleton at the Small Quarry, she had the chance to study vascularization for attraction, temperature control, and climate detection, all in a place that might have contained so many different environmental possibilities.

Mass drought, Rhiannon says. The ranger at the Small Quarry told us it might be what caused the stegosaur's extinction.

It's a possibility here, too, Angela says. That's what first led your mother here.

So she was studying Jurassic climate, too, Rhiannon says and Billie watches her connect a scattering of dots by the expression on her face.

Angela nods. Your mother thought there might be several environmental catastrophes across so much Jurassic time. So in a way, yes. She was studying Jurassic climate, too, through the plates themselves. She was looking into how stegosaur plates detected their environment over time, especially if there were multiple events.

Billie sits back, the mug of tea finally beginning to cool in her hands. A land of multiple catastrophes. Rhiannon sits in silence and the wind picks up and scatters dust against the trailer's small window. The planet's monsoons and tornadoes. So many planes. An earth the news speculates might be on the brink of another mass disaster. Billie tries to imagine her mother here re-envisioning what this land was even so many millions of years ago. A land of puzzles. A land she believed carried several disasters in the layers of its sediment. A land pocked by loss, what swirls in the atmosphere of every corner of the world around them, and what has drawn Billie and Rhiannon back here for a funeral.

When the sun begins to set across the valley below the quarry, casting the surrounding mesas in layers of lavender, Billie pulls the tent from the Mustang's trunk as Marcus emerges from the visitor center and locks the door behind him for the night.

What's that you got there? Marcus calls. A two-person tent?

Billie smiles. It's worked fine for us the past few nights.

Didn't Dr. Wallace tell you we have a trailer for you?

Rhiannon emerges from the backseat with their two paper grocery bags in her arms. We don't mind camping. We were expecting it.

Yeah, but we've been expecting you too.

Marcus tucks the visitor center's keys in his pocket and takes the two bags from Rhiannon's arms. In the fading light, Billie can see her sister's face stiffen. How uncomfortable it makes her to take help from anyone. How impossible it was to even picture her letting their father organize her pit crew on the raceway. Marcus motions for Billie to put the tent back in the trunk and she grabs only their suitcases and follows him down the trail behind the visitor center.

Next to Dr. Wallace's trailer sit four other small trailers, what Billie assumed this afternoon were the living quarters of other researchers. Marcus leads them to the front door of a trailer at the edge of all five. He pulls another set of keys from his pocket and hands them to Rhiannon.

This one is yours, he says. For as many nights as you want to stay. We have another paleontologist from the University of Utah, Dr. Torres, who usually stays here. He's back in Salt Lake City this summer with his family. The trailers are pretty sparse, but better than camping. The desert can get cold at night, especially at elevation.

Thanks, Rhiannon says. Which trailer is yours?

I'm right next door. Dr. Wallace, right next door to that, which you already know.

And the other two trailers?

Usually BLM workers, though neither of them are occupied right now.

Billie glances at Marcus. Do you know much about why we're here?

Dr. Wallace told me. I haven't seen your mother since last summer, but I know why she planned for you to be here.

Do you know when the funeral will be? Rhiannon says. We forgot to ask Dr. Wallace this afternoon.

I really don't know. Marcus sets the grocery bags on the metal steps leading up to the trailer's door. All I know is that she's planning to grill for all of us tonight.

Is she in her trailer right now? Billie asks.

I'm guessing so. There aren't a lot of hiding places out here. Anyway, I'll let you unpack and get situated. I'll be next door if you need anything. Just come out whenever you're ready and we can make dinner.

Inside, the trailer looks near exact to Dr. Wallace's living quarters. Small makeshift kitchen. Fold-down table. A narrow bathroom with a spray-handle shower. A tiny bedroom in back with a double bed shoved in, both edges lining the walls.

Looks like we're sleeping together tonight, Billie says from the bedroom as Rhiannon unloads the groceries into the overhead cabinets and dorm-size refrigerator.

I don't think we've slept in the same bed since I was in junior high. That time you watched *Carrie* at Nicole Sizemore's house and you were too scared to sleep alone. I think you were only in fifth grade.

Billie emerges from the bedroom. How do you even remember that?

Rhiannon looks at her. I remember everything.

Billie sits on a fold-down bench beside the kitchen cabinets and doesn't want to ask but asks anyway. Rhee, are you doing all right?

Rhiannon sets a can of baked beans down on the counter. It's just a lot, she says. All of these people who knew Mom.

I know.

First the woman at the Small Quarry. And now Dr. Wallace. And even Marcus — they all knew her. They all knew her in a way it seems we never did.

I never even knew about all those theories. Mom never said a word.

Rhiannon sits down on the bench beside Billie. I keep trying to remember that she was our mother. Not a colleague. That maybe she wanted to be a parent first. That she never wanted to bore us with her work.

Billie motions out the trailer window across from them, the sun's last light thinning across the mesa line. How is this boring? How the fuck is any of this boring?

We were kids. We were kids who became adults. It probably never even occurred to her to tell us about any of this.

But she brought me here. She brought me here once.

Rhiannon sighs. To make you want something. Not to let you know anything at all about her work. Did she tell you anything? About predators or bone plates or five different theories of why so many fucking dinosaurs disappeared in the same place?

We knew she studied plates. I feel like that's all we ever knew.

Now we know she studied climate, too. Climate sixty-five million years ago. And she was clearly aware of how the weather is changing now.

You think there's a connection.

I don't know. I'm tired, Billie. Not just from driving. I'm so fucking tired.

Billie leans against the wall and feels a weight descend on her shoulders. She tries to imagine how Rhiannon feels driving both of them across so many states in so many days only to experience another funeral, all over again.

How many days are we here? Billie asks.

We have to be back a week from now. It'll take three days to drive back. If we go nowhere else, we can stay here until Wednesday. If we even want to.

We made good time.

We made good time, assuming we're not headed anywhere else but here. Did you look? The journal. Did you look ahead at the coordinates?

I told you I wouldn't do that. I promised.

I mean the next page. Did you check to see if we're going anywhere else?

I don't want to know right now. But doesn't this seem like everything? Where the hell else could we go?

I don't know. But five days here is a long

fucking time. We could go back early. Though we don't even know when this supposed funeral will be.

Billie stands. I can go ask Dr. Wallace. I may as well right now, so we don't have to talk about it at dinner. Would you let me do that? You look like hell, Rhee.

Thanks. Rhiannon grins. That's nice of you to say.

Billie opens the trailer door and lets herself out before Rhiannon can say no.

When Billie reaches Dr. Wallace's trailer, the front door is already open. Angela sits inside at the fold-down kitchen table beneath a weak lamp, notes scattered before her, the table's surface a converted desk. The sunset's ghost lingers in the sky through the window behind her and Billie feels a faint catch in the cage of her chest. How wide open the desert is. How easy it is to forget that a week ago she was still locked inside a barbed-wire prison yard in the flatlands of the Midwest. She knocks softly on the open door and Angela looks up and motions her in.

I didn't mean to disturb you, Billie says.

Not at all. Just finishing up some field notes before we start dinner. You hungry? And did Marcus show you your trailer?

Billie nods. Thanks so much for hosting us.

It's no trouble at all. We have room, and you both are special guests.

Billie climbs the steps. That's what I came to talk to you about.

Angela stacks the papers before her and waves Billie toward the fold-down chair on the other side of the table.

Billie sits. The funeral. We forgot to ask you about it this afternoon.

What do you want to know?

When will it be? And what can you tell me about it? We don't know anything other than that this is a second funeral. So I could attend.

Angela smiles. That's the story, right?

You mean there's another one?

I don't really know. All I mean is that your mother was full of surprises, always. That seems evident by this trip she planned, and this journal she gave to both of you.

Did you really not know about any of that?

No idea. She didn't mention any of it to me. All she told me was that she needed help setting up a funeral out here. Only logistics. She knew I'd take care of it.

Any idea who left these boxes for us everywhere else, including here?

Not a clue. But I can tell you, your mother

had friends and colleagues everywhere. It wouldn't have been hard for her to find someone at each site to hide something for you.

Billie hesitates. What do you mean, my mother was full of surprises?

I mean she was full of life. Maybe that's a better word. She had a joy about her. To seek and explore. That's what I mean. This is a funeral, but it's also a road trip, right? This seems an extension of that. She wanted you to have some fun.

Despite a funeral being the end result, Billie says.

Angela reaches her hand across the table. A woman Billie barely knows. A welcome unfamiliarity. So few people have touched her in the past six years.

The funeral will be tomorrow, Angela says. Nothing extravagant. A simple ceremony. Small. It's not like there are many people out here. We'll close the visitor center for the day. We'll scatter ashes across the valley like your mother wanted.

Whose ashes?

It's just silt. Sedimentary rock from the dig site where your mother spent most of her life. Maybe remnants of a fossil or two. Nothing special, but special enough that it might hold some meaning for you and your family.

But why? Why spread anything at all if it isn't real?

Angela's grip tightens. So you can say goodbye.

Billie avoids Angela's eyes. Says nothing of watching her mother walk away from Decatur's visiting room for the last time.

Do you have a family? Billie asks. I'm sorry. I hope that's not too personal.

Angela laughs. I do have a family. My two kids are grown. My husband is back in Salt Lake and comes down on weekends when I'm here in the summer. He's a lawyer. Practices environmental law. Utah is the place to do it.

Billie nods. Wants to ask more. Wants to shift the conversation away from herself.

Your mother told me about you, Angela says. I'm not trying to impose. But I think it matters to say goodbye in the right way. It sounds like your sister got to say goodbye. Your father. This is just another way of doing that. In a place that meant something to your mother.

We didn't think to bring anything fancy. No dresses. I'm sorry we're not prepared.

You won't need anything but what you have.

Billie pulls back from the table. I should see if Rhiannon needs help unpacking before dinner.

Come out whenever you're ready. We'll have hot dogs and brats. And beer.

Billie turns and heads toward the door and when she's almost on the front steps, the desert breeze picks up and blows through the frame and Angela calls behind her.

You were the falconer, weren't you?

Billie stops in the doorway and turns around.

Angela smiles. It's an interesting choice.

Billie looks at her. Are you a birder too?

I'm not. I wish I was. But you and your mother share that.

She studied dinosaurs.

She studied stegosaurs, right. But they're ornithischians.

Billie knows the root word. Ornithology.

Bird-hipped joints, Angela says. Stegosaurs also had beaks. So much like birds, even though birds descended from lizard-hipped dinosaurs. A perfect inversion, you and your mother. Studying two sides of the same coin.

Billie nods. I'll see you at dinner.

As she walks back toward the trailer where Rhiannon will be waiting, Billie looks up at a wide moon rising over the desert and her legs feel like they might collapse beneath her. This landscape her mother's epicenter. Where she studied the age of giants that could never last. The age of Pangaea splitting off into separate continents, Billie remembers from elementary-school books, how something that large could break apart. An age of devastation and mass burial. And Angela's words: birds a tie that bound Billie to her mother, even if the era when she practiced falconry was marked by a similar devastation. Shoves. Broken bones. Billie listens through the dusk for any kind of call at all. But there is nothing, no sound she recognizes, every hawk bedded down until dawn.

BALDWIN, CHARLES. PHD. JURASSIC ECOLOGY. CAMBRIDGE: HARVARD UNIVERSITY PRESS, 1992. XVII-XX. PRINT.

CALL NUMBER: QE320 .G9 1992

JURASSIC ENVIRONMENTS

The Jurassic period, spanning from the end of the Triassic to the beginning of the Cretaceous, was marked at its start by the supercontinent Pangaea splitting into two separate landmasses, Laurasia and Gondwana. This resulted in more coastlines and shores, and more lush greenery by trading aridity for humidity.

Dinosaurs dominated the land of the Jurassic period, and it was during this time that birds were introduced. Conifers, ferns, ginkgoes and cycads filled the junglelike landscape. Oceans were inhabited by fish and marine reptiles, and streams and rivers by turtles and crocodiles. Algae first appeared in the seas.

Because the climate was warm during the Jurassic period, no ice caps existed on either pole of the earth. Additionally, there is no evidence of glaciers. Volcanic activity was common along tectonic plates given the shifting movement of Pangaea, and warming temperatures created rising sea levels.

39.3228° N, 110.6895° W: Cleveland-Lloyd Quarry, UT

The trailer's shower is small, so cramped Rhiannon can barely move, but a separate bedroom allows her for once to leave Billie behind to sleep. No tiptoeing around a motel room. No quick pull of a tent zipper to minimize noise. After she finishes showering, she makes coffee in the two-cup drip in the trailer's kitchen and steps outside as the sun breaks across a line of distant mesas.

You're up early, a voice calls and Rhiannon looks away from the valley to a picnic table where Marcus sits between his trailer and theirs in basketball shorts and a dry-fit T-shirt, nothing like his work khakis and beige hat the day before.

I could say the same for you, Rhiannon says. Coffee? I made enough for two.

Marcus shakes his head. I already had some, but thanks.

How long have you been up?

I always get my jogs in early. I like watching the sun come up over the valley.

Rhiannon sits across from him at the picnic table. How long have you been coming out here?

This is my third summer at the quarry.

So you worked with my mother for two summers.

She was here, in and out, for the past two summers, yes.

Did you work closely with her?

I mostly work with Dr. Wallace. But I did work with your mother a bit.

Did you know her well?

I didn't know anything you don't know.

Rhiannon sips her coffee. It doesn't feel that way.

Dr. Wallace told me about the journal. The coordinates you're following. Maybe it's not my place, but I think your mom has built an adventure for the two of you.

An adventure, Rhiannon repeats. She watches the horizon line of the mesas. I still don't know why she spent so much time here if she found an intact skeleton in Colorado. There aren't any here. There are barely any stegosauruses at all. Some adventure. An adventure based on everything she never told us about her career.

Marcus shifts on the picnic bench. I wouldn't look at it that way.

Then how would you look at it?

I'd look at it as parents not talking to their kids about their careers. I'd look at it as her making this trip as fun for you as possible, given the circumstances.

Rhiannon sighs. Billie said the funeral is today.

I don't really know anything about it. Dr. Wallace planned everything based on your mom's recommendations. I just know it's later this afternoon. Three o'clock.

Will you be there?

Marcus nods. I'm sorry again for your loss.

Rhiannon sets her mug on the picnic table, notices the humid ring of heat it makes in the wood. What brought you out here? she asks. From the University of Utah. Are you studying these five theories too of what happened here?

Sort of. I'm studying allosauruses, and Jurassic predators more generally. And also paleontological ecology.

You mean climate.

It's one of the best places to study it. There are fossilized bones here, but there are also plants. The theories Dr. Wallace studies are what happened to these dinosaurs, but for me, they're also figuring out what kind of climate might have existed across sixty-five million years. And what caused this mass grave of bones.

So you must have had some overlap with my mother. It sounds like she was studying climate too to see how stegosaurus plates responded to environmental change.

A little. Your mother was interested in similar aspects of the Jurassic climate here.

Rhiannon looks at him. Have you been watching the news?

You mean the plane crashes.

Yes. But all these weather events too. Tornadoes. Unexpected monsoons. We drove through that wildfire in Colorado.

We don't have televisions out here, but I heard about that on the radio. Marcus leans into his elbows on the picnic table. I've been paying more attention than I want to, despite the remoteness out here.

Rhiannon nods. Me too.

Marcus waves a hand toward the valley. This quarry opened in the mid-1960s. The University of Utah championed a team of excavators to figure out what happened here, wrangling in a few other universities. The University of Illinois was one of the other colleges. I'm sure that's how your mother got involved, if she found a stegosaurus skeleton in Colorado and the remains of four other stegosauruses were found here. Marcus pauses. I'm sure the weather was very different in the 1960s, before she first came here.

My mother was clearly paying attention, too. She said the wind and turbulence grew more violent out here the longer she traveled to this place.

I'm lucky I've been able to just drive down from Salt Lake City the past couple of years, Marcus says. My range of study is an entire Jurassic period. It's hard to imagine what might have happened to the weather across millions of years, compared to how quickly our climate has changed in just the past fifty.

It is hard to imagine, Rhiannon echoes. And I don't just mean the weather millions of years ago. It's hard to imagine that any of this is happening. That we haven't seen the sun in Illinois since winter. What's it been like in Salt Lake City recently?

Drought. There and in Nevada, where I'm originally from.

I know Nevada's speedway well, Rhiannon says before she can think. Vegas?

Reno. Your mom told me you raced.

I'm surprised she told you that.

She mentioned you had another job. Something with books?

Did she tell you Billie was in prison?

She was proud of both of you. I know that much.

Rhiannon wraps her hands around her coffee mug. Are you working today?

Marcus shakes his head. The visitor center is closed all day for you two.

What are you studying right now?

Marcus looks at her. Do you really want to know? It's kind of boring.

It's not boring to me.

I've specialized in Jurassic predators, which is what I've looked at every summer I've been here. This summer, since I'm nearing the end of my doctoral work, I'm focusing in on a subspecialty of paleobotany. Specifically, I've been looking at thallophyta this summer. Very simple, algaelike plant fossils.

Thallophyta. And what are you finding?

Not much. At least, not much yet. Through something so small, I hope to help Dr. Wallace better determine what kind of climate existed here during the Jurassic period.

She told us it could have changed dramatically across sixty-five million years.

Which makes it even more difficult to determine. That there could have been more than one major climate during that time. I'm just trying to figure it out based on the age and condition of the plant fossils in the sedimentary layers.

Rhiannon takes another sip of her coffee, the cup nearly drained.

I told you this was boring.

Not at all. But I should see if Billie's up. We have a hell of a day ahead of us.

Marcus stands and says nothing, not that he'll be here if they need anything, but Rhiannon knows it's on the edge of his tongue. This young man who's spent two concentrated years of his life studying a single ancient plant, far more attention than any newscaster or commentator has paid to the environment's rapid change. Who knew Rhiannon was a driver, even now, so many years after she set down her racing helmet. Who across the past two summers could have learned this only from her mother.

Inside the trailer Billie is already dressed, her hair slicked wet, the narrow double bed made. She wears what Rhiannon knows is the best outfit she's packed, a pair of jeans and a T-shirt that isn't a hiking tank top. She sits on a bench beside the kitchen counter, the coffee maker still holding one more cup of weak Folgers she hasn't poured. Her head is in her hands. She looks up when Rhiannon steps inside the trailer.

I don't know if I can do this, Billie says.

Rhiannon sits down on the bench across from her. I know.

I know they're fake ashes. I know it's just sediment and rock.

Did Angela tell you that last night?

Billie nods. I know it's just a symbolic ceremony. But I'm not ready. I thought I was. I thought it was going to be so much easier than this.

Rhiannon leans back against the trailer's walls. Tries to feel if she's ready despite a funeral she's already seen. March drizzle. Heels sinking into the damp earth, the only pair of dress shoes she owned. Her father standing beside her, his lower lip a thin stoic line. The featherweight of Beth's hand, so close but not touching hers. Her aunt's hand on her shoulder, an anchor tethering her to the ground so she wouldn't float away. The warble of the officiant's voice. And the cherrywood of her mother's casket: the one burned image she hoped to leave behind.

It's at three o'clock, is all Rhiannon can say. We have the whole morning.

Billie looks at her. How did you do it?

How did I do what?

How did you say goodbye to her? How the fuck did you say goodbye?

Rhiannon is silent. The solidity of wood. Watching it disappear one last time covered in silt. She'd thought of her mother alone in the ground for weeks. They'd abandoned her to a cemetery by herself beneath nothing but moonlight, to an earth that in the end would take all of them. Rhiannon's fingers grip the trailer's fold-down bench.

That's what this is for, Billie says. For me to say goodbye. For us to say goodbye together. We drove out here and I can't even do what I promised her I would.

It's an unkeepable promise. How can any of us keep that kind of promise?

Billie says nothing. Rhiannon hears the coffee maker buzzing on the counter.

I didn't, Rhiannon finally says. I didn't say goodbye. I was there and I saw her go. That's not the same as letting anyone go.

I wish I'd been there.

I know. But we're here. We kept a promise. We did what she wanted us to do.

I don't want to spread fake ashes across the fucking desert.

Then what do you want to do?

Billie looks up. Do I have to do anything?

We have all morning. We can do everything she wanted us to do but still make this day ours.

I want to get lost for a little while. I'd

rather see what she saw firsthand out here. By ourselves. No one else telling us what she did and what she studied. Just us. I want to know myself what it was that she loved.

Rhiannon stands. Come on.

Where do you want to go?

Put on your shorts. You won't need those clothes until later.

Rhiannon opens the bedroom door and pulls out Billie's suitcase, the sun already high beyond the thin curtains of the trailer's bedroom. The morning theirs. No coordinates. No drawings, no journal. Nothing but the fossil beds their mother once dug, the dust-caked trails she once took.

Once Billie pulls on hiking shorts and they sneak behind the visitor center toward the quarry's circuits of trails, the valley widens before them and the sky hazes with full sun and clouds of dust.

Where do you want to go? Rhiannon asks.

Anywhere. Let's just walk. I don't want to have a plan at all.

Rhiannon chooses a trail up the ridge of the quarry's elevated mesa. She knows it won't matter which path they take, their mother's footprint everywhere. She imagines their mother's first trip here, surely upon invitation in the 1970s after Marcus said the University of Utah's excavators began organizing multi-institutional teams. Surely after she discovered the full skeleton in the Small Quarry in 1992, her reputation preceding her, after she knew the red-rocked terrain of the West as intimately as she knew the alliums and poppies of their Urbana backyard.

Angela asked me about birds, Billie says. Last night. She asked me about falconry.

Marcus said something to me this morning about racing.

Did he say anything about prison? If Mom told them about us, I'm sure they know where I've been.

I'm sure they know. I'm sure it doesn't matter. Billie, there's nothing for you to be ashamed about.

I'm not ashamed of prison. Billie stops walking. But I felt awful when Angela asked me about the birds.

Rhiannon doesn't have to ask why. The same hollow she felt when Marcus asked about selling textbooks, a question she evaded.

You can do whatever you want now.

Billie laughs. It's going to be hard for me to get a job when we return.

I mean you can get another hawk. You can always start training again.

And you can always race again.

I'm too old, Billie. You're never too old to train a bird.

You just think you're old. Jesus, Rhee. You're only thirty-five.

That's ancient in athletics. Quarterbacks retire at thirty-five. Gymnasts retire in their twenties. Baseball players retire at forty if they're lucky.

You're not a baseball player. You're not a gymnast or a quarterback.

Rhiannon keeps walking and hears Billie fall into step behind her. She knows some NASCAR drivers have retired at forty, sometimes forty-five or fifty, but it's meaningless information. It would take her years to get back into training, to relearn the track, to retrain her muscles.

Our house has an enormous yard, Rhiannon says. Plenty of room for a hawk's weathering yard, better than that shit cage Tim built in Jacksonville.

You remember Alabama's cage?

I remember she had better living quarters when she lived with just you in Champaign. What was that guy's name? The one you trained with?

Bud. His name was Bud.

You could contact him again. I bet he still lives in Urbana.

What makes you think I'm staying in Urbana?

Rhiannon turns around, Billie's words hanging in the air. What Rhiannon realizes she's assumed: that they'll live together, that Billie will need her.

Where the hell are you planning on going?

I don't know. But nothing's tying either of us to Illinois anymore.

You're on probation as soon as you get back. This trip is an exception. You have to be there for your therapy sessions. You have to be there one week from now.

But you know that's only for a year. Not forever. I'll do what I need to do, but I'm not required to stay in Illinois past a mandatory series of sessions. I can even move out of state after forty-five days of supervision as long as I have therapy sessions set up for the year. And I can move anywhere in the state as soon as I want. So can you.

Rhiannon stops and looks out over the valley, the sun high above them. The dumb sound of Billie's words: nothing tying them to Illinois. What she hasn't thought until Billie says it. Rhiannon's job the only thing. The one stupid factor in a world of possibilities roping her to Champaign-Urbana, the same town she's known all her life beyond a blip of years traveling interstates to racetracks. Urbana bereft. Only a house, one that could be sold. No property of her own. No Beth, a cord she's cut, a relationship with nothing but a muddled future. A dead-end job: her only tether to home.

Rhiannon doesn't look at Billie. The wind pushes around them and scatters Rhiannon's hair across her face and she knows all at once that she's envisioned a life in Urbana with her sister beyond this trip. A life in their childhood home. Past the requirements of foraging through boxes, donating clothes, keeping what's theirs to keep. A life populated by something more than solitude, more than the empty rooms of a home holding the ghosts of her mother's voice and her father's voice and Billie's voice. A sisterhood beyond six years in a state prison. Something to beat back the soft devastation of losing Beth and her mother in the span of three months, to combat the nothing of a job, to ignore the dust gathering on a helmet in the garage.

There's nothing there for us, Billie says.

Beth's there, Rhiannon says. Beth is still there.

But you're not even with her anymore. Are you? Is that what you want?

Fuck, Billie. Rhiannon closes her eyes. I don't know.

Well, you better figure it out. Billie sweeps her hands across the valley before them. Look where we are. We're saying goodbye. We're saying goodbye to our mother in a place where she siphoned every last drop from the one short life she had. So you need to figure it the fuck out. We both do. I've already wasted six years of my life. And before that, four years with a complete shitbag who made me feel dead inside. I feel like I haven't lived. I feel like I haven't lived at all.

Rhiannon feels her breath leave her. The mesas on the other side of the valley shimmer in the early morning heat. This place her mother's church. Household name. Her mother's version of a racetrack's asphalt, a cockpit's compression. Nothing kept Rhiannon from pulling her helmet back on and getting back on the raceway. She'd siphoned nothing. Her mother squeezed everything from this landscape and Billie hadn't lived because she couldn't, not because she'd given up.

Do you really feel that way? is all Rhiannon can say. Do you really feel like you haven't lived at all?

I've been in prison, Rhee. That's not living. Neither is living with someone who tells you you're nothing. I don't have any more time to waste.

Rhiannon keeps walking. She can think of nothing else to do. She hears Billie calling her name behind her. The wind rising. The wind pushing grained dust and grit into Rhiannon's eyes and she keeps moving, her hiking shoes gripping the trail's ascending slope, her lungs scrambling to pull in air.

Jesus, Rhee, slow the fuck down.

Rhiannon reaches a landing on the trail. Her lungs screaming. Altitude. The pace of a hike. The effort of choking back a morning before another funeral, before releasing her mother to the earth again and again. She sits on a rocked ledge, the sun beating down against the back of her neck, the damp sweat of her skin.

Billie sits beside her. Be honest. Just be honest, Rhee. That's all I'm trying to do.

Be honest about what?

About what you want. About your job. About racing. About why you left Beth.

I don't know. I don't know what you want from me. I'm here, Billie. I'm here with you because Mom wanted us to be here.

You're numb, Rhee. You've been sleepwalking since she died.

Like you would know. You weren't there.

I wasn't where?

You weren't there with me to lower her down.

The words surprise her, the wide span of their mother's desert spread out all around them, words she didn't know were lodged in her throat. That Billie wasn't there. Their father and her aunt and Beth quiet beside her and Billie nowhere, Billie another half, Billie a twinned life growing up and out of their childhood home, Billie sharing not just T-shirts and combat boots and small rakes planting seeds in their mother's backyard garden but an entire foundation no one else on Earth could understand, the sole person on this devastated planet who knew their mother in the only way a sister could.

What do you want me to say? Billie whispers.

I don't want you to say anything.

Do you want me to say I'm sorry?

I don't need you to say anything at all. I just wish you could have been there.

As if I could feel any worse that I wasn't.

I'm not blaming you. I'm just telling you what I wanted. I wanted you there.

Billie clasps her hands together, her elbows bent against her knees.

I can't believe I fucked up my life so badly that I couldn't be there at all.

Rhiannon focuses on the valley all around

them. Sleepwalking. She wonders if it's true. If she's been doing nothing but basic functioning, just eating and barely sleeping. Since their mother died but so long before. Since Billie nearly killed herself just to live on her own terms.

When did you feel alive? Rhiannon whispers.

What kind of question is that?

You said you felt dead inside. With Tim. When have you ever felt most alive?

Do you know what a hawk feels like on your arm?

Rhiannon keeps her eyes on the valley, the scarlet slope of striated rock.

I was alive. With Alabama. Feeling her take off from my arm. I was so fucking alive.

Rhiannon is silent, Billie breathing beside her.

What about you? she hears Billie ask.

Rhiannon closes her eyes and lets her brain catch on the first thing that comes. One memory, maybe two. Her brain releases a flood. Opening the hood of a car for the first time inside their garage on Grove Street, her father letting her fasten and secure the prop rod. Following her mother around the backyard flowerbeds, a green plastic watering can in her small hands. Driving to high school in an old Honda Accord, Billie in the passenger seat, Billie still a freshman and Rhiannon a senior, the one year they shared the building's walls. Kissing a girl for the first time, the ocean heat of Atlantic City beyond the hotel room's window. Beth dropping her off outside her house, their first date. Chinese hotpot. Two cups of green tea. A May thunderstorm blowing in when Beth dropped her off afterward and leaned across the driver's seat before Rhiannon got out, lightning flashing beyond the car's windows. The damp-soft of Beth's mouth against hers. Beth calling the next morning. Beth calling every morning after. And the raceway. Talladega. Pocono. Indianapolis. Daytona Beach. The same thrill as the Mustang gunning them across Missouri and across Kansas straight into Colorado and New Mexico and now the layered rock of Utah where their mother stood and said *here.*

Right now, Rhiannon whispers. This trip. The chance to get back out on the road. It makes me want to disappear, Billie. She gestures toward the far-off mesas, the desert's bright sun spilling down over all of them. This land. This place Mom knew so well. That we have to bury her here. Again. All of it makes me want to die. But I feel alive. I feel so fucking alive for the first time in years.

Billie says nothing and Rhiannon wonders what it is that her sister feels. That she's out here, straight from prison to the desert's split-open sky visible for miles beyond the windshield of a car. Shared bathrooms, shared showers, shared cafeteria tables, stolen toilet paper. And out here, nothing. This hiking trail. The possibility of not seeing another human being for hours. The highway, so many mile markers of a radio's white noise.

I'm glad you're here, Rhiannon says. That we're out here together.

Rhiannon waits for Billie to say this valley and the small space of their trailer make her glad to be here. But Billie just stands and continues along the trail their mother once walked.

They hike in silence. Billie speaks only to point out loose rocks to avoid. They return to the quarry past noon, Marcus and Angela standing outside the cluster of trailers making lunch. Billie slips inside their trailer and Rhiannon approaches the picnic table populated with pickle jars, deli cuts, sliced bread.

Angela looks up. Good hike? I almost thought you two skipped town if not for your car still parked by the visitor center.

We had the chance to get out before it gets too hot, Rhiannon says. You have some great views up there along the ridgeline.

Your mother climbed all over this country, Angela says. Did you take the left-swinging trail? That view up there was one of your mother's favorites.

Rhiannon imagines her mother's hiking shoes gripping the ridgeline. What she must have done for years while Rhiannon was on the interstate. Marcus motions her over and opens a plastic cooler filled with aluminum cans of Sprite and Coke. Rhiannon never drinks soda, never drinks beer, realizes how much of both she's had in the past week. She pulls a Coke from the cooler and pops the tab and looks at Marcus, desperate to talk about anything but her mother.

Decent morning?

Marcus nods. I got a bit of work done in my trailer after my run.

Is most of your family still back in Reno?

My mother and father. I have a sister living out in San Francisco. The Palo Alto area. Silicon Valley. Marcus hesitates, a barely perceptible pause. And I have a partner. A boyfriend back at the University of Utah.

Did you meet him there?

He's a doctoral candidate in atmospheric sciences. We met through some overlap of research two years ago since I'm studying paleontological climate. His name is Jason.

Do you see him much over the summer?

Sometimes on weekends. He's come out here a few times to visit.

I'm guessing Salt Lake City isn't an easy place to meet people.

It's less conservative than you'd think, at least in terms of the dating scene. I was surprised by that when I moved there. I expected only white people and fundamentalists.

Rhiannon hesitates, unsure how much her mother might have told Marcus about her own relationship with Beth. If it ever came up. If it even mattered at all to mention.

Champaign's the same way, she finally says. You'd think it would be a red dot in a blue state, but I guess being a college town helps. It wasn't hard to meet Beth there.

Marcus looks up from the bag of chips he's opened on the picnic table. Is Beth your girlfriend?

Was. Rhiannon looks away. I don't really know what we are now.

How long were you together?

Over four years. We broke up a few months ago.

Marcus looks like he wants to ask more but Angela calls him over to help pull containers of potato salad and coleslaw from her trailer's small fridge, far too much food for the four of them to eat. Rhiannon stands beneath the Utah sun alone. She thinks again of first meeting Beth. An art opening at the University of Illinois she'd gone to with her mother after returning to Champaign off her final racing circuit. A Friday night, where some of her mother's colleagues would be, where she hoped Rhiannon would buck up and have a drink. Rhiannon was standing by herself in front of a red canvas with a plastic glass of white wine when a woman came up and talked a good five minutes about the piece before mentioning she'd painted it herself, a screen-print artist who'd branched out to oils and mattes just for this show. The woman's eyes a cutting blue, the shade of her hair a dirty blond. Her frame wiry and brittle, a type Rhiannon never went for: too delicate but for the pull of Beth's low voice. How it hinted at something tough.

Ready for a sandwich? Angela says, carrying a jar of mustard to the picnic table. Nothing fancy, but I promise dinner will be better.

Rhiannon feels a faint buzzing in her

brain. I just need to make a quick phone call. Is there service out here?

You have Verizon? Marcus says. It's the only service that consistently works.

Rhiannon shakes her head and Marcus pulls his own phone from his pocket.

Here. I learned last summer that I need the right service, if I want any chance at all of keeping up a long-distance relationship.

Rhiannon grips his fingers briefly as he passes the phone to her hands.

Behind their trailer, Billie still inside hiding out, Rhiannon takes Marcus's phone and dials Beth's number, one she knows by heart. She doesn't expect her to pick up, the number unfamiliar, but she hears Beth's voice after the second ring.

Beth, it's me, Rhiannon says. We're here. We're out in Utah.

You made it to the quarry?

We're at the quarry. The funeral's this afternoon.

Are you okay?

Rhiannon closes her eyes. I'm fine.

And Billie?

I don't know. She's had her ups and downs. We both have.

I'm sorry. I know it's a rough time for everyone.

Rhiannon leans into the shade of the trailer, its metal siding cool against her back. She wonders what Beth means. *Everyone.* If she's incriminating herself, if their breakup has been just as hard on her.

How are you? How's everything in Champaign?

Nothing's changed since you last called. How about there?

We've had a few detours. We got stuck in Colorado for a night, then we camped in Moab last night. But we're on schedule. We should be back to Champaign by Saturday at the latest.

Are you wanting to meet up when you get back?

I don't know. Are you?

Beth sighs. I don't know. Rhee, I really don't know what you want from me.

Rhiannon eyes the valley beyond the trailers. The vast span of land. So much daylight. A visibility she hasn't seen for months in Illinois, a bright-flooded light that illuminates every corner of her brain.

I don't want anything from you, she says. I wanted more from myself.

What? Rhiannon hears Beth sigh. I don't know what the hell you're talking about.

The irritation in Beth's voice breaks across the line and Rhiannon knows all at once that she's fucked with Beth for months since they broke up and for years before that. Never telling her what it was she was feeling or what she needed. *When were you most alive?* Billie pleading. If it's right now, Rhiannon has nothing else to lose.

I was a driver, she says. I was a race car driver.

Rhee, I know.

No, you don't. Listen to me. I was a driver. I was such a good fucking driver. I could have been a household name.

The words out there, the words Lucy used at the Small Quarry to describe her mother and Rhiannon can't believe they're coming out of her mouth right now. The valley below a gleaming landscape of marbled pink and purpling sun, a valley scoured beneath a white-hot sky that has bleached everything clean. Rhiannon feels the heat of the trailer's paneling against her back through her shirt and doesn't know why she's spit this out across the line except only that she must.

Rhiannon, I know. You think I don't? I know how good you were.

What do you mean you know?

Come on. I looked you up right after I met you. Doesn't everyone? You mentioned what you did but you never talked about how many races you won. I never thought you wanted to talk about it. You never brought it up.

Right after we met? The gallery opening?

Beth sighs. I thought you didn't want to talk about it.

Rhiannon slides against the trailer wall and sinks into the dirt. A shared pot of green tea. Steamed windows. Their first date, only days beyond the gallery opening and Beth's tongue pushing hard against her mouth and even then she knew everything Rhiannon barely brought up and rarely mentioned since. She knew when Rhiannon hauled a small carload of clothes into her apartment and she knew when they huddled on the couch beside each other, every night, every episode of *The Daily Show* and *Six Feet Under* and *Top Chef,* every single night across four years inside Beth's cramped apartment until Rhiannon moved out.

Why didn't you ever bring it up? That you knew I was good?

Jesus. How is this my fault? Why does it matter what I thought at all? Why wasn't it you who said something?

I didn't think you needed to know.

I didn't need to know? We lived together for four years and I didn't need to know that you could have made history?

You could've asked.

No, you could've said something if it meant that much to you. You never did. I thought you would and you never did and is it any wonder that you moved out?

What the fuck is that supposed to mean?

It means you're a fucking wall, Rhee. You never talked about it. Just like you never talk about your mother. Not when she first got sick and not now.

What the fuck was there to say? Beth, she's gone.

Yeah, she's gone. And how do you feel about that?

Fuck you.

The words leave Rhiannon's mouth before she can take them back and she feels her eyes smarting, her fists trembling.

Fine, Beth says. Fine. You know what? I walked on eggshells for years never knowing what I could bring up and what I couldn't. What you'd actually answer or what you'd keep to yourself because you could. Now I know. That you're incapable. That there are people surrounding you who love you and you refuse to let them in.

Maybe so, is all Rhiannon can think to say. She doesn't want to think at all about who surrounds her, what it feels like to be loved. If Beth loves her. If Billie loves her. If her mother loved her, what Rhiannon logically knew but never stopped to feel what that meant beyond a word.

Jesus, Rhee. Beth sighs. What the fuck does that say about us?

That we were strangers, Rhiannon says, words she doesn't want to say but there they are. That we were strangers for four fucking years.

Beth is silent for a moment. I guess we were.

Beth breathes into the receiver and Rhiannon feels her anger drain away and in its place there is only sadness, a wave that overwhelms her.

Beth, she hears herself say.

Don't, Rhee. Just don't.

Beth, I'm sorry. I'm so sorry I fucked everything up.

Beth sighs. You didn't. I know what you're going through right now is impossible. I just don't know why the past five years were so fucking hard for you too.

I wish I could tell you.

You still can. Rhiannon. You can still tell me anything.

Rhiannon watches the valley until her eyes burn, the bright of the desert blinking back in a film of blue. What Beth's voice sounds like: hope. That Rhiannon hasn't dug a hole so irreparably deep and unfillable. That there might be something waiting for her back in Champaign beyond her job, beyond Billie wanting to leave.

I wish you could've known me in a different time of my life, Rhiannon whispers. I wish you could've known me when I was so much prouder of myself.

I'm proud of you.

You don't have to say that.

I am, Rhee. I'm so fucking proud of you. Regardless of how good you were.

Rhiannon closes her eyes. The words find their place.

I wish you were here, she whispers.

I wish it too. I wish so badly I could be there for you.

Rhiannon opens her eyes and there is only the valley. Let's talk when I get back.

Okay, Beth says. Let's talk.

When Rhiannon emerges from behind the trailer and steps back into the sun, the midday heat warms her skin and flushes her face. Her stomach empty, a five-mile hike since a small breakfast of coffee and a single granola bar and her head fogged with what she wishes she hadn't said. *Fuck you.* She moves to the picnic bench where Angela and Marcus are waiting and her brain doesn't process at first who waits before her at the table. A familiar figure. Angela and Marcus sitting on opposite sides of the picnic table, a third person standing beside them.

Her father.

Here. Standing in the rock-cragged dust of Utah.

Rhiannon stops short.

How did you — she hears herself speak right as she hears the trailer door open behind her. She turns and Billie is standing on the front steps of the trailer, her body immobile, her gaze firm on their father.

Girls, he says.

His eyes on Billie. He takes a step toward her.

For a moment, Rhiannon expects Billie to be relieved. She hasn't seen their father for six years and now he's here, on this day. But before Rhiannon can move, Billie's hand is reaching back to the counter just inside the trailer door. A set of keys. Rhiannon steps toward her just seconds too late and Billie is running up the dirt path toward the visitor center, toward the parking lot, toward the Mustang.

SHAH, ERICA. THE PHYSICS OF AUTOMECHANICS. LONDON: MACMILLAN PUBLISHERS, 2005. 229–233. PRINT.

CALL NUMBER: QC124 .H32 2005

CAR ENGINES

To convert gasoline to energy and motion, automobiles require internal combustion engines, which place high-energy fuel in a cylinder with heat. The more cylinders a car contains, the stronger and faster its engine will be. Multiple cylinders create greater horsepower, or the amount of power an engine can produce against the load it bears.

NASCAR stock cars are capable of 850 horsepower, two to three times higher than the average civilian car engine. NASCAR maintains strict guidelines for engine design, and all stock cars must contain carbureted V-8 engines with iron blocks. Engine servicing is required in pit stops due to extreme stress on engines from constant acceleration around turns. The temperature of NASCAR engines can reach 2,000 degrees and pressures of 1,500 psi. For this reason, engine valves are made of titanium to resist heat, and engine blocks are made of cast-graphite iron.

39.3228° N, 110.6895° W: Cleveland-Lloyd Quarry, UT

Billie's hands cortisol-curl around the Mustang's sun-warmed steering wheel: the same as Rhiannon's hands. What she dreamed from the polyester sheets of her prison bed, her sister's fingers locked around the wheel, always Rhiannon she imagined and never herself guiding anything anywhere. Now there is nothing but an open road she knows she shouldn't be on without a license and with a criminal record. But it feels like something. It feels like every kind of rebellion.

Her father. Her father here. Her father here in this place that has become a space for her and Rhiannon alone. Her father in Utah, six fucking states away from Illinois but never once in the visitors' room in Decatur. And Rhiannon. Billie doesn't want to think of her as the Mustang finds the end of the quarry's gravel road and meets the highway. Who shuttled her out here. Who visited her every month even if she lied, every goddamn month except the last three of a seventy-two-month sentence. Who picked her up at the curb of the Correctional Center and made her a room back home. Who wants her to stay in Champaign beyond probation. And in thanks: Billie grabbing keys that aren't hers to grab and running toward a car that isn't hers to drive. But the impossibility of her father. A funeral. Every single one of Billie's muscles screaming no.

Billie wants none of it at all.

The desert is a panorama beyond the Mustang's windshield and her sneakers push hard on the gas, no cops and no speed limit signs in such a desolate place. No gas stations. No roadside dives. Barely any other cars at all. The sun slicks hot off the hood and the Uinta and Wasatch mountains span off to the north, so wide open Billie feels her eyes water just looking at them.

There is no aim. No place to be. There is nothing to do, nothing to find. There is only a car shuttling across the West, not the liberation their mother intended for them out here but the one Billie will take. Her mother. Her father. Rhiannon standing beside the picnic table. What their family is now. Billie presses the gas and feels her eyes sting and it is not for the beauty of the mountains.

Billie steers the Mustang until she sees a gravel recess marked as a scenic pullout. One tin-roof hut, no more than a glorified carport sheltering a single picnic table. Billie slows down and pulls in and lets herself sit in the shade on top of the picnic table beneath the lone hut, her feet resting on the bench. Before her lies a span of mountains beyond mountains. She lets her gaze fall out of focus against the line of Wasatch peaks in the distance. She exhales and closes her eyes. This week. More land than Billie has seen across her entire lifetime. Sun-saturated sky. Hawks wheeling. The muscle memory of Alabama on her arm, an arm once unscathed by gasoline burn. *When did you feel alive?* Her mother's hand passing a journal of coordinates across a prison table. This desert. This fucking light.

At the quarry after their ridgeline hike, she'd sat in the trailer alone. The window cracked open. Rhiannon on the phone below the window's screen, her voice drifting in. Calling Beth. What this trip had made her do. What it could make Billie do too. What their mother wanted her to feel standing at the quarry when she was only fifteen. IV drips. Catheter lines. Bags of saline and blood. What Rhiannon witnessed in the hospital room and Billie imagined from the prison yard pressing her hands to the chain links of a metal fence. To see her mother alive past a prison sentence, past the weight of her own mistake. To take back the gasoline and strewn books if she'd have known they'd cost her the nearness of her mother in the last six years of her life. The heaviness of her own stupidity is the only thing Billie feels at all out here. These breath-stealing mountains and apricot sunsets and colossal sweeps of open plains and even still she can't breathe, a landscape that meant everything to her mother, a landscape that only breaks Billie open.

And her father.

Her father there to see all of it.

To see her remorse. To feel vindicated that he never came once.

Billie hears the gravel crunch of a single car decelerate into the lot and come to a stop. She keeps her fingers to her forehead, her eyes focused on the wood of the bench beneath her sneakers. She doesn't look up when she feels a hand soft on her shoulder.

Billie.

She has known Marcus only a day but recognizes his voice.

Billie, it's time to head back.

She doesn't look up. How did you find me?

There's only one highway out here. Not many places to stop. And that bright-red Mustang. You're easier to find than you think.

I fucked up, she hears herself say. She doesn't know if she means the car and the keys or if she means everything at once, all six years of it. She looks up and wants Marcus to be angry. But he says nothing and extends his hand and Billie looks beyond him to his car and sees Rhiannon waiting in the passenger seat.

She knew you shouldn't drive back yourself, Marcus says. Without a license.

Billie nods. No words come out of her mouth.

Want to ride back with me? Or do you want to ride with Rhiannon?

Billie sees Rhiannon glance through the window and emerge from the car and Billie knows there is no choice, that she will drive back to the quarry with her sister.

I'm sorry, Billie says. The hum of the engine surrounding both of them as Rhiannon follows Marcus back to the quarry.

Rhiannon doesn't look at her. You don't

think, Billie. You just do.

Maybe that's not such a bad thing.

It is when you burn down a library. It is when you flee a bar and no one can find you until you get into a fight. It is when you take a fucking set of keys without a license and take off down the highway. Jesus, Billie. Do you think of anyone but yourself?

Billie leans against the passenger window. Her mother and father. Her sister climbing into a car with Marcus to find her. Billie thinking of absolutely everyone in her family and the impossibility of her own place within it. A family of doing. A family where she still would have fucked up if she'd never gone to prison, falconry still just a hobby. No place for awards or recognition, for ambition or drive. But she wants her mother here. Here. She wants her father here, too, despite everything.

Look, I know you're mad, Rhiannon says. I know you don't want to see him.

Billie looks at her. Did you know he'd be here?

I didn't even get the chance to talk to him, thanks to your bullshit. I have no idea why he's here. He should be in Colorado. He must have kept driving to be here for us.

For us. Billie can't help the salt in her voice. He's not here for us.

Then why the hell else would he be here? He's already buried her. He's already been to a funeral. Once is surely enough.

Maybe he's here for her wedding ring. You said he wanted it back.

He knows it's in St. Louis. Christ, Billie. You have every right to be upset but he's not a monster. Is it so hard to imagine that he's here for you?

Rhiannon steers the Mustang back up toward the quarry and Billie wants to tell her that it is. That he must be here for Rhiannon and not for her, a ridiculous span of miles from Illinois to Utah when he could have simply visited her in Decatur but never did. The last time she saw him at her sentencing, two guards dragging her from the courtroom and she'd glanced back to see both of her parents sitting in the front row, her mother weeping and her father watching her go, his face stonewalled and blank.

By the time they reach the quarry, the sun tilts west in the sky and Billie knows it is almost time for the funeral. The cold cuts and jars of pickles have long been cleared. Angela nowhere in sight. Marcus disappears into his trailer, leaving them to themselves. And their father: sitting alone, his hands folded on the picnic table.

Billie watches as Rhiannon approaches him and he draws her into a hug. Watches his face, lines worn and grooved. Hands, taut and leathered, clasping Rhiannon's shoulders. Gasoline-worn palms. A mechanic's world he thought their mother never understood, no more than Billie understood how a father could let his skin wrinkle and his hair lighten into white-dusted tufts without speaking to his daughter once.

She doesn't move. Stands in shorts and a tank top, scars currenting down her left arm in ripples of flame-hardened skin. Every evidence of what she's done. What's been done to her. A past she carries beneath a layer, her skin its own sediment. What her father can't see. The only layer he can: a flame she lit and threw herself. She looks at him and knows that all he understood was a daughter burning down her own life. A daughter thinking only of herself. What Rhiannon said. Running with boys all across high school through cornfields, always sneaking out, only to do nothing with her college degree but follow one more boy to Jacksonville.

Her father walks toward her, an arm's length away.

Billie, he says.

She feels her scars gleam in the heat of

the sun.

He says nothing. Not sorry. But he reaches toward her with the same hug that enveloped Rhiannon and Billie wants to stay planted but thinks of her mother and the ashes that will take to so much wind and for once she just wants to belong. She notices he still wears his wedding ring. She feels herself step toward him. His once-sweatshirt, the Illinois woods. His arms are around her and she lets herself be held.

What are you doing here? she whispers against the rough fabric of his shirt. What the fuck are you doing here?

Her voice on the verge of breaking but she won't let it. Steels herself. Hears him whisper back *I'm here for you girls, I'm always here for you* and she wants to scream. *You were never here* she wants to shout but feels her limbs slacken in his arms.

Billie can recall only one funeral in her entire life. Her uncle Mike, her father's brother. An unexplained heart attack in his early fifties. Billie remembers a quick ceremony in Pekin where her father's family still lived, a musty funeral home peppered with only two dozen people then a private burial with immediate family, a still-humid September day followed by a fast lunch at a

Hardee's along the highway. Fried chicken and instant mashed potatoes, tastes Billie still associates with loss.

She still doesn't know what's customary for a funeral but knows this one is more than ordinary. Angela has situated a small fire ring made of thick stones at the ridgeline's edge. Several bundles of sage smoke in the center, the grassy scent billowing off to the valley with the high afternoon winds. Five folding chairs circle the fire ring. The surrounding mesas, a panorama. And the ashes, what Billie knows are only bits of rock and dust, sit beside the fire ring in a green plastic urn.

Hell of a funeral, her father mutters beside her and Rhiannon, all three of them standing along the ridgeline waiting for Angela to begin. Where do you think someone bought that urn? At Home Depot? It looks like a watering can.

Billie doesn't want to laugh, doesn't want to give her father an inch but can't help herself, that they've all driven way out here for only burned bundles of weeds. Her mother's doing. She wonders if this, too, was intended as levity. Despite the mess of emotions swirling in her gut, she stuffs a brief burst of laughter back into her throat out of respect for Angela and Marcus, out of letting her father know that a single hug doesn't make them family again.

Marcus approaches and asks if they need anything. Bottles of water. Jackets to block the wind. Rhiannon shakes her head. Marcus moves to Billie's other side, just beyond earshot of her sister and father.

How are you? he asks. Feeling better?

I'm fine.

Marcus places a hand on her left arm despite its visible scars, her shoulders barely covered. Billie flinches in reflex but Marcus doesn't move.

Did my mother plan all this? she whispers.

The plastic urn was your mother's idea. But she's probably not responsible for the sage. Angela's a fan of burning it in her trailer. I think your mother found it calming too.

And the view? Why are we up here along the ridgeline?

Definitely your mother. I think Angela told you she loved the hiking trails up here.

Billie feels a pinprick pierce her rib cage. That Marcus knows what her mother found calming, even what she loved.

It's time, Angela calls to them from the fire ring. Come have a seat.

Billie follows her father and sister toward the line of chairs.

Angela sits beside them. We're gathered here to honor a mother, she begins. And a wife. And one of the best researchers I've ever had the privilege to work with.

Billie wants to be the bigger person but the word grinds, a metal she tongues inside her mouth. *Wife.* Her mother nothing of her father's wife, not since Billie was a sophomore in high school, a term he has no right to claim.

I don't have much to say, Angela continues. Margaret never sent me a script. But I can say with certainty that she'd have loved knowing all of you were here. She loved this place. The high desert up here spoke to her in a way I've never seen it do with any other researcher. She knew the land. It was a privilege to watch her skill at work, to see her uncovering so much that no one else would have noticed.

Billie glances at Rhiannon. Her sister's face unreadable. She sits in the folding chair beside Billie, leaned forward, her elbows on her knees.

But this ceremony isn't about me, Angela says. Rhiannon, Billie. Jim. Please feel free to say a few words.

Their father is the first to volunteer, a limelight Billie is sure he can't resist. I'm glad we can all be here together, he begins.

It's been so long since that was the case. Billie feels her palms curl around the seat of her chair, her knuckles tightening. As if it's her fault and not his that it's been so long. How they could have all been together in the prison's visiting center if he'd just come down from Chicago.

I'm glad we can do this, he says. For you, Billie. Since you couldn't be there.

Billie feels her teeth clench. Another dig. As if she hadn't wanted to be there. As if she hadn't pushed her palms against a prison-yard fence in the low March rain to press herself in the cardinal direction of home.

I felt it was important to be here, for all of us to be together for this. For you girls.

Girls. Billie closes her eyes. A word that meant something when they were small. A word that means nothing now, nearly as dismissive as *ladies.*

I've never been out here, he says, but I can tell by its light that it's a place your mother would have loved. She was always drawn to light. To life. To anything that lived.

Except you, Billie hears herself say.

Billie, Rhiannon warns.

This place was her life's work, their father continues. How special to be here all together, in a spot that meant so much to her.

Billie hears only that he's never been here in his life. That she's the only one. An easy excuse for Rhiannon, traveling always on a racing circuit. But her father, her mother's once-husband: it was his job to love what she loved. It was his job to know the chisels and dental picks she scraped across the earth, to know firsthand what it was to stand beneath shards of sunlight looking out across so many mountains and to uncover the first edge of bone that would become an entire skeleton, to know how it felt to stand here and see the age of so many rocks, a visual history, every mystery they held.

A jigsaw piece. *Paleontological puzzle.* Her mother's belief that this land held multiple disasters. Angela's words. Her mother resolute that across sixty-five million years so many bones might have undergone every ravage of flood and famine a population could take. The same as a marriage. Disaster. How her father's disinterest must have razed her mother. The same dismissal Billie always internalized from Tim.

Her trip here at fifteen only six years before she met him, how slim a window. She sits up in her folding chair and scans the ridgeline, mesas and mountains she barely remembers. Recalls only her mother showing her the process of excavation. How to detect bone. How to spot a fragment, the right shape and size. Tiny fossils. Crinoids. So small Billie never knew about the full-scale skeleton her mother discovered. No drills, no hammers. No boulder-size slabs of rock. Only a dental pick pulled from the pocket of her cargo pants and Billie crouching down to examine what her mother uncovered.

Fifteen, Billie sees now: just one year before her parents divorced.

She always sensed it threatened her father that her mother might know more about the world than he did. That she had a PhD, despite having the same blue-collar upbringing as him. The first complete stegosaur skeleton, what she and Rhiannon never knew. What Billie wonders now, watching her father drone on: whether he ever cared. If her mother brought her here at fifteen not because she saw Rhiannon take to racing and Billie take to nothing at all but because Billie was available, the one daughter she could show an entire world beyond the confines of a relationship, what a woman could do on her own and what Billie ignored, moving on to college and to a relationship that would break her.

How lucky we are to be here, her father is saying. To be where Margaret would have wanted us to be. To honor her in a way we couldn't before, all of us together now.

Stop, Billie says.

Billie, Rhiannon says again.

Her father keeps talking and Billie feels her hands leave the folding chair. Empty words masked as elegy. She won't take it. She stands and hears Rhiannon's chair scrape the gravel behind her but she is already crossing the fire ring through the smoke of so much sage and she is grabbing the urn with the same texture as the watering can in their Urbana backyard where her mother once grew poppies and she is pulling open the canister that carries nothing but pulverized rock and dirt and she is scattering what's inside across the edge of the ridgeline.

JONES, SHARMA. "MORRISON FORMATION." NORTH AMERICAN GEOLOGY OF PALEONTOLOGICAL SITES. ED. NICHOLAS RUFINA. SALT LAKE CITY: UNIVERSITY OF UTAH PRESS, 2012. 22–26. PRINT.

CALL NUMBER: QE170 .B18 2012

MORRISON FORMATION

The Morrison Formation is a widespread area of sedimentary rock that has proven most fertile in containing Jurassic period dinosaur bones. Spanning the states of Wyoming, Colorado, Kansas, Utah, New Mexico, Arizona, Montana, and Idaho, it covers approximately 600,000 square miles. Though a percentage of the formation has been excavated, 75 percent of its fossils are still buried within its layers of mudstone, sandstone, and limestone.

Significant sites of the Morrison Formation include Dinosaur National Monument in Utah, which contains over eight hundred paleontological dig sites; Cleveland-Lloyd Quarry in Utah, an alleged predator trap; and the Small Quarry of Colorado.

Many of the fossils found in the Morrison Formation are incomplete, but they nonetheless reveal telling evidence of the Jurassic period's flora and fauna. Much of the climate was dry, with fossilized vegetation found along former riverbeds. There is evidence of nesting as well, which suggests that the environment was suitable for long-term habitation rather than migratory patterns.

39.3228° N, 110.6895° W: Cleveland-Lloyd Quarry, UT

Rhiannon knows it's only rock. She's already buried her mother in the soft gray of central Illinois, drizzle pelting down on the sheltered tent beside a mud-slung grave. The rhythmic drip, a sound she wants to forget. The rain-damp cotton of her dress clinging to her skin. The weight of Aunt Sue's hand on her shoulder. Beth silent beside her. Her father speechless then and full of words now, here across so many state lines that have become hers and Billie's alone, a trip that leaves no space for their father and his hollow posturing around a fire ring that holds an empty urn that makes Rhiannon feel nothing at all. She knows it's just rock, pebbled gravel and the crimson rust of sandstone, her mother elsewhere deep inside the Midwestern land where she was born. But when Billie rips the canister open and scatters a cloud of ash that takes to the gaping valley Rhiannon rushes forward, her entire body encircling her sister from behind.

Nothing like embracing Billie awkwardly for the first time as she stepped away from the Correctional Center's curb. The empty canister limp in Billie's left hand, scars rippling down her forearm that Rhiannon feels. Billie trembling. Rage or devastation, Rhiannon can't tell. She feels through her sister's skin every ounce of regret for her absence from a March funeral and still Rhiannon wants to drag her to the ground, make her understand she's not the only one gutted by loss.

Rhiannon can take a bar fight. The joyride of a car across an empty highway.

She can't abide six states for a ceremony Billie has destroyed on impulse.

She feels Billie struggle against the wrench-locked grip of her arms, Rhiannon's mouth pressed to the back of Billie's sun-soaked shirt. Get the fuck off me, Billie whispers.

Get ahold of yourself, Rhiannon says, her mouth a line of teeth.

Get ahold of myself? There's nothing in this fucking container. There's nothing at all here to bury and we have to listen to him drone on like he gave two fucks about Mom or about us?

Not everything is about you.
No? Then who the fuck is this about?
Rhiannon lets her go and Billie pulls away and drops the urn. Rhiannon glances at Angela and Marcus, still sitting in their folding chairs, both looking at the ground. Rhiannon at once embarrassed. Her father standing beside his own chair, his eyes hard, the sage bundles smoking in the ring between all of them. The plastic canister rolls side to side in the ridgeline's wind, vacant and weighted with nothing.
You should be ashamed of yourself, their father says and Rhiannon knows he is speaking to Billie.
Billie raises her eyebrows. Should I?
They planned this for you. He motions toward Angela and Marcus. Your mother planned this for you. All of this, Billie. All of this is for you and your sister.
And we're all so glad you've made it about you.
Oh, I'm the one who made this about me?
You weren't invited. You're not supposed to be here.
What in hell is that supposed to mean?
It means why are you here, Dad? Billie shouts. Why the fuck are you here? Why do you think we care at all what you have to say about Mom? This was ours. You've never

even been out here. Not even once.

Rhiannon watches her father's mouth break into a crude laugh. You think you know everything? You know everything about your mother and me and what the hell went on between us? Let me tell you something. She didn't want me out here. She told me not to come, not even once. She said this space was hers and hers alone. But she wanted me here now. She said I should be here. She wanted me here for you girls.

Rhiannon glances at Angela and wants to ask if this is true, if Angela knows anything of who their mother asked to be here. If she ever spoke about why her own husband never visited Utah once and why it would matter to her if he visited now.

She never said anything about you being here for this, Billie says. Not when she gave me the journal. Not once when she came to visit in her last months.

She didn't want you to know. She said she wanted us all to find ourselves here, together again.

Billie smiles. Together again. A big happy family. Without her.

I can't speak for your mother. All I know is she wanted me here. She wanted all of us here on this land that meant something to her.

And how about Decatur? Rhiannon hears Billie say.

Rhiannon feels her jaw clench. Billie.

No, really, Dad. Was Decatur a space that was mine and mine alone, too?

Jesus, Billie, their father says. Not now.

Why not now? You made it all the way out here. Where the fuck were you then?

Rhiannon watches their father and despite Billie turning their mother's ceremony toward this, now of all moments, she finds herself curious: she wants to know. Wants to hear what her father could possibly say, beyond the excuses she's given Billie across six years for their father's absence. Being busy. Being out on the road. Being unsure of what to say. Rhiannon waits for him to speak and realizes she has no idea at all why their father never came beyond any excuse she could give Billie to make it right.

I'm telling you, he says. Drop it.

Oh, I assure you, I won't.

He looks at Billie. Fine. But you're not going to like it.

There's not much left to like about the last six years.

He keeps his eyes on Billie. Your mother told me not to come.

Billie laughs. You expect me to believe that? You weren't even married anymore. What difference would it make to her what you did or didn't do?

I don't care what you believe. It's the truth. Your mother told me not to visit you and I respected her wishes, just as I respected them by coming out here.

Why would she do that? Rhiannon blurts.

She knows her father. She knows by his voice that he isn't lying. He looks at Rhiannon, as if he's forgotten that she, too, is standing by the fire ring.

I don't know. Your mother had her preferences. And her secrets, as you good well know. I don't know why she didn't want me there. At the prison, or out here when she was working. But she didn't. He looks at Billie and runs a hand through his thinning hair. I figured maybe you told her you didn't want me there at the prison.

Who gives a fuck what anyone told you? Billie shouts and Rhiannon hears the hurt in her voice trying to be anything but hurt. Who cares what Mom told you to do, or what you thought I wanted you to do? I'm your daughter. You could've come. Regardless of what anyone told you to do or not do.

You think I didn't want to come?

She wasn't your wife anymore. What would it matter if she asked you not to come to see me? And now, all of a sudden, to come way the fuck out here? What about doing what you want?

Rhiannon speaks up. Stop. Please. Let's not do this right now.

Angela looks up and meets her eyes. Marcus keeps his gaze on the ground.

This isn't what she wanted, Rhiannon says. Please, let's just do what she wanted.

Their father nods. His fists balled and perched on his hips. He slides back and takes a seat in his folding chair and Rhiannon remains on the other side of the fire ring, waiting for Billie to move.

Billie, Angela says softly. Billie, you're welcome to say a few words.

Billie says nothing and stands firm beside the ridgeline, the urn rolling in the gravel, and Rhiannon feels her own rage drain away, replaced by nothing but a hollow in her chest. That they're here. The urn empty, carrying only rock but carrying something. That in the end, it doesn't matter who was where. Their mother is gone.

It is a miracle that Angela and Marcus still set up the post-ceremony reception. Rhiannon helps them pull food from their trailers' small refrigerators, Billie sitting outside at the edge of the picnic tables alone, surely readying to disappear into her own trailer. The only place on this entire quarry to be alone, a land that for once seems too open and vast. Rhiannon feels for her sister. That their mother kept something from her, too, for reasons Rhiannon can't understand. Even still she doesn't want to be near her.

While Marcus and her father set up the food, Rhiannon drifts to the parking lot and sits inside the only other solitary space she knows: the sealed shell of the Mustang, engine off, every window rolled up tight. The visitor center dark and unlit, the sun shifting west beyond its roof. She sits with her hands clenched to the wheel as if she were on the raceway, as if she were in control. She flexes her fingers against the sun-softened padding, a thin disc she's piloted across an entire country in the past week.

Rhiannon felt nothing watching the urn's rock blow in dusted sheets across the valley. Billie scattering its contents. The rest of the ceremony mechanical, nothing more. Rhiannon's own brief-whispered eulogy. *We love you, Mom.* The words hollow capsules. Everything inside of her spent. Her own grief numbed by the time March ended and pushed her from Beth's apartment back to her mother's home. Let Billie feel what she feels, the ceremony for her alone if Rhiannon's already felt everything she needs to feel.

Let Billie throw dust and rock.

Let Billie do whatever the fuck she wants.

The Mustang's door creaks open, a quick puncture in the sound-dampened womb of the car, and Rhiannon's father climbs into the passenger seat and closes the door behind him. He sits beside her, eyes forward, hands resting on his knees. Rhiannon doesn't look at him. Their positions beside each other reminiscent of so many years shuttling down so many highways. The Mustang immobile. Not windswept and throttling across open plains, not zipping along the yellow dash of a center line to outgun a thunderstorm developing in the black-clouded distance. Rhiannon listens to her father breathe. She doesn't move when he places a hand on her shoulder.

I'm sorry about that, he says. I'm sorry about all of it.

You have nothing to be sorry about. None of us do.

Rhiannon hears her words and knows she means Billie, despite everything.

I should've told you, he says. I should've

told you your mother wanted me out here, and that she didn't want me in Decatur at all.

You said you were going to Dacono.

I'm still going. Bryson's already there. I just made a detour along the way.

Rhiannon looks at him. Did she ever tell you why? Did Mom tell you why she didn't want you to see Billie for six whole years?

He shakes his head. Not really. For a long time, I thought she was protecting Billie. That Billie told her she didn't want me there. I can see now that's not the case. I don't know if your sister wanted me there or not, but it's clear she didn't know.

Neither of us did. I always thought you didn't want to see Billie that way.

I didn't. Did anyone? But I would've been there. I would've been there every week. I wrote letters sometimes, birthday cards. I threw them all away. I thought six years was nothing, that we could celebrate so many more birthdays once your sister got out. I wanted to respect what I thought wasn't just your mother's wishes but your sister's, too.

Rhiannon props her elbow against the driver's-side door and leans her head against her palm. She imagines Billie sitting across from her in the industrial furniture of the Correctional Center's visiting room, chairs and tables built in the 1970s, their mute-brown lining and split-pea upholstery matching the drabness of Billie's navy twill pants and cream starched shirt. The same uniform, the same furniture. Every single time. Through the windshield Rhiannon watches the sun wink above the quarry's visitor center and knows her own complicity, that she could've asked. Her sister always so guarded and so unflinching, so good at seeming like she didn't care that Rhiannon never thought to ask their father why he never came.

Why didn't Mom say anything to us about any of this? Rhiannon says. Why didn't she want you there?

I don't know. But I'm here now. Regardless of whether you and your sister want me to be here.

Billie didn't mean that. She's just upset.

Her father takes his hand off her shoulder and Rhiannon notices he's still wearing his wedding ring. I know what your sister's going through. She wasn't even there to say goodbye in March.

That doesn't mean you know what she's going through.

Look, I know I wasn't the best dad. At least to Billie. And I know I wasn't the best husband at all. But I loved your mother.

This isn't easy for any of us. And it matters to me that you and Billie know I'm here for you, always. Regardless of what you think.

Rhiannon can think of nothing to say in return. She knows this. Knows her father as a constant presence beside her in their family's garage, teaching her to read a tire's pressure, pointing out every fluid gauge beneath the car's hood: radiator, transmission, brake. Beside her on the road between raceways. Guiding her pit team, making split decisions. Her father always there, a pillar of her childhood and her career before its quick fade, so much that she forgot he sometimes wasn't there for Billie or her mother.

But he's here. Now. He's the only parent Billie has left.

Rhiannon pulls her head from her hands and looks at him. Did you drive because of the weather?

I'd have driven anyway. We always drive the circuits. You know that.

How's Bryson doing?

Probably running speed trials in Dacono right now. I drove separately to get down here. He's good. And I can tell he'll be great.

Rhiannon glances away. How's Chicago been? Is the airport closed there?

O'Hare was open when I left. Midway's

probably back open by now too.

Does all that worry you?

To be honest, not right now. I was more concerned about getting here on time. And you know me. I've never paid much attention to the weather, being on the ground all the time. Your mother was far more concerned about all that.

Rhiannon watches the sun sink at last beyond the windshield, the afternoon's breeze dying down beyond the car's windows. The valley visible just beyond the visitor center, the line of mesas shading lilac in the disappearing sun. *All of that.* An entire planet, what it hides in the strata of rock. Her mother always holding a hand to the pulse of the earth and her father here at last despite knowing nothing at all about weather or fossilized bone. What surely threatened him at one time, what her mother knew and he didn't. What Rhiannon herself doesn't know, what newscasters don't know, what broadcasters don't know across so many states of public radio affiliates. Rhiannon leans back. Forgets the weather. Forgets her mother's reasons for planning a ceremony this way, her father's arrival a secret. Forgets why her mother might have kept him from so many prison visits, Billie in the dark for six years. Forgets everything but the narrow view of her fingers stitched to the wheel, some small semblance of control.

When Rhiannon at last leaves the car and treks back with her father to the congregation of trailers, the sun is nothing but a whisper of thinly lit clouds. Billie sits beside Marcus in the same folding chairs pulled from the ceremony's fire ring to the reception. This postfuneral party: a new cluster of trays and platters spread across the picnic table. Deviled eggs. Olives and cheese. A serving dish of pink shrimp and cocktail sauce. Fancy finger foods Rhiannon has no idea how Angela got here and when, the nearest grocery store at least thirty miles away. Angela crouches beside the picnic table pouring bagged ice into a cooler filled with beer and bottles of white wine.

She looks up when Rhiannon approaches. You want something to drink?

Rhiannon takes the beer Angela hands her. A Uinta pale ale, the same beer she and Billie drank in Moab only two nights before, what feels like years ago. Rhiannon bottle-opens the cap and stays planted in the dirt beside Angela, a stranger to them until yesterday, a woman who planned an entire funeral for two people she's never met.

How are you doing? Angela asks.

Fine, Rhiannon whispers. I think we're all fine.

Angela sighs. Look, I know the ceremony was hard. I know it feels like there was nothing in that urn. But maybe this will help. This isn't the place or time to get scientific, but the land here is part of the Morrison Formation. The same swatch that contained the stegosaurus skeleton your mother found in Colorado. I thought you should know that you two scattered rock that meant something to your mother.

Rhiannon glances at Billie across the clearing. Rock her sister scattered, no one else. She won't tell Billie, even out of spite, that the urn she spilled held the sediment of her mother's entire career. Her father approaches the picnic table and Rhiannon watches as Billie stands and makes her way toward him. Rhiannon traps her breath tight inside her lungs but Billie only extends her hand and briefly holds their father's hand and Rhiannon knows the word *sorry* will never find its way from Billie's throat and that this will have to do, this brief point of contact before Billie pulls her hand away. Rhiannon doesn't wait to see if Billie will look her way, too, if she will offer another apology. Rhiannon wants none of it. Not now.

Come on, Angela finally says. Food's ready.

Rhiannon grabs a paper plate. Keeps her eyes on the platters scattered across the picnic table. Blue-cheese olives. Mushroom puff pastries. Toothpicked gouda and butter-knifed brie. A final celebration in the center of a landscape none of them will have any reason to visit again. Their mother's legacy left behind, fragments of bones gathering dust inside a visitor center. A set of fossils that could bury themselves again beneath wildfires and dust storms, the same tempest of flooding or drought that tidal-waved across a landscape sixty-five million years ago. Leaving mystery. Leaving nothing. The same disasters of climate now, removing all evidence of anything they ever did. Talent and accomplishment. If it matters at all. If in the wide span of geologic time anyone will care if Rhiannon raced or didn't race. Her mother buried in Illinois. Folded back into the soil of the state where she was born despite everything she achieved. The taste of beer bitter in the back of Rhiannon's throat as she fills her paper plate. Debris falling from the sky. So many black boxes. Just like the unreadable orientation of so many bones out here. A predator trap. Horizontal bones. Vertical bones. None of them matching, none of them indicating anything at all. Flood or famine. Poison. Drought or turbulence. Rhiannon wonders if it matters. Regardless of stegosaurus plates attracting mates or sensing danger, every single one still perished in the end. She watches the ghosted sun marble the clouds against the jagged line of mesas and sees nothing but the scattered jigsaw of an impossible puzzle, nothing but an earth ready and waiting, always, to claim every one of them.

After the reception and after she's helped Angela clear the table, Rhiannon watches Billie recede to their trailer. Their father stays seated at the empty picnic bench, the only light the blinked-on bulbs gracing the front steps of each trailer. The night sky speckled with stars. The afternoon's winds diminished to the faint pulse of a breeze blowing up from the valley, what feels like an intermittent hand against Rhiannon's skin.

She sits down beside her father. Both of them look out across the valley.

You doing okay?

He nods. As good as can be expected.

That turned out all right. Better than I'd have thought.

Nobody punched anyone. No one stole any cars. A civil reception.

How long are you staying?

Leaving tomorrow. I need to get back to Dacono. You girls?

We don't know. Maybe tomorrow.

Any more plot points on your mother's journey?

Rhiannon leans back against the picnic table. We didn't even look. But I'm guessing we're heading home. Billie's got to be back within two weeks for mandatory check-in, and I can't get any more time off work.

Her father glances at her. How's it going? The job?

It's not awful.

Not too late for you to get back out on the road.

That's one thing you and Billie agree on. She said the same thing.

She's right. You could still race.

Rhiannon watches the dark wash of the valley so she won't have to look at him.

I know you miss it, he says. You don't have to say so. I can see it in your face.

Rhiannon thinks of Beth's voice on Marcus's cell phone, her knees stiff from crouching in the shade of the trailer's hot-metal siding.

How did you manage a career like that while you were married? she asks. How did you make it work to be out on the road, doing what you loved?

I really didn't, did I? Your mother got tired of it. But she was traveling too, always out here where she didn't want me to be.

Is that why you got divorced?

It's as much my fault as hers. I was gone a lot. We both were.

Rhiannon thinks of Beth's lithographs. Her show this September in Detroit. That should've made your relationship stronger, she says. Right? That you both actually did something you loved.

There's more to it than that.

Like what?

Your mother and I came from different worlds. Her father sighs and gestures toward the darkened valley. Look at this place. She was far more worldly. She knew so much more about everything.

I don't think that matters.

Oh, you don't? Try going to faculty parties for twenty years. See who will talk to you if you don't have a formal college education.

Rhiannon smiles despite herself. I don't

know if Beth's art friends ever even knew I raced. I don't know what they would have thought.

Yeah, but come on. It's not like anyone ever looked down on you.

Rhiannon looks at him. How would you know?

Her father leans forward on his knees. Goddammit, Rhee. You were good. You were so fucking good. There was no reason at all for you to give it up.

The picnic table's wood is cool against Rhiannon's back and she thinks of the gas station attendant in Colorado, a boy who recognized her, how many more people might have if she'd just stuck with it. If it mattered whether they did. If it mattered more whether she could have said herself that she was proud of everything she'd done.

Dad, Rhiannon whispers.

He says nothing beside her.

Dad, I don't know what the fuck I'm doing with my life.

The valley is an ocean of darkness beyond the picnic table, every mesa disappeared to an expanse of black. No rush of cars. No distant highway. No cricket hum, no cicada drone. Nothing but the spackling of constellations, a paintbrush smear of the Milky Way faint above them. A sky like nothing Rhiannon has ever seen in the Midwest, overwhelming as her father reaches over and takes her hand.

You know what you're doing, he says. You don't think you do. But you know.

Rhiannon doesn't want to tell him that she doesn't. That she feels nothing out here but an ending. She imagines the dust and rock Billie threw across the ridgeline settling somewhere down in the sandstone bed of the valley, a valley her mother surely knew like the short lifelines of her own palms.

After her father disappears into his trailer, Rhiannon sits on the picnic bench alone. The thought of returning to her and Billie's trailer still too raw, a dim square of light through the small bedroom's window letting Rhiannon know Billie is still awake. The same in Angela's kitchen window: a thank-you Rhiannon knows she needs to extend. Rhiannon leans her palms into her knees and stands. The lights in Marcus's trailer gone dark. She will remember to thank him tomorrow.

When she knocks, Angela opens the door.

Come in, she says. Was just wrapping up for the night.

Rhiannon steps inside and sees Angela's

computer and a scattering of notes spread across the small kitchen table. Continued fieldwork. Of course. What Rhiannon realizes Angela has set aside for the entire day to accommodate their mother's wishes. She sits down at the table and Angela gathers the documents into a pile and shuts her laptop.

Want anything? Tea?

Rhiannon shakes her head. I'm good.

Hanging in there?

Look, I'm sorry about what happened today.

No need. Funerals are messy.

I think Billie's having a harder time than she'd ever admit.

And what about you?

Rhiannon looks up. I just wanted to thank you.

Really, it was no trouble at all.

I can see it was. Rhiannon gestures toward the stacks of paper and Angela's closed computer. I know even two days off can be tough if you're in the middle of work.

Your mother told me you were a driver. And now what? Textbooks?

Rhiannon wants to ignore the question. I guess I just gave up.

Angela surprises Rhiannon by laughing. Tell me about it. Try being a woman in paleontology. All these male scientists getting their feathers ruffled at every little challenge to their work. And a black woman on top of that? Forget it. You know how many times I thought about giving up? You know how many times I've been mistaken as someone's assistant?

I got that too sometimes. Maybe not the same as you. But it's easier selling textbooks. The world doesn't expect much more from me.

Oh, come on. That's too easy. You don't actually believe that.

Rhiannon meets her eyes. Despite Angela's warmth, Rhiannon sees she isn't afraid to push.

It was so hard being a woman in that field, Rhiannon says.

I know, Angela says. But you go after it. Everything else is just noise.

Rhiannon watches her. How do you know what you want?

You just know. Or else you know what you don't want. It sounds like textbooks aren't what you want.

They're nothing like being on the road. Rhiannon waves a hand around the trailer's interior. Or being way out here. You must be energized out here, all of the time.

It's hard work. There are days I hate it,

every last shred of it. Especially the conundrum of what happened here. It baffles me to exhaustion sometimes, when I'm here in the summer and when I'm back in Salt Lake City.

But you love it.

Angela levels her eyes at Rhiannon. Yes. I do.

Did my mother? Did she really love what she did?

It's an unfair question, she knows. A stupid question. Rhiannon already knows the answer in having observed her mother for so many years despite the ways she kept her profession separate from her home. And these highways and coordinates: the precision their mother put into letting them finally see this lifelong love. The gleam of a Kansas riverbed. The ascent of sandstone trails. The tornado-swirl of bats lifting from a cave. Southern Utah sun, buttes and red-rock formations. A landscape devoted to John Wayne and European explorers and the myth of cowboys and men. A land their mother studied but never tried to own. The same as Angela. The same as Beth: landscape art. Midwestern lithographs. The Spiral Jetty, what Rhiannon still doesn't know if Beth has ever seen. Billie's birds. Work in tandem with the earth, even if the earth could take everything from them completely.

Yes, Angela says. I've never seen anyone more in love with what they did.

Rhiannon wonders if Angela is embellishing for her sake. She guesses Angela's passion matches what her mother carried across her life, digging out here side by side as if nothing else mattered. Rhiannon feels her lungs falter, Angela's words a slow blow that halts her breath: she wonders if anyone could ever tell just by looking at her what it was that she loved. The raceway. The road. A thought that buries her with grief, the first wave of sorrow she's felt all day. Not the sage smoke of a fire ring. Not makeshift ashes thrown in frustration across a valley. Only that someone could so easily tell that her mother loved what she did and that Rhiannon knows without Angela having to say anything at all that the same isn't true for her: that no one can tell just by looking at her what she does or does not love.

GARCIA, BUD. A BEGINNER'S GUIDE TO FALCONRY. COLUMBIA: UNIVERSITY OF MISSOURI PRESS, 1990. 25–29. PRINT.

CALL NUMBER: SK322 .Q2 1990

BEGINNING FALCONRY EQUIPMENT

Beyond adequate weathering pens and mews for falcon housing, as well as a proper diet of quail, rats, mice, chicks, and rabbit for high, medium, and low caloric value, birds of prey require a standard set of equipment for beginning falconers.

Scales maintain a hawk's flying weight, which must be measured every twenty-four hours. All hawks require perches, and broadwing birds such as red-tailed hawks require a rubber-topped bow perch that can be staked into the ground. A leash secures the hawk from the bow perch to the falconer's glove. To tether a hawk to the glove, a set of jesses is affixed directly to a hawk's legs and unlatched when the hawk is released for flying.

To train a hawk to grow comfortable leaving the glove, a falconer needs a creance, a spool-like lure that will grow gradually longer as the hawk grows accustomed to flying longer distances. A lure is also necessary, with food attached to a dummy bunny to train the hawk to hunt. The creance and lure are required for use until the hawk is comfortable hunting on its own, and so the hawk does not get lost.

Because hawks often do get lost at least once for every beginning falconer, bells strapped to the hawk's jesses are advised, as is a system of telemetry. A small transmitter is affixed to the hawk, and the falconer keeps an aerial. Through signaling between the transmitter and the aerial, hawk and falconer may find their way back to each other if the hawk is lost.

39.3228° N, 110.6895° W: Cleveland-Lloyd Quarry, UT

Billie stirs in the sun-warmed sheets of the trailer, daylight slatting through the blinds of the bedroom's lone window. Rhiannon sleeps beside her, turned away. Billie's eyes half crusted, a hard night past a harder day. Stolen car. A funeral. Scattered rock. Her father. And that her mother kept him from her for six years: inexplicable. She doesn't remember falling asleep or hearing Rhiannon come in. She sits up and rubs the scabbed sleep from her eyes and creeps beyond the bedroom. She thinks to make coffee and doesn't, her mouth cotton dry from taking too many beers from the cooler at the ceremony. She grabs a water glass instead and through the window above the rush of the kitchen sink watches a swelling disc of sun crest above the valley. She sets down the glass. Watches the light splinter across the jagged curves of each mesa and define their peaks. It steals her breath. A land so wide it almost makes her afraid beyond the closed space of a correctional center bunk bed, a communal cafeteria, the poplar tree line of a prison yard. If nothing else, she has seen sun-dusted rivers, a swirl of bats. She has seen the remnants of red dust on her sneakers and it is something.

The bedroom door creaks behind her and Rhiannon squints out against the sunrise filtering through the kitchen window.

Morning, Billie says.

Rhiannon disappears into the bathroom. Billie doesn't want coffee but knows Rhiannon will. She rummages in the cabinets until she finds a bag of grounds and fills the coffee maker, its staccato drip echoing through the trailer when Rhiannon reemerges.

Hungry? Billie asks.

Rhiannon sits at the kitchen table and rubs her face. Not really.

You want coffee?

Rhiannon glances at the coffee maker. I guess.

Billie sits across from her. You want to ignore me for the rest of this trip?

It's kind of early for a fight.

I'm not fighting with you.

I don't know what you want from me, Billie. I've done everything I can for you.

Billie holds her tongue, the disappointment in her sister's voice nearly unbearable.

I picked you up, Rhiannon says. Drove you out here. Paid your way, your motel rooms, your meals. I barely balked when you took my car for an ill-advised joyride. But the funeral? Come on. Be better. You can do better than that.

Billie sighs. There wasn't even anything in that urn.

Who cares?

I fucking care.

The coffee maker growls a prolonged groan, the pot finished, and Billie gets up and fills a mug and slides it across the table's chipped veneer.

Rhiannon cradles the cup. We knew coming into this that there'd be nothing here. Nothing to bury. It's the ceremony that counts. It's what Mom wanted for you.

Billie plants her fingers on the table so her voice won't waver. No, what Mom wanted was for me to be at her funeral in March.

There's nothing you can do about that.

And fuck, how I wish there was.

Rhiannon lets out a long breath. Is that what this is about?

I don't know. Fuck, Rhee. I don't know.

Then what, Billie? Figure it out. You can't just go around for the rest of your life doing whatever the fuck you feel like doing.

What, because you didn't?

What the hell is that supposed to mean?

Billie shakes her head. Doesn't want to start a fight. Doesn't want to rip another chasm wide open between herself and someone else.

It means nothing, she says. It means it's hard enough knowing just how badly I fucked all this up by not being there for the real thing. On top of Dad being here. On top of him saying Mom kept him from visiting me for six goddamn years. Jesus, Rhee. Six years. I don't know how to feel about either of them right now. Give me some fucking slack. None of this makes any sense.

Rhiannon nods. I know.

Why would she do that? Why keep him from me? Why keep him from me for six years only to have him come now, at the worst possible time?

Or the best. Maybe she thought you'd need him the most right now.

Billie looks up and feels the urge to say what's gridlocked beneath her tongue: that it's Rhiannon she needs right now. Rhiannon the most. A sister who's barely spoken to her since she threw an urn of rock and gravel across a valley and Billie wonders only here in the trailer whether this second funeral means more to Rhiannon than she let on. Whether a proper goodbye in an Illinois cemetery was no fail-safe at all.

How are you doing? Billie asks.

So good of you to ask.

I mean it. Are you okay?

Honestly, I feel nothing.

I heard you talking to Beth yesterday. Is everything okay?

Rhiannon sighs. This has nothing to do with Beth.

Then what does it have to do with?

I don't know. I just know I'm ready to go home.

Look, I'm sorry. Rhiannon. I'm sorry I did what I did.

I know.

The rising sun filters light across the table and Billie hears the fight drain from her sister's voice.

I meant to be better, Billie says. To do what Mom wanted us to do out here. But it's just too much. That guy in Colorado Springs. The hawk feather Mom left me. This place. This place that meant so much to her. And now Dad being here. It's just too much.

I know.

When's he heading back?

This morning. He's heading up to

Dacono.

And us?

I don't know. I'm ready to leave as soon as you are.

Billie stands. Retrieves her daypack from the trailer's bedroom. Tries to remember what day it is: Sunday morning. She's nearly lost track. She hasn't opened their mother's journal since they arrived at the quarry. She pulls the journal from the daypack and brings it back to the kitchen table.

This has to be it, Rhiannon says. We made good time, considering. We have until this coming Saturday to get back. At this point, I'm fine with heading home early.

Billie thumbs through the journal's pages to the last one they opened. The allosaurus: what stood in the visitor center and marked their arrival to the Cleveland-Lloyd Quarry's coordinates. What led them here to Angela and Marcus. To their father. Billie turns the page and half anticipates a blank sheet of paper, the journal at its end. What she sees instead is an image that briefly stops her breath, that there's any image at all.

An oval. Almost rectangular in shape. She hears Rhiannon set down her mug. And beside the drawn oval: another coordinate scrawled in the corner of the page.

Fuck, Rhiannon whispers.

What do you think this is?

It looks like a racetrack. It better not be. Dacono is the nearest one. We better not be heading there with Dad.

Billie thinks of the locket meant for both of them. The laser pointer and the tail bone for both of them. But not the hawk feather. Just for Billie. This oval, if it's a raceway, just for Rhiannon. Billie watches her sister but Rhiannon's face is impassive.

Well, we have time, Billie says. Mom must have known we'd budget our time well.

Flip the page. Come on, Billie. Just look ahead. The funeral's over. I want to know if that's it. If this is the last coordinate we have to find.

We can't do that. I promised. She wanted us to not know where we're heading. She knew how much time we'd have. She knew we'd have to get back. This has to be the last one.

You're not the one driving, Billie. I'm fucking tired. I'm ready to go home.

It's Sunday. We've only been out a little more than a week. We have time. Come on, Rhee. What do you have to rush back home for? Isn't this better than your job?

Beth wants to meet up when we get back. She wants to talk.

I'm sure she'll still be willing to talk on Saturday.

Rhiannon grips her fingers around the perimeter of her mug and Billie can see them clench, the only outward flinching Rhiannon reveals.

Fine, she finally says. Fine, we can go. But I mean it, Billie. This has to be it.

Billie showers first and packs her bag. Strips the bed, cleans the kitchen sink, places their washed dishes in the drying rack. While Rhiannon showers Billie steps outside to stretch her legs before another day in the car. Not even eight o'clock and the sun pulses down in thin waves of heat. June in Utah. The first official day of summer, Billie realizes.

The picnic table is deserted, each trailer in the cluster quiet and closed. In the bright morning sun Billie can't tell if there are lights on inside any of them. Their father. Dacono. A racetrack she's heard Rhiannon talk about before, a speedway she's never seen. On impulse Billie crosses the gravel clearing and knocks softly on her father's door.

She expects to wake him but he pulls open the door fully dressed. Blue-faded jeans and a plain white T-shirt. The scent of coffee. The trailer's space immaculate and clean behind him, ready for leaving.

What time do you have to be in Dacono?

Midafternoon. Races begin tomorrow. Come on in.

She slides past him through the trailer door and sits on a thinly upholstered loveseat beside the kitchen sink. He offers her coffee and the cobwebbed dehydration in her throat has diminished just enough that she accepts.

He sits on a folding chair across from her. When are you two taking off?

This morning. As soon as Rhiannon's ready. I just wanted to let you know.

You heading back home?

She thinks to mention their mother's drawn oval, the possibility of a racetrack, the slim chance that they're headed to Colorado too. But she says nothing. Wants this trip to stay between her and her sister.

Eventually. I guess Mom has at least one more plot point for us to visit.

Her father looks up. Where you headed?

We don't know. I'll map the coordinate once we get in the car. We have to be back regardless by this coming Sunday.

Probation?

Mandatory therapy starts as soon as I return.

You heading through St. Louis on your

way back?

Billie reclines into the loveseat. Rhiannon told you about the ring.

I don't need it anymore. It's yours. Clearly your mother left it for you both. I just want to make sure someone keeps it safe.

We will. I promise, we'll take care of it.

Rhiannon said you're picking it up from Tim's brother.

Billie hears the caution in his voice. Dad, we'll be fine.

Just want to be sure it's all right for you to see him.

Billie stops herself from spewing something smart. Meaning what?

Her father hesitates. Meaning I was up all night. I couldn't sleep. I was wondering why in hell your mother never wanted me to come visit you, since you clearly didn't know she told me not to. And all I can think is that she thought it'd hurt you to be around me. Around anyone who could've done better by you. Maybe around men at all.

Billie doesn't look at him. Holds her coffee mug, its temperature matching the rising heat in her chest. Birds and trees. The Illinois woods. Her father maddening but also perceptive, able to hear the chatter of chickadee calls high in the trees. She sits still. Imagines her mother telling her father not to come, the possibility that she meant protection instead of pain, a mother bear instinct. What she never told her mother. What she never told anyone. What her mother must have intuited anyway, trained to dowse fossils from the earth and the worst of secrets from her own daughter. Billie closes her eyes against what she knows her father is readying to say.

Billie, did he hurt you?

She keeps her eyes closed. Nice of you to care about this now.

I mean it, Billie. Did he hurt you?

She opens her eyes and her father is leaning forward in his chair.

Tim, he says. Is he the reason you did what you did?

Billie says nothing, her silence the only admission her father needs. He sits back and exhales hard and Billie hears the wind of his breath pushed from his lungs.

What did he do to you?

It was a long time ago. There's nothing anyone could've done.

Bullshit, Billie. What did he do?

You want me to talk about this now? Now and not six years ago? It doesn't matter anymore. All that matters is that I had a reason. That should be good enough for you. Since nothing else is.

What's that supposed to mean?

It means I know you didn't visit because you were ashamed of me. You and Mom both, you've always been ashamed of me.

How can you say that?

Billie doesn't stop herself, this flood of words. I can't do what you do, she says. I can't do what Mom did. I'll never do what Rhiannon did.

You think we care about that? That we care at all about what you do or don't achieve? God, Billie, we just want you to be happy. And being in prison sure isn't a way to make yourself happy.

Like I planned it that way. Like anyone does. Things happen. You meet terrible people. You let them tell you what you are.

Just tell me what he did, Billie.

Why? So you can find him and beat him up? Jesus, Dad. This isn't about him. This is about me. This is about me and what he did to me.

Why didn't you tell us?

Billie meets his eyes. Why didn't you come for six fucking years?

For the first time since his arrival at the quarry, despite everything, her father's eyes rim red.

I'm so sorry, Billie.

I needed you.

The shock of these words falling from her tongue. She lets herself say them.

Her father places his head in his hands, and despite everything, Billie wants to apologize. For the ceremony. For the rock-strewn urn. That she still carries a rage that makes her want to destroy everything around her to avoid feeling destroyed. Her father imperfect, head bent, the sheen of his scalp visible through so many thin strands of gray hair. Billie watches him and something falls away in the pit of her stomach, how easy it is to aim her anger at him so she won't have to think about anything else. Despite his shortcomings. Despite never visiting, a lack that might always ache. She watches him and knows that her anger with him is nothing compared to the heavy weight of what she's dragged around a prison cell for six years and across so many highways to this place, this moment: that in the end she is most disappointed in herself, no one else.

You did the best you could, she says.

I can do better. If you'll let me.

He glances up and Billie knows he means when they're back home, Chicago and Urbana only hours apart, a clouded future Billie can't imagine from the quarry's heat.

She knows he means a spool of years unraveling before them and Billie doesn't know what they hold, doesn't even know where the afternoon will take them from a scrawled coordinate on a notebook page. But she looks at him and nods and it feels like something, the same something of Utah's light breaking across the desert rock.

Rhiannon is waiting at the picnic table when Billie steps from their father's trailer. Showered. Her hair nearly dry, their suitcases gone. Already situated in the Mustang's trunk, Billie guesses. Her daypack the only remaining piece of luggage at Rhiannon's feet, what holds the journal and the GPS and the afternoon's coordinates.

Their father emerges and embraces Rhiannon. Sleep all right?

Rhiannon nods. You heading out too?

It's a seven-hour drive to Dacono. I better get on the road.

The door to Angela's trailer squeaks open and she treads down the small set of steps fully dressed. She approaches the picnic table and hugs Rhiannon and a flood of gratitude washes through Billie for everything this woman has done for them.

Heading out? Angela asks.

Rhiannon nods. Our mother left us one

last coordinate.

Angela glances at Billie and pulls her into a hug. I told you she was full of surprises.

Thank you, Billie whispers into Angela's shirt. Thank you for everything.

Billie pulls back and lets herself glance at the valley beyond the picnic table, a view her mother once awoke to every day she was here. Trails and precipices. A view Billie's grown accustomed to across only a span of two days. One she wonders if she'll ever see again once she and Rhiannon drive away.

Marcus descends from his trailer's steps and stands off to the side of the picnic table, his hands in the pockets of his cargo shorts. It was a pleasure to meet all of you, he says. And truly, it was an honor to know your mother.

You take care of yourself, Rhiannon says. And thanks again for everything.

Billie seconds her sister's words, these two responsible for every detail of the ceremony and reception. Billie feels her heart pooling, a wave of sadness for what two strangers have done to soften their grief.

You all drive safe, Marcus says. And please do keep in touch.

Agreed, Angela says. You're welcome back here anytime.

They walk together along the gravel path

to the visitor center where Marcus heads to reopen the doors for the earliest nine o'clock patrons. Once they reach the visitor center, Billie watches her father throw his backpack into the trunk of an old-model Dodge Charger, less flashy than Rhiannon's Mustang but still capable of speed. Angela and Marcus wave their final farewells and disappear into the visitor center, Billie assumes to leave the three of them alone for their own goodbyes. Rhiannon embraces her father one last time and disappears into the driver's side of the Mustang where Billie can see her situating her smartphone and its digital map. Her goodbye casual. The nonchalance of knowing she'll see their father again: so many years of regular visits between them. He stands beside his driver's-side door and reaches out his hand.

I'll see you soon.

His voice firm to let Billie know he means it this time.

Billie lets herself take his hand and he draws her into a hug. She doesn't pull away until she hears the rev of the Mustang's engine behind her, Rhiannon telling her it's time. Billie climbs into the car and glances toward the ridgeline behind the visitor center. A place of heartbreak. Multiple disasters, her mother believed. Tim. Prison.

Losing her father for six years. Losing her mother forever. Rhiannon steers the car away from the quarry and down the long gravel drive and Billie sinks into the passenger seat, their father's car following behind them.

Looks like you two made up, Rhiannon says.

Billie watches the visitor center recede in the side mirror.

Could you map the coordinate on the GPS? Rhiannon asks. I can recalibrate the map on my phone when we're back in range on the highway.

Billie pulls the GPS from her daypack. Opens the journal again. Plugs in the coordinates. Eyes the oval drawn across the center of its page.

North, Billie says. Looks like we're heading north this time instead of south.

How far? And where?

Not sure yet, but looks like it's about a three-hour drive.

Salt Lake City.

How do you know?

Rhiannon smiles. Come on, Billie.

Her sister has memorized America's highways and every one of its racetracks and they are headed to Salt Lake City, not Dacono as they thought. When they reach the end of the quarry's gravel road for the beginning of a paved two-lane highway, Rhiannon steers the car north and Billie watches their father's car turn south, his hand waving in the Mustang's side mirror.

He's taking I-70, Rhiannon says. South and straight across Utah to Colorado.

And what are we taking?

You tell me. What does the GPS say?

Billie squints at the console. Highway 191 then I-15 all the way north.

Salt Lake City. I told you.

Is there a racetrack there?

Rocky Mountain Raceways. A smaller track. I've done minor circuits there before. They have a drag strip, but also an oval series.

An oval series. Billie barely knows what this means but it's a clear match for the drawing in the journal. Salt Lake a city she's barely thought about from the flatlands of the Midwest. A city far bigger than Carlsbad or Cañon City or any other destination their mother has led them beyond St. Louis, a city Billie maps as their father disappears in the rearview mirror, the dim taillights of his Charger fading south.

Rhiannon keeps the radio on as they travel north, ranges of mountains rising along both sides of the highway. Peaks Billie remembers as still snowcapped in mid-March when she flew into Salt Lake City in high school, now razored and burnt brown beneath a diffuse June sky. Summer solstice. Talk news cuts in and out across waves of static as the highway winds through mountain passes, roller-coaster curves and sloped switchbacks that carry them through the ranges. A local NPR host intones what they've missed while at the quarry: the FAA has officially designated the Frontier airline crash between Los Angeles and Houston as weather related, the black box indicating no pilot error and no storm but only clear-air turbulence, the worst and most unexpected kind. The same as four of the other crashes. The investigation nearly complete in Arizona, a scale of funerals Billie can't begin to imagine. One hundred twenty-six passengers. Incomprehensible beyond the single funeral she and Rhiannon have attended. The weather calm in Utah except for occasional gusts of wind across the morning, nothing like the wildfire in Colorado or the thunderstorm in Missouri or the onset of monsoons the radio's now reporting across central India, far earlier and heavier than any other year, and the beginning of hurricane season across the eastern seaboard expected to be the most intense on record. Billie watches the mountains rise in the distance beyond the car and listens to the broadcaster announce that every U.S. airport has reopened.

That seems unwise, Billie says.

What do you expect them to do, suspend all flights forever?

If it's dangerous, no one needs to fly. We all made it out here in cars.

We did. But Dad and I are used to highways. And you and I have two full weeks.

Rhiannon turns off the radio and Billie presses her hand against the window, already sun-warmed before noon.

I'm starving, Billie says. We forgot to eat breakfast.

We can stop for lunch as soon as we arrive in Salt Lake City. It isn't far. Your choice. Anything you want before we find this coordinate.

The two-lane highway widens as they approach and pass through Provo, more lanes and cars than Billie has seen since they wound through Albuquerque. Midmorning traffic, a flow of sedans and semis that only grows as Provo blends into the sprawl of southern Salt Lake suburbs, a flattened valley gridded with streets and surrounded on all sides by mountains. When the rising buildings of Salt Lake City's downtown appear against the foothills of the Wasatch, a range Billie remembers, she notices the sheen dome of the Capitol building and the arched spires of the Salt Lake Temple, what looked like an ice castle from the plane when she flew in at fifteen. Rhiannon decelerates and pulls off the highway and glides into the city's central corridor, the GPS inching closer and closer to their coordinate and destination.

What kind of food do you feel like? Rhiannon says.

Not bar food. No hot dogs or burgers.

Billie eyes the buildings beyond the windows as they travel down the widest road she's ever seen. She spots a sign for a restaurant called Himalayan Kitchen.

There, Billie says. God, I haven't had Indian food in years.

Inside the restaurant, Billie expects a thin crowd, near noon on a Sunday in one of the most devout cities in the country. But the tables are packed with fine linens and tablecloths and people dressed in skirts and khakis and Billie feels out of place in her hiking shorts and T-shirt. Rhiannon follows the host to a window booth and Billie situates herself across the table from her sister.

I forgot how massive the streets here are,

Billie mumbles. To turn oxcarts, right? When Brigham Young first settled the city.

Rhiannon peruses the menu. You'd know better than me. What are you ordering?

Billie scans the menu and wants everything on it. Chana masala, she finally says. And the Himalayan vegetable platter to start, if you're game. And a mango lassi.

Rhiannon rolls her eyes but when the server comes, she orders everything Billie wants, plus coconut curry for herself. Billie watches her sister unfurl her napkin and feels the air still stiff between them despite the morning's drive.

How's Beth? Did it feel good to talk to her yesterday?

It did. Not that I have to tell you. I think you heard everything.

I wasn't eavesdropping. I barely heard what you were talking about.

The server brings Billie's drink and Rhiannon glances out the booth's window. We talked about racing. Just for a bit. But it's the most we've ever talked about it across our entire relationship.

And what did she say?

Rhiannon sighs. That I've been too shut off. That I should've talked about it long before this.

I could have told you that.

Thanks, Billie. That's a helpful thing to say.

I just mean you should talk more about what's bothering you. With everyone.

Rhiannon stays silent and Billie sets down her glass, condensation already building against the cold of the creamed mango, the afternoon's heat pushing into the restaurant as the server sets their platter of appetizers on the table.

How are you feeling? Rhiannon grabs a pakora from the plate. About Dad.

I told him about Tim this morning. About what happened. He guessed. I couldn't make myself lie.

That's good. And?

And he thinks that's why Mom told him not to come. I never told her what Tim did but she must have figured it out. He thinks she was protecting me.

Rhiannon leans back in the booth. Do you believe that?

I don't know what to believe. Nothing else makes sense.

Rhiannon nods. I'll be honest, that sounds extreme. But Mom had her reasons, clearly for everything. I always just assumed Dad was busy. Distracted. I'm sorry, Billie. I didn't even think to ask him, or ask how you felt that he didn't visit.

I don't know if I would have told you anyway.

Then that makes two of us. Rhiannon eyes her. And anyway, I was distracted too. I never guessed Dad not visiting had anything at all to do with Mom.

Well, whatever the reason, I'm ready to move on.

Are you?

Dad's not perfect. You said so yourself. But at least he's trying now.

Rhiannon watches a gridlock of cars stop and start along the boulevard with each stoplight.

What about you? Billie tries again. How are you feeling?

Fine. I'm feeling fine.

Billie hesitates. How will you feel if this oval's a racetrack?

Rhiannon doesn't look at her. I don't know, Billie. I don't know how I'll feel. Like I said, I don't really want to be on the road anymore. I thought the quarry was it. But I'm here. I'm here because Mom obviously still wants us to be here.

Why do you think there's more? Why not just end at the quarry?

What, you think I know? After hearing yesterday that Mom kept Dad from visiting you, I don't know anything anymore. I don't know what she wants from us. I don't know what a laser pointer means or a locket or a wedding ring. I'm tired, Billie. I don't want to think about any of this anymore.

Billie doesn't push any further. Are you seeing Beth when you get back?

I guess. I don't know where we go from here. God, breakups are so messy. Do I move back in with her if she wants me to? Do I stay in the house forever, unpacking boxes and feeling sorry for myself? Both feel like moving backward. And I don't even know if she's interested in being with me anymore.

And are you? Interested in being with her?

Rhiannon finally looks at her. I think so. I think I always was. I just fucked it up by not wanting anything else I have in Champaign.

Don't you think that's understandable?

Beth probably doesn't think it is. I jerked her around for so many years.

She probably doesn't see it that way. It sounds like she wants to see you when you get back. Rhee, you'll figure it out. Beth. And everything else.

Everything else. Rhiannon smiles. Like finding another job? Champaign's such a small town. I hate that I can see why you might not want to stay there. There's nothing there anymore. Jesus, Billie. I thought this trip would be good for me. But I feel even more lost than I did before we left.

Billie pulls a samosa from the platter. She doesn't want to talk about whether she will or won't stay in Champaign, a question she hears on the tip of her sister's tongue. She wishes Rhiannon could just talk about herself for more than a few short minutes.

What about you? Rhiannon asks. We're getting close to heading home. Have you thought about what you want to do?

Billie opens her mouth, words halted by the arrival of their entrees. Spiced chickpeas. A plate of vegetables, Rhiannon's coconut curry. They lose their conversation to lunch, neither of them having eaten since the funeral's reception, but Billie knows that even if she'd answered Rhiannon's question she doesn't know what she would have said.

After lunch, Rhiannon steers the Mustang down the boulevard toward the coordinates, indicated by the GPS as only a short distance from the restaurant. Salt Lake City is small, Billie realizes, despite the seeming size of its downtown. Rhiannon drives with the windows rolled up, the air-conditioning blasted on high, the afternoon heat visible on the blacktop in mirrored pools beyond the windshield. They drive past what Billie sees is Salt Lake City's main public library, a swirling marvel of nautilus-shaped architecture, and on past a water tower marked TROLLEY SQUARE, what looks like an outdoor shopping plaza. Rhiannon turns south and travels three blocks until they dead-end in a parking lot, the GPS inching toward but not yet reaching a destination.

Rhiannon cuts the engine in the parking lot. This isn't a racetrack.

Do you remember where the racetrack was in the city?

South, now that I'm thinking of it. Rhiannon sighs. I don't think that drawing meant a racetrack at all.

Rhiannon gestures beyond the windshield and Billie sees a canopy of greenery past the dead-end lot: a public park. A walking track circling the outer perimeter.

The entire park an oval, the shape of the drawing in the journal.

Liberty Park, Rhiannon reads from a wooden sign staked in the grass beyond the windshield. This must be it.

Rhee, I'm sorry. I thought it was a racetrack.

Why are you sorry? We don't even know what's here.

The coordinate's showing a little farther

into the park.

Fine. Ready to do some walking?

Rhiannon leaves the Mustang's windows cracked to diffuse the heat and Billie follows her into the park with the GPS in her palms. Rhiannon says nothing and Billie can't tell if she's disappointed or relieved that they're somewhere other than a raceway. Rhiannon walks ahead of her as they move down the park's central thoroughfare, a paved trail lined on both sides with tall rows of cottonwoods. Leaves lime bright against the fallow blue of the western sky and Billie still can't believe how vivid the colors are out here in the absence of low clouds and rain. They head away from the park's perimeter populated by joggers and a few in-line skaters and move into the interior, past basketball and tennis courts toward a playground filled with children. Jungle gyms and swing sets bloom with toddlers. Concrete channels of rushing water surround the playground, man-made creeks where kids splash in swimsuits and plastic floaties. Rhiannon glances back and Billie shakes her head, the GPS still charting them toward the other end of the park. The heat dampens any talk between them and Billie walks behind her sister in silence. They pass signs for a public pool, a greenhouse. They keep walking until they ascend a sloped hill to a glittering lake on the other side, mallard ducks kicking through the water. The light beats off the lake's ripples and glints from the peaked mountains in the distance, visible from the lakefront. Billie breathes. A manicured landscape, no less beautiful in its own way than a red-rocked mesa or a trail spiraling up a mountain switchback. This park the polar opposite of a prison yard, nothing more than dirt mounds of anthills and thin patches of crabgrass. They keep walking down the path along the edge of the lake until the GPS beeps, their destination finally reached.

What the hell are we supposed to find here? Rhiannon says. This lake is huge.

Billie shakes her head. I guess we should've driven to this side of the park instead.

Do you see anything? Anything at all that looks like something Mom would mark?

Billie holds a hand over her eyes and sees a family of five on a blanket spread in the grass. The reflection of trees shimmering in the water. Canada geese. Mallard ducklings. The arch of a footbridge leading from their side of the lake to a shaded island in the middle. Everything sky blue and lush green that she doesn't even think to look away from the lake.

Billie, Rhiannon says.

Billie looks up and Rhiannon's eyes are fixed on the other side of the path. When Billie follows her line of sight she sees what Rhiannon sees and knows immediately.

Tracy Aviary.

A menagerie of birds. Its entrance wide, its sign huge. What Billie can't believe she missed. What she knows for sure is the destination their mother intends for them, or else for her alone: not a racetrack at all.

Billie glances at Rhiannon, her face indecipherable.

It looks like a big place, is all Rhiannon says. How the hell are we going to find anything in there?

Billie says nothing. Billie knows exactly where to look.

After Rhiannon pays their admission and they move along a boardwalk that takes them across a lake filled with pelicans and beyond another shallow pool crammed with neon-pink flamingos, Billie follows the map the attendant gave them straight to the exhibit she knows to seek. Utah's raptors. The main attraction a lone bald eagle, not what their mother has led them here to find. Billie moves past the eagle and past the turkey vultures and the American kestrels to the exact enclosure.

The red-tailed hawk. Mottled auburn. Russet feathers. Coffee-colored irises bearing down from a perch, Rhiannon and Billie the only patrons in the entire exhibit. Despite the ferruginous hawks pinwheeling above the western highways of Utah and New Mexico and despite the few pigeons and cardinals she saw flitting against the Midwestern gray from her small bunk window in Decatur, Billie hasn't seen a red-tailed hawk since she left Jacksonville.

Alabama.

The aviary's hawk looks exactly like her.

Goddamn, Rhiannon whispers.

Billie says nothing, a cyclone whirling inside the walls of her chest. She knows they'll find the plastic box here, what she dreads to open and see what her mother has left. Because it will be for her, as crushing as the blade of a hawk feather in Carlsbad. Because it won't be for Rhiannon, two talismans planted for Billie and none for her sister. Billie glances at Rhiannon squinting beneath the sun, her face betraying nothing. Billie bends below the sign that describes the red-tailed hawk's range and eating habits and scans the wooden fence that separates the walking path from the hawk's chain-link enclosure. Her hands almost touch the cage's rusted metal, the hawk's beaded eyes flickering with her movements. Her hands find nothing. Her hands continue trawling the edge where the enclosure meets the grass, dragging through tall weeds until they meet rough plastic.

Billie closes her eyes. The unclouded afternoon sun magenta hot through the shade of her eyelids. She grabs the box and stands. Gray plastic. The same as every other box they've found. A red-tailed hawk feather in Carlsbad: her mother already twisting a knife. Her mother telling her father to never visit. And now here: Billie has no idea what else her mother can say about her once-life and every way it failed.

You want me to open it? Rhiannon asks.

Billie shakes her head. The sun directly overhead, heavy on her scalp and shoulders. Billie squeezes the box, the plastic clasp popping open. Inside, the small sheet of paper. A sketched oval upon it. The drawing in the journal. The matched coordinates scrawled beside it. And beneath the paper, what Billie knows by touch alone before she pulls them from the box: two jesses. The thin silk of leather straps sliding through her fingers, straps Billie once attached to Alabama's feet to keep her perched and secure. Billie pulls them from the box and holds them to the sunlight, the red-tailed hawk in the enclosure blinking down at them. Two straps that tethered Alabama to Billie's arm before Billie untied them the night Tim broke her brow bone, the night she watched Alabama hesitate only a moment before taking noiselessly to the sky.

Billie turns them over in her palms. A small *A* branded into the tail end of both straps. Her mother must have kept them. Slid them quietly into her pocket when her family cleared all her things from Tim's house in Jacksonville.

Billie, Rhiannon says.

Billie shakes her head. Doesn't want to hear Rhiannon say a word. The mess of the funeral, her mother telling her father not to visit, all of it sharpening the jesses into blades. She holds the straps limp in her hand and slides the plastic box into her pocket, the afternoon sky sweltering, more unbearable than the ridgeline of a quarry. A funeral not enough. No ceremony enough to remind Billie of everything she left behind, everything she fucked up. A feather in Carlsbad inadequate. Too weak a reminder. The jesses in her hands, something she owned. Something she fastened to Alabama's talons. Something she untied herself, her mother no longer twisting a knife but driving it right in.

A line of pool tables. Budweiser awnings shedding cones of light above them. No windows. A tube television above the bar local-broadcasting afternoon golf. A dive called X Wife's Place across the street from Liberty Park, the nearest bar open on a Sunday in a liquor-lawed city. Rhiannon asking through the heated haze of the aviary if Billie wanted to take a break, spend the night in the city. If she wanted to look ahead at last in the journal to see if any coordinates were left, if she wanted to take off down Interstate 80 toward home, straight across Wyoming and Nebraska and on to Iowa and Illinois. Billie shaking her head, the journal buried in her daypack. No decisions. No thinking at all. She sits across from Rhiannon in a scarlet-vinyl booth in the corner of the bar, two whiskeys on the table between them, the jesses still curled in her palms against the condensation of her glass. She knows they must pierce Rhiannon just as much, her sister expecting a racetrack, but she can't find the words to ask.

I'm sure she didn't mean any harm by these, Rhiannon is saying.

Billie nods. Maybe not, she thinks. But there it is. Her father's presence at the quarry. Her mother's six-year secret of keeping him away from Decatur. A man in Colorado Springs. Gnarled-up cunt. A man in Jacksonville, a man who nearly killed every part of her. A man in Cortez, a moonlit pool not enough to forget. Billie feels the tide of grief pressing in at last, the jesses its final pull. Her mother keeping her father away to shield her from every single man, even the one who made her. How it meant her mother knew what Tim did, even if she never said a word. A line of women keeping secrets. A line of women avoiding words too fucking hard to say. The only thing left in Illinois when Billie returns a cemetery that awaits her long-due visit and out here in Utah only carefully placed relics, a bread-crumb trail she and Rhiannon have followed across the entire West to arrive where, Billie doesn't know, the jesses clutched in her hands.

I know how you feel, Rhiannon says. Maybe she thought these reminders of our old lives would be rejuvenating. That they would set us back on the right paths.

I don't know what the right path is.

I don't either. I don't feel anything but exhausted.

Billie sips her whiskey, a sugar burn creeping down the trail of her throat. Do you really think it's clear? That she meant this trip as a reminder?

Rhiannon sighs. At this point, I have no fucking idea what she meant this trip to be. We've retraced so many of her pivotal steps, Billie. We've been reminded the entire way of our own steps, how we aren't following them anymore. What else could it be?

No, my steps, Billie says. Me specifically. That I'm not following them anymore. She's left nothing for you, Rhee. And I'm sure on the surface that looks bad. But to me it seems like she's saying that you don't need any help at all.

Rhiannon is quiet and Billie listens to the drone of golf announcers on television, the whir of two standing fans circulating air through the swampy bar. The smack of pool balls breaking across a table. The suede-smooth texture of the leather straps in her hands. She pulls her daypack from the vinyl bench and reaches her hands in and scatters across the liquor-sticky table everything they've gathered, everything their mother left them across seven days of states. The locket: its short gold chain, the cherubic portraits of her mother and her aunt sealed inside. The fossilized tail spike of a stegosaurus. The thin blade of a red-tailed hawk feather. An astronomer's laser pointer. A jigsaw puzzle's lone piece. The ghost of a wedding ring the only absence, what Billie will face when they meet Oscar in St. Louis. And now, here: Alabama's jesses. Rhiannon looks away and Billie plants her hands on the table.

Tell me, she says. What the hell kind of story do these things tell you?

We don't even know who left these. We've already been to her funeral and we don't even know how all these things got out here.

Rhiannon avoids her question. Billie won't let her. Does it even matter? she says. I don't care who left them. We're here. We're here with these things and I'm so fucking tired of trying to guess what she wants from us. So tell me, Rhee. What kind of story do we have here?

Rhiannon doesn't meet Billie's eyes, her jaw clenching inside her closed mouth.

Fine, Rhiannon finally says. The locket. Mom and Aunt Sue. You and me. Mom wanted this trip to begin with us, both of us traveling together, both of us on the same page. For me, that's why she also began with their wedding ring. Their marriage, yes, and where she started her graduate work and career. But also where both of us began.

Where she met Dad. We wouldn't have been possible without it. The stegosaurus fossil. The beginning of her life's work, of proving another scientist wrong and setting down her own path. The hawk feather. Your path. What used to make you happiest. The laser pointer. Fuck if I know. Being out in the wild, being free. Looking up at a clearer sky than anything we could have seen in Illinois. The jigsaw piece. That a degree of mystery might be worth something. Even if it drove her crazy throughout her career. That she didn't know the answers to everything. That she spent her life searching regardless. And now Alabama's jesses. You again. Your path. What you left behind. You.

Billie hears the strain in her sister's voice, the only hint she'll give. That among every one of the objects Rhiannon has listed, none of them are for her.

And what about your path? Billie says.

I don't think this trip is about me.

I think it is.

Rhiannon rolls her eyes. You just said it was. Your steps.

Yeah, I think it's a reminder of where I went wrong. But it's about you, too. It's about both of us. So tell it to me again, Rhee. Tell me the story here.

I don't know the fucking story, Billie. A

hawk feather. Two jesses. Those messages are clearly for you. That's the story.

You really think that's true?

Yes, goddammit, Rhiannon nearly shouts. And you're crazy if you think Mom brought you all the way out here just to make you feel like shit. They might be a reminder. But you heard Dad tell you himself. She meant to protect you. For six years. And now she wants you to take control of your own future. And what about me, Billie? What the fuck is out here for me?

Mom wanted you out here. All these other objects were for both of us. I just need more help. It's obvious. But she wanted you out here too.

Yeah, as your driver. To shuttle you out here. I already said goodbye in March.

Did you?

Rhiannon says nothing and Billie pulls their mother's journal from the daypack and slides it across the table.

Open it, she says. To the next page. Just open it.

It's not my journal. She didn't give it to me.

She gave it to both of us. So open it. We might not be done. You might get the last coordinate of the entire journey. Open it, Rhee. Tell me if we're going anywhere else.

Rhiannon looks away, lines of tension chiseling her jaw. So many objects, what Billie guesses can have only been left by BLM workers across so many states. Everyone her mother knew. Favors pulled. How someone at almost every location knew of her mother and her work. People who knew her work better than Billie ever did. Rhiannon finally sets down her whiskey glass and pulls open the journal's pages, past the first T. rex sketch, past the drawing and coordinates for Carlsbad, what Billie can see from across the table. Rhiannon turns the page past the drawn oval for Salt Lake City and tilts the journal toward herself and Billie can't see what the next page holds.

What? Billie says. What is it?

Rhiannon looks up, her face blank. Rhiannon's gaze drifts past their corner booth and beyond Billie's head to the small rectangle of the tube television above the bar growing louder. The bartender aiming the remote and raising the volume. Rhiannon's attention vanishing from the objects fanned across the table. Billie looking up at the television, Sunday golf suspended. The bartender standing below the television, neck craned up, knuckles resting on his hip bones. The tower fans whirring. The crack of pool balls halting. Everyone in the thin crowd of the bar looking up.

Breaking news. Another plane.

A newscaster standing in a field above the televised headline: EIGHTH PLANE CRASHES IN WYOMING.

Along Interstate 80. The same highway Rhiannon mentioned taking back to Illinois right before they headed to the bar.

Billie looks back at her sister, Rhiannon's eyes still fastened to the television and her hands loosened from the journal and Billie sees the next page splayed wide open on the table, a page with no coordinates or drawings, a page filled only with blank space.

ALEXANDER, KATE. "RISING TURBULENCE REQUIRES BETTER IN-FLIGHT DETECTION." HUFFINGTON POST. 15 JUNE 2016. WEB.

Rising Turbulence Requires Better In-Flight Detection

Given the recent crashes of seven commercial planes, half of which are assumed to have been caused by what is known as clear-air turbulence, it is to our benefit to not only discuss probable cause but engage in possible prevention. This week marks the closure of most major world airports, including international hubs such as London's Heathrow and Tokyo's Narita International. Rather than risk continued closures and declining airline sales, discussion of turbulence prevention is imperative.

Most commercial airplanes detect turbulence in cloud-covered areas, but not in seemingly clear skies. Computer models can be improved to more accurately discern areas of clear-air turbulence. Dr. Caroline Moreno, a researcher with the Department of Meteorology, has proposed a laser-based system equipped to the nose of all commercial airliners that would identify clear-air turbulence along the plane's path before dangerous air is reached.

While some climatologists suggest that the increase of carbon dioxide in the atmosphere due to global warming will increase flight turbulence, there is no evidence at this time correlating an unfortunate string of air tragedies to climate change.

40.7608° N, 111.8910° W: Salt Lake City, UT

The late afternoon sun is white hot beyond the bar's front doors. Rhiannon sees only burned afterimages when she blinks. Traffic shuttles beyond the curb, the routine of early rush hour, as if the news has stayed inside the bar. Rhiannon wonders if each car is filled with news radio, every single driver coming to the realization that random catastrophe has become an unquestionable pattern. Billie emerges behind her, her daypack slung across her shoulder.

Rhee, Billie says.

Rhiannon closes her eyes. Another one.

I know. Take it easy.

Fuck, Billie.

We'll find another way home. Another route if the highway's closed.

I don't care about the fucking highway. People are dead. More people are fucking dead. And there's nothing left in that journal. We have nowhere else to go.

Rhiannon tries to remember what the breaking-news broadcaster said before she fled the bar: a United route between Minneapolis and Las Vegas, a flight number she can't remember. A crash outside Laramie, Wyoming, along Interstate 80 at the edge of Medicine Bow National Forest. An estimated 214 people on board. The flight path normal if not slightly northern, what the newscaster claimed was avoidance of a thunderstorm system sweeping across Nebraska. A wall of black clouds spanned across the highway: what Rhiannon knows from their own drive across Missouri. Heavy wind. Enough to blow a semi off the interstate. Enough to push a plane out of the sky. Or else the same kind of turbulence she experienced on the flight that made her never fly again: blue skies. What this plane surely sought in avoiding thunderstorms. A clear route. The unexpected shaking of a plane's cabin, a cockpit's black box going silent. The notebook's empty page flickers in Rhiannon's brain, so inconsequential to the wrangle of metal on a television screen but she feels her lungs break inside her chest and can't tell if it's the plane or the journal.

The end of the coordinates. The last one, for Billie. None of them for her.

Rhiannon wishing for days that they

would just head back to Illinois.

Rhiannon surprised at how much it kills her that they will.

We can go home, Billie says softly. That's where we can go.

Rhiannon turns and looks at her. What home? The one filled with boxes we're supposed to sort through? The one with nothing left at all but what our family no longer is? You haven't lived there for years, Billie. Mom's gone. Dad hasn't lived there since you were in high school. I'm only there because I have to be. Because I fucked everything up with Beth. You and I don't have a home. We don't have anything. Not even any idea what the fuck we should do next.

Billie places a hand on her shoulder and Rhiannon flinches away.

She left one last note for you, Rhiannon says. She left nothing for me.

I wouldn't call it a note.

At least she left something. For you. Billie, there's nothing left of her at all. Except for this stupid fucking road trip that's clearly been all about you.

The journal doesn't mean anything. It's just a blank page.

Then why did we follow it if it doesn't mean anything? Of course it means something. It means everything. It means all the life she had left to live that she didn't get to live so she sent us instead. To see everything she was able to see while she could. To say goodbye. To let you see so many states of this fucking country after seeing only one small corner of the same state for six years. But guess what. That's it. You. This was all about you. I'm just the vehicle. The driver. The one who got you out here. This was always about you, the daughter she missed for so many years while I was always right beside her in Champaign.

What, you think she took you for granted?

Maybe. Maybe she did.

She talked about you every time she visited.

And told you what? That I sat by her bedside in the hospital? That I held her hand through chemo treatments that in the end only made her sicker?

She told me she was glad to have you close. She never took you for granted.

Rhiannon stands by the curb beneath the oppressive heat and imagines a hospital room, drawn curtains, the low hum of the craned television in the corner. *I Love Lucy.* The room's lights dimmed, black and white flickering blue through the dark. Her mother asleep, hands folded like wings across her lap. Antiseptics and IV bandages and the incessant beep of the heart monitor. Her mother's life ticked down to seconds. Rhiannon doing nothing but sitting in a stiff hospital chair and watching it happen.

I was only a caretaker, she whispers. I was only there to watch her go.

You weren't, Billie says.

Then what the fuck was I?

You were a driver.

Rhiannon looks up and Billie is watching her.

You said so yourself. You're the vehicle. You're the driver. Fuck you.

Billie says nothing but doesn't back away and Rhiannon realizes too late, the words already spit, that Billie means something else. Not picking Billie up at the curb of a correctional center. Not this trip. Not a vessel for transportation and meals and funds.

A driver.

What she used to be.

What her mother knew she did best.

Beyond coordinates and drawings and plastic geocached boxes. The simple fact of moving across pavement. Of accelerating, the engine's drone a rough lullaby. Of logging miles, of watching a speedometer's count grow across a wide road. Of letting the landscape track through a windshield and recede in a rearview mirror. Of feeling wind whip across the side mirrors and into the open windows of the car's cabin.

Rhiannon feels the sun's heat pulse down on her face and hears the television murmur through the bar when a patron opens the door. Two hundred and fourteen passengers. Two hundred and fourteen lives. And what the fuck was she doing with her one small life. Avoiding everything. White-knuckling her last flight before taking to the road, not for races but for the dulled drone of delivering textbooks. Not the wheel of a stock car. Not the face of a woman she loved but couldn't make herself hand over everything completely. Two hundred and fourteen passengers. So much devastation Rhiannon feels sitting hard on her breastbone. Interstate 80 closed. Their only route east. And west: she knows America's highways like a lit constellation.

A driver.

West on I-80 instead, the opposite direction of where they need to go to get home. Rather than heading east toward Wyoming and Nebraska and Iowa and finally Illinois: go west. Toward Nevada. Toward a place she once passed on a race route but never stopped to see, a place she can't believe is this close, her mother's doing in bringing them to Salt Lake City. She pulls the Mustang's keys from her pocket and heads across the street toward the car and hears Billie follow.

A driver.

She will show her mother just how good.

West. The highway a vector straight across Utah. An interstate bending only once, a dip south around the Great Salt Lake before straightening into an arrow shot direct from Salt Lake City to the Nevada state line. Rhiannon keeps the radio off and the car stable, Billie silent beside her. No questions. Rhiannon's turn to take the car where she will.

The sun slices down the horizon straight ahead and sinks toward the mountains, jagged peaks of cobalt. Flat plains of red rock surround the car and grow whiter as they travel, dotted by green tufts of marsh grass. As if they were driving into the ocean. All of western Utah a former ancient sea. Lake Bonneville. What once spanned so much of the American West, Rhiannon remembers Billie telling her, before receding with the last Ice Age and leaving behind only salt.

Their mother. Their mother in a hospital bed. Hooked to a heart monitor that skyrocketed then plateaued before slowing to a flatline. Rhiannon still holding her hand.

Every nurse ready. Rhiannon the only one in the room who wasn't. An end. An end in a hospital room and an end beside a grave and an end on the quarry's ridgeline, none of them closure, none of them any kind of goodbye. What still feels undone out here across the desert, her mother leaving Billie jesses and Rhiannon nothing, nothing but the face slap of a blank white page.

Two hundred and fourteen passengers. Inconceivable.

She and Billie's destination now: a place she and her father never visited.

A place she's only dreamed but never seen.

It doesn't take long to get there. Ninety minutes from Salt Lake City. Past clumps of marsh grass and puddles of saltwater along the highway. Low water levels making this landscape ideal for summer racing, marsh water receded by May. Summer. Rhiannon realizes it's solstice, the longest day of light. And now, deepest darkness. The longest possible day for two hundred and fourteen families waiting to hear from their loved ones. Changing weather. What her mother knew. Rhiannon wonders if water levels have been low not since May but since January or earlier amid so much drought. This level desert making this place a hallmark of racing since the turn of the twentieth century.

The Bonneville Salt Flats.

One of the flattest, most windless landscapes on earth.

Land-speed records. Stock cars and motorcycles making pilgrimages every summer. Kitty O'Neil. A woman's highest land-speed record set in Oregon's Alvord Desert in 1976. Five hundred and twelve miles per hour. A speed the Mustang will never reach, a street vehicle without a stock car's capacities. No women's records set here. Just Lee Breedlove, 1965, three hundred and eight miles per hour. Only occupying the flats on her husband's orders to fend off his competitor. Rhiannon wants to try regardless. Wants to show her mother. Wants to think of nothing, wants to blast her brain apart with speed. Wants to feel her automobile gunning across salt, wants to feel the engine rattling and reaching its limit at last.

Billie says nothing as Rhiannon decelerates and pulls off the interstate to the eastern edge of the Salt Flats. The season just readying to begin, no crowds or cars in sight. Where Rhiannon knows NASCAR stock cars and piston engines and rockets have made their way across the past century to break barriers of sound and speed, racing season July through October, the flats at their hardest and driest. She pulls into a sand-scattered parking lot bereft of vehicles, a wooden Bureau of Land Management sign the only occupant: BONNEVILLE SALT FLATS INTERNATIONAL SPEEDWAY. Beyond the sign spans a wide bed of dry salt and cracked blue, as if they've parked on the beach of a seashore. This place nothing like the Chicagoland Speedway or the Colorado National Speedway or any other track Rhiannon has ever raced, deep grooves cracked through the salt like reptilian patches of dinosaur skin. Rhiannon blinks back the blank notebook paper, the lack of any last coordinate. She shifts the car into park and leaves the engine idling, bands of the day's last light breaking across the low mountains beyond the windshield.

She glances at Billie. Get out.

The first words she's spoken since they left Salt Lake City.

Billie doesn't look at her. I know what you're doing.

I don't care what you know.

I'm not moving. I'm coming with you.

No, you're not. Get out.

Why should I?

Because I don't want you hurt. You have no health insurance. It's not the kind of liability I need. You already took the god-

damn car, Billie. Just give me this. Just let me do this on my own.

Rhiannon's hands clench the steering wheel. The engine hums through the dashboard. Billie watches the spanned fields of white salt.

I don't want you to do anything stupid.

What, like you? Like stealing a car? Like scattering an urn across a fucking cliff? It's my turn. I haven't done anything stupid in six years.

Rhiannon looks at her sister. Her head half shaved. Her limbs so much skinnier, her left arm rippling down in wound-hardened waves. Rhiannon's assumed always that they're nothing alike, that they could've been born to different parents, but in the car beneath the fading sun Rhiannon takes in Billie's short-sloped nose, the same as hers. The same dimpled cheeks catching Utah's setting sky. The same chestnut eyes, same dark hair despite so many years of Billie dyeing it anything but its natural color, anything to separate her from everyone in their family. Billie keeps her eyes forward. The engine drones and Rhiannon wonders if they'll sit in the car forever. But Billie nods. Almost imperceptible. Grabs her daypack and slips out the passenger door.

Rhiannon watches in the rearview mirror as Billie walks across the parking lot and stands in the distance, her hands shielding her eyes. The cabin silent. Radio off. No news. Rhiannon tests the gas pedal, the car idling. Watches the tachometer spike. A speed race: what she hasn't done since she spun out on the racetrack in Indianapolis. The Mustang always only possibility, only knowing what a car could do without testing its limits. V-8 engine. Eight cylinders. Zero to sixty in four seconds, zero to one hundred in ten. Intake and exhaust valves and camshafts designed for maximum lift. Four hundred thirty-five horsepower. Four hundred pounds of torque. A six-speed manual override from the automatic Rhiannon's used across six states of highways. And speed: Rhiannon knows the Mustang can top out at 164 miles per hour. Nothing to a stock car. Nothing to a 512 mile-per-hour land-speed record, but something. The sun knifes down the horizon and breaks into shards across the jagged graph of the mountains. Rhiannon knows she needs a permit, the Salt Flats operating under BLM land requirements. But she knows the land as desolate. Two minutes, tops.

Two minutes of speed and wind and light.

She shifts the transmission into manual

and lets her foot fall from the brake and the Mustang rolls onto the crunch of the flats, Billie receding behind her in the rearview mirror. No helmet. No gloves. No racing suit. She wants to feel empty. This entire trip for Billie, as if Rhiannon could stomach and stand the short months of their mother's decline. As if her grieving ended in Illinois. As if a blank page could speak in the absence of directions. *Go west, daughter.* As if any number of funerals was enough to lose the memory of a heart monitor flattening, her mother whispering her last words hours earlier before she lost the ability to speak. *You girls are so loved.* Rhiannon steers the Mustang across the pocked flats and the tires crackle, salt splintering beneath them like the fissures of a frozen lake. She faces the car west toward the vanishing point of the surrounding mountains. The sun sinking. Pulses the engine. Checks the tachometer's revolutions per minute. Glances out the driver's-side window one last time, Billie barely visible across a field of sun-spiked salt.

She shifts the car into first gear and lifts her foot from the brake.

The Mustang is a rocket, a shuttle launch spiraling out across salt. The tachometer spikes, the speedometer rising as Rhiannon

shifts into second and third gear. Sixty miles per hour. Seventy. She keeps her hands locked on the wheel. Muscle memory. Her body an archive. A record of tendon and bone. A record of grief. Eighty miles per hour. Ninety. Rhiannon shifts gears again and the car bullets across the flats.

Two hundred and fourteen passengers. Unfathomable.

The world a well of loss.

The world a lack of any preparation for goodbye.

Twenty seconds until the Mustang reaches maximum velocity, twenty seconds everything, enough time to break the world apart: the time it took for a heart to flatline and for a plane to shuttle to the earth and for Billie to light a match and for Rhiannon to feel the heavy weight of so many goodbyes rattle through her body behind the wheel.

The scent of burned rubber. The salt-damp of sweat, a racing suit clinging to her limbs inside the stock car's cockpit. Crowds filling stands and spilling from the infield, tailgates and shuffleboards and bean bag tosses. Her foot harder on the gas pedal, ninety-five miles per hour, ninety-eight, one hundred. Goodbye to the welcome silence of the highway and the wheat-dusted hills and the prairie dog mounds of Nebraska

and the sunflower-strewn fields exploding across Kansas and her father shuttling her across so many states and Wendell Scott and a portrait pasted to her bedroom wall. Every barrier she never broke. One hundred ten miles per hour. Fifteen. Salt spraying up from the Mustang's tires. Goodbye to Billie: orange prison jumpsuit. Billie led away by the elbow in the courtroom, hands cuffed behind her back. One hundred twenty-five. A house in Jacksonville that Rhiannon and her parents cleaned out. A red-tailed hawk. Two jesses her mother must have kept in her pocket.

Her mother.

Goodbye to what it was to be alive.

Goodbye to a stock car spinning out and a helmet hung just to gather dust and an art opening and a first kiss fluttering against her mouth and her mother's hand on hers when she first said the words out loud: *Rhee, I'm sick.* Goodbye to the slowing beat of a heart monitor and the shoveling of earth in a cemetery that nauseated Rhiannon, the Mustang shotgunning across the flatlands of a once-sea. Goodbye to a backyard garden and her mother's watering cans and the sun filtering down through a green canopy of summer oaks and the gasoline scent of a garage and the cool shade of slid-

ing beneath her father's car on a wheeled dolly and the damp Midwestern humidity billowing in from their driveway's scorched blacktop that was the same wafting heat of every raceway ahead and the bright blue dream of breaking records scrolled out before her.

One hundred sixty-four. Maximum velocity.

The Mustang shakes. Weightless. Floats across a surface of salt. Rhiannon leans back in the driver's seat, the sun gone. Solstice. The longest day. The sky a marble of lavender and coral. She closes her eyes and feels nothing but the engine's pulse, the same as her own heartbeat. She could drive forever if she knew the Mustang could endure it but feels the car sputter and can still see the dim outline of Billie waiting for her in the parking lot. She lets the car run until it slows completely to a halt, her breath the only sound. The mountains a silhouette. Her hands still gripping the steering wheel.

Daughter, go west.

Goodbye to an empty page.

Her mother knowing her better than she thought: that it would enrage her. A parent knowing the depth of a daughter's sorrow and how to bear down upon it. How to tap a well. How to activate control, the only

reflex Rhiannon knows. How to begin again. Rhiannon watches the faded sun blur through the windshield's glass and pulls her palms from the steering wheel and holds her face in her hands.

The night sky is a lacework of stars. Even brighter than Moab, a full moon bouncing light off the phantom white of the Salt Flats. The desert silent and dark. No trees. The faint rush of cars shuttling on the interstate, the black silhouette of mountains poking up in the distance. Rhiannon takes in Utah's quiet as she walks back from squatting at the edge of deserted BLM land, no restrooms and no facilities, only the small glowing orb of their pitched tent for what feels like miles. Billie unfurling their sleeping bags inside by the spark of a single flashlight. The Mustang parked beside the tent, dim but visible in the sky's wide moonlight. Its windows open, dome lights extinguished. The weak buzz of news radio billowing from the stereo's speakers. No firewood, no grilled pits. No cooked hot dogs or cans of beans. As Rhiannon approaches the tent Billie emerges with her daypack and the last of their food.

How about trail mix and beers for dinner? she says.

Rhiannon nods. Camping is exactly what we packed them for.

Billie pulls a container of dried cherries and a canister of mixed nuts and a bag of barbecue potato chips from their groceries. She drags two bottled beers from the bag and cracks their caps, the carbonation lukewarm but welcome. Rhiannon takes the bottle Billie hands her and sits on the Mustang's hood, the engine still warm through the metal.

Billie perches beside her. You doing okay?

The car's heat pools against Rhiannon's bare legs. The radio drones through the open windows. Two hundred and fourteen passengers and crew confirmed dead.

I don't really know.

It was good to see you run speed again.

A passenger car isn't really built for that kind of speed.

Billie glances at her. How did it make you feel?

Good.

Billie laughs. Good?

Rhiannon watches the patchwork of constellations above them. I haven't felt that good in years.

Billie grabs a handful of chips, their crunch the only sound above the drone of the radio. A newscaster reports scattered

debris nineteen miles west of Laramie. Knadler Lake. Just south of Wyoming's Bamforth National Wildlife Refuge. Interstate 80 closed indefinitely for the work of investigation crews and cleanup. Detours scheduled. No black box yet recovered, only speculation of another weather-related crash. Speculation as to whether airports across the world will close again.

I can't believe this, Billie says.

I know.

What now?

We can route south to I-70, back through southern Utah. On toward Denver and across Kansas.

I mean for you. Rhee. What now for you?

Rhiannon leans back against the car's hood. She imagines trekking back across Colorado, across Kansas, on through Missouri and back to Illinois toward textbooks and a clapboard cubicle only to watch nine hours tick away every day. Nine hours to twenty hot seconds, the velocity of an engine rocketing across salt. Twenty seconds: enough time to know the impossibility of returning to a desk beyond the sweep of the western desert.

I don't know, Rhiannon says. All I know is I can't go back there. Not now.

To Illinois?

Rhiannon thinks of Beth. A talk that awaits her when she returns. Not Illinois, she says. Illinois is home. Billie, I can't imagine leaving. But my job. Fuck.

Billie smiles through the dark. Leave that shit job, Rhee. Leave it now.

It's not that easy. It's good money.

What, you think I don't know that? That I won't be in a position to take any job at all that will pay me? I get it. I get the practicalities. But you can leave. You can leave that place and find something else.

I know.

Billie looks at her. Think you'll race?

Billie, no. I'm too old.

You're never too old.

Rhiannon pictures the race routes, capillaries of highways webbed across the entire country. Beth in Illinois. A home that was hers. A home she never let herself make.

I don't think highway life is for me anymore.

What, you haven't had fun out here on the road?

That's different. We're just out here for two weeks. I don't know if I'm built for constant travel. I always thought I needed it. I don't know if I do anymore.

You could do what Dad does. Coach. It seems to satisfy his need to race.

I have time to figure it out. But I can't stay at that job anymore. I can't.

Then don't.

Billie is watching her and Rhiannon looks up at the network of bright stars peppering the dark cloak of Utah's night sky. The faint band of the Milky Way beginning to shimmer. A wide-open dark so different from the thick gray of Illinois cloud cover, a clear expanse that across a week has allowed her to imagine other skies, other lives.

Birds navigate by constellation, Billie says. They follow the orientation of stars during seasonal migration. They know north and south by memorizing the patterns of constellations.

What are we looking at right now?

Billie pulls the laser pointer from her daypack. Circinus, she says. Those four stars. They're faint. But out here with no light pollution, they're clear enough to see.

Rhiannon points toward the far mountains. There's the Big Dipper. No pointer needed. At least I know that one.

The radio wafts through the dark: airports deciding again whether to shut down. Rhiannon watches the laser's light flicker across the points of constellations and feels a wash of sadness. As they travel east across Colorado the winds will pick up and wildfires will only continue to flare and in Missouri the horizon will flood with thunder and lightning and once they arrive back in Illinois the sky will fill with mist and clouds.

Mom knew, she hears herself whisper. She knew this would happen.

Billie shuts off the pointer, the sky lit with nothing but its own stars.

This whole trip, Rhiannon says. Driving instead of flying. Her work at the quarry. Uncovering the mystery of another climate that eradicated every living thing. She knew the earth was changing. She could have predicted that wildfire in Colorado. She could have anticipated these crashes. She made us drive. Rhiannon sighs, presses her knuckles against her eyes. She also knew I'd be so fucking angry that she left me a blank page. She timed it right. Salt Lake City. She probably knew I'd make my way out here.

Did you ever talk to her about the Salt Flats?

I think I did. And she knew about them anyway, being out here so often.

This trip is about both of us, Billie says. Equally.

What is she trying to tell us?

Isn't it clear? To do what we want. To get back out there.

But what about the quarry? The mystery

she and Angela were studying.

I don't know. Maybe to take notice. To see it happening. Billie tilts her chin back and looks at the stars. To take stock of this planet before it disappears.

The radio statics across the Salt Flats. Two hundred and fourteen dead. On top of hundreds, the eighth crash, other families and other investigation sites radiating waves of heartache spiraling out across so many coordinates across the world. Coordinates her mother never mapped. Their current coordinates nothing, just one small pinpoint of grief on a worldwide map of devastation, the scale unimaginable. Rhiannon watches the winking light of every constellation, the moon spilling down across the bright-white specter of the Salt Flats. The visibility endless. The red rock of Utah receding in the rearview mirror when they wake in the morning. All the stars and mesas and bats and limestone, everything their mother has shown them on this trip. Drought and storm and fire. The chance that all of it could completely disappear.

I didn't know it was possible, she whispers.

Didn't know what? Billie whispers back through the dark.

I didn't know a landscape could break your heart too.

In the thin light of the night's stars, Rhiannon sees Billie's eyes glisten wet.

I watched the same square of window from my dorm for six years, she says. I watched the hills beyond the prison yard change from green to brown every fall.

I bet it was still beautiful.

Billie smiles. It was. But not like this.

What about you?

What about me?

Rhiannon imagines the journal burrowed down in Billie's daypack, so many pages of blank white paper beyond their last coordinate.

The hawk feather, Rhiannon says. The jesses. What are you going to do now?

Billie is silent and Rhiannon studies her face in the light of the moon, the anger that chiseled out her features in Liberty Park smoothed away.

Maybe I'll go to Alabama. My bird's namesake. I've never been there. Not once. But Rhee, I don't want to do much. I'm tired of doing. I kind of just want to be. Billie hesitates for a moment. How long until we need to get back?

Five days. It should only take two or three to make it back to the Midwest.

Billie nods. There's one more stop I want to make, if that's okay.

Rhiannon doesn't ask. If she's dragged them west from Salt Lake City to the Bonneville Flats, Billie's earned one unscheduled stop. She lies back on the warmth of the car's hood, the constellations above them a blanket of light. Billie sits beside her. Rhiannon's limbs swim with the lingering lull of the car's movement, the same as sinking into every motel bed along a raceway route and still feeling a car's pull. The radio drones from the Mustang's interior. An earth spun beyond control. The same mass devastation her mother once studied. But out here: only silence. Only stars. Only the lit ghost of the Salt Flats. Only the pulse of her own skin, the hum of an engine beating back inside it.

HERRMANN, JEAN. BEAR RIVER MIGRATORY BIRD REFUGE. WASHINGTON, DC: NATIONAL GEOGRAPHIC, 1999. PRINT.

BEAR RIVER MIGRATORY BIRD REFUGE

The Bear River Migratory Bird Refuge, a seventy-four-thousand-acre preserve on the northeastern edge of the Great Salt Lake, is home to over 250 species of migrating birds. A critical habitat for winged creatures on the Central and Pacific Flyways of North America, the refuge contains a variety of habitats including wetlands, grasslands, open water, and mudflats. Millions of birds pass through the refuge each year including trumpeter swans, bald eagles, pelicans, and snowy plovers.

The refuge is surrounded by desert lands, making it an important oasis for birds. Because the refuge is vulnerable to flood and drought, this land must be preserved for the continued survival of birds on their migration routes.

41.4462° N, 112.2622° W: Corinne, UT

There is no need for a journal. No coordinates. Billie maps them on the GPS once they wake at dawn upon the Bonneville Flats, the sun a semicircle rising above the stark plains of cracked salt. Straight back across Utah from the near-border of Nevada, rounding up through Salt Lake City and on past Ogden. The peaks of the Wasatch lining the right side of the highway as they travel north, the alien coral blue of the Great Salt Lake spanning off past Rhiannon's driver's-side window. Beyond a Denny's brunch off Interstate 80 in the middle of central Utah, a hollandaise omelet and a side stack of three pancakes and two cups of coffee, Billie leans back against the headrest as Rhiannon veers around the northern edge of the lake. The radio off, news Billie knows they'll listen to all the way home. Devastation Billie can't comprehend. In her hands: the red-tailed hawk feather. Billie runs her fingers across it, a worry doll. Rhiannon at last pulls the car off the highway and steers them down a two-lane road toward brackish marsh and patches of salt grass.

Billie can already see them in the distance: shorebirds. A flock of black-necked stilts nesting in one of the mirrored ponds surrounding the road. The Bear River Migratory Bird Refuge. One of the country's main flyways, a crucial stopover for so many birds in migration. What she read about in a dimly lit corner of the Decatur Correctional Center's library, a children's book on the Bear River Refuge. Dewey decimal number 598. The only book in the entire library on birds and their habitats, surely left behind by another inmate's visiting child. Billie remembers the facts, what she scanned over and over for lack of any other reading material on birds. Seventy-four thousand acres established in 1928, surrounded by the Wasatch to the east and so many hunting clubs everywhere else. Strategically protected land along migration routes, information that seemed irrelevant from the walls of a prison library but out here, the eighth plane crash in less than four months, the fact takes on a somber note. Hunting clubs. Jet engines. Monuments in every state they've seen devoted to men who claimed discovery. Everywhere out here: evidence of human hands bending the earth to their will. Billie watches the black-necked stilts preen themselves, summer their breeding season. Building their numbers before the mass migration of heading south come fall, a clockwork Billie guesses will be altered despite what news pundits are already denying on the radio's reports. Changes in so many climates. What Billie can only assume will become a norm. She cranes her neck up and looks out the window, the sky marine blue and cloudless, an endless span hiding its danger.

The Mustang rolls over gutted roads flecked with potholes until a parking lot appears. Only a few other cars, one couple wandering around with binoculars and a tripod. Bird-watchers. Billie recognizes their equipment, the feather still in her hands. Rhiannon pulls into a sand-dusted parking space and pulls a pair of sunglasses from the overhead visor, the full summer sun beating down upon the open water.

We're here, she says. Now tell me why.

The reason Billie came back to the book again and again: a small section on the refuge's predator species.

One page devoted entirely to the red-tailed hawk.

Hawks breed and hunt here, Billie says. I thought we'd see one. Mom might be happy if I do something with the feather and jesses.

It's a lie. One she's sure Rhiannon can hear, the feather and jesses useless out here. She's already seen a red-tailed hawk in the enclosure of an aviary exhibit. She's already seen ten thousand bats spiraling from the open mouth of a cave. There is nothing at this refuge that she hasn't seen except this: the flat pages of a child's book come to life.

Six years of dreaming from a prison library made real.

She walks over an embankment beyond the parking lot and past a field of tall grass dotted with picnic shelters, the air thick with swarms of birds. Small swiftlets. Starlings. Their summer nests stuffed into the shelters' eaves. Rhiannon follows her beneath a thick sky teeming with hundreds of circling birds as they make their way down to the boardwalk beside a shallow lake. Billie can identify every species. American white pelicans. A cluster of cream-colored tundra swans. The slim beaks of white-faced ibises, their snouts nearly as long as their fluffed bodies. And a fluttering mass of American avocets, crane-thin legs, wide wingspans of white and black feathers.

Billie squats at the edge of the boardwalk and drags her fingers through the water. A woman sits in a folding chair farther down the boardwalk, a tripod stationed beside her. Ready to wait. The kind of bird-watcher Billie once imagined she'd become, so much more patient than the person she turned into, a can of gasoline in her hands. Someone who couldn't wait anymore. She lets her hands skirt the surface of the water, concentric rings forming like pools of skipping stones beneath her fingers. Rhiannon sits down beside her and dangles her feet in the water.

Hawks aren't shorebirds, Rhiannon says. I don't think you'll find one over here.

Billie smiles.

Come on, Billie. I know birds too, almost as well as I know you.

Fine. It was a book. On this place. The only book on birds they had in prison.

Rhiannon nods and Billie doesn't speak. There is no way to say it, the sun glittering across the water, a huddle of peeping snowy plovers gliding beneath the boardwalk. That this place is more than anything she imagined in the pages of a book, this entire trip a wide span of country she forgot. A wall of sunflowers rippling along the highway across Kansas and on toward Colorado. The blue of a pool. The malt taste of beer. The sugar-tart of whiskey. A man's hands circling her waist in the water. A man's hands at last welcome. Diner food. A cone of bats. A ridgeline. A pocked sky filled with stars and a once-sea of endless salt, small crusted peaks of white crystal spreading in fields toward distant mountains and the open highway rolled out like a carpet billowing west, so many miles she can't believe she's traveled across.

I'm here, she says. I was there in Decatur. And now I'm here.

You're here, Rhiannon repeats.

Billie closes her eyes. Hears nothing but the sound of swiftlets, their soft wings beating against the light wind.

What are you going to do? she hears Rhiannon ask.

The same question. What Rhiannon has already asked. What Billie doesn't know. But where there was fear sprouted to anger the last time her sister posed the question, there is now only calm: if nothing else, their mother's work done through this.

Red-tailed hawks can live up to thirty years, she says. Alabama was a fledgling when I got her. Maybe she's still flying around in Illinois somewhere.

Rhiannon smiles. Maybe she is.

Billie watches a pair of cinnamon teals slide cautiously from the shore into the waiting lake, water slicking across their feathers. She doesn't know if she wants to train birds again, if she even wants to stay in Illinois. The gray of the sky. A land of ghosts. Her memories caught in every cornfield. But it is enough to know she could. The feather, Alabama's jesses in her bag. The span of shorebirds beyond the boardwalk. It is enough to know she holds a pilot flame inside her, the memory of muscle. That she'd still know gauntlets and hooks and anklets. That she'd know how to draw a falcon back to her arm.

After they've stayed by the lakefront until the sun pushes toward late afternoon, Billie sits beside Rhiannon inside the car with the engine off but the radio on, a salted breeze blowing in through the open windows. The voice of an NPR broadcaster reporting exclusively on the crash in Wyoming: airports shut down. Every single one in the continental United States. A black box recovered, far more quickly than any of the other seven planes, investigators moving fast given the frequency of their work across the past four months. Confirmed: clear-air turbulence. Loss of control. Despite the flight's routing around thunderstorms sweeping the plains of Nebraska. Interstate 80 closed indefinitely for debris and cleanup. Every family notified. And accompanying the newscaster's voice: a guest spokeswoman for the EPA. Her voice asserting that beyond all reasonable doubt every single crash is due to shifting weather, no matter what analysts or talk-show hosts speculate to say. *We are facing a global crisis,* Billie hears the woman declare. *We cannot ignore this any longer.*

Fuck, Rhiannon breathes.

They're just going to stop all flights?

Rhiannon looks at her. What else can anyone do?

Billie watches out the window as a flock of Franklin's gulls lifts from the lakeshore and takes flight, a bird she knows winters in Central and South America. A bird she wonders while the radio drones whether it will make it to Argentina this year. Warming temperatures. Light pollution. Constellations a bird can't see if city lights and thick thunderstorms block them out.

I don't know, she says. Maybe there's nothing anyone can do.

Rhiannon watches the waterfront through the windshield. Mom couldn't have planned this. She couldn't have known this would happen while we were out here.

But she knew it was happening. It was already happening when she got sick. And long before that. Rhee, it's clear she was at least partly studying climate at the quarry.

But what are we supposed to do with that?

I don't know. Like I said, maybe she just wants us to pay attention.

Like paying attention is going to bring back all those passengers.

Billie sighs. What do you want to do, Rhee? Head back now? Make it as far as we can and stop for the night?

I guess I-70's the best route, even if it's a detour. It will take us right to St. Louis. Rhiannon looks at her. We don't have to stop for Mom's ring. If it will bother you to see Oscar. I can just drive down sometime after we're back.

That's pointless. We'll be passing right through. We may as well stop.

Are you okay with that?

Why wouldn't I be?

The words spoken out loud let Billie know it's true. Oscar's face: everything like Tim's, but nothing more now than another face. A man decent enough to take a phone call, to track down a plastic box. Nothing else. And Tim: another life, one Billie can't believe she once lived.

How long will it take to get back to Illinois? she asks.

I mapped it this morning. From Salt Lake City, with a detour south adding a lot of extra miles, twenty-five hours. Sixteen hundred miles. We can do it in three days, getting us home on Thursday night just liked we planned. Or we can push it if you really want and get back on Wednesday night. Rhiannon gestures toward the radio. Assuming nothing else happens along the way.

There's no rush, Billie says. Let's just do it in three.

What Billie doesn't say: that she'd rather prolong this trip if she can. That she prefers the highway to mandatory therapy. That even in the grief of their reason for being out here, there are still salt shores. There are still mountains and birds.

What will we do with Mom's ring? Rhiannon says. Dad said we could have it.

I don't know. Billie sighs. How about you keep it. For now. If you know you're staying in Illinois. It should be kept near home.

Rhiannon says nothing, doesn't ask where Billie will be if not Illinois. The radio hums through the silence that forces its way between them until Rhiannon leans forward and shuts the dial off.

There's one more stop I want to make, she says. A quick one. It's not far, so long as we're north of the Salt Lake. We may never be out here again.

Billie nods. Whatever you want to do.

Rhiannon's mouth curves up, a smile tinged with sadness. She turns the key in the ignition and pulls away from the parking lot and Billie watches the birds recede.

GILLESPIE, JIM. THE SPIRAL JETTY. LOS ANGELES: TASCHEN BOOKS, 2000. PRINT.

THE SPIRAL JETTY

The Spiral Jetty is an earthwork sculpture constructed in 1970 by American sculptor Robert Smithson. Part of a land art movement, Smithson created works beyond the confines of museums that responded directly to the landscape.

Located on the northeastern shore of the Great Salt Lake, the Spiral Jetty is a fifteen-hundred-foot-long, fifteen-foot-wide coil rotating counterclockwise out into the lake. Built of basalt rocks, salt crystals, and mud, all materials from the Great Salt Lake itself, the sculpture's visibility fluctuates with Utah's climate, submerged when the lake's water levels rise above 4,195 feet. Because the sculpture depends upon weather, preservationists have taken interest in the climate's effects of flood and drought.

Widely influenced by geology, paleontology, and astronomy, Smithson described the land sculpture as documenting the earth's history, as well as the lack of predictability in the earth's processes. Smithson has said the sculpture responds to the landscape rather than imposing upon it, and that the artwork is meant to be engaged with rather than beheld.

Cultural criticism of the Spiral Jetty suggests that walking into the counterclockwise coil signifies traveling back in time and into the earth's history, and that walking out clockwise signifies moving forward in time.

41.4377° N, 112.6689° W: Spiral Jetty, UT

The Mustang contours farther down the road from the Bear River Refuge instead of routing back toward the interstate, a paved highway that becomes a dirt path that becomes windbeaten sand and dust. Rhiannon's choice for their trip's last destination: only forty-five minutes from the birds Billie chose. If Billie is surprised, she says nothing. The Mustang bumps across uninhabited miles of jagged roads, so far that Rhiannon wonders if they've made a wrong turn. Out toward the northern edge of the Great Salt Lake, the blue peaks of low mountains blend into pale sky on the opposite shore's horizon, an azure gradient that reminds Rhiannon again of the ocean against fields of sand and salt, the lake's water levels low. The shore itself all salt, the same makeup and bright white of the flats. What Beth told her about for so many years. An art book always situated on their coffee table. What

Rhiannon never thought to open. What she realized at the Bear River Refuge was so close, a place she never thought she needed to see until now. Coiling out from the shore of the Great Salt Lake, visible from the rocked road: a wide helix of mud and basalt rock and salt crystal.

The Spiral Jetty.

An earthwork sculpture Beth described from their Urbana apartment, built with six thousand tons of basalt from the Great Salt Lake. Art made from the land, what Beth intended to do with her own work in Illinois. The bark of oaks and hickories. Her show this September. And out here, the black rock of a once-seascape. A sculpture in flux with the earth and with visitors, a curved fiddlehead meant to be walked out to the center. What Beth called *land art,* what never held Rhiannon's interest until she realized how close she and Billie were to the sculpture. Rhiannon watching so many birds spiraling beyond the parked car and all at once she felt homesick, not for Beth's apartment or the sweeping cornfields of Illinois. Homesick for a different kind of planet. One that could keep so many starlings swirling. One that could keep travelers alive. One that held human striving and the earth in one soft hand.

Rhiannon cuts the engine, the Mustang parked at the edge of a path leading down to the water. The shoreline deserted, no other cars. Beyond the windshield, the sculpture's counterclockwise coil rotates out into the dried lakebed.

Billie leans forward beside her. What is this place?

The Spiral Jetty. Beth talked about it for years.

Can we actually walk on it?

Rhiannon nods. Come on.

When Rhiannon opens the driver's-side door, a gust of wind pushes across the shoreline and dishevels her hair. The lake floods with sunlight, shorebirds surfing through the air in the distance. Rhiannon remembers what Beth said: a sculpture meant to respond instead of impose. Not domination. Not a landscape named after an artist or an explorer. A site intended for active walking, not a work to stand by and watch. Rhiannon leaves the radio's news behind, what's billowed through the car's speakers from the Bear River Migratory Bird Refuge to the isolated edge of the Great Salt Lake. She closes the Mustang's door and begins walking toward the shore and Billie follows her, the daypack slung across her bare shoulders.

The basalt rock forms a raised path and Rhiannon steps onto it, a curled spiral rotating straight out and to the left. The dried lake a desert surrounding the sculpture, and beyond the desiccated sand, the Salt Lake an endless blue. The horizon marbled in purple and the pink against the mountains in the distance. Rhiannon walks. Closes her eyes. Hears the pulse of the wind and Billie's footsteps following. Their mother. A constellation of coordinates shot across the country, like the points a laser located in the sky. A lit pattern. A journey. A way of making meaning from nothing. Navigation. A way home. Rhiannon walks the jagged rocks as they curve toward the spiral's center. An IV drip. The slow leak of life from her mother's palms. Dental picks. Rock axes. Crinoids. The smallest fragments of stegosaurus plates, what lined the desk of her mother's home office. Tango lessons. Plant identification. Alliums and daylilies and daffodils. A car's garage. The scent of diesel. Oil and dusted rags. Summer humidity. The Mustang gunning across a dried sea at maximum speed. *Daughter, go west.* If Rhiannon keeps her eyes closed she can almost hear her mother say it. How their mother has pulled them from the rockbed of Illinois and thrust them into the other-worldly ridgelines and campgrounds of the West, a place that was never theirs but out here walking the thick band of a spiraled path feels almost like home.

Their mother's playground. A place she didn't even want her husband to visit, a place all her own. A salt raceway. A western landscape humming Rhiannon back. Billie's birds. Alabama's jesses. Hawks swirling above the highway, swiftlets circling above the refuge's boardwalk. Rhiannon follows the path as it grows tighter in concentric rings toward the center. A to B. How she might have driven straight across the country if Billie weren't here. The sound of her sister's footsteps beside her blends into the roar of the wind, a sound like the pulse of a sea's waves.

A once-ocean. The mystery of flood or famine or poison. Their mother's lifework. The eighth plane. Rhiannon walks and wonders if this is the beginning of their own age of mass devastation, a mystery for another era to mine. A planet beyond tilt. A planet leaving no trail of bread crumbs behind, only metal and wreckage. Only debris. A closed highway. Everything shut down. Only notified families. Rhiannon feels her hand travel to her chest, an ache beneath her breastbone as she walks.

Mother.

She almost hears her mouth form the word.

She wishes she'd said it back.

Mother, you are so loved.

The basalt path coils to the bull's-eye center and Rhiannon stops when she can't walk any farther, Billie standing beside her.

Goddamn, Billie whispers. A hand shielding her eyes, her gaze on the distant line of blue mountains, the rippled waterfall of scars pouring down her bare arm. Rhiannon stands where they are. A Kansas riverbed. A cone of swirled bats. A mountain valley. So many ridgelines their mother once walked. And from the Jetty's center, a span of sea salt and coral and blue.

Did you know only brine shrimp live in the Great Salt Lake? Billie asks.

Rhiannon shakes her head.

Billie points to the sky, a flock of beach-white birds. Western sandpipers, she says. This lake sees five million shorebirds each year on seasonal migrations.

Rhiannon says nothing as Billie pulls her daypack from her shoulder and rummages through its contents. Billie takes none of the objects from the bag but Rhiannon knows everything their mother left for them has traveled with them to the center of the spiral except her ring. Two jesses. Jigsaw piece. Astronomy pointer. Hawk feather. Fossilized bone. Locket. Billie pulls out the GPS instead. Presses buttons. Waits for it to calculate before unearthing a pen and their mother's journal.

Rhiannon watches as Billie crouches in the sand and opens the journal and flips it to the blank page beyond their mother's last entry. An open white sheet that threads the hurt in Rhiannon's chest. What seemed like a slight. Billie glances up at Rhiannon. Leaves the sheet blank and turns to the next open page.

Rhiannon watches as Billie marks the coordinate: what the GPS reads, the latitude and longitude of standing in the spiral's center. She draws the laddered slats of the Bear River Refuge's boardwalk. Beside it, the nautilus scrawl of a backward coil.

She marks her initials, the same as a hiking ledger, and extends the journal and pen up to Rhiannon, in Billie's care since they set out in Illinois. The wind whipping between them, the scent of salt and sea swirling in the desert heat. Six states. Eight planes. A trail of coordinates across so many western highways. There is no geocached box left to find. Rhiannon takes the journal from Billie's hands. From her mother's hands. The ghost of her fingerprints everywhere, upon the dust-gray plastic of hidden boxes and upon the scrawled drawings and coordinates of a notebook. What she once held. What she slid across a prison table to Billie's waiting palms.

Rhiannon takes the pen. Marks her initials. Squints across the sand and salt of the Jetty. Lets herself stand beside Billie in the silent blue.

Mother, we were here.

ACKNOWLEDGMENTS

Thank you, Kerry D'Agostino, for your unwavering support of this book and of my work, and for believing always in the journey of this novel. Thank you to Margaux Weisman for acquiring this book. Thank you, Jessica Williams, for giving it a home, for such a thorough and razor-sharp editorial hand, and for teaching me the skills of compression, brevity, and letting the words gleam. Thank you to the entire team at William Morrow, including Julia Elliott for her assistance with this novel and Laurie McGee for careful copyedits. I am boundlessly grateful for such a dream team.

Thank you to the Santa Fe Public Library for providing me with manuals, textbooks, and even children's books on falconry and NASCAR racing, including Jeff MacGregor's *Sunday Money: Speed! Lust! Madness! Death! A Hot Lap Around America with Nascar,* James McKay's *Practical Falconry,* and

Corona Brezina's *Falconry and Game Hawking.*

Thank you to Terry Tempest Williams and Robin Wall Kimmerer, two guiding lights leading the way of this book.

Thank you to the city of Santa Fe, and to the immeasurable inspiration of my students and colleagues at Santa Fe University of Art and Design as I wrote this novel. You taught me a lifetime in two years. Thank you to Moab and Salt Lake City, and to the bright blue solitude of the Spiral Jetty. Thank you, infinitely, to my colleagues and students at Hamilton College.

Thank you, always, to my family. Mom and Dad, you are the very best, as is your love of records and the University of Illinois. Michelle, though these siblings aren't us, thank you for teaching me what love between sisters means. All my love to Jeff, Noa, and Salem.

Thank you to Josh Finnell, first reader and bedrock, who has driven this entire country beside me and who was there beneath all that desert light.

ABOUT THE AUTHOR

Anne Valente is the author of the critically acclaimed novel *Our Hearts Will Burn Us Down.* Her short story collection, *By Light We Knew Our Names,* won the Dzanc Books Short Story Prize. Her fiction and essays have appeared in *One Story, The Kenyon Review, The Southern Review, The Believer, Catapult, The Rumpus,* and the *Washington Post,* among other publications. Originally from St. Louis, she currently lives in upstate New York and teaches at Hamilton College.

The employees of Thorndike Press hope you have enjoyed this Large Print book. All our Thorndike, Wheeler, and Kennebec Large Print titles are designed for easy reading, and all our books are made to last. Other Thorndike Press Large Print books are available at your library, through selected bookstores, or directly from us.

For information about titles, please call:
(800) 223-1244

or visit our website at:
http://gale.cengage.com/thorndike

To share your comments, please write:

Publisher
Thorndike Press
10 Water St., Suite 310
Waterville, ME 04901